CROWNKEEPER

ANNE WHEELER

ISBN: 978-1-951910-21-1 [ebook]
978-1-951910-22-8 [paperback]

narcienne
cresquel river
Mencote Desert
tourmel mountains
kalcine river
bra
winson lake
Coalwood Basin
bolcour mountains
ed
inn
heosta
n
w
e
s

THE KINGDOM OF
MEIRDRE
vistel
lochfield castle
arsele forest
zen
elternow
the moors
harnow
Galban Ocean
windersay

Part 1

Treason's Crown

PROLOGUE

LAURENT

Slivers of light fell across Laurent's boots as he paced across the ballroom, roaming his kingdom—at least, the version of it inlaid into the floor in the form of an intricate map, shades of light and dark wood indicating mountains, villages, borders. As he strolled, the piercing afternoon sun illuminated the wear from his frequent rides on Foxfire, but no one had seen fit to look at him as anything but a well-dressed king, so he didn't care that he should have replaced them long ago.

Those old riding boots which had seen better days traced the map in a circle, starting on the northwest border with Nantoise, always a problem with their raids and piracy. From there he walked west to where Iraela lay, and he stared at the inset wood that made up the border for a long time. The bargain he'd made with the Iraelan king—his mother's new husband—had it been as injurious as he'd suspected? Likely so, but Iraela wasn't even the worst of his worries. No, he decided, as he traced the border south, that would be Vassian, with an army that could march right over Meirdre if they put their mind to it.

Of course, he had more immediate problems than border raids and an army that far surpassed his own—for Lochfeld

Castle's priest had coerced him into a meeting this afternoon, when he should have been in his office working figures once more.

"Sire!" Father Gerritt's rumbling baritone interrupted Laurent's rambling thoughts.

And here he was. Laurent turned toward him, trying to forget the map that laid bare all Meirdre's vulnerabilities.

"Father." His voice echoed as he crossed the ballroom and dipped his head slightly at the priest. "You wanted to see me?"

Gerritt shrugged. "You look worried, sire."

"Always." There was no point in hiding his concern. About Lochfeld, about Meirdre, about his future, about his family's future. With his father gone and his mother married off once more, it fell to him and his younger sister, and he wouldn't allow her to suffer that responsibility of leading a kingdom if he could help it. "I'm afraid I'll never become used to this duty."

"Perhaps that's because you're not intended to be burdened with it on your own." Gerritt gazed at the map, then looked back at him. "In case you were unsure, you are old enough to marry, sire," he said with a chuckle.

"Marry." Laurent scoffed. "Don't you think I have other problems? Bigger problems? Courting a woman is hardly a priority right now, Father."

Gerritt's brows rose. "So you don't court."

Laurent circled the kingdom of Meirdre on the floor once more, considering that. His parent's marriage had been arranged—his mother's second marriage had been as well. He'd arranged that marriage himself. But his own? Marriage wasn't about love, but still . . .

"What other option do I have?" he asked, barely concealing a laugh. The slivers of light through the narrow windows were withdrawing, which meant he needed to withdraw too, back to real duties. "Surely you aren't suggesting I ride off to the countryside and ask a peasant girl to marry me."

"In fact, that's exactly what I'm suggesting."

Laurent blew out a breath. "With all due respect, Father, that's ridiculous.

"Ridiculous? On the contrary, it might just save you and Meirdre." Gerritt's focus fell to the map. "Have you ever heard of a crownkeeper, sire?"

CHAPTER ONE

THE LAST OF THE FIREPLACE EMBERS WINKED OUT AS I PULLED MY shawl around my shoulders. The day had sped by, and I wasn't unhappy for the prospect of the relative warmth of my bed, for even the single candle next to me could scarcely keep burning in the draft leaking through the crack in the room's sole window. It had been there for two years, ever since the incident with the deer, and Papa couldn't afford to repair it, just like we couldn't afford to repair most things. The draft made winter evenings even more miserable than usual, but Mama insisted I complete my needlepoint before bed, and I had never been one to argue. I also wasn't given to ingratitude, not usually. At least we had glass, I continually reminded myself—some in our hamlet of Elternow had resorted to oiled animal skins across gaping holes in their walls.

I'd done enough spring flowers for one winter night. I licked my chapped lips, then set the thread and hoop in the basket next to my feet and rubbed my sore neck before shivering again. The wind was not the only evidence of the storm the neighbors had predicted yesterday; wet snow was beginning to hit the window. Papa would struggle to reach the barn and feed the horse and cow in the morning, especially with the inflammation which had turned his fingers and knees into knotted messes. I was not allowed to help him any longer, and selfish though it might be, I was grateful for Mama's recent insistence on more feminine pursuits. Needlepoint and baking were tedious, to be sure, and her marital plans for me frightening, but at least they didn't involve trudging through snow.

I glanced at the candle, burnt to the bottom, but before I could blow it out, there was a knock on the door of our low stone house. A pounding, really. I called for Mama even before springing to my feet. A visitor in this weather, this time of night . . . Something was wrong. It was always that way. A poorly positioned calf, fire consuming a thatched roof, or even an intractable fever. Terrible things happened at night.

It had been night when they'd taken Thomas, after all—a warm and breezy late autumn midnight, not like this wintertime evening—but night all the same. We'd heard the horses, which wasn't so unusual by itself, even in a poor village. But these had been more than a few lost travelers looking for shelter in the wildness of the moor. We'd huddled in this very room, Mama and Papa and me, knowing King Laurent had sent his men for a reason. And in the morning, when Elternow was down three men including Thomas, we learned what that reason was.

Would it be the same tonight?

I threw open the door, bracing myself against the cold, praying it wasn't something that required me and my nascent medical skills. My down blanket was calling me louder and louder by the moment, but more importantly, Mama would be furious if I left tonight to help. Every healer and midwife in Elternow was a woman, but that wasn't good enough for her. It wasn't *feminine enough.*

But this time, outside our house, fifty paces from the village proper, it wasn't a worried father who stood there, or even a villager covered in soot.

It was six of the king's men, snow swirling about them.

They weren't as flashy as in the paintings I'd seen in school, but I suspect that was due to the weather. Heavy wool cloaks, lined with fur, covered their brocade tunics. I could imagine them anyway: royal blue silk, with a sheen unheard of in the fabric we spun here, laced with gold embroidery finer than I was capable of. I was stuck between fear and interest until my gaze landed on their swords.

My throat closed up at the sight of the polished steel. Mama and Papa had done no wrong, even though doing no wrong was harder and harder these days. The taxes were always paid on time, difficult as that order was, and they never spoke a word against the king.

None of us did. None of us associated with those who did.

Well.

Most of us didn't.

I stood there silently, my failure darting about in my mind, and one of the men, about the same age as my twenty summers, looked worriedly at the one with gold cord on the shoulders of his cloak.

"Do you think she's mute, Captain?" he asked. "He won't be happy."

I don't know what I expected. I held my breath, my eyes wide, just standing there in the doorway.

The captain burst into laughter. "I doubt she's mute." His amusement faded. "But if she leaves us standing here in the cold, I may cut out her tongue."

My imperiled tongue darted to my lips once more, and somehow, I found the courage to speak. "You honor us with your presence, Captain. Please, do come in and warm yourselves." After what had happened to Thomas, I was nothing if not specific with the correct responses—when they finally came.

He nodded with the lightest of smiles, and six sets of boots tromped in behind me as I lay a forbidden extra log into the now-cooling fireplace. The coals caught at once, and I couldn't help but think that if a visit from our enemies was what it took to find extra warmth, maybe it was worth it.

"Riette!" My mother's shock was palpable behind me. I spun around to see her clutching a spare piece of fabric around her, her lips moving in a silent prayer. "What is this? What have you done?"

The captain interrupted before I could reply.

"Your daughter is showing us the hospitality the king requires of you. I urge you to do the same, Madame . . ."

"Kaleveld." Mama's hands fluttered as she pushed by me and set another log on the fire, more, I suspected, to distract attention from her mistake than to warm the room. The space had already grown sweltering with the eight of us. "And of course, Captain," she went on. "Anything you need."

"I need to speak with Master Kaleveld." The captain cleared his throat. "All of you."

"I'm here." Papa's voice was even as he entered, though wary. "It's ghastly weather for a ride from Lochfeld Castle, sir."

I brushed sweat from my forehead as the room closed in around me. If only I could wipe it from under my arms as well. Thomas was there, in the king's dungeons. We'd been seen together by neighbors and strangers alike before the royal guard bore down upon Elternow to arrest him for treason. Could these men be here—

"It was urgent," the leader said. "Even through a snowstorm. Next week is the Feast of St. Margaretha, you know."

"I am aware." Papa's wariness increased at the non sequitur.

"King Laurent needs a wife by then."

"A wife?" Something cold slunk down my spine.

"It is—" The captain looked at me, as if down his nose. "Difficult to explain. A tradition, if you will."

The explanation wasn't mocking, exactly, but confused me, nonetheless. The feast, yes, we all knew of that. But poverty muted that ancient celebration these days, and it was doubtful anyone in Elternow planned on celebrating at all—the pardon of criminals was an all but assured aspect of the festivities, although Thomas would never be absolved of his crimes.

"And you're coming for her?"

Mama had asked exactly what I was thinking. King Laurent's father had married a common woman, but that had been years ago, and it wasn't exactly something discussed on a routine basis. Perhaps it was some odd family preference.

Perhaps we were simply easier to control than noblewomen.

"It is not for me to question the king. Nor any of us. He will explain further if he deems appropriate." The captain looked around, his gaze landing on me. "But this is not a foregone agreement. You may say no."

Mama gasped. "And if she does?"

He held out his hand. A gold coin sat there, and I looked away in pain as the fire caught the edge, flashing like the light of sun directly into my eyes.

"If Miss Riette refuses, nothing will happen. We'll move on to the next house down the road. But if she says yes—this coin, plus more." His gaze fell on the window. "No broken glass. No rationing firewood. No gruel for dinner. Medicine for your husband, Madame Kaleveld. You'll be taken care of for the rest of your lives."

"Which is how long?" I broke in. "A week?"

He raised his eyebrows, half in amusement, half in exasperation. "You read too many novels, Miss Riette. As long as your parents are loyal to the crown, they will stay alive, just like before. This is no trick."

I didn't bother to tell him that all our books had long since been burned for fuel, including the one with the paintings of the royal guard. "I suppose when you have a million times what your subjects have, it wouldn't be."

"Riette!"

If Mama didn't stop saying my name like that, I was going to scream.

"Please forgive my rudeness, Captain." Thomas's face popped into my mind, and suddenly, harassing them didn't seem wise any longer. My heart ached at the memory of his lips on my cheek. "I'm simply overwhelmed."

"Best become un-overwhelmed, then. I need your answer now. It's a long ride back, and I don't want to delay."

"Now?" My teeth chattered in contrast to the growing, uncomfortable warmth.

"You may discuss with your parents first, if you must."

As if that were possible with half the royal guard standing in the same room. I looked at Mama and Papa, unsure of what to do. They stared in return, as if they weren't sure what to say, either—like they hadn't imagined this situation in a thousand years of dreaming.

"He said medicine." Tears formed as I made my decision, then I shrugged. "I can't say no."

"You needn't worry about that." Papa clasped his hands behind his back so I couldn't focus on his knuckles. How much longer would he be able to milk with those fingers? "I want this to be your decision. If one has to be made, you make it alone. Not me, not your mother."

"I'll go." I prayed he wouldn't ask me to explain the decision, because I didn't want to explain it to myself. "I don't see any other way. And it'll be all right."

Mama kissed my cheeks, tears streaming down her face. She didn't say anything, and her emotions irritated me. She had what she wanted for me—a husband, one better than I could ever find in Elternow. What was there to be this upset about it? King Laurent was horrid to our people, yes, and I didn't suffer any delusions that my future as his wife would be joyful, but my decision would benefit all of us in various ways. Why couldn't she see that?

"It's settled then." Papa grabbed me by the shoulders, like his hold would stop me from leaving. "What does she need to bring?"

One of the men, silent until now, chuckled. "I daresay she owns nothing worth bringing."

I ignored him and scooped up my embroidery basket. The once-hated pastime had become a lifeline to my entire world. "This. I'm bringing this."

The captain nodded. "I'm sure he'll allow it."

He swung the front door open again and gestured outside before I could grab my cloak. The heavy fabric around my shoulders, I swallowed, clutched the basket to my chest, and told myself that the chill which ran down my spine had everything to do with the way winter reentered the cottage—not with his words.

CHAPTER TWO

LOCHFELD CASTLE LOOMED HIGH ABOVE US, AND I SETTLED BACK in my saddle to gaze up at the craggy cliffs upon which it sat. My bottom had become numb the day before, and the rest of me wasn't in much better shape, even though the snow had stopped, leaving the darkness streaked with the stars. The horse Captain Willem had set me on when we'd left Elternow was well-trained, and he ambled beside the group with little input from my frozen hands. A warhorse, yes, perhaps, but it seemed tonight we both wanted the same thing—a bed and warmth.

Willem gave another order, and we headed up a narrow trail in the rocks. I clung to the horse with all the strength I had left— I'd never been a particularly strong horsewoman—but my mount was steadier than I imagined. Hooves clopped as we climbed, scattering what rocks remained after the first half of winter. The wind was my enemy now, and on the unprotected hill side, it bit, fierce and raw, into my bare cheeks. I couldn't help but imagine what the king would say if he saw me looking like this. He'd not find me attractive, surely, and for some reason I found myself wishing he would.

Soon enough we reached the top, and from closer up, the castle didn't appear as foreboding as it had from below. Spires rose from the towers, sheer decoration rather than functional battlements. Candles flickered in most of the towering windows, and a few chambers were lit more brightly.

Fireplaces. In the past few days of riding and small fires at night, I'd almost forgotten what they looked like.

Willem eased his stallion over to me. "You'll not see him tonight. We'll need to get you thawed out and cleaned up, and if I'm not mistaken, you could use some sleep."

I concealed my panic at his use of *we* as we ambled across a stone bridge I could barely see through my fatigue and sudden anxiety. Surely this group of men wasn't going to take care of my toiletry needs. It'd been bad enough spending last night alone in a tent while they camped nearby.

I needn't have worried, because when we hurtled through the gate and into a small courtyard, a servant waited—a woman—fur around her shoulders. I slid from the saddle, limp, and she fixed Willem with a glare I'd have never been brave enough to attempt.

"Captain!" The woman wrapped her arm around me, and I practically fell into her warm embrace. "You shouldn't have ridden the child through that weather."

"It wasn't as though we could stay out there in that." Willem slid from his horse and shrugged. "She's used to it, anyway."

"I doubt that." The woman pushed me away to look me up and down. "She's not very sturdy."

"She made it this far, didn't she?" Willem grunted. "He'll make do."

Sturdy? That's what she expected? That's what the king expected? Of course I wasn't sturdy. We've been starved for the past twenty years.

The servant made a noise of dissent and motioned me into an alcove, then up a set of stairs. "It seems we have work to do. Let's get to it, then."

"It was a long ride, ma'am." Her rudeness regarding my disheveled appearance wasn't the last thing I expected, but it wasn't the first. I hated explaining myself, and the reason for my disheveled appearance should have been obvious, but perhaps it wasn't. Perhaps she'd never ridden two days through a snowstorm.

She eyed me sideways. "None of that ma'am nonsense. I'm Sara."

"Sara." I tested the name. It was so normal. "You've been in the castle long?"

"I was born here." We turned down a corridor lit with oil lamps, and I tried to ignore the muddy tracks I left behind us. "During the first King Laurent's reign."

"I see. You served his wife?"

"Until her death, yes." Her eyes brightened a bit. "It will be nice to have a queen around the castle again. It's a different feel, a better environment. Loneliness doesn't become a king, after all, and Lochfeld has been too empty of late."

For some reason, the word *queen* unnerved me, like I hadn't made the connection between it and my upcoming marriage until now. I fell silent as I followed Sara down empty corridor after corridor until we arrived at what I assumed would be my new home. She threw open the door, and my mouth fell open at the sight which greeted me.

Not one but two fireplaces burned inside. A silk rug the size of our living room back home lay before one, and a wooden tub full of steaming water sat in front of the other. I drew my stare from the water long enough to take in the canopy bed and matching silk chair beside it. Both were a shade of red rarely seen in Elternow. Dye that vibrant was too expensive to use for anything except selling to noblewomen passing through our town on their way to something better. I must have looked like a fool staring as I was, but I couldn't take my eyes off it.

Sara clapped her hands, and with a shock, I realized there

were two other servants in the room, their heads close together as they giggled. Hoping they would blame the flush on my cheeks on the fire, I looked down at my sodden shoes.

"Get her in the tub," Sara ordered. "There isn't much time until sunup, and she needs some rest before then."

Feeling the order was meant for me as much as the servants, I stripped off my muddy dress. Sara clucked her tongue, likely at how my ribs were much more prominent than any woman would prefer, then poured a glass of wine from the decanter on a nearby table. I ignored her unspoken commentary and sank into the water.

Bliss.

She shoved the glass into my hand. "Drink this. Soak for a while, then we'll get you cleaned up."

It was a simple enough order. I obeyed, though the wine was stronger than anything I'd ever tasted. Papa kept malt in the barn for medicinal purposes, but he'd always forbidden me from drinking it myself, though I suspected he partook some nights. If it tasted anything like this, I couldn't blame him. The spice rolled around my tongue, and my eyes grew heavier. Soon, they closed completely, and I basked in the certain knowledge my attendants would never let me drown. Maybe being taken care of wouldn't be so awful after all. I was seconds away from falling asleep when a shout echoed outside.

"Sara—he wants her now!"

It was Willem, and he sounded panicked. I jerked upright, alarm likely written all over my face. The way the two younger servants were flailing about only added to the commotion, but Sara clapped her hands again and began to issue orders. I was pulled from the tub, hair damp but without soap, then forced into stays much lovelier than the ones I'd left at home. One of the girls pinned up my hair in a rather haphazard fashion to keep it off whatever dress they planned to shove me into, and my breath became short.

I'd hoped to have more than an hour to adjust to my new situation, and it seemed as though Sara had expected the same. But they drew a heavy velvet gown over my head, and I realized this was for real. The king had summoned me in the middle of the night—of course someone had informed him I'd arrived—and I was to meet him, frightened and exhausted and wet as I was. I shook with that understanding as one of the girls pinned my hair up, Sara giving her suggestions the entire time.

"It's still damp," she said, biting her lip so hard it turned white, "and we'll need to have your things fitted better tomorrow, but I suppose there's nothing to be done about that now. He'll be understanding. There was only so much we could do to prepare."

"Sara—" I hesitated before I asked the stupid question. "What am I—how am I supposed to act?"

She stared at me, her lips still pressed together in frustration.

"Two days ago, I'd had no thoughts of ever meeting any king," I added. "I don't want to make a mistake."

She grabbed me by the shoulder and ushered me out into the silent corridor. "Stay silent. Curtsy before him. Low. He'll tell you when to stand. Answer his questions and say nothing else until you're dismissed. And for heaven's sake, try not to stare like an awed peasant."

She rattled off more rules as we raced down the stairs. I tried to listen, but between my growing headache and trying not to stumble in my new shoes, it was a losing battle. By the time we arrived at the iron door of the throne room, I was out of breath and half asleep.

The two guards on either side of the doorway wore the gleaming uniforms I'd imagined the night the soldiers had arrived on my doorstep. They opened the door as we approached, and though Sara took a step back, I peered inside. The space was smaller than I believed a throne room should be, but if the silk in my bedroom had been a surprise, the deep blue fabric covering every bit of the walls made my heart race. A carved chair sat at the end, though I couldn't identify any of the designs from this distance, and on it—

On it sat a man.

CHAPTER THREE

I COULDN'T SEE MUCH OF HIM FROM THE DOORWAY—IN FACT, HIS indigo tunic all but blended into the silk walls—but his body language gave him away. He was impatient. That was clear from the way he'd placed a hand no-so-casually on the arm of the throne when the door had opened, and I froze, without regard for his upcoming annoyance.

"You'll go in alone," Sara whispered in my ear, drawing back. "This is not a place for me. Go!"

Fine. If I could survive everything I had so far in life, I could survive this. Resisting the urge to pick up my long skirts, I walked inside, my head high. I might not own much of anything any longer, but I had my pride.

The throne was farther away than it'd appeared at first, and I kept my eyes on it as I went. Analyzing my situation with a detached appreciation was easier than actually experiencing it. In the corners of my eyes, oil burned within glass sconces—the sheer number lit seemed odd for the middle of the night, but I knew their purpose at once. He wanted to see me, and not in the dim of an unlit throne room. A figure stood next to him—he didn't want to be alone with me. Something sparkled on the throne—had he dressed up for this introduction just like I had?

Sara's warnings flickered into my head, and I came to a stop at what appeared to be an appropriate position, then held a low curtsy. I doubted Papa would have approved of the action, but then, he'd have done the same regardless of his feelings, wouldn't he? Thomas wouldn't have, and that's why he was locked up in a cell somewhere.

A tear ran down my cheek at his memory, and I lowered my head further.

"Riette."

Fabric rustled; wood creaked. King Laurent was standing. My heart pounded so hard he must have been able to see it, but I took a breath and remained still.

"Straighten." His voice was colder than when he'd said my name. "Let me see you."

I did so, praying he didn't notice the tear. He circled around me, and as his shadow drifted to my side, I chanced a look up. The figure next to the throne was Willem, and he jerked his chin downward, so I did the same. An insolent order it was, but I would take whatever help I could get.

"Your hair is wet," the king went on.

From so close, I could study his clothing—from the knees down, at least. His boots were worn, which I found strange. Perhaps he enjoyed riding. His breeches were of the finest leather, though, and it was impossible to keep my eyes down instead of appreciating whatever luxurious fabrics made up the rest of his clothes. Realizing I'd been staring even if from under my eyelashes, I swore in my mind, words I'd picked up from listening to Thomas's men.

"I am sorry, sire. We didn't realize—"

"Silence! There will be no excuses. The next time you enter this room, you will be presentable."

Heavens. How long would I suffer this embarrassment? Fifty years? More?

"Yes, sire," I replied, making a mental note only to wash my hair when he was away from the castle. What else could I say? Anything else would be an excuse, though I desperately wanted to tell him the other option would have been for me to have appeared before him covered in mud.

"Good." His shadow retreated a few paces, then he stopped. "Come. Sit."

Willem pulled a plain wooden chair up beside the throne as I approached, and I was acutely aware of the intentional contrast between it and the ornate chair on which he sat. I adjusted my skirts and took a seat, keeping my eyes lowered.

"So. This is Riette Kaleveld. She is rather lovely, don't you agree?"

Willem made a non-committal noise, and I cringed at the idea of them talking about me like I wasn't there.

"Though I should have known her hair would be brown. They always are from Elternow."

The comment wasn't directed at me. Further, it sounded like he knew me—knew *of* me, that was—and tendrils of fear curled about my spine. Or was it just the bones of my stays?

"Yes, sire, it seems they are." Willem, to his credit, agreed without a wisp of irony.

"And her eyes are blue."

"They are."

"You know of my preferences. She is not it."

"It was the first house. She was the first one to agree. You know the law, sire."

In the corner of my vision Willem shrugged, and I envied his indifferent tone. Would I ever be able to effect such a manner in the king's presence? I doubted it.

"Yes. I know it." King Laurent sighed. "She'll have to do, then."

"I'll have to do?" It took a moment before I realized the words were mine. "You don't need to treat me like I'm your last choice!"

His eyebrows flew up, and I focused again on the marble floor, waiting for a slap on the cheek—or worse. Instead, I heard laughter.

"Perhaps you would be, if things were different. But the law is specific, and here you are." I must have looked confused, even staring at the floor, so he went on. "You don't know why you're here, do you? It's very simple. I'm not growing any younger, and I have no wife, no heirs. A king without either is a liability to his own self. Weak-appearing. Someone his rivals can jump on. My advisors have convinced me of this truth, and what better time for a wedding than the Feast of St. Margaretha?"

He cleared his throat. "As for my choice of a bride, my line has selected from common women for the past five generations. The pool of noblewomen is shrinking by the decade, and if we wish to continue with strong heirs—well, your father is a farmer. You can figure it out—or ask one of the servant women later if you must."

I had assumed it was something like that, but hearing it explained so bluntly, especially in front of two men, made me blush anew. There had never been any question that I was to become the neighbor's stallion, borrowed to inject new life into an old bloodline, but—but his candor was intolerable. I hated to destroy my parents' dreams of a better future, but I couldn't subject myself to this humiliation, even for pretty dresses and medicine.

"I'm sorry sire, but—is this agreement permanent?" The question flew out before I could stop myself. I wanted to flee, but I'd do it safely.

"Do you take me for a monster?" He lounged back on the throne as I swallowed, hard. "No. Not until the ceremony. I'd be disappointed, naturally, but I realize this life isn't for everyone, so until then, you're free to leave."

My shoulders relaxed.

"But I doubt Willem told you all of what you'll gain after the wedding. You may have been the lucky first, but you don't know all of what I'm offering."

"He showed us the coin." The image of it laying in Mama's palm made me second-guess my decision to flee. Why must these decisions be so difficult? "We are grateful for it."

But we wouldn't need it if you didn't treat us so poorly.

"And the extra head of cattle and medicine for your father, yes. But I think I can offer you something you'll appreciate more than money and pretty dresses."

I looked at him then, and really saw him for the first time. He might have had ten years on me, but no lines showed in his face—the product of better food, more sleep, and less work than anyone in Elternow would ever experience. His hair was shorter than most wore it these days, and I couldn't understand his issue with my eyes, since his were just as blue. He wasn't unattractive in the least, especially with the thick lashes that framed his eyes, and I could have stared at him for hours had he been anyone else. Instead, I found a crack on the floor and spoke again.

"What else can you offer me?"

"Something I think you'll find very difficult to turn down." He chuckled. "On the eve of every royal marriage, the bride chooses a prisoner to free."

"The—the bride?" My answer was uneven.

"You know where the tradition of clemency during the Feast of St. Margaretha originates, do you not?"

"I do not, sire. I'm sorry."

He might have huffed at my ignorance had he been anyone else. Instead, his explanation came as tolerantly as a patient schoolmaster.

"Five hundred and seventeen years ago, the war between us and the Duchy of Conzell reached its fiercest point. Almost a stalemate. King Arend had captured the Duke of Conzell, but at what cost? The duke's army was stronger, and our people were starving—it was very likely Meirdre would come to ruin. So, they made a deal, in the very dungeon below this castle—a treaty, if you will. Arend would marry the duke's daughter, incorporating the duchy into Meirdre. Hostilities would cease, our people would have food once more, and there would be peace."

"What did the duke get from that?" I asked. "It doesn't sound like a sensible proposal."

"His life, I suppose, even though he would have lived it out in a cell. He was a coward and gave up his lands—and a war his people could have won—to save himself. 'Twould have been better for him to die with honor."

I could understand the duke's desire to live. I hated having what the king surely would have believed to be dishonorable thoughts—rebellious ideas seemed too dangerous here in Lochfeld Castle—but I could understand it.

"On the eve of their wedding, the story goes, Arend asked his new bride why she looked so unhappy. It was a rather silly question, since her father was being held hostage three stories below where she'd said her vows—and through her tears, she told him so. Unfortunately, there wasn't much the king could do. If he released her father, he would appear weak, and fragility was the last thing he needed to show in the wake of a war." He smiled. "But his bride proposed a solution. She would select a prisoner to be released as a wedding gift to her, allowing both her father his freedom and her husband to save face."

"That's rather romantic." It *was*, if you ignored the whole dungeon and prisoner and death part of it.

"They made a tradition of it from then on, one that's been passed down through the ages, eventually conflating itself with the Feast of St. Margaretha. In recent years my advisors have taken on the role of selecting prisoners, but I usually have one or two names who are, of course, added to the list. This year . . . well, I have no problem showing that I can be capable of mercy when it suits my need. And I must confess, I do prefer the original—and as you say, *romantic*—tradition."

He was speaking in circles. "I don't understand."

"For this celebration, I'm doing something different. The choice has been given to you. Like Queen Katrien, I want this to be a wedding gift from me to you. Choose a prisoner."

Choose a prisoner.

I gasped. The words floated between us, making my head spin. Had I really heard them? Perhaps escape was the wrong plan of action.

He took my hand, then continued evenly. "Anyone. Even a traitor from the hangman's noose."

CHAPTER FOUR

My shoes, I realized for the first time, were embroidered with stars, the quality far beyond my own capabilities. I tried to count the stitches as the king let his comment hover in the smoky air of the throne room, but they were so delicate I gave up and met his stare.

"Choosing a prisoner to liberate must be a difficult decision, sire," I said. "I can only hope I do our people justice in choosing."

His eyes sparked with amusement, like the stars on my shoes. "Is it so difficult, Riette?" he asked. "I've recently learned you have a favorite among that unfortunate group—but perhaps I was given poor information."

His confirmation should have been a warning, but instead it emboldened me. His men had tortured Thomas, Thomas had given up my name. King Laurent was no longer simply the king, and I was no longer cowering—we were two equals on solid footing, negotiating with all the information. Chance and tradition had brought us together, and he wouldn't squander the opportunity.

"Thomas Wennink? He's hardly a favorite, though I won't

deny I know him. I even believed I loved him once," I said. "But childlike love means nothing in the grand scheme of things."

Whatever King Laurent thought of that statement, it wasn't a betrayal of Thomas, not exactly. Our relationship had always been fleeting. I'd had stars in my eyes at the idea of the leader of Elternow's rebellion group paying attention to me, and he enjoyed the kisses he was able to steal when I led the cow to pasture. It gave me a particular status in the village and him some pleasure in a life that was otherwise uncertain.

Did I truly love Thomas? Maybe. Most of the time, I believed I did. But marriages were rarely based on love, or I wouldn't have agreed to Willem's invitation so easily.

Did I believe Thomas would be the one to help overthrow the throne and restore peace and prosperity to our kingdom? Yes. Most definitely.

The king looked at me with fresh interest. "I won't permit adultery. If you think this will enable you to take advantage of my generosity and be with him as well . . ."

Offended, I lifted my chin. "I uphold my oaths."

In truth I'd never spoke one, and I had the sudden realization that I had no intention of doing so in the future. There was no way the king would let Thomas go, no matter the tradition, even if I married him. I knew now that I was being lied to. But I was here in the castle now, a place I'd never gain access to otherwise, and I could do something about his imprisonment. I had always known I'd risk anything and everything to free him for the sake of the rebellion, and now I had my chance. I would free Thomas or die trying.

"I believe you—though I shouldn't. We have an agreement, then?"

I nodded, even though my heart hadn't stopped pounding. "We do. I marry you; you release him."

"It's settled, then. The feast is in five days, if you can be ready by then. Anything you need to prepare, the servants will help you with." His eyes sparkled with as much humor as I suspected he ever deigned to show. "Make sure your hair is dry for the ceremony."

Five days. My heart thumped against the stays. Thomas might be doomed, but he would be alive for at least another five days, and that gave me plenty of time to figure something out. Images flooded my mind as the hope began to build. Thomas and I, riding down the trail cut into the cliff. Presenting him to his resistance group, now broken up and in hiding. Saying goodbye as they rode off to do whatever it was they did. Watching him drive a sword through the king's chest.

King Laurent stood, interrupting the vision, and I flinched, unsure of what to do with him hovering over me. "Willem, send her back to her room. Make certain she gets some sleep and for heaven's sake, ensure she dries her hair. She can't be seen around the castle looking like this."

"Of course, sire."

I curtsied quickly. Willem gestured toward the rear doors, and I didn't risk a look back as my shoes padded away on the hard stone, though I could feel the king's stare on my back. Did he suspect what I had planned? The castle appeared so deserted that I must have a chance, but then again . . .

My hope flitted away like the smoke from the oil lamps above us. It was the middle of the night. Naturally the corridors of the castle were empty. There was no doubt the place would come alive soon—in the next five minutes, for all I knew—and my plan which had seemed effortless and certain in the throne room was already in danger. For now, I would also ignore the fact that saving Thomas would take away my parents' newfound financial prosperity and Papa's medicine.

Sara clucked at me when Willem left me in my room once more.

"Keeping you up half the night. Far be it from me to question him, but he should have known better," she said, tugging the heavy dress over my head. "The sun will be up soon, and then you'll need a tour and introductions, but first . . ." She frowned at my stays, then began to undo them. "One hour to rest, my lady. Then I'm afraid you'll have to begin your new life."

I muttered my thanks and slid into sheets that were quite possibly more expensive than the dress she'd yanked so unceremoniously off my body. As my eyes closed, I wanted, more than anything, to dream of home and the cracked glass in the living room window.

Instead, I dreamed of oubliettes and screams.

CHAPTER FIVE

It wasn't Sara who woke me, but a rooster somewhere far below my window. Morning was always a time of renewal, and today was no different, even in the castle of a man I hated. I whispered a quick prayer before slinging my feet to the floor and letting my toes dig into the rug. As the first knock came, I tried to tug the yards of fabric over my head, but only succeeded in tangling myself in velvet. When hands gently lifted it off me again, I froze.

"Apologies." The owner of the hands spoke. "But you didn't answer, and by the sound of fabric catching on goodness knows what, it seems you needed help."

"I—I'm Riette." The fabric cleared my head. She was my age, though more fashionably dressed than I'd ever been before yesterday, and her educated accent unnerved me. "And I'm not used to such a dress. I'd appreciate the help."

"So I see." She laughed and unceremoniously dumped the dress over my head, then arranged my skirts and tied the back with more skill than I possessed. "And I'm Juliana."

"Not a servant." Her gown, all velvet and silk, and the enormous emerald on her left hand belied her status. This was a courtier who would have sneered at me yesterday.

"Aren't we all servants to the crown?" Juliana laughed again, making me doubt my previous accusation. "I'm to keep you company. Show you around and make sure you're comfortable. Help you set up the rest of your household—that sort of thing."

"I appreciate that." She finished fastening the dress, and I turned to face her. "I'm to have my own household?" It was an overwhelming thought.

"You didn't expect the king to share your quarters, did you?" Juliana smiled, but there was no malice behind it. "This room is yours—he's not even allowed in. He's close by though, for—for after."

I reached for the glass of water that someone had filled while I was asleep. "Not allowed? I'm surprised anything is forbidden from him."

She waved an indifferent hand. "I suspect the ban is of his own making. He's not interested in whatever goes on in women's lives. That part of the castle will fall to you."

"Perhaps you should show me around?" I suggested. "It was so dark and quiet when I arrived last night—I'm afraid I have no idea of where I am and where anything else is."

"Patience." She gave the door a sharp look, and as if on cue, it opened, admitting Sara, who carried a tray of fruit and bread. "Let her do your hair. You should have something to eat, then we'll be off."

Reluctantly, I sat before a large mirror, but I couldn't do much more than pick at a few dried strawberries while Sara arranged my hair on top of my head. It was the pins she used which were responsible for my distraction—the perfect tool for breaking into a dungeon. I answered her questions about the preference for my hairstyle and Juliana's innocent questions of my life before coming to the castle, but my soul was screaming for escape. No one would have understood my desire to flee if I'd spoken of it, and it took an entire five minutes to understand my motivation myself.

My own impatience was my biggest threat.

Finally, Sara released us, and I scampered down the stairs next to Juliana faster than I had when King Laurent had summoned me. More guards filled the corridors at this time of day, and they bowed at Juliana while giving me the briefest of nods. She was someone of importance based on how they treated her, but I didn't dare ask who or why.

"These are the stables." As we walked out an open doorway to one of the sizeable courtyards that made up the castle proper, Juliana waved at the long, tiled-roof building in front of us. "My Starduster is there, and if you're willing to ask the king for your own, we can go for a ride one day."

I hated telling her that I had no uses for horses except as a fast way to warn Thomas's men that the royal guard was coming. Spilling my secret at a resistance lookout seemed a good way to end up with a rope around my neck. Instead, I nodded.

"I would like that. Is there much time for such pursuits?"

"More than you had before, I would guess." Her forehead creased, and she ducked her head to the side before continuing. "I'm sorry. I'm afraid I'm going to step all over myself for the next few days. It's a fault of mine. I didn't mean—"

As we'd ridden up the cliffs last night, I'd decided I wanted to hate anyone who lived at Lochfeld. But Juliana's embarrassment was obvious and earnest. How could anyone hate her?

"I'm not offended," I replied. "I was hardly a laborer before, though I thought as much most of the time when Mama ordered me to do embroidery and read music and practice my language work." I laughed for the first time since arriving. Mama had done the best she could, expecting me to catch no more than a farmer with two horses, and here I was, about to marry a king.

"Oh! You can embroider?" Juliana's sweet face became, if it was possible, even more animated as she grabbed my arm. "We'll have to find you supplies for your needlework. You've never used silk, have you?"

"No, no, Juliana." Even though I'd brought my own thread, the horror of being forced into more embroidery practice before my escape was worse than almost anything else. Knowing she'd never understand that, I stumbled through an explanation. "I'm not good at it. Rather slow actually. Anyway, there's a piece I'd like to finish before I start anything else, and I'm afraid the silk would clash with what I've been using."

"Oh. Yes, of course." She pulled me along, and her smile brightened. "Perhaps after you finish, you can select something from my stock."

"That would be lovely," I managed to stammer. The idea of having someone to share my pain with wasn't wholly without charm, but I would be gone long before I finished the flowers on which I was already working.

We passed by the stables and into another wing of the castle, and I pulled her to a halt as a barred door passed off our left side. The corridor on the other side was lit with lamps even at this time of day, but it became dark toward the opposite end where only a single tread of a stairwell was visible. A cool breeze brushed my cheek when I walked by, and my intuition told me what was below.

"Juliana"—I tugged her to a halt at the door—"what is that?"

She blinked and tried to pull me forward, but I ground my feet into the stone.

"The stairwell to the dungeon, naturally," she said, tugging at my sleeve.

I held my breath. The first step of my plan would come sooner than I expected. "Could we visit?"

"Visit!"

"The king told me last night that I'd be selecting a prisoner to release on the eve of our wedding. In my mind, the best course of action would be to speak with the jailer and learn who is most deserving of that mercy."

Her rosy cheeks went pale, and she jerked forward, away from the dungeon door. "That would be inappropriate."

"You're afraid."

"Hardly." Her footsteps grew heavier and her breath rapid as she led me out another door into yet another courtyard. I'd never learn my way around the castle at this rate. "Well, fine. I *am* a little afraid. Who wouldn't be?"

"Have you ever been down there?" Even a basic map of the underground prison would be useful.

"Once." She sighed and leaned against a stone wall, only to pick at a sad-looking pear tree that, sheltered under an overhang as it was, had somehow survived this late into the season. "King Laurent had gotten some notion into his head that prisoners would be allowed to celebrate Sommermas. I took a basket of spiced peaches down and gave them to the jailer. That was all. It was duty, and it was—it was horrible. It took the servants two weeks of trying to get the stench out of that dress. The king hasn't suggested such a thing since, and I haven't been back. I wish I could forget the things I heard and saw there."

She sounded traumatized, but she was a sheltered noble-woman. I'd been raised on a farm outside of a small village. I could handle it.

"Spiced peaches," I replied. "How odd."

"Probably poisoned. I didn't ask, and I'd rather forget." Juliana dropped the rose leaves to the ground and pointed out another wing. "That's the chapel over there—where you'll marry. Let's go see."

She was changing the subject, and I didn't want to think about someone poisoning Thomas under the guise of charity, so I followed her through a narrow alley and into the building. The single church in Elternow had glass—uncracked, we always made sure of that—

but there wasn't any to be found in the walls here. Consistent with the castle's original use as a fortress, even a place meant to worship God was built like the rest of the castle, with thick stone walls and no entry points for arrows or enemies or bullets to enter.

The constant reminder of war and strife was depressing in a way, but I attempted to focus on the good. A chamber organ sat to one side, a stack of paper on top. I had no idea how to read music, but for the first time since I'd decided to rescue Thomas instead of marrying my sovereign, I wished I could stay and run my fingers over those keys until I could manage a song. For now, I'd enjoy the daydream and the sensation of something holier than myself.

I turned toward the altar, trying to decipher the saints portrayed on the icons surrounding. St. Margaretha at least should have been familiar, if not out of actual familiarity, then gratitude. She'd brought me here, after all—she would be responsible for Thomas's release. Squinting at the squares, each engraved in gold, I mouthed the ones I recognized.

"Riette." Juliana hissed my name, and when I turned from the altar, she was standing beside a side table that held—

I gasped, my eyes wide.

Two crowns.

One of them was large, heavy, studded with blue stones that I assumed were sapphires. Not that I'd ever seen such a thing, but the other girls talked about them sometimes. It was obviously King Laurent's, and I didn't give it much more thought than that.

Because the one that sat next to it took my breath away.

Lighter than the king's but hardly delicate, it was a subtler gold, rimmed with colored stones of all hues. From the azure of the sky, the emerald of the woodlands, and the rose and amethyst of the blossoms that dotted the moors around Elternow, it was the Kingdom of Meirdre turned a priceless work of art.

Soon to be *my* crown.

Juliana waggled her eyebrows in enthusiasm and pointed, but I shook my head. "I can't touch that!"

I backed away, more disturbed by her excitement than anything else. It seemed to be some grave offense to try it on, especially since I had no plans of ever wearing it on my head for more than thirty seconds.

"Please," she insisted. "It's absolutely stunning, and I want to see it on you. And this wing is empty—no one will see!"

It was empty, like she said. Emptier than I thought it would be, which was strange. Shouldn't a castle be filled with advisors and courtiers and nobles? So far there'd only been a few servants, the king, and Juliana.

It didn't seem appropriate to ask about the state of the place, so I forced myself to smile before I crossed the marble to take a closer look. Juliana was right—the crown was stunning. At home, its gems would have been ostentatious, but here, they were understated.

"I do wish I could try it on." I glanced sideways at her. Grave offense or not, it was so tempting that I almost felt as though the crown was calling to me. And why wouldn't it? I'd never owned so much as a gold ring before.

"You should." Her smile grew broader. "After all, we'll have to see how it looks on you so we can figure out just the right way to style your hair. The fashions in the paintings aren't in style anymore, and Sara will need direction."

"You're so practical." A chuckle burst forth from my lungs.

"Always. Here, turn around."

I obeyed, with one last touch of my unadorned hair. Weight settled onto my head, and I laughed again.

"What's so funny?" Juliana sounded disapproving this time, and I wondered if I'd insulted her.

I couldn't have explained it to her, didn't know myself. "I'm not sure," I said. "I think I'm just thinking of the headache I'll have after wearing this for hours on my wedding day."

She made another noise of disapproval and came around in front of me. "It's enchanting," she replied, tucking some of my curls back while pulling others down. "Like it was made for you. I wish you could see it right now."

I glanced around, but there were no mirrors in the chapel, naturally. It was a place to focus on God, not on such silly things as looks, and while Juliana continued to express her admiration, I decided that was for the best. I'd stand here for an hour staring at myself if I could, and the weight was already bothering me—not to mention I was enjoying the approval and wealth more than someone of my status should. Than any woman should, really.

"Juliana—take it off, please." I rubbed the back of my neck, the pain increasing by the second. "We'll have to find some other way to figure out how to do my hair, because this thing is hurting me already. It must be pulling on my hair or something."

"Strange." She did what I asked and placed the crown back on the table, then went back to fussing with my curls. "It's really very light."

"I'm not used to having anything on my head." Not something this uncomfortable, anyway. "I suppose I'll just need to get used to it."

At that, Juliana frowned in my direction. "Are you feeling all right? You've gone quite pale." Her hands began to wind in and out with each other. "Oh, no—I should have never been so selfish. I've overdone it, and you with hardly any sleep for the past few days. Let's get you back upstairs to lie down for a bit."

I wanted to snap at her that I felt fine, that I wasn't so weak that a few nights of poor sleep were going to do me in, but the truth was, I wasn't fine. The icons surrounding the altar had disappeared into a chaotic vision of wavy lines and sparkles, and looking at the white marble floor instead didn't do enough to steady my balance. If this was nothing more than a headache, it was proving to be an unusual and terrifying one. I'd have to ask Sara to find a surgeon who could procure some herbs for me, and on my first day no less, like some invalid. Surely the king wouldn't want a convalescent as a wife. Would he send me home before I had a chance to save Thomas?

Lost in those fears, I clung to Juliana's arm as she led me through the castle, my vision growing worse by the second. Fatigue? Dehydration? Stress? All of them and then some? Being able to identify the cause while being unable to treat myself would have been amusing if my sudden pain and the spots that floated through my field of vision weren't such a vexation. Nausea joined the undulating lines, and I focused so hard on not throwing up that I couldn't tell if she was retracing our steps or not.

Soon enough, the hard stone under my feet turned soft, but not rug soft. Wood? I blinked down at my feet, and to my surprise, my vision had cleared. The headache still raged somewhere in the background, but I was able to ignore it enough to bask in the return of my sight. Juliana came to a stop as I did, and I looked cautiously at her through my eyelashes, praying the awful sparkles wouldn't return.

"Where are we?" I asked. "This pattern—it's so random."

Juliana ran her fingers across my forehead and squinted down at the floor. "This is the grand ballroom. It's a map of Meirdre. See?" She skipped a few steps to my left, caution still written all over her face. "Here's Lochfeld Castle. The cliffs you rode up are here, and this"—she stepped back a few more paces—"is Elternow."

I massaged my temples as I looked around. When I stepped back and looked at the floor as a whole, it made sense. "That's why it seemed so random," I replied. "I was staring at the border with Iraela."

Juliana pointed. "And Haszen is over here."

"This must have taken months to create." Of all the things I'd seen since arriving at the castle, besides the queen's crown, the map was the most impressive. Each boundary, each mountain range depiction, each village and outpost had been created by small insets of darker and lighter wood. Light oak ships floated through a sea of ebony to our east, and the forests were painstakingly arranged in a bark that shone a vague green. I paced along the border of Nantoise, to our north, my headache forgotten.

"It's exquisite, isn't it?" Juliana asked.

I nodded, fascinated, as I traced the path of the Charmont River that separated us from Nantoise with my foot. A small segment of the border north of the river sparkled in the light of the lamps above us, drawing me closer.

"What's so special about this section?" I asked, kneeling.

Juliana frowned from above. "Nothing that I'm aware of. Why?"

"The craftsman set this piece with diamonds." I'd never seen diamonds before an hour ago, but I suspected that's what they would look like in a floor. "Look, right here on the border by the sea. How odd."

"Diamonds?" She lowered herself to the floor next to me and ran her fingers over the glittering line. "Riette, this is mahogany."

"No, no, it's—it's lit, as if from within." It was too hard to explain what I was seeing, so I sat back on my heels and rubbed my head. "I'm seeing things again. I think my headache's coming back, and worse than before."

"Time for a rest then, and no argument." Juliana pulled me to my feet and eased me toward the door. "We don't have much time before the festivities begin, and we need you in perfect shape. The king will be furious if things are delayed because I've made you ill."

I looked back once as she dragged me from the ballroom.

The border was still glowing.

CHAPTER SIX

I HAD JUST POKED MY FINGER FOR THE THIRD TIME IN FIFTEEN minutes when Sara came knocking on my door. More than happy to set the needlework aside, if only for a moment, I sprang from my chair, a smile on my face.

Juliana had forced me to bed immediately after reaching my room, and while I lay on my back with a cool rag over my head, she'd found two servants to keep me company and take in a few of my new gowns. It wasn't the way I'd wanted to meet my future helpers, but she wouldn't allow me back on my feet. Instead I'd closed my eyes and listened to them chatter about court intrigue while they tailored my clothing—intrigue which to their minds, appeared to involve which new courtiers were single and if said courtiers would *ever* make an appearance at Lochfeld.

My headache was gone by the time Juliana ushered them out, so she'd shoved me into a chair and placed my embroidery basket in my lap. I hadn't been certain staring at my hoop and fabric was any improvement over my headache, but I counted and knotted and cut thread with a diligence Mama would have been proud of.

"He wants to see you at once," Sara whispered, undoing my gown and yanking it off my head as she spoke. She hadn't glanced at the hem, yet she seemed to know how muddy it would be. Juliana and I hadn't been careful on our tour. "At least your hair will do tonight. We'll just get you into something clean and be off."

I didn't protest as she attired me in something more appropriate for a formal ball than an afternoon meeting. He was the king, and I would appear exactly as Sara decreed necessary. She knew better than I did, and after his comments about my hair last night—or had it been this morning?—I would do anything to avoid his ire. And to tell the truth, I was rapidly getting used to fine velvet and silk.

Still, my palms were sweating on said velvet as I curtsied in his office ten minutes later.

"I heard you were asking about the dungeon, my dear," he greeted me, leaning back in his chair.

Juliana. I could scarcely contain my fury, but at least I knew now who not to trust. That was valuable knowledge, even if I'd pay for it now.

"No, sire," I said, staring just over his shoulder. A painting hung on the wall behind his ornate desk, and I met the subject's gaze instead. A dead king was less intimidating. "Not really. Simply about the identity of the door—she was taking me on a tour."

"Is that so?" He stood and offered his arm. "Perhaps I was remiss in not doing the task myself. Juliana is quite competent, but your introduction to the castle should have been performed by someone more familiar."

"Sire, that's not necessary. I would not take you away from your duties." I couldn't imagine what those duties might be, but ledger upon ledger covered the top of his desk, along with a few rolled maps. Tyrant or not, his responsibilities must have been great.

"Nonsense," he replied, guiding me toward the door. "Welcoming you properly was my greatest duty, and I failed."

The guards outside fell in behind us, and I shut my mouth as we meandered through corridor after corridor in silence. Village girl or not, I wasn't naïve enough to not know where he was taking me. By the time we arrived at the barred door, my imagination had conjured up enough dismal outcomes to fill a library's worth of novels.

He didn't even need to order the guards to unlock the door. One did, then stepped back as he ushered me inside. We were alone in the corridor to the dungeon then, and against my better judgment, I clung to his arm as the door swung shut behind us, alerting everyone within hearing distance that someone had entered the dungeon.

"This was part of the original castle," he began in a conversational manner. I was beginning to understand that he fancied himself a storyteller, and had he been anyone else, I might have hung on his words—they were simply that powerful and intriguing. "Seven hundred years ago, when this place was nothing more than a hillside fortress, we didn't have the ability to store ice in the summer, so the basement was used for food storage. During one conflict or another, the cellars were repurposed for prisoners of war, and, eventually, our own criminals. Thieves, murderers —traitors."

"Fascinating," I murmured, though I was anything but fascinated. Apprehensive about seeing Thomas, that I was.

"Isn't it?" he asked. We reached the top of the stairs, and his hold on me grew firmer, as though chivalry existed in a place like this. "Of course, its current use is rather unpleasant, and I'm afraid you're about to see some things that will shock a lady."

I steadied my knees. "I've seen hogs butchered."

He stared at me for a moment, then burst into laughter. The sound was impossibly loud in the closed stone stairwell, and I flinched, missing the last step. He grasped my elbow, and I somehow managed to find my feet on the slick floor.

Water—it had to be water I've just stepped in.

"These are not hogs here, my dear," he replied.

"Sire!" A rotund man hurried down the corridor to greet us, cutting off whatever else the king had planned to say. "You honor us with your presence." He shot a glance at me. "And the presence of your lady."

"A brief visit only, Hek. We're here to see one of your guests—Thomas Wennink."

I stiffened.

"Ah. He is—well, come, come."

He is what? I freed myself from King Laurent's hold and picked my way along the rough stone, stumbling the entire time. The dungeon was quieter than it was in my nightmares, but the smell of urine and mice was almost overpowering. There were no cells in the main corridor, but my quick glances to the left and right filled in the rest of the picture—any prisoners were down the hallways perpendicular to us, though I couldn't see much more than a few iron bars lit by a single torch.

"Here, here."

Hek motioned us left down the third cross-hallway, then stopped us before an arched doorway covered by bars. I blinked, trying to adjust to the darkness beyond them, but it was no use, even when Hek placed an oil torch in the holder outside.

"Thomas?" I called.

A scuffling sound came from within, then he appeared in the shadows deep inside.

"Riette?" More scuffling, then a curse. "What are you doing—" His eyes landed on my dress. "What are you wearing?"

He sounded weary but not broken, and my heart skipped a beat. Maybe he hadn't talked. Maybe the rest of his men were still safe. Maybe there was still hope.

"It's a long story," I said, still too close to the king. "The Feast of St. Margarethae—I'm to select a prisoner who deserves clemency."

There was a lengthy silence. I crept closer, lifting my skirts from the mud and water and heavens knew what else that flowed out of his cell through the channel drains on the floor outside. Childish infatuation or not, I badly wanted to reach in and touch him, but the chains around his ankles and neck prevented that—not to mention King Laurent's presence at my side.

"I've prayed for you since you were taken," I said, when he didn't reply. "For whatever that's worth." That was mostly a lie, but it sounded like something I was expected to say—by my parents, by the king, by God, by Thomas himself.

"That's enough for tonight, my dear." The king guided me backward with a light touch on my elbow. "The betrothal ball is tomorrow night, and you need your rest."

"Betrothal?" Thomas lunged at the bars, only to be brought up short by the length of the chain. In the dim of the dungeon I could see the delayed understanding in his eyes. "You—that dress? You wanted nice clothes and more food that badly?" He twisted toward the king. "You bastard. It's not enough for you to take our food and money. You have to take our women, too?"

I hadn't known King Laurent was carrying a sword. I should have noticed it earlier, but I'd been so distracted by the prospect of a visit to this horrid place that I hadn't paid attention to anything he was wearing. And if Thomas's reach didn't extend to the bars, the king's sword certainly reached inside. The point hit Thomas's neck, drawing a drop a blood.

"Questioning me is what got you here in the first place," the king snarled. "I would avoid any further missteps if you want to die with your tongue attached."

I held my breath. Interrupting this disagreement could be fatal; I certainly didn't want that sword under my throat. Thomas, after what seemed like an eternity, took a step back, and the king sheathed his sword once more.

"Good. At least you've learned something." He turned to me. "Come, Riette."

I wanted to kill him, or at least strike out at him. I could have struck him, too, because Hek had departed as soon as the king had drawn his sword. And even though he would overpower me almost immediately if I did, I was certainly the last person he'd expect to slap him or scream at him.

Instead, I meekly took his arm and walked out.

There was only one thing left to do.

CHAPTER SEVEN

I DIDN'T KNOW WHAT THE APPROPRIATE ETIQUETTE WAS WHEN greeting someone who had threatened to stab one of your friends. Thankfully, the man who'd done that was a king, so etiquette decided for me, just like it had decided on my gown, a deep ivory velvet that likely weighed more than its wearer.

Ignoring the stares of the hundred strangers crammed inside the throne room, I curtsied, then breathed a sigh of relief as he stood and offered his hand. As protocol demanded, I kissed the back of it, then took his arm. It was unnerving to be so close to someone who could kill me with a single move of his sword—or a single word—but it was either focus on him or the throng of eyes on me.

I chose him.

"I was beginning to think the castle was empty," I whispered as we proceeded out the throne room and into the ballroom. "Where did all these people come from?"

"Most of my advisors live elsewhere. Out of necessity. The courtiers too, for a long time now." If my breach of protocol in the form of speaking before the crowd irritated him, he didn't show it. "Perhaps someday . . ."

"What kind of necessity?" His wistfulness intrigued me.

"Shh." He placed a tender finger to my lips. "There will be no talk of politics tonight. This is a celebration."

Hardly offended by his completely logical reminder, I resisted the urge to turn back and stare at the crowd. "Do you ever get used to being the center of attention?"

"Never. If you could feel my heart, it would beat so quickly against your hand you'd think me ill." His lip turned up. "You just learn to live with it."

"Tell me how?"

He beamed at me as we passed through the grand doors. "You ask too much, my dear. Or at least, you ask for something I'm no expert in. You'll learn, same as we all do."

I wouldn't, but I couldn't say that, nor let on that my immediate future plans didn't include him. Etiquette—there was that word again—demanded we spend the evening together anyway, so I was stuck with him for now. There was, evidently, some tradition about proving to the people that we loved each other enough to spend a few hours together, even though our arrangement had nothing to do with affection, and everyone here knew it.

Juliana ran up to me as I was contemplating the horror of an upcoming dance with my new betrothed, wearing a gown which put my own to shame and clasping the hand of a young man whose blond curls were almost longer than her own. She curtsied for the king and nodded at me, then smiled.

"Sire, if you don't mind the interruption, I've been wanting to introduce Riette to Berend since she arrived."

King Laurent's brows rose. "Berend. You've returned from Brannitz later than scheduled."

Juliana shot me a look. *The king controls the conversation,* she seemed to say. *You'll get used to it.*

"Snowmelt made the Kalcine impassable for almost a week,"

Juliana's companion replied. "We finally managed to ford it just a few days ago—it was a difficult ride back."

"I'm glad you made it when you did. Juliana has told you of my news?"

"She has." To his credit, the man turned toward me, including me at last. "And I wish both you all the happiness we've found."

I smothered a giggle. *Happiness.* Did we all play the same game, or were he and Juliana truly content together? She was staring up at the young man like he was the only person in the room, so perhaps they were. Jealousy replaced my amusement. I would never find that. Not with King Laurent, my betrothal vow being the lie it was. Maybe not even with Thomas.

"Thank you." King Laurent drew my hand up and kissed it. "Berend, this is Riette. Riette, the Duke of Athnard, Juliana's husband."

Juliana was married to a duke? That explained much. With flushed cheeks, I gave him a short curtsy, acutely aware that a week before we'd never have been standing in the same room, and he wouldn't have bothered speaking to me.

"I'm so pleased to meet you, Your Grace. Juliana has been quite welcoming. She's made my transition as pleasant as it can be."

"She doesn't argue when I choose her clothes, and that's good enough for me. It's almost like dressing a doll." Juliana sidled up to me and favored King Laurent with what I felt was an overly intimate, pleading expression. "Please, dear brother, might I borrow her for just a while?"

My breath caught.

Brother?

I hadn't been aware of the certain angle of their chins before, but it was there, along with the same long, dark lashes that had caught my attention when I'd first met the king. They'd looked incongruous underneath Juliana's blonde curls, but it now it was all too clear they'd both inherited the look—probably from the man hanging on the wall in the king's office.

"You know the rules. Betrothal festivities." Her husband chuckled before King Laurent could respond. "And I have missed dancing with my wife."

I gave her an apologetic look as he dragged her off, leaving me alone with the king once more. "Juliana's your sister," I said. "I had no idea."

"Younger by seven years." He gave her a look at she walked away, and I suspected he'd barely avoided rolling his eyes. "A former handful, she was."

"A family trait, sire?" Heavens, had I just flirted with him?

Surprise flashed across his face, like I'd just accused him of something worse than treason, then faded into amusement. "No. Not exactly. Though I suspect I was a disappointment to my father in other ways."

It was the wrong time and wrong place to ask him why—for that matter, I doubted questioning his comment would ever be appropriate. Still, it stabbed at my mind, breaking loose curiosity I didn't know I had. I knew his father had died when I was a toddler, his regent had been an uncle who'd died ten years ago, but I had little knowledge in the way the Meirdrean court had worked when he was a child. Growing up in a village on the moors didn't help with that.

"I'm sorry to hear that," I replied.

"Ancient history. We all make do with the situations we find ourselves in today."

I was about to open my mouth to reply when a brilliant glare caught my gaze, like the light of our fireplace had reflected off the coin in Willem's hand that night. Fire? My heart skipped a beat, but there seemed to be no panic in the ballroom to suggest such. I turned toward the light, and as I did, it focused itself on a single spot on the floor.

On the spot due west of Lochfeld.

I rubbed my eyes, and King Laurent caught me gently by the forearm. "My dear, are you quite well? You've gone pale."

I looked up and down the ballroom, mostly filled with velvet and silk. Outside of the hundreds of candles that illuminated the space, nothing else glowed. It was the diamonds I'd seen, and Juliana hadn't, the sparkling that I'd blamed on the headache the crown had given me.

The crown . . .

"No. I'm fine. It's just—your map. It—" I shook my head and twisted my wrist from him. I couldn't confess to what I was seeing. He'd think me mad, would send me from the castle at once, and then Thomas's fate would be sealed. "It's beautiful."

"If only I had the ability to create something so lovely, I could die happy. But it brought you to me, you know."

"How?"

"I threw a coin." He grinned, somehow shy. "It landed on Elternow without rolling, so I sent Willem there to select a wife."

Becoming a king's bride because of a coin toss was more than a little amusing. He led me onward, introducing me to advisors and dukes and counts—all the while smiling graciously as I floundered about, pretending this was somewhere I belonged, feigning that I couldn't wait to become an official member of the court. In truth, I wanted out of this ballroom and away from its maddening map, and I wanted out of the castle.

By the time he pulled me into an alcove and offered me a small glass of wine, my feet were sore, my head was beginning to ache from the cacophony of a hundred voices in an enclosed space, and my soul ached to examine the wood floor. In short, both my body and mind were failing me. Our token privacy might have the slightest hint of impropriety to it, but no one would question the king needing time with his betrothed, and I needed the break. Settling on the bench there, I moved my toes back and forth in their silk prisons until the blood began to flow again.

"You've done wonderfully tonight." He traced a finger down my cheek. "I am so very lucky they went to your house first."

His touch made me shiver like Thomas's kisses once had, and I hated him for that. "I'm pleased I've done right by you, sire."

"You certainly have." His smile slipped. "I know you don't love me now. But could you ever?"

It was the last thing I'd expected him to say when he'd escorted me over here. The alcove, though open to the ballroom, became a sweltering furnace, and I was certain he could feel my unwelcome reaction. I lowered my gaze to my shoes, but there was no way he took that for demureness, either.

"I wasn't aware a fondness for each other was a prerequisite for a royal marriage," I replied.

Or any marriage.

He sat back and examined me. "My parents did not love one another. Can you imagine what it's like to grow up watching that? To wonder if that would be you one day? To wish you could find something more?"

"No," I said quietly. My parents had loved each other—for the most part. Marrying for love wasn't common in their generation either, though sometimes I believed they'd grown into their love. "I can't."

"Juliana found happiness. My mother has at long last, even though it's in another kingdom. And I wish the same for myself." I didn't reply, and he coughed, once. "But I'm aware such things can take time. I won't rush you."

"Sire!"

A man in a cream and navy uniform—cavalry, I thought it might be—darted toward us, and the king stood, his forehead creasing in concern as his fingers brushed mine.

"Lieutenant? I trust you're not interrupting my respite to discuss strategy."

The lieutenant bowed rapidly, more out of breath than he should have been from an evening on a ballroom floor. "Sire, we've just received word from our scouts of Nantoisens skulking near Vilstel. They've crossed the border!"

I glanced up, alarmed. Vilstel was a fishing port, and an important one at that. We'd never traded with them, but much of the kingdom did, and an attack on the shipping and fish markets there would be devastating.

The king waved his hand. "Another raid. It's as if they know we're otherwise occupied this week."

"Not just a raid this time." The lieutenant's lips thinned. "They destroyed sixteen ships two days ago. The people are frightened, riots are beginning. If left unchecked—"

"I see." King Laurent's face had gone grave, and a small cluster of questioning men in uniform had surrounded us. "You've saddled Foxfire?"

The lieutenant nodded.

"Riette." The king turned to me and gave the slightest nod of his chin. "I'm afraid I must ride tonight. Some things must be taken care of in person. I'm sorry to delay to our nuptials, but another few days will seem like an hour in the end."

He kissed my hand, and as Juliana took his place and patted away what she doubtlessly thought should be tears, I celebrated inside.

I had at least three days to figure out a way to free Thomas.

And find out why the map on the ballroom floor was glowing in the exact place where the Nantoisen raiders had crossed the border.

CHAPTER EIGHT

Juliana fell to her knees beside me in the empty ballroom, a look of skepticism on her face.

"You had a headache, Riette," she said. "Even the surgeon said it can sometimes cause vision disturbances. Just like you described—shimmers and sparkles and wavy lines. You ought to know that as well"

I could hear the doubt of my healing abilities in her tone, and maybe she was right. "The headache ended when we stepped inside here—and my sight became better. It was only this small piece that sparkled."

I brushed my fingertips over the wood of the Meirdrean-Nantoise border, but it was dark, like the rest of the outline. The diamond-like glitter that had drawn my attention before was gone, and as much as I blinked and rubbed my eyes, it refused to reappear.

"And it's not now?" she asked.

I knelt back. "It's not now. And I don't understand."

"You were seeing things." Her admonition was kind but firm. "You just needed rest, and no one would blame you for that."

"Maybe." I had less desire to argue—or even speak with her—now that I knew she was the king's sister.

"Well," she replied, pushing herself to her feet, "I'm in need of some fresh air. Would you care to join me for a stroll through the east garden?"

I shook my head. A thin layer of snow had fallen last night, and my body hadn't yet forgotten what *too cold* felt like.

"I think I'll retire for a few hours. You're right—maybe I just need some rest."

Juliana didn't argue, and once she'd stepped outside the ballroom, I second-guessed my desire for a nap. After a few days' time, I would never have the chance to visit a castle again. Perhaps my new surroundings had sparked a hitherto undiscovered sense of adventure. The east passage from the ballroom led to the stairwell that would take me straight to my room, so I chose the west corridor, narrower and dark in the late afternoon, yet still lit with the ubiquitous oil lamps. The stone walls eventually opened up into a small courtyard which was probably lovely in every other season. Today the walls blocked nearly the entire sun, and I shivered as I hurried across, cursing my decision to not bring a cloak.

So intent was I of reaching shelter that I didn't see the patch of ice until it was too late. My elbow slammed into the stone first, followed by my hip. I lay there for a moment, stunned beyond words, until the chill of melted snow began to seep through my bodice.

Soaked.

I pushed myself to my feet, finding yet another injury as I did so. My ankle refused to hold my weight, so I leaned against the nearest wall and lifted my gown just enough to see a brilliant red mark under my stocking that was sure to become a bruise. Too bad I couldn't do much about it without the stash of herbs I'd left in Elternow.

"This certainly wasn't the way I expected to meet his betrothed."

I dropped my skirts and screeched. The owner of the voice—who'd now seen more of my leg than was proper—was dressed in black robes and carried a half dozen leather-bound books under his arm. His attire gave him away at once, and no matter that religion had been an afterthought in a village where growing food was more important than anything else, I was just pious enough to be humiliated at the predicament he'd found me in.

"It's strange," he began, helping me stand with his free hand, "how many react to my appearance with that very reaction."

A flushed spread across my cheeks, the only warm thing in the courtyard. "I slipped on the ice, Father. My ankle is—not broken, I would think, but I'm not sure I can make it back to my room."

Not up all those stairs.

"Lucky for you that I was a physician before joining the church. Yours is not the first ankle I've seen, nor will it be the last, I'm sure." The corners of his eyes crinkled. "I lit the fire in the library an hour ago, and it must be blazing by now. Please, come warm up. You appear to need it."

I hobbled inside, fully intending on finding the closest chair to said fireplace—but froze in astonishment once we crossed the threshold. The castle had impressed me from the first hour, with its silken walls and arched ceilings and marble floors, but the library was something out of a dream.

Ornate rugs lay on the wood floor, tempering their high polish. Several brocade chairs were clustered around the fireplace, a typical arrangement for this time of year—likely they'd be moved to the overhang outside in spring. The ceiling was carved in the same style as the throne room, but this time I could pick out the stories told in the mahogany and ebony: fairy tales. Princes and kings who wielded magical swords, malicious ghouls who made deals with malevolent fairies, princesses who saved their land from evil.

And the books? It wasn't difficult to tear my stare from the ceiling. I'd never seen so many. Had never imagined so many existed in the entire kingdom.

The priest helped me to a chair, and I fell gratefully into it, thankful for the ability to take weight off my sore ankle. His books hit a table somewhere behind me, then he appeared again, this time with a tumbler of clear fluid.

"Oh," I said. "Thank you, but I couldn't possibly—"

"Medicinal," he replied, taking a seat next to me. "If anyone bothers you about it, tell them I ordered it."

Whatever liquor he'd poured burned my throat going down, but a pleasant warm sensation welled up in my chest, and I decided he was right. Melted snow soaked the hem of my gown, my left sleeve in not much better shape, but until I warmed enough to stand the feel of ice on my bare foot in private, I wasn't going anywhere. Fire and liquor, it was.

"So," he went on, "you were it."

I didn't have to ask what he meant. The story of my arrival must have been going around the castle for days.

"Yes." I sucked down the rest of the glass and set it aside. "I must confess, though, we don't learn of these royal traditions where I'm from. I was shocked to find the king chooses a bride from the nearby villages."

"Did he explain why?"

I flushed again, hoping he'd blame it on the flames and drink. "Yes."

"All of it?"

"I'm not sure what you're implying, Father . . ."

"Gerritt Rasch. But Gerritt will do." He gave me a quiet smile and crossed an ankle over his knee. "Meirdre's troubles are nothing new. Our location between the Tourmel Mountains and the sea puts us in an excellent—and precarious—position in this part of the world, and this narrow plain on which we exist doesn't help matters. Good, heavy rainfall, ideal for crops and livestock, plus access to the open ocean which allows for fishing and trade. Some would prefer not to trade, instead taking what they want without giving us compensation in return."

I raised my eyebrows. "You're a teacher as well as a priest and physician?" I asked skeptically.

"Just setting the stage." He peered at me oddly, like he knew a secret. "Border raids turn to skirmishes, skirmishes turn to battles, battles turn to all-out wars. Seventeen were killed in the village of Granbar last month over their grain stores. I'm afraid it'll get worse before it gets better."

I shivered, but it had to be my damp clothing. "We've always been insulated from the border raids in Elternow. I didn't realize it was so bad."

"The king does. He might be a difficult man—believe me, I know he's hardly someone to hold up as the paradigm of virtue— but he cares what happens to this kingdom and its people."

A noncommittal sound rose in my throat, eased onward, I supposed, by the liquor.

The priest laughed out loud. "Oh, he adores his power as well. Thankfully, that works in all of our favors. It behooves him to keep his borders secure and his people safe and happy—relatively so."

Did he know his king had a rebel locked in an arctic dungeon not so far away from where we sat in front of a blazing fire? None of us in Meirdre were safe. Happy? Well, that was debatable. I wasn't unhappy exactly, but anxious for the future? Yes.

"I can see you disagree with much of what I've said. No matter." He stared into the flames for a long time. "Back to why the king needed to marry a common woman, then."

"I think we've established why."

"Not entirely. Your parents have always been farmers?"

"Yes."

"And you were born and grew up in the meadows of Elternow."

"Yes." I drew out the word.

"Hmmm." He stared at me, a finger on his cheek. "Then there's a chance you're a crownkeeper."

My forehead creased in what was probably a most disagreeable manner. I'd never heard of such a thing, and it sounded vaguely superstitious and nonsensical. But he looked serious, so I forced the same expression to my face.

"I don't know what that is."

"Most don't." Father Gerritt tapped his fingers on a book on the table between us. "For reasons which will soon become apparent. You've seen the map in the ballroom, of course."

The question made me wish for another drink. "Of course."

"Well, then . . . every so often, a child is born with a particular connection to Creation. Several a year, in fact, though they usually go unknown, unaware of their gift. It benefits our sovereign to choose one of these women, even if most times, they do not."

Maps, peasant children, the king's choice of a bride. It made no sense.

"But why?" I asked.

"There is an additional gift granted to these children, bestowed upon their marriage. Or coronation, in the case of monarchs in their right, though I know of no cases where a royal child has been born with the necessary bond. They're referred to as crownkeepers—but only in private, you understand. They can feel when Meirdre is in danger, can warn of wildfires, border raids, epidemics. And the map speaks to them, shows them where misfortune is happening."

My eyes grew wide. "But that's witchcraft!"

He chuckled. "Hardly. Who do you think bestows that gift upon them? The evil one cares not for protecting something he only seeks to destroy."

I moaned in dismay. It all sounded . . . too coincidental?

"Why so disheartened?" he asked. "Most would be flattered to be granted a gift like this—and truthfully, I may be explaining this to you for no reason at all. We have no way of knowing if you're one of these children until you're wed."

"Father—" Did I dare speak of what Juliana and I had done? I didn't want to, but I could still see the undulating lines in the ballroom when I closed my eyes. "If I confess something, you'll keep it in confidence? Even to the king?"

He spread his hands. "Naturally."

I took a deep breath.

And then I told him about the map.

CHAPTER NINE

For the next day, I was in such knots about Father Gerritt's revelation that I scarcely thought of Thomas. When I wasn't in the chapel pleading to be released from this unwanted power, I was in the ballroom, forcing Juliana to teach me the dances I'd be expected to know on my wedding day. Thankfully, I was becoming a rather accomplished actress, and she had no idea of my true intentions. The map refused to glow again, however, and I constantly questioned the things Father Gerritt had told me. Had I slipped on the ice that day, hit my head, and imagined it all?

Earlier this afternoon, she had ridden off with her duke husband, making an excuse about needing sunshine and fresh air. I'd sat in my room embroidering for three hours before the light had become bad and my back stiff. It was becoming a routine of sorts, and I was grateful for anything that reminded me of home and took my mind off . . . whatever I'd turned into. A princess, a monster? I didn't know. Thomas was no doubt furious I was living in luxury, and my parents would be frightened of this new power I'd found.

And the king—Juliana's brother, I kept reminding myself— would have me hung if he knew my plans.

Later that afternoon, I found myself before the door to the dungeon, anyway, having cornered a sentry on the way down. I'd picked a young and nervous one, too, to verify my story with Captain Willem. I'd told him that the king had allowed me to bring a prisoner some food and gave him my best fake smile, though I was cringing inside. Flirting had never been a strength of mine, even when the first part of my plan depended on it.

"I'm so glad you could escort me," I said, peering through the bars. "The king will be relieved to know everyone in the castle is being so helpful."

"It's no issue at all, uh . . ." He trailed off, perhaps realizing he had no idea what to call me.

"Riette." My smile faltered, and I waved toward the door. "Can we get this over with? I'm anxious about going down and just want to be back up as soon as I can."

He nodded, practically falling over himself in an effort to unlock it. "I'll be waiting here when you get back. Good luck— and make sure you stay far away from those cells." His eyes widened. "They can grab you, even from inside."

"I'll keep that in mind," I whispered. I was only after Thomas, but if anyone else occupied those cells . . . yes, that worried me.

The hair on my forearms rose as I descended the stairs where the king had led me just a few days before. I popped a dried strawberry from the basket in my mouth, desperate for the tang to cure the dryness which had taken up permanent residence around my tongue. The sourness worked, and focusing on it allowed me to walk the rest of the way without panicking at the sound of weeping coming from somewhere farther below.

"Miss Riette?" Hek's question boomed off the stone walls as he approached; in the background, the weeping became louder. "What in the heavens are you doing here?"

I lifted the basket and prepared to lie once more. "In honor of our betrothal and the Feast of St. Margaretha, the king has asked me to bring these down so the prisoners might be able to see a taste of what they are missing because of their crimes."

Hek's broad face broke into a smile. "And you volunteered so you might speak to one of them alone before his execution, yes?"

"I—"

"You have nothing to fear from what he's confessed here. We know you refused to be a part of his treachery. He said you would have turned him in had you had the chance."

Thomas had protected me? Through torture?

Well, of course he had. Making these kinds of decisions, even during his own suffering, was why he'd risen to his position.

"I did." I forced a modest expression. "I am loyal to our king."

"He must love you to protect you after all that."

"He must," I murmured, understanding we were talking about Thomas again, though I wondered if that was true. Thomas was more about duty and loyalty than anything else—though I supposed there were some feelings there somewhere. "Can I speak with him?"

Hek reached for the basket. "Second corridor, turn left, fourth cell. Five minutes."

I relinquished the dried berries and crept off down the stone tunnel, my heart thumping. What was I supposed to say to Thomas? *I'm planning to get you out of here?* If they tortured him again before murdering him, he might not be able to keep my secret again, and then we'd both be dead.

The thought of standing on top of the scaffolding overcame me, and I stopped to rest my forehead against the cool wall. Mildew. Blood. Urine. Focusing on the smells that washed over me didn't do anything to block my fears, nor the crying which had turned to moans.

What am I supposed to do?

Whatever it was, leaning against a wall wasn't it.

Mustering all of my courage, I proceeded to Thomas's cell.

There was no torch here as there'd been before, and it was only the light from the main corridor which allowed me to remain on my feet. Clumsy I was not, but the uneven stone would make even a swan ungainly, and my sore ankle didn't help matters. At the fourth cell, identifiable only because it was darker than where I stood, I stopped.

"Thomas?"

Something shifted beyond the bars at my whisper, then moaned.

"Riette? What are you—"

"Shush. I only have five minutes, and we need to talk about getting you out of here."

"Getting me out? Don't tell me you have some sort of plan."

"No," I admitted, pressing my face against the bars and squinting into the darkness. "But I have hairpins. I wasn't sure I'd even get this far, so—"

"Toss me one. Just straight forward. I'll find it."

I pulled one from my hair and did so. A rattling echoed from inside—shackles releasing? I glanced frantically behind me, certain the noise would bring guards, but the corridor remained empty. Rattling shackles, I realized, weren't given a second thought down here.

Thomas appeared at the bars a moment later, his rough palms on my cheeks. The touch of his icy hands was chilling, but I didn't pull away—he'd doubtless been through enough that seeing and feeling another human who didn't intend him harm was more healing than anything else I could do.

"I've missed you," he whispered.

"I've missed you, too."

I'd have kissed him had we had more space between the bars. As it was, I squeezed his hand, luxuriating in the sensation of his calluses. They meant something—that he was still the same boy who'd climbed trees with me as a child and helped Papa with the plowing and taught me basic swordsmanship.

He picked the lock to his cell with his free hand as I remembered the weight of that first sword in my hand, and before I could protest that we had more urgent matters, his lips were against mine. I kissed him back, though Hek's return was at the front of my mind.

"Sorry." He tucked the pin back in my hair. "I needed to do that before anything else."

I grinned at him. "I'm not complaining. But Thomas—I wasn't planning on breaking you out today."

"Have to take the chances as they come," he said, pushing me behind him. "There may not be another. You gave me a way out of the shackles and this cell, and that's not something I thought I'd see when I woke up earlier. What time is it?"

"I don't know," I stammered. "Late afternoon, I suppose. Or early evening."

My heart fell. He was going to try to run, and I couldn't see him hurt.

Silly girl. Would you rather see him swinging?

"Then you have wonderful timing." He gave me another kiss on my cheek, and I didn't fight that one, either. "An escape at dark is what I've been dreaming of."

"But I have no plan. King Laurent is still gone, but—"

"That's all right. Just turn around and walk out. I'll take care of everything else."

He sounded casual. Too casual. Was it possible he never meant to walk out of here at all? Had he decided to martyr himself in this dungeon, to become an inspiration for whoever was willing to follow him?

I wanted to ask, but as I tiptoed toward the main corridor, the light grew brighter, and Hek and whatever other guards roamed the dungeon would hear anything I said. I kept my head up and a light smile on my face, wondering what he was up to.

Until a dagger pressed across my throat.

CHAPTER TEN

I GASPED OUT LOUD AS THE WEIGHT OF THE COOL BLADE SETTLED against my skin, and Thomas laughed.

"That's right. Just keep walking, girl. Slowly now. Keep your hands in front of you and don't struggle."

His voice was icy, and I understood at once. I slowed, both to give him another few moments to prepare and to slow my own racing heart. Hek must have heard, for boots echoed at the end of the corridor—several sets. He'd brought guards.

"Back off! Unless you'd like to explain to your king," Thomas hollered at him, "why his betrothed's blood is coating the floor of this place."

"You won't escape." Hek didn't back away, but his sword lowered a fraction. I was more worried about the three guards behind him whose swords didn't move.

"You can't let him get away," I added lamely. A skilled actress, I was not.

Thomas pinched the back of my arm through layers of fabric. I flinched, then shut my mouth. I could take a hint.

"You could have waited, Wennink!" The shout was louder

than before. "Rumor was that you were to be released in celebration of the feast."

"Is that true?" Thomas asked under his breath.

I froze, and he crashed into my back. I'd already told him this. What was he playing at now?

"No," I replied quietly. "They're lying."

The truth would have to come later. Thomas would be furious I'd kept important information from him, but if it mattered that much to him, he should have asked for all the details before he kissed me and put a knife to my throat.

"I thought as much. Wouldn't expect anything else from the king's men." He stopped us just short of striking distance. "I'm walking out of here with her. One of you"—he pointed—"will proceed us. I want a horse. I was riding by the time I turned two, so don't try to stick with me a lame one. She comes with me. I'll leave her on the trail halfway down the cliff. Unharmed."

Hek shifted from foot to foot. "I can't agree to that."

The point of the dagger turned inward, and I squeaked in shock. Thomas knew better than to rely on my acting talent. If I didn't trust him so implicitly, I'd have been terrified.

"If the rumor you spoke of was true, you have nothing to fear by letting me go, do you?" Thomas asked. "I'm simply earning my freedom a bit early."

"And hers? You will guarantee she'll return?" Hek called.

"You'll have to take that chance I won't need a hostage for long." Thomas smirked. I couldn't see him, but I could hear it in his voice.

"That's not what I mean." Hek sheathed his sword and held his hands out to his sides. "She may prefer to follow you, and you understand that I can't allow that."

Yes, yes, I do!

"She'd be a fool to follow someone who doesn't love her," Thomas said, pushing me forward once more. I stumbled on an uneven stone, and he yanked me up so hard I cried out. "I don't think you have anything to worry about there."

At least one of us could act.

✳

The unarmed guard who led us through the castle fulfilled his duty well. He followed the more remote passageways and knew which chambers would be empty, and where we would encounter servants instead of soldiers and guards. I stumbled along, Thomas's feet a continual hazard, and by the time we reached the ballroom, my sore ankle was aching once more.

"Thomas," I gasped. "We have to stop."

"No."

He pushed me forward, through the open doors. I tripped and limped behind the guard, focusing on my feet—and then something else.

A glowing piece of wood.

Regardless of what Thomas wanted, I stopped. The glowing area wasn't an area of the kingdom I knew, but he wasn't going to wait for me to call for Juliana and have a conversation about geography. It was near the castle, yes. Between Elternow and where we stood atop these cliffs. West of the Arsele Forest, east of the Kalcine River.

Thomas pushed me forward once more, toward a door on the long end of the ballroom, and I ignored everything but the map. Committing to memory what I had seen seemed important, and I mentally recited the location over and over as the guard led us into a courtyard where official visitors stabled their rides. Whether I'd remember it in an hour was another story, but since I couldn't tell the king, I could tell Thomas—he'd help.

The guard pointed to a chestnut stallion, saddled and apparently docile. Thomas nodded—the horse looked like any other horse to me, but he'd seen something in the animal that met with his approval, and I didn't argue. He looked like he was capable of carrying both of us back to Elternow, and that was all I needed to know.

Well, that and what was going on in that piece of land near the castle, between Elternow and where we stood atop these cliffs, west of the Arsele forest, east of the Kalcine river.

"Riette!" Juliana dashed toward us in her riding clothes, flushed and sweating, even in the cooling evening air. "What's going on? I heard such a commotion—" She focused on the dagger in Thomas's hand. "Who is this man? Has he harmed you?"

"Juliana," I managed to stutter, "I'm sorry."

And I was. She'd been kind to me. She couldn't help who her brother was.

Her eyes widened. I couldn't tell if she had any idea what was going on, but she darted toward me, her skirts flying. The guard moved to grab her, and Thomas, taking the opportunity, pushed me up on the saddle, then jumped up behind me with a shout to the horse.

Hooves flew. I grabbed the pommel with my fingertips. Thomas wound a hand around my waist, and for the first time since I'd come to the castle, I felt secure.

Confident.

Safe.

Behind me, Thomas gave a shout, and then we were gone.

He slowed the stallion to a walk as soon as we entered the woods below the cliffs. The trail was wide—used by the army as it was—but the cover surrounding us was heavy. No one seemed to be pursuing us, and for the moment, we could breathe easier. I leaned back against him, trying to adjust for my poor seat.

"Thomas, we've got to find another horse for me. I'm afraid he's not going to make it much farther carrying both of us."

Thomas whistled at the drenched stallion, and we came to a halt in a clearing, obviously created to make use of the spring to our left. Yawning, he slid from the saddle and tossed the reins in my lap. For a man who'd spent a while in a dungeon, he didn't look bad—he'd lost weight, yes, but he appeared lithe rather than sick. His beard wasn't scraggly in the least, and while the breeches he'd likely been wearing since he'd been arrested were dirty, they weren't covered in the blood I'd feared.

"You're going back," he said. "I'll walk. Rorswil isn't far, and I can pick up another mount there."

"Go back?" I twisted toward him and flicked the reins, enough to let the horse circle and catch his breath.

"You are to marry King Laurent, are you not?"

The stallion and I circled around him twice.

"Of course not," I said with all the courage I could muster. "I had no intention of doing so. Well, perhaps at first, when they told me what the marriage would do for Mama and Papa, but once we arrived at Lochfeld and I realized you were down below . . . I always meant to leave with you."

Thomas threw back his head and laughed. "You don't love me, Riette."

It was a slap, just like I'd felt back in the dungeon. "If we're going to make those accusations, I would think you're the guilty one, Thomas." The horse's ears flicked nervously at my sharp tone.

"Well, you're right about that. You didn't think I'd settle down and marry you, did you?"

I yanked on the reins harder than I should have and the horse gave a snort. The words were heavy. I *had* thought that. Of course Thomas would grow weary of fighting a never-ending battle. I had assumed he'd slink off to another village, another kingdom, one where he wasn't known, and that we'd begin our new lives together. After rescuing my parents from Laurent's wrath, of course. The feelings we had for each other were enough. We would grow to love each other in time, and if we didn't? Our history together would be enough to bind us in mutual respect, and even if it never turned to love, *that* would be enough.

Wouldn't it?

The question—and the answer I didn't want to admit to myself—exhausted me. I leaned forward against the horse's neck and closed my eyes.

"Heavens, Riette, you did." Thomas appeared at my side. "I had no idea. I never meant—"

"How many men do you think I've kissed?" I asked, digging my fingers into the horse's mane. He must have been well-trained, for he did nothing but snort and toss and his head.

"I never gave it any thought, truthfully."

"One. You, Thomas. It was just you." I made a sound of frustration, and the stallion snorted again. Nervous he was not, but my anger was bothering him. "I thought we had an understanding. I thought we had a future!"

He looked up at me, steady as he could be. "My loyalty is to Meirdre and her people. There is no room for anything else."

His claim slammed into me, almost unseating me. Even though we'd just agreed we didn't love each other, I could scarcely believe what he'd said. I could scarcely believe what I'd *heard*. The reins loosened in my hands, and the horse, freed from the pressure, began to paw at the ground.

Thomas caught him by the bridle. "I care for you. But being saddled with a wife isn't something I can do now. Likely not ever."

My cheeks grew red, even in the chilled air—then the rest of me followed, hot and trembling, as I realized he was right. What else was there for someone like me? We grew up—if we were lucky—we married, we had babies, we strive to provide enough food for all, we grew old, we died. In Meirdre, no one of our status ever dared to hope for more.

"I never wanted you like that." My reply was childish, but I wanted to hurt him as much as he'd hurt me.

"Riette . . . we're going to pretend?" His hand fell on top of mine. "Even now?"

I dug my heels into the stallion's side. He reared, and Thomas took a step back. Into a mud puddle, I was glad to see.

"What else do you expect me to say?" I asked.

"I don't know." He sighed. "You won't go back?"

"To marry that man? Never."

"Then where? I can't just let you ride aimlessly about the countryside—and think of your parents! What do you think he'll do to them when he finds out you're gone?"

"We'll leave Elternow. He won't search for us forever." The idea of King Laurent finding Mama and Papa and me made me want to curl up and die in terror. "He can't."

"Riette." His chin fell to his chest. "I can't let you do that."

"You—" I gave a little pressure on the reins. "You have no authority over me."

"That doesn't mean I don't care about you."

I brought the horse to a halt, more to show Thomas I had some skills than anything else. "Prove it."

"Prove it? Even if I was able to—"

"I need you to take me somewhere," I interrupted.

"Where?"

I closed my eyes and spouted off the directions I'd memorized. "Between Elternow and where we stood atop these cliffs. West of the Arsele forest, east of the Kalcine river."

"That's an interesting way of giving directions." He narrowed his eyes at me. "But that's Haszen. Got to be."

"Fine," I said, reaching down a hand in invitation. "Then take me to Haszen."

Haszen.

Near the castle, between Elternow and the cliffs, west of the Arsele forest, east of the Kalcine river.

I repeated the words over and over as we ambled down the footpath. Thomas had only agreed to throw any pursuers off our trail—of that I was certain. They'd expect him to head for his woods near Rorswil, but we'd turned west, out of the woods. No hoofbeats followed us as we headed through a vast countryside of rolling hills that seemed to stretch forever in every direction. In the summer they'd likely be as green as the emeralds in what would have been my crown, but now they were dead. Brown. Crisp. Several haystacks sat at the top of few of the hills, and even from this distance, they were black.

"Soldiers burned them." Thomas spoke for the first time since we'd rested the horse a half hour ago. "Soon as they were stacked."

"Why?" My voice was a whisper.

"Starve the people and their livestock and they can't rebel." His bitterness carried on the icy wind that whipped around us. "Maybe you did the right thing by not going back."

"It looks like mold." I squinted at the haystacks, then at the river in the distance, spilling out of its banks even in the middle of the winter. "Lots of rain here."

"It was fire," he snapped. "You can tell by the color."

I couldn't, but his tone bade no argument.

"I'm afraid," I said, changing the subject. "Something's going to happen in Haszen. I—I feel it somehow."

"Reprisals?" he asked sharply.

Was his rebellion the only thing he thought about?

"I don't know," I admitted. Why wasn't the cursed map color-coded? "It's just a feeling. Perhaps if we could ride about town a bit, see if anything looks unusual—"

"No." His reply was piercing. "There's a house where we'll be protected. We'll hide out there for now and figure out what to do next. I may have to take a side trip to Elternow and make sure your parents are safe before we head that way."

"Thomas—"

I was trapped. Father Gerritt had made one thing clear—the enchantment of the map was a secret. I couldn't speak of it to Thomas lest he laugh at me and call me silly, but I couldn't search an entire town alone, either. I wasn't *meant* to. No queen could protect the entire kingdom—but she could pass down valuable information and let others do the foot work.

And because I'd left Lochfeld, I'd have to figure it out alone.

We fell into silence then, shivering as the horse slowed to walk on the hard ground. We'd been pushing the stallion too hard, but the deepening clouds to the north spoke of more snow. Being caught in the hillside when it came could be life-threatening.

And Haszen was hours away.

CHAPTER ELEVEN

By the time we rode into Haszen, the flurries danced around us, and despite the snow, my eyes were wide. Compared to Elternow, the town was sprawling. I'd never imagined a church so tall, or houses so close together, or streets without the stray horse or cow. A fortress sat upon the hill to the north, crumbling with disuse, and as we wandered across a wooden footbridge over a thin, frozen stream, bells rang.

The entire scene was enough to warm my soul, if not my body.

Thomas brought the stallion to a stop outside a house on the end of a low row of buildings. The timber door was worn and scratched, but smoke rose from the four chimneys. I shivered as the warmth of his body left me, and I could not follow him inside quickly enough.

Somehow, I'd expected an inn, but when I shook off the little snow that had settled on my head and looked around, I realized it was a private home. That made sense—if Thomas was wanted in Haszen, this was safer. I didn't particularly care what we were doing here, because the fire across the room was roaring, the meager table in between was set with wine and bread, and my fingers were already thawing. Figures moved somewhere in my corner vision, but I was too focused on the fire to pay them any heed.

"Thomas." A man's voice broke through the chill that still hung about me. "Wasn't expecting to see you here. Or at all, truthfully. Who's the girl?"

"This is Riette." Thomas shrugged off the cloak he'd stolen from a barn hours before, and I turned toward the man he was speaking to.

"Strange," came the reply. "Riette is the name of Laurent's new betrothed."

It was the first time I'd heard someone speak the king's name with such utter casualness. The speaker was older than Thomas, perhaps closer to Papa's age, his scraggly gray hair almost shoulder-length. Fine—some didn't have time for hygiene. But it was the way he held himself, as if he expected to spring toward anyone at any second, that set my teeth on edge. Well, that and the fact he'd somehow put together my appearance and Thomas's escape with nary a question or confusion.

"She had a hairpin." Thomas glanced at me, then nodded. "She's from Elternow. We grew up together."

No mention of any relationship. I couldn't determine what that meant.

"You trust her?"

"Yes."

"Hmm."

The man stared at me, and in my gown, I felt like he was seeing someone I wasn't. A woman who belonged in another world, one with silk sheets and dungeons and ballroom floors that sparkled. How was I supposed to convince him that wasn't me? That I might have lived there for a time, but my body and mind belonged somewhere else? Heavens, my fingers were still callused from milking, and the dress I've chosen because Juliana was away from the castle was hardly the height of fashion.

"She should go upstairs," he went on.

I hadn't realized there were people higher in the rebellion than Thomas, but this man's tone left no room for doubt. With a slight smile, I headed upstairs, wrapping the blanket around myself as the warmth of the kitchen turned to ice in the stairwell. But there was a fireplace in the first room I found, and it only took a bit of effort to light a small fire with what little wood remained inside.

It was no royal bedroom in a castle, but after riding for a long while through the frozen meadows of Meirdre, it might as well have been. The mattress on the floor smelled like fresh hay, and even though there was a small pile of screws in the corner which spoke of the fate of the bed, I collapsed on it, exhausted. Things must have been bad in Haszen if the residents were burning furniture.

My own situation was even more immediately concerning. Had I done the right thing?

Leaving with Thomas had been my plan since I'd met the king that first night, but as soon as he'd put a dagger to my throat, all my plans had seemed foolish and hollow. I'd gone along with anyway, because there hadn't been another option at the time—at least, not one that my mind had come up with immediately. When he'd admitted he'd never loved me, it had sealed my confusion. Was it the fact he'd taken advantage of the situation instead of waiting for me to come up with something that wasn't quite so . . . dangerous?

Or was it just that we'd finally become honest with each other?

It didn't matter. Whatever he'd said, whatever he'd thought about us, I'd been convinced we'd marry one day. He'd never said as much in so many words, but his actions had spoken for him, hadn't they? The kisses, the smiles, the small gifts of eggs and milk he'd left for Mama some days . . . had they been a lie?

I rolled to my side and closed my eyes. There were too many

questions to contemplate right then, especially when we'd chosen Haszen as our haven because of the map. It wasn't anywhere near a border, so we were protected from raids. Wildfires? Perhaps, though the amount of snow and water in the creeks made that unlikely. What else had Father Gerritt mentioned?

Illnesses.

Earthquakes.

Floods.

Blizzards that put the entire region at risk.

Not for the first time, I couldn't help but wonder what the purpose of a vague glowing area on a map was. They obviously didn't expect a queen to know, but how could we decide whether to send soldiers or physicians? Perhaps the scout party traveled with an array of skilled men to handle whatever came up.

Warmth settled over me as the heat of the newly stoked fire began to fill the room, and my eyes grew heavy. Moments from drifting off, map or not, I jerked awake at the sound of voices below. A knot in the wood floor? I rolled off of the mattress and found it, smaller than a finger, but any void was enough to let the words of the angry man downstairs fill my ears.

"You should have known better than to bring her here, Thomas."

It was the man who'd sent me upstairs in the first place.

"I couldn't very well leave her in the woods." Thomas's placating tone was something I was intimately familiar with. "Not with the weather this time of year."

"Better the wolves get her than get us."

My cheeks flushed, and not from the fire. He dared to wish for my death when I'd done nothing wrong? I'd acted as a lookout for Thomas on more than one occasion—how could this man question my loyalty like he was?

"Riette's no wolf, that's for certain." Thomas's laugh echoed; I heard it through the knothole and from outside the door. "Just a child trying to find her way in a world she has no control over—

though she thinks she does. She'll find out she's just as weak as everyone else in Meirdre, and that unless we prevail, that won't change."

I pulled away from the hole and turned to bury my face in the blanket. Screaming was out of the question, but in all my life, I'd never wanted to shout and cry and stomp and slap someone this badly. This was what he thought of me? Everything else had truly been a lie.

A child.

Weak.

No control.

I leaned back on the mattress and squeezed my eyes shut, then rolled to the floor and put my ear back to the hole.

". . . suppose it won't matter in another few months. Once you let the armies of Vassian in, he'll be dead, and you'll be a hero."

Thomas laughed, but it sounded morose through the ceiling. "Not if I can't get there. King Damir has refused to authorize an invasion unless I personally assure him Laurent is dead, and the people will peacefully exchange his rule for another. He's not interested in a war, nor can he afford one."

I covered a gasp.

"No one will agree to another despot," a third voice replied.

"Doesn't matter." Thomas went quiet for a moment. "After Laurent is gone, they'll believe anything we tell them, no matter how erroneous it is—and it's not as though Damir won't reward us for presenting him his new domain. No more hunger, no more scarcity. Can you imagine?"

"When you put it like that . . ." It was the first man, the one who—probably rightfully, at this point—hadn't wanted me around. "All right, Thomas. You may proceed. When it's safe, head for Vassian and make your deal with Damir." He chuckled. "But I want to be named in your list of those who receive the earnings."

"Always, Lennert."

I sneezed, then froze.

"Thomas . . . go check for eavesdroppers."

Thomas sighed, and a few seconds later I heard his footsteps on the stairs. Flinging myself over on the mattress, I closed my eyes and concentrated on my rapid heartbeat. Thomas wouldn't touch me to verify I was asleep, would he? The door opened, and I tried to slow my breathing. The fire was still roaring, and I hoped the crackling hid my short, distressed gasps for air.

"Riette?"

I didn't move. Boards creaked as he moved toward me, and a finger hit my temple.

In, out.

Breathe in, out.

Just like he'd come, he'd disappeared.

"No eavesdroppers," I heard through the floor. "She's fast asleep—not used to riding like we did."

"Good. Because if she learns of your plan, it won't take long for the king's inquisitors to pry it out of her—if she doesn't tell him herself first. You'll have to make sure she dies before that happens."

"You won't need to worry about her. I'll do whatever it takes."

I woke the next morning, stiff from the hours in the saddle and heartsick over Thomas's betrayal of Meirdre—and of me. My feelings for him mattered little at the moment, though, since any indication I was aware of his plot would be the end of my precarious grasp on life. His leader had convinced me of that. Besides, I had more immediate problems.

I needed to find out why the map had led me here.

I located the chamber pot, and then splashed a little icy water from the wash basin on my face, which went a ways into shedding the rest of my fatigue. I'd need all my wits to pretend to be

Thomas's jilted but surviving lover, sticking by his side because I was convinced his cause was right and just, although the smells of sausage and eggs from down below made that pretense easier. I crept downstairs, wondering how they'd greet a woman they'd so easily sentenced to death the night before, but to my surprise, only Thomas sat at the long table, a full plate across from him.

"It was a late night," he said, pointing to the food. "The others are still sleeping, so I went ahead and made something for you."

Part of me wondered if he was making up from what I heard last night, but I sat, the rich smell of butter impossible to ignore.

"I appreciate it. After yesterday—" I closed my mouth.

"It was a long day," he said all too calmly, wiping more butter on a piece of brown bread without looking at me. "We both said hurtful things."

"Yes." I speared a piece of sausage with my fork. "But I was wondering . . . if I could borrow the horse. Take a look around town."

"Why?" His gaze was sharp.

"I have to settle somewhere. This looks populated enough; my parents and I might be safe."

Thomas leaned back and folded his arms. "It's too dangerous."

I couldn't argue with someone who was more than willing to kill me to further his own aims. Still, I couldn't get the map out of my head.

"Then I'll go for a walk."

"Rieeeette." It was the same pleading tone I recognized from our childhood, when I'd insisted on climbing trees, and he'd thought it a silly pursuit.

I shoved a roll in my mouth and stood.

I hated having Thomas behind me as we rode through central Haszen. There could be a knife in my kidney before I knew what was happening, but I knew there'd been no leaving the house any other way. He kept his hands to himself though, and I was grateful for that.

The brief snowstorm which had caused us such concern yesterday had blanketed the town in white. The weather had warmed too, and when Thomas said that was usual here this time of year, I realized he hadn't spent all his time in Elternow—more secrets.

Would they ever end? I felt like everything I'd lived so far, everything I'd believe, had been a lie.

"This is where they store what little grain they can." Thomas pointed from behind me.

I made a noncommittal noise. A tour guide wasn't exactly what I'd been after when I'd gone downstairs that morning. He seemed to sense my irritation, for he didn't speak again when we ambled Laurent's expensive horse over the river that separated the town from the sprawl of shacks and cottages to the west. Only a third of them had smoke drifting from their chimneys, and I shivered at what the residents must be feeling. Even on our worst days, Mama and Papa and I had always had wood.

There was no way to know why he'd brought me here. Perhaps he meant to show me this was where my parents and I would be living, once I made my way back to Elternow and convinced them to leave. He was probably right. I stared at the compact houses with a critical eye. There were so many that the king would be hard-pressed to find us.

A few people waved at us as we passed, and I did the same in return, my lips pressed together. Our horse was well-fed; I couldn't help wondering if they were hoping he collapsed in the middle of the road so they could partake. How could Laurent justify feeding these animals when his people went hungry?

I pushed the question to the very far corner of my mind. How could anyone justify half the evil things they did? I'd never know the answer, and searching for it would only drive one mad.

"This isn't so bad," I said over my shoulder. "Lots of places to hide."

"Mmm. I think you'd survive here, yes."

A chill ran down my forearms at his mention of survival, but before I could come up with a reply that didn't let him know what I'd heard last night, the horse stumbled. I grabbed at the reins in Thomas's hands, pulling us to a stop. The horse was too trained to falter, and it only took a moment to realize he hadn't.

The earth was moving.

Thomas seemed to sense the tremors a fraction of a second after I did. He kneed the stallion again, sending us flying down the street toward the empty fields in the east. I didn't argue. The ground rolled and slid underneath us, making anything faster than a walk difficult, but the way the two-story homes swayed on either side of us was a greater concern.

As when we'd rode out of the castle, I clung to the front of the saddle, my bare fingers numb. Thomas urged our mount on. A scream echoed somewhere behind us, followed by a sound I could only describe as the end of the world.

I looked back, knowing what I'd see. Wood and stone lay in the road where we'd been walking just a minute before. Two homes or three? I couldn't tell through the haze of dust.

"We're almost out of the center of town." Thomas spoke loudly in my ear; the sound of screams and lumber cracking was almost ear-splitting.

I nodded, then froze upon the frightened horse. I'd known this was going to happen. I'd come here because the map had warned me—running away was out of the question. Another shriek cut through the dust, followed by sobs. A woman was dashing down the street, covered in dust, her eyes wide.

There was no time to think. I yanked on the free side of the reins, then slid from the saddle, almost reaching the ground before Thomas's hand clamped down on my arm.

"I have to go help them!"

He yanked me back up by my wrist, and I cried out.

"You'll sit right there. They're vermin, not worth saving."

"Not—" In front of him once again, I twisted backward the best I could, praying I'd misheard. His face, cold and unemotional, told me I wasn't. That woman's expression would haunt me forever, and he was . . . he was ignoring it all, just to save his own skin. "They're people, Thomas!"

"And your pity is slowing us down."

He whistled, loud, and the stallion bolted. Not knowing what else to do, I clawed at him, screaming at him to let me go. I didn't need him. I didn't need the horse. I'd find my way back to Elternow and save Mama and Papa from the king's revenge all on my own.

"Fine."

He called me a name under his breath, then shoved me, hard, and I slid off the saddle. It wasn't the first time I'd fallen from a horse—though it was the first time I'd been *pushed*—and I rolled to the side before clasping my hands over my head. As soon as the hoofbeats grew distant, I looked up.

The earth had stopped rolling, but that was all I could determine. Dust flew through the air, and I coughed as I checked my injuries. There was a scrape on my temple, and I'd landed oddly on my ankle again, but nothing seemed to be broken. I lay there, waiting for the ground to resume pitching, but it stayed still. The deathly silence that had followed the earthquake turned to screams and shouts.

I pushed myself to my feet, ignoring how the dust had turned the light coating of snow into a sticky mess. I could help. This was what I'd been sent here for, and the purpose revitalized me. Picking through the rubble, I made my way toward where I'd last seen the woman. I might not have been a mother, but my heart understood somehow. I could search, I could hold her while she cried, I could—

"Well." A man's voice cut through the panic all around me. I tore my gaze from the commotion down the street. "What have we here?"

I looked up, my body knowing before my mind.

Willem.

I hadn't seen the captain of the Meirdre Royal Guard since the night I'd met Laurent in the throne room. He had a line of dust down his uniform—even he hadn't escaped the tremor unscathed —but like me, he appeared otherwise uninjured. I stared at the silk of his jacket, unable to reconcile it with the surrounding disaster, unable to force my feet to run.

He grinned at me—or maybe my motionlessness—then pulled my arms behind me, lifting me off the ground. I kicked and screamed then, but none of the people who passed us on the streets paid me any heed. One more distraught woman, hysterical over the loss of her home and possibly her children—why would they care?

"You can keep fighting," he snarled in my ear, "but it won't change a thing."

He shoved me around a corner, toward a waiting cart with tall sides and no roof. I'd expected soldiers, but there were none, and I flailed, my confusion slowing my reflexes. But that also meant there was a chance I could talk myself out of this mess. I couldn't escape from a squad of men, but I maybe could convince Willem to let me go.

"Captain." My breath was short, from the dust that still hung around us and my own fear. "You don't understand. You have to listen. They need assistance. Medical help. I can save people, if you'd only let me—"

"I understand well enough. You brought him a dagger, then escaped with him. You thought you'd get away with that?"

I hadn't brought Thomas the dagger—there was no doubt he'd picked it from a careless guard—but Willem would never believe my pleas. With a firm hand on my arms, he pushed me into the cart and shoved me to the floor. I landed on my side with a grunt and examined my routes of escape. The wood was already cold under my hip, and it would only get worse as we began our trek back to the castle and frigid air began to flow around and under me.

"You had so much," Willem said, yanking chains from a pile in the corner. "And you threw it all away. And for what?"

"I—"

I slammed my mouth shut at his accuracy. Or maybe it was the weight of the chains he'd secured around my wrist and ankles. They hung heavy about my joints, and even before he fastened an iron collar to the opposite end to a catch on the top of the wagon, I realized there would be no escape.

"Quiet." He pulled a sack over my head, and darkness joined my silence. "You can tell the inquisitors."

CHAPTER TWELVE

I KNELT ON THE STONE FLOOR, WAVERING FROM SIDE TO SIDE IN fear. The iron around my wrists and ankles had rubbed my skin raw during our trip, and my muddy dress did nothing to shield me from the cold of the throne room. Blind though I'd been on the trip, I'd still been able to tell that it had been snowing so hard that drifts formed in the open wagon around me, and I'd be lucky if I kept all my toes.

Not that keeping them would matter for much longer. Frostbite or no frostbite, they'd march me to the execution chamber all the same. Not until the snow ended, naturally, since Meirdrean executions always took place on a clear night—legend had it that there was a tunnel in the ceiling of the death chamber, a hole in the layers of rock above the dungeon that allowed the condemned to see the stars one last time. Such were the whispers, but I was going to learn the truth. It might have been snowing when they'd brought me back, but this time of the year the storms would be waning, which meant my remaining days were few. Willem had reminded me of my fate when he'd hauled me out of the wagon upon our return, and I had no reason to doubt him.

It would be Thomas's fate, too.

For after Willem had found me, my heart hadn't had the chance to stop pounding before Thomas had been shoved into the cart as well—and judging by his sporadic unconsciousness, he might have fought harder than I had. Not that I'd been all that surprised at his capture. I wanted to look at him, kneeling next to me, but I could only focus on Laurent's boots as he rose from his throne and walked down the stairs.

"I suppose there's no accounting for taste." His tone was smooth, unbothered, almost bored. "Though I admit I'm surprised you chose him over me."

I looked up then, but he turned his attention to Thomas before I could plead for my life—or tell him that I'd chosen no one.

"Thomas Wennink," he said, "Do you have anything to say for yourself?"

Thomas swore at him, but the words were so slurred I couldn't understand them, which was probably for the best. He'd barely closed his mouth when the hilt of a sword in his abdomen silenced him once more, and Laurent's boots turned back toward me.

"And you?"

I wasn't stupid. Even in the midst of my desperate fear and frantic desire to beg for leniency, I'd known, as every Meirdrean subject did, that anything I could say would be grounds for capricious and arbitrary torture before the imposition of my sentence. I swallowed my fear, along with the last of my hope.

"Nothing? I think I deserve an explanation of why my betrothed rode off with a known rebel. Someone"—his voice rose to a shout—"who would see me dead!"

I jerked upright, and though I'd wanted to hide my fear, I could feel it on my face. I could sense it, and for some reason I wanted Laurent to see me as courageous.

"Will—will my explanation change anything?" I asked quietly.

He stared at me, and for a fleeting moment I saw the man who'd asked if I could ever love him. The one who'd wanted a marriage—a genuine one. Would I live after all? I took two quick breaths, savoring the hope that had filled my heart, then his expression turned as hard as the sword at his side.

"No," he replied slowly, shattering my courage. "It will not."

I lowered my head.

"You have both," he went on, "been found guilty of high treason. Therefore, as is my duty as the King of Meirdre, I sentence you, Thomas Wennink and Riette Kaleveld, to death—as soon as the snow ceases."

Light glinted against the stone outside as I tried to wedge a fingernail into the shackles once more. Footsteps approached, and the lock clicked, but I was beyond caring if the visitor saw what I was doing. I didn't look up. Whether I was bound for the torture room or the hangman or managed to free myself by my own efforts, I'd be free soon, though I'd never be able to rescue Thomas now. I could hear him somewhere in the distance, his screams alternating with moans, and for some reason I felt pity for him, even after what he'd done to me and tried to do to Meirdre. For a long while I'd sat with my hands over my ears, but that hadn't been nearly enough to drown out his sounds of agony.

"Riette, stop."

I yanked my bleeding fingers from the shackles and looked up at Father Gerritt. He settled down next to me, apparently not caring that his robes had already become soaked with mud and the melted snow I'd dragged in. The white execution gown I wore couldn't look much better, but I'd been beyond caring what I looked like as soon as Hek had handed it to me.

"I have to get out of here," I said.

Thomas's earlier screams stopped, filling the cell with silence, and Father Gerritt didn't answer as he unpacked the small bag at his waist. I'd hoped for a key to the shackles or maybe a dagger, but as near as I could tell in the shadows of my cell, it was only a bottle of oil. I could do nothing but stare at his hands, spotted and wrinkled, as he prayed over it. Mine would never look like that, for I would never grow old enough for them to age. This was it. There was no escape, and even he knew it.

"Father—"

"In a moment—let me do this first. He said he wouldn't interfere."

His firmness silenced me. Was he so concerned they'd come for me before he finished his ritual? Even the king knew better than to interfere in the administration of last rites—he'd never cross a priest, would never be responsible for the damnation of my soul, I supposed.

I wanted to laugh at the hypocrisy.

Cinnamon and myrrh overtook the stench of sweat and urine as he swiped the oil on my forehead, and some of my terror turned to anger. What did he think this would accomplish? That it would save me? Heal me in advance from the mortal injuries they meant to impart on my body? If the past few weeks had taught me anything, it was that life didn't happen like that.

His palm settled on the top of my head, and I fought the urge to scream at him.

"Receive her into Your merciful arms and permit her to walk in Your light forevermore," he murmured. "There. I would be remiss in my duties if I didn't take care of that first. You have something you wish to confess?"

"Confess?" My voice cracked, and I shook my head. He was so close to finding out the truth, and though I'd been ready to tell anyone, now that I was standing on the brink, it was impossible. I would take the secret of Thomas's treachery to my grave. "Father, I've done nothing wrong."

"We've all done something," he pointed out. "Even me, believe it or not."

The cackle that sprang from my throat was perhaps inappropriate, but what did it matter anymore?

"I doubt you know anything about sin," I replied with no small amount of spite.

"It's funny you use those words. Doubt. Sin." He eyed me with more than casual interest. "Doubt can be a sin, you know."

My religious education had been sparse enough that I only had the vaguest idea of what he was talking about. I made a noise of assent anyway. If he believed this was his final chance to save my soul, I'd let him try. It couldn't hurt.

"Then we're in agreement on that? Good—though I don't think you suffer from that particular malady."

My eyes grew hot. As it wasn't bad enough to be waiting on my certain death, he was confusing me, and my confusion only added to the humiliation. I wasn't unintelligent, but I wasn't educated either, and his reminder that I lacked something most others in the castle possessed fell harshly upon me.

"Father, I don't know what you're trying to get at."

"Well, let's start with your theft of the horse."

"I didn't steal anyone's horse. Thomas did. If I'd tried to change his mind—"

For the first time since I'd entered the dungeon with the berries, I realized any escape might not have ended the way I'd have hoped. Thomas didn't love me. He'd used me. Would he have truly cut my throat if I'd fought against his plan? Likely he would have. He'd told Lennert he'd kill me if I made my way back to the castle and told anyone of his plans for Meirdre. Yes, he'd have doubtless killed me if I'd tried to escape. More heat joined the tears, only this time, it warmed me to my core with fear and rage. I'd trusted someone who would have sacrificed me for his cause.

"Father—I do have something to tell you." The story tumbled

out. Vassian, Damir, how Thomas planned to use them to over-throw Laurent, only to leave our kingdom in the same poverty as before—perhaps worse. "I tried to tell Willem, and he didn't listen, so now . . . I don't see any way around this. We're both going to die."

"There." He reached out a hand to my upper arm. "That wasn't so hard, was it?"

It hadn't been, but my confusion didn't abate.

"But I didn't confess to anything."

"You just confessed to trusting the wrong person. Not that you did anything wrong in doing so, but I suspect you needed to acknowledge it yourself. For your own peace of mind, you understand. No one should go to eternity holding a secret like that. You can't forgive him if you can't accept what he did to you and planned to do to Meirdre."

I drew my knees to my chest, the shackles clanging against the chain which held me to the wall, then laid my head down on them.

"I was so stupid," I whispered. "So naïve."

"We all have our moments," he replied easily. "Now, the treason."

I didn't answer. There was no point. Depending on what else I said, they could still torture me, and why would I subject myself to pain like that?

"I do not think," he began, "that we have time to address whether the general crime of treason itself is a sin, though I have my own opinions, of course. In a thousand years, men much more learned than I haven't been able to agree." He leaned back against the wall and folded his arms, a casual gesture I didn't particularly care for at that moment. "Your individual treason, on the other hand . . ."

"Spare me," I spat at him from my hunched position, my throat half closed. "If you'd experienced half of what I did as a child—"

"Who says I didn't? I rather think you're not familiar with my entire history."

I shut my mouth, and he went on.

"I was born in Saalben—yes, that Saalben you know as one of the poorest villages in the realm. My mother was practically a child herself, unmarried and young. They took me from her and left me on the steps of the local church one winter night, hoping I'd die—but that they could assuage themselves of any guilt by making certain I passed as physically close to the Lord as possible."

He cleared his throat. "Only I didn't. I spent my first years in an orphanage. If we had little food, discipline wasn't in short supply. I'll spare you the remainder of the details, but I learned to hate King Julian, and later, his son Laurent."

"You don't seem like you hate him now."

"Saying otherwise would shorten my life, would it not?" He gave me a slight smile. "None of us are wholly sinless or wholly evil, and I do what I can to make sure the balance of his heart and works are tipped toward good. It's never-ending work, believe me."

"I can imagine." I didn't hide my bitterness.

"And it's drudgery we all share a responsibility for."

He was probably becoming tired of my hateful laughter, but I couldn't stop myself.

"You can't possibly believe I have any responsibility for that man's evil deeds," I replied, "nor the power to persuade him to act otherwise."

"Maybe. Maybe not. I'm no seer. I can't predict the future, and I can't hazard to guess what may or may not have happened had you chosen to go forward with a marriage you consented to. I do know you were chosen for one reason or another, and that you decided to throw that summons away. That's the treason I speak of. Not against the king, but against Someone infinitely more powerful and merciful."

How could he speak of God now?

"Thomas and I are both going to die now, Father. There's no way around it."

"There is." He sounded too confident. "And I think you know what you need to do to save yourself."

"I won't do it. I don't care what happens to me in this life or the next." His figure disappeared into a blur of dark tears. "I helped save Meirdre from Vassian by telling you what I did, but I won't help Laurent oppress my own people. I won't wish for his death, but I also won't help protect him. Someone else can take up that obligation, because I refuse."

"Oh, child." The disappointment flowed from him, landing heavily on my shoulders. "You think this gift that's been bestowed upon you was meant to protect *him*?"

CHAPTER THIRTEEN

THERE WASN'T MUCH ONE COULD DO IN A DUNGEON CELL ON THEIR last day of life but cry and pray, and as much as I'd sworn to be brave when the time ultimately came, it was a foolish optimism. Some could walk to the chamber without sobbing and with their head held high, but I, it turned out, was not one of them. By the time the king swept in, two guards at his side, I was limp with exhaustion and dehydration. The floor beneath my cheek was soaked with my tears, and when I lifted my head at their entrance, a puddle remained, proof of my cowardice.

So much for valor.

The king looked down at me, his lip twisted in disgust. "Pleading and weeping for mercy is a waste of breath." He gestured at the guards. "They'll drag you out if they must, but I would hope you have enough honor to walk yourself."

Even if I'd wanted to, I was too numb to plead. And I didn't as they removed the shackles, or as I stood and crept forward to where the ceiling allowed my full height. But when they fastened my hands before me with a rough cord, the tears returned. They didn't stop when one of the men slipped the noose around my neck, scratching my skin, and I closed my eyes in fear. He tossed the free end to the ground, and I fought for air, though I was almost certain my inability to breathe was panic, and nothing more.

They weren't done with me yet.

I was certain of that when they pulled me into the corridor and my eyes adjusted once more. Thomas was there, surrounded by guards, likewise restrained, though livid bruises showed on his exposed skin. We were both pushed forward without ceremony, and somehow my legs kept moving.

Stone.

Mud.

Melted snow.

Stone.

I stared at them alternating under my bare feet, watched the hem of my gown grow dark as the rope trailed along behind me. Thomas's moans sounded in my left ear, in my right, the quiet prayers of Father Gerritt. No one else spoke, and even though I wanted to scream, something kept me quiet. Fear? Acceptance? I'd come so far from the girl who'd promised to save Thomas or else.

Still, watching him die and then hanging myself was better than what Father Gerritt had suggested. I knew, behind the traditional prayers, that he was asking for me to change my mind, but there was no chance of that. I'd made my decision.

My guards pulled me to a halt and bound my knees with a rope. I forced myself to look up as they did, at the gallows in the center of the chamber, a hole over it. No snow fell to the floor, no rain dripped from the opening. There might have been stars somewhere up there, but I wouldn't know for certain until they stood me underneath. Even so, I could see them in my mind, brilliant and dazzling, like someone had flung a handful of diamonds into the heavens. A vast and eerie darkness stretched between them, incandescent with unthinkably distant stars.

While two others pushed Thomas underneath the scaffolding, I blinked away the vision of the heavens. He stumbled then, whether out of fear or pain I couldn't tell. His rope was flung over top, and I closed my eyes, unable to watch the rest. Forcing me to watch Thomas's execution before my own, I'd finally realized, was another part of my sentence, one I would not willingly participate in. But my lack of vision made me unsteady, even with them holding on to my arms, and I opened my eyes almost immediately.

The executioner began to speak. "Thomas Wennink, having committed treason, your life is forfeit unless the king, in all his mercy, wishes to grant you clemency."

There was a pause, a heavy silence in the stone chamber, but his suggestion was a formality. The king rarely—if ever— witnessed executions, and his presence at my side wouldn't change the outcome.

"Then may you be forgiven of your crimes and be returned to the arms of the—"

"Stop!"

My heart thudded at Thomas's scream; I grew light-headed, even in the chill of winter that drifted through the hole. So dizzy I sagged against the wall, against the guards who'd grabbed me. It didn't make sense, and that was the only thing I could repeat in my mind as my surroundings blurred. I might not have courage, but he did, more than anyone I'd ever known. He wouldn't have begged them to stop. He wouldn't have humiliated himself like that.

And then I realized, as I was jerked back to my feet and the chamber sharpened about me again, that the scream had been mine.

King Laurent waved his hand at the executioner and turned to face me with a new and frightening interest. It was that curiosity that kept me upright, even though I had no faith that I had stopped anything for long. In giving me the attention I'd screamed for, he was merely toying with me, like a cat might with an injured bird.

"Stop?" he asked, so close I could see the blood pulsing in a vein in his neck, could smell that he'd had a glass of wine with supper. "You order me to stop, standing here bound and half strangled? Just who do you think you are?"

I wanted to duck my head away, but the heavy rope prevented much movement. Fine, then. If that's what it took to impart me with artificial bravery, I would take it, however reluctantly.

"I have a deal to make with you," I said. Swallowing was difficult with the rope pressing on my throat; saliva welled up in my mouth. "Here. Now."

"A deal?" he scoffed. "A peasant girl whose life is forfeit has nothing to offer me."

I did, though. I did. But which was worse? Falling into eternity with the knowledge I'd failed my kingdom—or making the decision to save it, knowing I'd be forever bound to a man who'd once wanted me dead?

"You said I could save a prisoner by marrying you." I gasped the words. "I will still do so."

He laughed. "You're more foolish than I thought. You think I would marry you now?"

I couldn't breathe any longer and shrank back against the wall, sending a violent shiver down my spine. "Take this off my neck and I'll tell you."

"No." The answer was immediate, but his curious gaze didn't falter.

"You can always," I whispered, "hang me when I'm done talking."

"You demand too much." He gave the guard a sharp order, anyway. The man wasn't gentle about removing the noose, and he'd probably left splinters of rope in my skin, but I didn't care. Thomas, I noticed over the king's shoulder, was watching with his mouth open, the rope still tossed over the top of the beam.

"Riette, you can't do this!" he shouted. "Not for me. There will be others. Don't give that man—"

"It's not only for you," I interrupted before the guards could hit him again. I wanted to tell him so much more, but now wasn't the time. I doubted it would ever be the time, so I focused on the king again. "You don't want him hearing this. Or the guards."

He narrowed his eyes and tilted his head before ordering the guards and executioner out. They dragged Thomas with them, and as the chamber emptied, leaving me alone there with Laurent, I suddenly thought better of my abrupt bravery.

"So?" he asked, when I didn't speak. "You had something to tell me?"

"I'm a—a crownkeeper." I looked past him, at the stone wall on the far side of the chamber. "The one you've been waiting on, the one you never actually believed you'd choose out of all the girls in Meirdre, the one our people need. Kill me if you must, but you'll regret it. Maybe one lonely night while you're staring at the ceiling wondering what you could have done better for your people. Or maybe only when you have to tell your advisors that you murdered the one person who could have given forewarning that your borders have been breached."

"You're no crownkeeper." His smile grew. "You're not only a traitor but a liar. That power is gifted only to queens. Connected to Creation you might be, but without our marriage, you're nothing but a might-have-been. And since the law forbids divorce or the execution of a royal wife, I certainly won't take a chance on marrying a charlatan now."

"Juliana and I—" My chest was so tight that I might as well have been immured, stealing my last oxygen all on my own. "We were in the chapel. She thought it would be amusing to see what I looked like with—she put the crown on my head. And ever since, I see the cracks in the borders. I see raiding parties assembling. The earthquake in Haszen. That map on the floor of the ballroom —it shows me everything."

"Who told you about the map?" I didn't answer, and he stepped even closer and shouted in my ear. "Who told you?"

"No one told me. You know what a closely held secret it is, just like I do now. Juliana led me through the ballroom right after we visited the chapel, and it was lit like diamonds, right at the border with Nantoise. I didn't even know what I was seeing. It confused me, and then it terrified me, and now . . . it calls to me."

I hadn't even realized until now. Maybe it was the magic, but I rather believed it was my own stubbornness. But that was gone now, leaving me empty—and only one thing could fill that void.

"I don't believe you."

"But you can test me," I answered quietly. "If the map is lit, send scouts. You can verify what I'm saying is true."

"And if it's not lit?"

My head fell to my chest. I didn't answer. I knew what his response would be.

He hollered for one of the guards. To me, he added, "You have one chance. If the map isn't lit, or if I found out that you're lying about this power, I'll make you wish you died today."

My weak legs made it difficult to climbs up the stairs, even with guards on each elbow. Thomas had been returned to the gallows, insurance against any thoughts I might have of escape. One shout from my companions would end his life, so I walked quietly next to them, through empty stone corridors and the occasional storage chamber.

The servants were gone. *Celebrating the eve of the feast,* the king said as we walked, as though he was introducing me to court life and not putting me to a test that could end my own. I scarcely heard his words, could hardly see anything in the fog that hung around me. The men pulled me to a stop, and I looked up, confused, only to see myself standing in the center of the ballroom.

"Look around your kingdom." With no small amount of mocking, Laurent threw his hands in the air and spun in a circle. "See anything?"

I wanted to rub my eyes, but the guards had a vise grip on my arms. I blinked, the dizziness and nausea almost unbearable. They spun me, slowly, after I kicked my feet out the side in a silent order to let me turn, and I stared.

And stared.

And stared.

At Meirdre.

At Vassian.

At the Kalcine River.

At Elternow and Haszen and the Arsele Forest.

There was nothing. The map was as quiet and still as the stones that made up the dungeon where I would now die. My eyes, filled with fear, met Father Gerritt's, and he shook his head. It was odd, but I felt like I'd let him down more than anything else. Would he continue to pray for me as they walked me back to that chamber? Or had even he given up hope?

"She doesn't see anything. Hang him. Immediately." Laurent made a disgusted noise, then stroked a few fingers under my chin. "And take her back down and prepare her for her own execution."

He hadn't pressed on my throat, but the ballroom began to spin. It'd done that the first time I'd seen the map glow, but this time it was panic and nothing more. He was going to take me away from the map, and right now staying with it was the thing I wanted most. More than saving Thomas. More than hurting Laurent.

"No. Stop."

My voice broke as I yanked myself away from the guards. They didn't catch me quickly enough, and I fell to my knees, tears dampening the marble. They'd have to lift me up, carry me back to the dungeon, and I didn't care who heard my cries. Let Laurent cleanse the mess he'd created.

"Get her up."

A deep pain shot through my elbow as one of them yanked on my wrist. My feet slid on the polished floor, and I tried to claw at the wood with my free hand. Anything to buy myself more time. The guards dropped me, and I grunted as I hit the ground, blinking furiously. There was something—

"Stop!" The entire wing had probably heard my scream. "You have to stop. It's there. It's right there."

"What?" Laurent's shadow hovered me. "What's right there? You see something?"

Tears streaming down my face—from relief now, not fear—I pointed at the shimmering piece of wood not a foot from where I knelt, though I knew no one else could see what I saw.

"Harnow. Something's happening at Harnow."

CHAPTER FOURTEEN

I HADN'T SPOKEN SINCE THE KING AND HIS MEN HAD RIDDEN OFF. Not to Hek, not even to Father Gerritt, who'd stayed in this dank cell with me for the past two days, promising me it was no worse than the vigils he'd kept in the past. I hadn't replied to that argument, and eventually, he'd given up trying to force me to speak and had resorted to praying over me—when he wasn't making me drink what little water I'd been allowed. I did that, grudgingly. It was the only thing keeping me sane, especially I hadn't slept at all, too consumed with the threat Laurent had left me with.

If you're lying, I'll make you regret it.

I believed him. I believed he was angry and frightened and was capable of almost anything.

Father Gerritt finished his latest prayer and shifted closer to me, taking my left hand in his. He'd extracted a promise from me —a nod, at least—that I wouldn't try to unfasten the shackles, but he must have known I'd break it. My prior attempts had left my fingers bloody and swollen, and he shook his head as he washed them again with a rag and a little water.

"You're going to die of an infection if you don't stop this," he said.

The calm prediction almost made me scream.

Almost.

I jerked my hand away and fell to my side in a silent command that he stop his suggestions, the chains rattling as I did. What did it matter if I died of an infection? Would it be more painful than the noose? I doubted it, though it wouldn't matter in the end. In any case, death was so near that I was more in need of his prayers for my soul than his medical care.

He scooted back into his corner. Maybe Father Gerritt had seen something in my hands that I hadn't. I was finally warm, after all, and down here that meant one thing: a fever. Then—the jingle of keys sounded outside. No, the noise had to be a hallucination.

But the door was hauled open, and in the light of the lamp outside, I saw a single shadow. Not Hek, since he'd never appeared without a guard, and I still had what he considered adequate water. Likely not the executioner, not here on his own. I wanted to claw at the collar in one last effort to free myself from the chains which held me to the wall, but I held my breath and clawed at my palms instead. The hours of thirst and pain and fear made it too burdensome for me to speculate further.

"It was just a few cases," the figure said as he entered and sat the oil lamp on the floor. "Just a few cases."

He limped, as if days in the saddle had been unkind to him, and straightened even more sluggishly. The words were listless. Not drunk, but exhausted, like the speaker had used all his energy on what he'd seen. He stopped just short of where I huddled, hands on his hips. He might not have been able to see me, but I had grown used to the gloom of the dungeon, and I could see him.

Laurent.

"Measles, in several young children," he went on, as if to himself. "It was beginning to spread."

I told you so was less than helpful. Instead, I pressed my lips together and waited for whatever came next. I recognized his expression—the realization had dawned on him as he'd ridden back to the castle. He knew I was telling the truth, and he was furious and resigned and hopeful all at once. I'd given him a way to protect his power, and I could only pray he reached for it.

"The villagers quarantined themselves two weeks ago. Not even a scout in or out. There's no way you could have known," he said to himself as much as to me. "Unless you saw it in the map."

"I wasn't lying." My mouth had become so dry I could barely speak. The way he was looking at me was just like I used to look at the slivers of dried beef Mama would pull from some dark corner of the cellar after a long winter—I'd hated them, even though it wasn't their fault they were the only meat left. "I will not swear much to you, but I swear that."

"I still don't need to marry you," he replied with a glance at the chains. I didn't like the contemplation I saw in that glance. "I could just as easily keep you down here. Build a duplicate of the map in stone. You'd have no choice but to watch it for me."

We both knew it was a lie—I could see it in his eyes. Not lust, not exactly. Lonely desperation for the wife he'd lost even before securing her. He wouldn't get that love and companionship from me, but if he thought he would? Maybe that would be enough.

"Or what? You'd have me tortured?" I bit off the words, regretting them as soon as they tumbled out. They hadn't done it so far, and I wasn't sure I could survive it. Putting the idea in his head was dangerous, no matter what he thought he felt about me.

"It doesn't matter," Father Gerritt broke in. "She needs contact with the land in order for this to work. The sky, the ground, the snow, the mountains. And she needs the original map, not some poor reproduction created so you can abuse the crownkeeper sent to you. Don't tell me you don't have a clue how the magic works, sire. She's willing to honor your original agreement in order to prevent harm to this kingdom, and I know you want the same, if only to preserve your power. If you allow harm to come to Meirdre—and you would be doing so if you murder her—I doubt your position would remain secure for much longer."

Laurent's sword clattered at his side as he spun around toward him. "You knew about this, didn't you?"

"It was not my secret to tell." He shrugged. "You've been given a glorious gift, sire. The first crownkeeper to appear in over a hundred and fifty years, if I'm not mistaken. I suggest you not squander this gift out of some misguided yearning for revenge."

"And I suggest you keep your nose out of business that doesn't concern you, Father."

The king turned back to me, his expression hard, but we all knew the power in the kingdom had shifted. I could practically see the futures playing out in his mind—did he grant me mercy, solidifying his hold on Meirdre, or did he let his need for vengeance get the best of him and force me under the gallows, ridding himself of my ability for the rest of his reign?

"And as long as we're being honest, there's something else you need to know," I added. "Thomas, he—he planned to hand Meirdre over to Vassian. He'd made an agreement with Damir." I quickly related what I'd heard through the knothole at the house in Haszen, watched Laurent's cheeks grow red in fury—and no small amount of fear, I suspected. "I hadn't known what he'd planned. I didn't realize he'd sacrifice Meirdre to elevate his own status. That's not something I can support. It's not something I can allow to happen. I tried to tell Willem, and he—"

"And you want me to free this man."

I shook my head. Naïve I might have been at one point, but even I knew Thomas would never leave this dungeon alive.

"I know he can never be freed." My voice cracked for the last time. The words were so heavy. So final.

"No." His immediate agreement made my stomach turn. "He cannot."

The cell fell quiet. I had saved my life—probably. But I hadn't saved Thomas, and that was why I was down here in the first place.

"But he can live," I replied.

"No," he repeated. "He cannot."

"He's not a threat to you while he's imprisoned. As long as he can't meet with Damir, there's no risk to you, no threat to Meirdre."

"Has your captivity addled you, my dear? That's not the tradition, and outside of that, I have no reason to allow it. He's to be freed or executed, as was his sentence prior to your arrival. And he will not be freed." With that decree, he turned back toward the open door, snapping his fingers at a guard outside. "Bring him to the chamber at once."

"It's the arrangement King Arend made in his original surrender agreement with the duke," I called after him without thinking. "I'd argue it's more of a tradition than the one you celebrate now."

Laurent turned, a strange sort of delight in his expression. "You remember the story."

"I do," I said, frowning at his expression. He was pleased I'd remembered?

He paused, backlit there in the doorway. "And if I agree to save his life, you agree to marry me? You will live at Lochfeld, will watch the map for me, will protect Meirdre until you die?"

I nodded. He hadn't mentioned loving him, and I could easily agree to everything he *had* asked for.

He crouched before me and ran a shaking finger down my jawbone. "Why would you do this?" he asked. "You don't love me, and you don't love that man. You have no reason to save either one of us. Are you that afraid of death?"

Telling him how I felt called to protect Meirdre was too intimate. He hadn't earned that trust and likely never would—nor did I particularly feel like vocalizing it to myself. Acting on it was one thing. Admitting it was something altogether different and frightening.

"Yes." The lie slid through my lips. "I am."

An oppressive quiet fell heavy on me as he watched my breathing slow. I couldn't tell what he was thinking. Of all the powers I could have been gifted, why couldn't mind-reading have been one of them?

"There will be no formal ceremony," he said at long last, standing suddenly, as if to make the difference in our circumstances clear one last time. "As a reminder of what you've done, you will marry me as befits a traitor—in that gown you're wearing now. Here. Down below."

Hope. I felt it for the first time, and when I glanced at Father Gerritt, his head, lowered in relief, only served to confirm my optimism. The king's words sounded like a threat, something demeaning, and maybe they were partly that—but they were also so much more.

He had made his decision. I would live. So would Thomas.

I knew, because he was negotiating with me now. Not with a peasant, not with a prisoner, but with an equal, as he had the first night I'd come here. His desire for equilibrium was his strength, though I'm sure he'd consider it a weakness if he stopped to think about.

"I don't care what I wear," I replied. I wanted to stand, to equalize us even more, but the clanking of chains would defeat the purpose, so I remained still.

"No?" His brows rose. "You will never hold the title of queen while I am alive. I'll find some lesser title to satisfy most of the gossip. Still, the court will wonder why, and I will forbid you from explaining."

"Let them wonder." He certainly didn't know much about me

if he thought I cared. "I only ask that my parents do not suffer on my account."

"Our original agreement regarding them stands," he said without hesitation. "You needn't worry about your parents."

My shoulders sank even further in relief.

He grinned, and for the first time I worried he had the upper hand somehow. One-sided negotiation it was to be, then. No matter. He knew what I had to offer and what I could take away. Any threats and propositions from his side would be laughable.

"Thomas Wennink was sentenced to be whipped before his execution. A hundred lashes. I commute his sentence, if you take his place as punishment for your treason. Agree to *that*, dear Riette, and you have your bargain."

My pulse quickened, and a foul sensation overcame my stomach. I hadn't noticed the whip in the executioner's hand that day, so distraught had I been by the gallows, and the sickening truth hit me like a bolt of lightning. They hadn't intended to make Thomas's death easy. They'd planned to whip him as he stood under the noose, knowing once he could no longer remain on his feet—much sooner than a hundred lashes—he'd slowly strangle all on his own. The entire performance was more macabre than I'd ever imagined.

"Ah." His grin fell, an odd gravity taking its place. "Not so easy to agree to my conditions now, is it? You shouldn't have shown your hand so early, my dear."

I turned my face into the shadows so he couldn't see the tears running down my cheeks. A hundred lashes would kill me. It was enough to leave a powerful man half dead—though it wasn't as if they cared what happened to someone who already had his head in a noose. Did I care enough for Meirdre—for Thomas—to allow him to do this? I'd made my peace with marrying a man I didn't love in order to save the kingdom, but no one had ever told me the sacrifice would be physically painful as well.

The king knelt again and turned my head to face him once

more. "So? The executioner is in the chamber waiting for your decision. Who will it be? Both of you, to the death . . . or just you, until you beg me for mercy?"

"Ten," I whispered, not caring that I'd truly failed at bargaining with him. "Ten lashes, and I'll agree to your conditions."

"Ten? I couldn't possibly absolve you after such trivial suffering. Whatever would you learn from such a lenient sentence?" He wiped my left cheek dry with a tenderness that felt out of place. "Fifteen."

Relieved, I swallowed. He was trying to save face, not harm me—not seriously, at least. I could work with that.

"Twelve," I replied. "In private."

"Do you think I'd have my future wife whipped in front of the court? Only the ones here will ever know of your crimes—that's not a factor you can bargain with. It'll happen right here, this very hour. Thirteen."

He was simply being cruel now, and I knew we'd reached an impasse. Most of me wanted to tell him to go to hell, that he needed me more than I needed him, but the smallest whisper in the back of my mind was afraid he was holding something over me. I couldn't imagine what that could be, but every negotiation came to an end, didn't it? Most of the time both lost something, but sometimes . . . sometimes only one did.

But none of that mattered.

I could protect Meirdre.

I was destined to protect her.

My heart thumped once, and I spoke before I lost my nerve.

"Thirteen."

CHAPTER FIFTEEN

THE EVENING WAS WARM FOR LATE WINTER, AND I WAS GRATEFUL for it as I watched out the open window wearing nothing but a thin chemise. Goosebumps dotted my arms, even in the mild weather, but I had cried out in pain when Juliana tried to dress me properly, so nothing but the chemise it was—and would be for a few days. At least it was silk, and I'd embroidered snow-drops along the hem that reminded me of spring on the moors. It was something, at least. The exquisite stays and gowns? Those would have to be abandoned for at least a month while I healed, something which grated on my new husband.

If I'd only known you would have to dress like a servant for so long, I'd have told the executioner to go easier on you.

He'd told me so as I lay on my stomach on the floor of the dungeon, sobbing from my wounds. A surprising emotion had welled up at his statement, and I'd tried to swallow my reaction before I could anger him even more. The pain had dulled my focus though, along with all my common sense, and my tears had turned to laughter just long enough for him to stomp out in disgust. The willow bark he'd gone to procure for me had taken away enough of the pain that I eventually stood—with his assistance—and then, with Father Gerritt as a witness, I promised to love and obey someone I hated.

I had to admit he'd come up with a foolproof story. The official account was that I'd been too distraught over my treatment at the hands of my abductor to participate in a formal wedding ceremony. Hek, the executioner, and Willem's royal guard had been silenced by threats of their own demises, and Laurent had carried me up from the dungeon himself, allegedly after I'd identified my captor who'd immediately been hung for his offenses.

Before he'd done that, however, he'd shown me Thomas's new abode—a hole scarcely large enough for him to stand or lie down. I'd leaned against him, too frail to stand on my own. I heard chains, and the drip of water, and the occasional moan, but I hadn't been able to see inside, and that was for the best. I still wasn't sure if the stopover was meant to be a threat or reassurance, and I chose to see it as the latter. It was the only way to quell my fear, to convince myself I'd made the right decision.

Juliana hadn't questioned the story. She'd embraced me with the caution my injuries demanded, then ministered to me as best she could, all the while cursing the man who'd harmed me so. Sara hadn't asked questions either, and I doubted any of the rest of the servants would ever mention the situation again. Not in front of me, at least. For once, rumors and gossip worked in my favor.

"Are you done watching the moon rise?" the king asked from his position by the door.

"Yes." I eyed him warily. It had been an excuse, but I needed time to accept what I'd done.

"Then come to bed, my beloved wife. We have a wedding night to enjoy."

The sneering wasn't going to end anytime soon, then. That was fine—vows or no vows, I didn't feel any particular marital feelings toward him, either. Moving as quickly as my injuries allowed, I perched on the edge of the bed and stared at my hands, clasped in my lap.

The king sank down beside me, and I held my breath, anticipating his touch. Juliana had said it could be pleasurable, but she loved her husband. She'd never imagined intimacy with someone she hated, nor not being able to lie down properly. I'd begged her for more instruction, but she'd demurred, likely having no further suggestions for my battered body.

One palm cupped my cheek, and I closed my eyes as the other settled behind my neck. The caress was gentle—might have been arousing on any other day, even from him—but I arched my back in dread of the moment his touch would reach it. That involuntary motion hurt more than his hands on me, and I cried out as my skin pulled across the fresh wounds.

He frowned, then removed his hands and placed them in his lap. We sat there in silence, next to each other but miles apart, as the moon rose higher out the window, casting a glow on his face and strange shadows in the corners. I couldn't tell what he was thinking. Learning to hide his emotions must have been one of the first things he'd been taught as a child.

But if he was sitting there expressionless, I knew exactly what was running through my mind—how he'd asked me the night of our betrothal ball if I could ever love him. After I'd knelt on the icy stones before the whipping block, after he'd watched without compassion as I screamed in the chains which held me immobile, I suspected he knew the answer to his question then. No willow bark, no soothing bandages, no kind words could ever make up for what he'd done, would ever change my feelings for him.

"Beautiful as you are, I won't take what you're not willing to give without reservation," he said at long last. "And I won't be responsible for causing you further pain. So if I might make a suggestion, it's that we both go to sleep. When you feel differently, you may ask for an audience and inform me."

His pretentiousness almost made me laugh once more, but

before I could, my words caught at the obvious guilt in his voice. He didn't deserve to feel guilty about what he'd done to me, but I couldn't very well tell him that, so I only nodded.

"I think that's a fine idea, sire."

He nodded once in return, then scooted to the far side of the bed, burying himself in layers of velvet and wool. After a moment I swung my legs up and joined him, for no other reason but to warm myself. He flinched but didn't pull away as I crept up to him on my side. If I was to share a bed with him tonight to make the servants believe nothing was amiss between us, I was going to get something practical out of it. Warmth was enough.

I stopped before I touched him. Even though his feelings in the situation mattered little to me, he had frightened me enough that crossing him seemed unwise, and I wasn't entirely sure how far I could push him. Even so, as I began to shiver in the cooling night air, and his breath remained that of a man who hadn't yet been claimed by sleep, I pulled his blanket across myself.

He still didn't stir, and I wondered if he was staring at the opposite wall, his eyes open, thinking about what he'd done. Was he feeling guilty for ordering abuse to the woman he'd thought he could love? Or was he simply hoping I'd fall asleep without speaking to him again?

We lay like that for what seemed like an hour. Finally, just as I'd despaired of him ever leaving me to my thoughts, even in sleep, soft snores filled the bridal chamber. I stared at the moonbeam that glinted on the far wall, and a smile spread across my face. He would never believe it was a real one, and he would never believe me if I told him the reason for it, but I knew, and that was all that mattered.

I was alive.

The king was displeased.

And Meirdre was safe.

Part 2

War's Crown

CHAPTER SIXTEEN

Today, the map was quiet.

I circled the ballroom once more, my feet trampling the map inlaid on the floor, pretending to practice a waltz with a non-existent partner. In truth, I was eyeing the mahogany borders and oak cities and pine mountains beneath my silk shoes, searching for any indication my kingdom was in trouble. I'd been born one of those exceptional children, gifted with the connection to the kingdom, and the map—it spoke to me and had since I'd put that cursed crown on my head during my betrothal period. It showed me Meirdre's misfortunes, as it showed every crownkeeper.

But married now, if not Queen of Meirdre, I'd quickly grown used to the strangeness of my power since arriving at Lochfeld Castle. I joked to myself that my ability to see the map's sparkles and shimmers that warned of danger was bizarre enough to make my other situation—that of a peasant girl yanked from her home and brought to a castle to marry a king she'd never before seen—not *quite* so odd. Not that I'd forgotten Mama and Papa in the least, but the much-needed comfort secured for them by my marriage had a way of softening homesickness. They had coin and several healthy head of cattle, and I had . . . well, warmth and fine dresses, if not love.

My gaze swept from the far western border, out past the Tourmel Mountains, then all the way back to Lochfeld where I stood, and then, finally, to my erstwhile hometown of Elternow. I'd worried about Elternow incessantly when I'd first arrived, even more than the sovereign's castle. But the wood throughout the kingdom remained glossy and dark, not sparkling and glowing, so I lowered my arms and settled into a chair by the window for a short break. Anyone who looked inside would see me a fool, constantly dancing with myself, and I needed to be seen as anything but a fool here, in King Laurent's court.

Though to tell the truth, I felt a bit like one today, even as I rested and my breathing became regular. Not much sun shone through the thick, impenetrable glass today, and no one danced in a dark ballroom, especially without a partner. The spring rains of central Meirdre hadn't quite moved on, and heavy clouds hung above the castle towers. The dreary weather wouldn't normally affect my mood—a farmer's daughter never cursed the arrival of the light showers that followed our harsh winters, naturally—but here in the castle, it was another story. I needed the happiness of the sun. Silk gowns and sufficient food or not, the sunlight was my only happiness some days. With a sigh, I tucked a stray piece of hair behind my ear and searched for the very slightest hint of a sunbeam that might lift my mood.

There was none, so I looked back at the map. From my position at the window I could see the entirety of the kingdom—no waltz about the expansive space required—but the king had been the one to place the chair here, so I objected to using it more than necessary. It turned out that being married to a man who didn't love you made having certain principles easy. Besides, my dancing skills were much improved after practicing hour after hour.

It wasn't as though the king helped with my waltz skills,

either—not that I especially wanted him to. I'd have to dance with him eventually, I knew, and the idea made my hands clench into fists. Thank the heavens Lochfeld wasn't known for its social engagements and galas. At least, not anymore. The castle was almost empty except for the king, myself, his sister and her husband, and the bare minimum of servants. Courtiers and advisors were rare, unless they had a reason to be here.

As the memory of dancing with the king at our betrothal ball floated into my mind, the faintest glimmer of light caught my eye, and I leaned forward, trying to shove the memory aside. He'd almost kissed me that night—had touched my hand, anyway—and I'd take any distraction to dispel the heat that suddenly flashed in my cheeks. King Laurent could not be allowed to affect me like that. Not after what he'd done to me.

I blinked away his memory. Once more, it was Harnow that had caught my attention, sparkling like a diamond. They'd had an outbreak of measles months before—in fact, the very same outbreak that had proven my map reading ability to the king, the crisis that had confirmed me a crownkeeper. After the way the king had treated me then, I didn't like to think of either the measles or Harnow. I was certain that for the rest of my life I would connect the small town with my wedding night. Not the wedding night of most queens of Meirdre, I'd spent it lying awake next to my bridegroom, tears in my eyes as the wounds from the whip had pulled at the skin on my back. The only thing that brought me some relief was the remembrance that the king hadn't slept well, either.

But I had a job to do, as distasteful as it sometimes—most of the time—could be. With a short glance at the door for any witnesses, I crept up to the miniature house inlaid on the floor, the mark that symbolized Harnow. Still cautious of the power I'd been granted, I knelt to look closer. Yes, Harnow, shimmering like a rainbow washed in rose, was definitely in trouble.

But what kind of trouble, I had no way of knowing.

There had to be some kind of pattern to the flashes and colors the map in the floor radiated, but so far, I hadn't figured it out. The last time Harnow had made its problem known, it had been white, like diamonds. Today it was still white, but there was something odd about it—small rosy flashes in the glittering map symbol. I mentally marked the image to add to my journal later, then shrugged it off. Likely colors meant nothing. Just one more oddity the Creator had bestowed on the map. But with time, and luck, and meticulous recordkeeping, I'd be able to determine if there was a pattern. It wasn't as though I had much else to do. No baking, no escorting the cow to the pasture, no climbing trees. No acting as a lookout for rebels who turned out to be anything but.

Regardless, the king would need to be informed.

Standing, I ran my hands over my gown and checked my image in the mirror. Sara, becoming a friend more than a servant, had chosen something a little more velvet than the balmy yet dreary weather had called for, but King Laurent would appreciate that I looked like I'd made an effort, and one of the things I *did* focus on these days was avoiding his cutting comments about my looks. My hair wasn't quite as elegant as the dress, but perhaps he wouldn't notice. I prayed he wouldn't notice.

That risky decision made, I headed to the king's private office. The ability to see him there instead of the throne room was a benefit of my marriage that I hadn't expected, but quite appreciated. His Majesty in the throne room was the tyrant who'd sentenced me to death; King Laurent in his office was the civil administrator who dealt in paperwork and coinage. Bothersome, yes, but not a threat. At least, that was what I had convinced myself.

A sentry nodded at my approach and reached for the door. I steeled my back, preparing for yet another disagreeable conversation once he opened it. Conversations with the king, if not always brief like I preferred, were always unpleasant. Had been ever since our wedding in Lochfeld's dungeon.

"Her Grace, sire."

I tiptoed inside at the introduction and curtsied in front of the king's antique desk before meeting his gaze. At first, he was barely visible behind the stacks of parchment and other books, though it wasn't quite as disorganized as my imagination wanted, and he shoved a few aside, clearing my view completely as I straightened. Dark circles surrounded azure eyes in his face, and I looked away for an instant, toward the window that overlooked what had once been the bailey. He had no right to be exhausted. If anyone slept well at night, it was the imperturbable King Laurent of Meirdre, who never deigned to trouble himself with the plights of his subjects.

"Yes, my dear?" he asked, evening the stack of paper to his right without giving it so much as a glance. "Something is happening?"

Of course something was happening. We didn't speak otherwise. Yes, sometimes we ate together, but we never conversed, sometimes we even shared a bed to fool the servants into thinking our marriage was solid, though we never touched or even spoke when that happened. Our sole verbal interaction—truly our sole interaction beyond painstakingly avoiding and ignoring each other—was when I informed him of trouble. Sometimes I wondered if he'd rather not speak to me even then. What would he do if I sent a written message with a servant or one of the royal guards?

I decided I'd find out next time.

Maybe.

"It's Harnow, sire," I said, clasping my hands in front of me and giving him an even, small smile. Not a happy one, because I didn't want to encourage him or seem foolish, but a frown implied . . . the wrong things. What wrong things, I wasn't exactly sure. "It's glowing again."

The word *again* was a mistake, but it came without warning from my subconscious. Perhaps his affectionate form of address had rankled me more than I'd appreciated. The use of *Her Grace* certainly had, and it wasn't because I had any desire to be queen. The desire to be respected and loved, yes, I had that, but that simply wasn't King Laurent, and there was no use hoping for something that would never happen. At least, that was what I told myself. What woman didn't want her husband to value and admire her as something more than a tool to keep his power secure?

"Hmm." The king set down his pen, folded his hands in front of him, and stared at me over the desk. "Harnow again. What do you think is the problem there? You've spent so much time watching the map since arriving at Lochfeld—you must have some idea."

"I—" I shut my mouth and frowned. This was new. He'd never asked for my opinion before, simply acknowledged my information and dismissed me with an offhand wave. "I have no idea. Perhaps the outbreak isn't over."

"Hmm," he repeated. "That would be . . . unfortunate."

Unfortunate? What kind of response was that? I shifted to my opposite leg and switched my hands behind my back, frantic for his dismissal. Since my other reports had been met with indifference—though each one was investigated, I was sure—I hadn't planned on standing in front of him for so long.

And that was a problem, for the longer I did, the more chance for him to comment on my hair, messily braided in a style I knew he disliked. But the map had shown me a dust storm in the Mencote Desert just last week, and though I knew the map didn't keep any kind of a set schedule, I'd never thought something else would be happening so soon after that storm. If I had, I would have made certain to be more presentable.

Then again, why should I have bothered impressing the king with my looks? Many women had and did, I knew—I saw the looks of the daughters of nobles who visited, even after our marriage—but since he and I scarcely spoke, I didn't see it as a priority. He might be my king, yes, and I afforded him the grudging respect his position demanded, but he wasn't truly my husband.

Not when I didn't love him.

Not when he'd punished my childhood friend by proxy—with my body and a whip.

Not when he'd refused to give me the title of queen.

Not when—and we hid this secret from the entire court—we were husband and wife in name only.

When I didn't reply to his comment about a measles outbreak with the possibility of killing dozens as being *unfortunate*, the king broke his gaze and began to shuffle and restack some of the paper in front of him. Had I actually succeeded in making him uncomfortable? Just by standing here thinking to myself? It was something to remember for the next time. Anything that made him feel awkward meant I'd won a little something, and in the strange new world I currently inhabited, that was never something to discount.

"I will send out scouts," he said, as I began to wonder if he'd notice if I simply walked out. "Hopefully it's nothing, but . . . the map is so rarely wrong that we shouldn't begin to ignore it now."

"Thank you, sire. I'm sure the people of Harnow will be grateful for whatever help their liege is willing to provide." That flattery complete, I took a deep breath. "May I go?"

His eyes landed on my hair, and I clenched my fingers even tighter, daring him to say something about the curl that had somehow managed to escape and was hanging across my forehead. He picked up his pen and shifted a document in front of him.

"Yes," he replied, without looking up. "But next time, my dear, have Sara do your hair."

CHAPTER SEVENTEEN

THE SINGLE BEST THING ABOUT LIVING IN A CASTLE, BESIDES THE sumptuous gowns I was rapidly becoming used to, was having unfettered access to a better-quality horse than I'd enjoyed at home, a horse meant simply for pleasure riding, not farm work. The one which had stolen my heart was the brindled mare who whinnied when I appeared in the stables and nuzzled at my hand when I approached. She made an acceptable replacement to the mare I'd been forced to leave when I'd arrived at Lochfeld Castle to marry the king, and I was grateful for her affection as I edged into her stall one gray spring afternoon.

As the lone stable boy saddled Skylark, I tried to ignore the fact I hadn't seen my husband in almost a week—the day after I'd informed him of Harnow's newest difficulties. He'd appeared in Lochfeld's chapel for a private liturgy that morning, given me a quick nod as I stared in surprise at his appearance, then disappeared to his rooms once more. I dared not intrude on whatever solitude he wanted, but there was a small part of my soul that resented the distance. He had hurt me, he had insulted me, and he dared treat me like I was something to discard? If anyone had implied that, it should have been me.

My skirts whipped around my ankles as I urged Skylark away from the castle. Not down the trail that led to the cliffs and then onward toward my hometown of Elternow, but north, across the open field that sat atop the mountain. The flat ground allowed Skylark's rare gallop, allowed me to breathe in the chill that still clung to the hills in places. Outside was the only place I could breathe these days. There was no royal guard directly at my back —though two sets of hoofbeats followed somewhere behind me, publicizing their distant existence—no Juliana, questioning why her brother and I seemed so aloof on the rare occasions we were together, and no memories. Not of my past life in Elternow, not of the emotions I'd thought I'd felt for Thomas, and not of my punishment at the king's command.

The broad meadow gave way to a line of trees ahead, and I slowed Skylark to a walk. She tossed her head, irritated at how quickly I'd ended her run, but my legs were aching, and the forest was calling to me. I wouldn't run her through the stumps and roots, though, so I muttered a few reassuring words under my breath and guided her toward the narrow trail that led within. We could race back to Lochfeld later, but right now I needed to enjoy the beauty of nature at a speed that allowed me to see it.

My guards hung back the appropriate distance as the cloudy afternoon became even dimmer in the heavy cover of limbs and leaves. Shadows cast their gloom across my path, but it didn't bother me in any way that truly mattered. Even in spring this wood was thick enough to block most of the sun, which was why the trail led this way, I'd been told. The castle might be cool enough to bear when summer eventually arrived, Juliana said, but the spring a five-minute ride from where I sat was even cooler.

Skylark tossed her head and whinnied again, making her displeasure at the cancelled run evident. I ignored her and guided her farther inside, indulging in the sensation of freedom I'd thought I'd lost when I'd first come to Lochfeld. Right now, there were no servants, no king, no map, no responsibilities, no reminders of how I'd failed myself and my own desires. Just the distant hoofbeats of my guards, and they wouldn't dare interrupt my private afternoon.

I spun backward in the saddle as the whinnies and hoofbeats of more than one horse grew louder, but I couldn't see any riders. Were my guards so distant? The trail had turned though, heading west, so perhaps they were behind me on a curve. No matter. Nothing would ruin this ride, even if Skylark was less than thrilled about the change in plans.

I twisted forward again to continue deeper into the woods, then screamed as a figure smiled at me from one of the deeper shadows. My heart threatened to explode, then settled again. It was Captain Willem who sat astride his horse in the middle of the trail, his hands folded on the saddle in front of him and a wry expression on his face.

"You ought to be paying more attention to where you're headed, Your Grace."

I swallowed down the remainder of my abandoned scream and gave him a baleful glare. The captain of the royal guard knew he'd snuck up on me, had probably planned it once he'd heard Skylark coming down the trail, but he'd never apologize. That wasn't worth arguing about though because his very presence here could mean only one thing.

The king was somewhere deeper in the forest.

"And you could have made your presence known," I said, as steadily as I could. Willem wasn't the issue. And he couldn't know I was becoming distraught at the idea of encountering his master. That was King Laurent's order—no one could know how much we hated each other. I wondered if he honestly believed it was that much of a secret.

"It's hard to hide a horse on dry earth in the forest," he replied, "especially the way the wind is making everything echo today. If you were not paying attention to your surroundings, Your Grace, that is your fault and your fault alone. Perhaps more education in your own security is in order. We'll work on your knife skills tomorrow. And the next day as well, if I don't feel you've improved enough."

My mouth fell open at his reprimand. He was right, of course, and my security was something I couldn't ever take for granted now that I'd married the king, but what woman wanted a lecture?

Captain Willem shrugged as I sat there silent and motionless, then guided his mount around me. Turning around and following him back to Lochfeld would have been the prudent decision, but before I could, his royal charge cantered up to us on Foxfire, the stallion who hated me almost as much as his master did.

Trapped and silent, I clenched my jaw as the rest of the royal guard trailed him.

King Laurent pulled Foxfire to a stop and looked me up and down, somehow both expressionless and mocking, a paradox only a few men in the kingdom could manage.

"Out for a ride, my dear?" he asked. "It certainly is a pleasant day for it."

What tripe. Through the trees, the clouds were suddenly gathering above us, and if I wasn't mistaken, a raindrop had just landed on my head.

I lifted my chin and tried to relax my jaw. "Yes, sire. I've been enjoying it."

The king's gaze dropped to his hands, wound oddly tight in the reins. "Willem," he said to his nails, his tone sharp. "I will escort her back. The rest of you are dismissed for the remainder of the day."

"But I don't want to go back!" My protest surprised me as much as his appearance had.

He watched the rest of the guard head out of the forest before speaking again. "I would think you'd have learned by now that your desires are rather low in importance, all things considered."

His tone wasn't unfamiliar, but I stiffened my spine at the distaste in his comment. He couldn't even pretend to be civil to me now, even after he'd pretended in front of Captain Willem and the others? The disparity was disheartening.

"And I've also learned that I'm allowed an afternoon ride," I retorted.

Or had he changed his mind about how much freedom I was allowed?

"Not today." The king turned Foxfire toward the castle and nodded at me to follow, like I was an old hunting dog. "You need to check the map. Something might be happening, and I won't have you miss it because you were rambling around the woods."

Skylark moved to follow her stablemate. I yanked on the reins —harder than I'd intended—to stop her. "I checked this morning. There was nothing."

King Laurent stopped, then twisted slowly in his saddle as if he couldn't believe I'd refused his order. "Things may have changed since you were last there."

"They may have, but you can't possibly expect me to sit in the ballroom all day, every day, sire!"

Or maybe he could. After all, he'd married me because I had the power to see those dangers, and I'd agreed because I needed to protect my kingdom along with my own small family. I was an effective prisoner now, but I didn't need to be treated like one, did I? Couldn't I go for an afternoon ride? The magic was so particular that I believed the map would call to me if I was needed. The king didn't know that part of it, and although I wasn't certain, I was confident enough in the magic to risk a ride.

"I'm not expecting you to sit in the ballroom all day, every day. But as I said, things may have changed."

I opened my mouth to argue, then stopped as a flush crept up my neck. I hadn't lied, not exactly, but forgetful was as bad as falsehood when a kingdom's security was at stake, wasn't it? Or maybe it was King Laurent's fault for making the days all blend together into one.

He was still glaring at me from astride Foxfire, but I had to admit that he wasn't an unattractive man, especially seated on a powerful horse, his sword hanging at his side. He'd lost a bit of weight since winter, and though he could scarcely afford the loss, it had somehow emphasized the curve of his calves through his fitted breeches. Flushing, my gaze moved upward.

"What are you staring at, Riette, dear?"

I gasped at his question and brushed my hair back. How long had I been staring at those thick lashes and azure eyes?

"Nothing," I stammered. "Nothing."

"Really."

It wasn't a question that time, and my flush grew deeper. "I'm tired. Were you saying something?"

His eyebrows rose. "I was telling you that you're needed back at Lochfeld. But if you're so exhausted, perhaps a casual ride through the grove would be better for you. Everyone deserves some rest, and the fresh air might do much to aid your fatigue. Maybe I've asked too much from you, after all."

I narrowed my eyes in return. It was like the king to offer me only enough to keep me content, but I was no fool. He had an ulterior motive today as well, though I had no idea what it was. Perhaps he simply didn't want to argue? Indifference was more his style than anger—and had been since our wedding.

"There's a spring," he added when I didn't reply. "I've just come from there, and I thought—"

"You thought what?" I demanded more rudely than I'd intended.

"I thought we could spend some time together while you rest."

"I do not require your presence in order to rest, sire."

The opposite, in fact.

"Yes, well . . ." He trailed off for a long while, and as a bird sang a rain song above us, my disloyal gaze fell to those calves once more. "That may be so. But I think I would enjoy your company today, and as my wife, I thought that perhaps—"

I didn't let him finish. I didn't need to in order to figure out what he was going to say. He wanted to spend time with me at long last, and that meant—that meant the cold distance between us might dwindle. It meant I might trust him, if not for the rest of my life, for a span of five long minutes.

And that couldn't happen. I wouldn't *let* it happen.

I dug my knees into Skylark's sides and bolted.

King Laurent didn't follow.

CHAPTER EIGHTEEN

IF THE KING WAS SOMEONE I WANTED TO AVOID AS MUCH AS possible, his sister, thank the heavens, was not. From my first day at Lochfeld, she'd made me feel welcome, and after my unusual marriage? She hadn't acted as though my relationship with her brother was anything other than normal, as if I hadn't come back to the castle a few weeks ago on Skylark at full speed, minutes before my husband, and then locked myself in my room all day. Perhaps that was because love didn't usually exist among royalty, but I suspected she was simply polite and kind enough to not bring attention to anything untoward. Whatever the reason, I loved her for it.

Today, as we relaxed in her parlor, the spring sun spilling through the narrow windows, I loved her even more for choosing a pastime that didn't put me in as much of a disadvantage as it could, given my upbringing. It was always possible she was letting me win on purpose, but her facial expressions, amusing and despondent at the same time, told another story. It was hard to believe a relative of the king lacked strategic skills, even in something as innocuous as chess, but Juliana had clearly focused her educational pursuits elsewhere. She wrinkled her nose at me as I moved my queen, and I grinned in return.

"Checkmate."

She toppled her ebony king with a light finger. "I don't believe I have much else to teach you. You're too fast a learner—and my chess skills are sorely lacking."

"Hardly. It took me almost a month to figure out how to beat you." Satisfied in my charity, I tucked my feet under me in the deep chair and arranged my skirts. Unladylike, yes, but we were alone in the parlor. A few days ago, she'd commented that her servants had become a burden and that she preferred the solitude of doing everything herself. It'd been a strange comment, but not one I could argue with. "At least I've been successful in learning something."

"You'll get there." Juliana eyed me critically. "I hear you've been spending quite a bit of time in the library, anyway. Soon you'll know more about Meirdrean history than Laurent."

She wasn't wrong about my time in the library. I could read, but my few years of schooling in Elternow seemed woefully inadequate now that I was married to her brother. Despite her poor chess skills, she could speak of things with more cleverness and grace than I could—science and history and politics. It was a good thing the castle was as empty of advisors and courtiers as it had been when I'd first arrived. I couldn't imagine having to show my ignorance in front of even more people. King Laurent was bad enough.

"It's quiet," I replied. "And I can read without anyone knowing I'm doing it."

"Laurent, you mean."

I nodded. Truly, I'd been hiding so he couldn't see me learn *anything*. History, writing, numbers, all of it. The shame of my husband knowing my math skills were limited to what I'd needed to know in order to sell milk and wheat rankled me. My confidence was growing as I learned more and more, but not quickly enough for me to feel I truly belonged at Lochfeld.

"Well," she went on while packing away the chess set, "there's no reason to be ashamed of it. I'm sure he knows your education was—"

"Your Grace!"

The door must have opened silently, for we both spun around at the interruption. Willem strode across the parlor, paler than I'd ever seen him. Juliana jumped to her feet, then as if she realized I should be the one to reply, lowered herself slowly back down.

"Yes?" I asked through gritted teeth. I wasn't exactly required to greet the king when he came home from wherever it was that he disappeared to, but things seemed to go better for a few days when I did. Sometimes I even received a smile from him. "I wasn't aware he had returned to Lochfeld."

"He's upstairs." Willem's voice shook. "Ill. Both of you need to stay away from that wing. Your Grace"—this was addressed to me, I assumed, since our rooms were next to each other—"I'll move your things. Is there anything specific you need for the next few weeks or so?"

"I— why do you need to move my things? How bad is he?" My chest tightened, and I couldn't understand why. Meirdre needed a king, and King Laurent had no heir, but someone would take his place. I shouldn't care what happened to him as a person.

"Measles," Willem replied. "We can't take the chance it'll spread to you."

I moved toward him in relief, while in the corner of my eye, Juliana stood and retreated from the room—rapidly.

"I've had the measles," I said.

"Good. That's good. Do you mind?" His shoulders sank as he waved a hand at the nearest chair.

He looked exhausted, and I nodded as he fell into it. Juliana would have it burned, but I couldn't very well say no.

"But how did he contract the measles?" I asked. "Has someone else in the castle . . ."

I trailed off. We would have heard long before now if one of the few residents was ill. Was this related to wherever the king had disappeared?

My heart skipped a beat.

Harnow.

Had he ridden for Harnow himself the day after I'd encountered him in the forest? Part of me had wondered if King Laurent hadn't in fact left Lochfeld at all, that perhaps he'd been holed up somewhere in the castle these past weeks. Or maybe he'd gone on some scouting trip around the Nantoisen border. I really didn't know, and hadn't cared, beyond assuming he was gone. But then again, I hadn't had a compelling reason to look for him, even when he'd disappeared shortly after our ride.

Was his insistence on spending time with me in the woods because he'd intended to ride for the stricken town shortly afterward?

"No." Willem folded his arms. "No one in the castle has it or has been exposed, and we must keep it that way. I shouldn't have brought him back, but—but he insisted. I'd thought him delirious enough with fever that I could convince him the camp we'd stopped in on the way back was Lochfeld, but I wasn't that lucky. He wants to die at home."

I gasped. Men like King Laurent didn't die. They lived forever to make their wives and kingdoms miserable.

"He's bad off, Your Grace. I wouldn't expect a miracle."

Time stood still as I rose to my feet, and my loathing for my husband cracked. I could feel it somewhere deep in my soul, like the glass in our house in Elternow had shattered that one night. Had I brought this upon him with my refusal to forgive him? That wasn't how life worked, but I couldn't shake the feeling this was my fault. But it wasn't as if I had sent him to Harnow.

"Then I want to see him," I replied quietly. "Right now."

Willem's brows drew together—no doubt he was well-aware

of how little the king and I cared for each other—but he nodded and motioned me into the corridor. I kept up with his stride, long, yes, but slow from exhaustion, as we climbed the stairs to the wing in which Laurent and I had rooms. Two servants were heading in the opposite direction, their expressions grim. Were they gathering supplies for their return, or was I the only one in the entire castle who wasn't susceptible to the disease? The sudden weight of responsibility fell on me like an entire haystack as I peered into his room.

The window was open, and the heavy velvet drapes blew in the spring breeze, though someone had tried to tie them shut. The sun had moved on past this side of the castle, so it was hard to see the figure lying in bed, especially with the pervasive oil lamps extinguished and only a few candles for illumination. I clasped my hands to my sides to avoid lighting a few more. Laurent, if he had any senses left now, probably had a ruthless headache. It was one of the few things I remembered from my experience years ago.

"Riette." The tall figure on the other side of Laurent's canopied bed rose into the light and frowned. Father Gerritt's easy tenor and the cautious movements of his elderly body would always be familiar to me, but I could scarcely recognize him through the gloom. "You shouldn't be here. Go, now, and don't come back."

"You're certain it's measles?" I asked.

"Can't be mistaken for anything else, even by a novice." He nodded at Laurent's bare arms, covered in an angry red rash.

"Then it's fine." I slunk toward the bed, cringing inside. Tyrant and awful husband though Laurent might be, I, unlike Thomas, didn't necessarily want to see him dead. Just . . . away from me. I shouldn't have been fighting with this compassion I didn't understand. "We didn't have the luxury of avoiding disease in Elternow."

If Father Gerritt was offended by my comment, he didn't

show it. "The king will be angry you were allowed in here, even immune—though I suppose he's not in any condition to find out now. Perhaps we can keep it our secret."

A chair appeared behind me, and I sank into it as Willem disappeared back into the corridor. While my eyes adjusted, the reason for his and Father Gerritt's alarm was obvious. Laurent hadn't brushed off the disease as I had, like most of the children in Elternow did. The raised rash covered every exposed area of his skin, and though his eyes were closed in what appeared to be a fitful sleep, he shook with the pain of a man wracked with fever. His nightclothes were damp, and the bedsheet pulled halfway over him, clean though it looked, was just as drenched.

"Yes," I murmured, reaching for Laurent's hand, for reasons I'd never be able to explain. It was cold in mine, even with the fever. "I suppose we can."

"It'll have to do." Father Gerritt reached for a rag in a bowl of water, then sighed. "He didn't want you to know where he was or what he'd been doing. Said it wasn't any of your business, and he'd have the head of anyone who spoke of it to you. Thankfully, he's so out of it that I feel my head is quite safe."

"And he was where and doing what, exactly?" I asked as he ran the cloth across Laurent's head.

"Harnow." He peered at me in that peculiar way he had, like he could see into my mind. "Doing what he could for them during the outbreak."

I gave a sudden bark of laughter, only cutting myself off at his disapproving expression. Knowing Laurent had ridden for Harnow was one thing, but being told he'd done it out of his own kindness was something else entirely.

"I'm sorry, Father," I replied, "but His Majesty was not in Harnow tending to ill children."

He shrugged and wrung out the rag, unperturbed once more. Since I'd been at Lochfeld, I'd come to understand that nothing bothered him.

"Well, tending to ill children might be a bit of a stretch. But delivering supplies directly to homes and overseeing the hospital tent, yes. You can believe me or not," he said at my obvious distrust, leaning back in his own chair, "but I saw it with my own eyes."

I dropped Laurent's motionless hand and stared at the priest. I'd been so caught up with Juliana and chess and Skylark and the joys of spring that I hadn't noticed Father Gerritt had been away from the palace along with Laurent. And truthfully, his library was more intriguing than his God who had brought me to Lochfeld in the first place. His empty library? Well, I didn't question my good fortune when that happened, which was frequently. He was the only priest in the immediate Lochfeld district and often traveled the countryside, offering prayers and absolution.

"So that's where you've been," I replied. "I'd assumed you were somewhere close by."

"It was a long few weeks, trust me. But he asked me to accompany him, and it would have been foolhardy to say no. Doctors were needed, even old ones like me. And selfishly, I rather enjoyed throwing myself in the middle of medicine once more."

I sighed and brushed my fingers against Laurent's cheek, which was almost too hot to touch. *I do what I can to make sure the balance of his heart and works are tipped toward good*, Father Gerritt had once told me. He had a relationship with my husband that I didn't understand—and probably never would. But the fact he still tried meant there was some part of Laurent worth saving, and I wasn't going to be the one to pray he met his end now.

"Is it truly as serious as Willem suggested?" I asked.

Father Gerritt reached for the rag again.

"I certainly hope not," he said to the floor.

CHAPTER NINETEEN

Laurent's office was silent and dim, but a few candles took care of the latter problem. The lamps that normally lit the room would have been preferable, but I didn't want to broadcast my presence more than absolutely necessary, for now that Laurent had returned to Lochfeld, the royal guard had also returned in force. Captain Willem and his men were the last people I wanted to see. Was rummaging through the king's personal documents considered treason? Perhaps—but I'd fought that battle when I'd first arrived at Lochfeld and won it already.

I shouldn't be here, but Father Gerritt's explanation of Laurent's disappearance and subsequent illness simply made no sense. He had advisors he could have sent to Harnow in his stead. For that matter, Meirdre had an army at the king's disposal, though they were rarely seen away from the borders and coast. Still, I wasn't about to accuse a priest of lying to me, especially one who had a hand in me still being alive, so I'd slipped into Laurent's private office unseen. There had to be something in here that explained what he'd been doing in Harnow.

As brave as I considered myself for being here in the first place, I didn't sit behind his antique desk. Instead, I pulled up a chair on the opposite side. My side. The safe side. The side where I belonged. If I was found on his, it would be obvious I was searching through his things, and some part of my soul wanted nothing to do with the responsibility of his side.

All these documents . . .

His seal sat on top of a mess of papers. Captain Willem had likely replaced it first thing after they'd carried Laurent upstairs. I lifted it from the right-hand stack of books and letters and placed it cautiously on the sliver of mahogany left exposed through the mess, half expecting a lightning bolt to strike me down as I did. There was no sound though, not even the creaking floors that signaled the sentry's passage outside, so I flipped open the first book underneath and rotated it toward me.

A calendar, it appeared. I knew Laurent's handwriting, and the last date was a few days after I'd left him sitting in the forest atop Foxfire, hollering after me. There was nothing to suggest he'd been headed for Harnow then, and I hated myself for accusing Father Gerritt, however silently, of lying to me. With a sigh, I closed the calendar and unwrapped the book beneath it. A few weeks of dust coated it, and I sneezed when I blew it clean. There was more writing in this one, hurried and squashed together, and I squinted as I tried to make out the lettering.

I will never understand why this responsibility was put to me—an irresponsible and selfish man. I haven't worn the duty well, that much is clear from the lectures I still suffer from Father Gerritt and the way Riette looks at me whenever she stands before this very desk.

I slammed the book closed on my finger and threw a cautious glance over my shoulder. Why hadn't Laurent brought his journal to Harnow with him? Had he left in a hurry? Forgotten it? Knew he wouldn't have time to write in it? The very fact I couldn't answer that question proved how little I knew about him. Would the journal answer any of my questions? I couldn't decide, but I flipped it open once more.

I've done wrong by her—by almost everyone in Meirdre. I know that. It was too late to earn Riette's trust and love as soon as I made that fool decision to have her whipped, and imagining I'll have the adoration of everyone in Meirdre is a delusion I won't allow myself. But it's not too late to do right by the people in Harnow, even if they'd rather see me underground than riding into their village. I can't cure whatever has befallen them this time—especially, heaven forbid, another outbreak of the measles—but I can manage supplies, pray, hold hands, and dare I say . . . help morale? Whatever needs to be done, I'll do it.

Unbidden, I rolled my eyes at his lie. Laurent, thinking he could help morale in a town full of peasants and commoners? I couldn't believe that motivation, and I found it hard to believe he could convince even himself of the words. Was it possible he was so paranoid someone would read his journal that he wrote falsehoods like this, hoping to cast himself in a positive enough light? That didn't exactly sound like him either—he rarely seemed to care what the court thought of him.

I flipped backward, finding the date when I'd first come to Lochfeld.

No matter what I told Willem last night, I'd be fooling myself if I didn't admit in private that she is attractive. Perhaps once she doesn't carry herself like a child playing dress-up, she'll become an asset to Meirdre—and me.

My lip curled. Too far back. I didn't particularly care to read what he thought of my body or my awkwardness at wearing nice clothing—though it was a relief to read that we had the same thoughts of each other. I would become the wife and mother of his children that his position required, and he would provide for my parents. Before I could lose my nerve, I flipped to the day after our wedding.

I have to admit, it wasn't the wedding night I expected. The girl cringes whenever I so much as look at her, so any intimacy is out of the question. She blames me for ordering the whipping, of course, but in time she'll come to accept that her choices were her own, and the conse-

quences, too. Though I doubt she'll make the same decisions again. Even a peasant girl can learn what—

"And here I thought you scarcely knew how to read."

I gasped at Willem's voice and twisted around in my chair, my cheeks blazing. He strode inside, slipped around my frozen body, and gazed down at the book with a certain amusement in his expression.

"Instead, I find you so intrigued by the king's journal that every horse in the stable could have ambled in here without rousing you," he went on, lifting his oil lamp and focusing on my reddened face. "You must be fond of that dungeon."

I straightened my back at his threat. "Perhaps he should secure his personal documents better."

Willem cackled in a disapproving manner. I'd meant what I said, and he of all people knew I was anything but the king's perfect wife. Hadn't he shackled me in the back of a wagon halfway across the kingdom not so long ago? Delivered me to said dungeon himself?

"Maybe he should," he replied. Then, after a moment, "Though I see no reason his wife shouldn't be looking through his documents to make sure everything that must be done while he's indisposed is finished. It's a major reason a man suffers a wife, after all."

"Flattering." I straightened the books, only because my hands needed something to do but shake. "Thank you. I promise my intentions are all noble."

"You're welcome. Just be quiet about it." He turned to go. "It would be hard to keep the servants from gossiping, and I know you don't want that."

"Captain, wait," I called out to him. I didn't know why the question had appeared in mind—probably because I *had* snuck in here without anyone seeing me—but it had, and I wasn't going to let the one man besides Laurent who might very well be able to answer it get away. "Why is Lochfeld so empty? Your men, a few servants, a priest. But courtiers? A militia? Entertainers? Advisors?"

His forehead wrinkled. "He didn't tell you?"

"I asked. Once. He didn't answer, made up some excuse, and I never asked again."

"I'm sure he didn't." Willem shuffled his feet, then sighed. "The truth is, he can't afford anything else."

"Can't afford it?" I asked. "I don't—"

I wanted to laugh, but he sounded too serious. How could the king of Meirdre not be able to afford an entire court? Lochfeld had been built for more people. It could support more than the few dozen who currently occupied it. The books I'd seen as a child implied that a castle was full of people, royal and not.

"Then I can assume your meddling hasn't yet made it to his ledger?"

I shook my head.

"I expect the answer to your question can be found there."

With that evasive response, he slipped back out the door. I heard the hushed sounds of conversation, my name, along with an unexpected admonition to not allow anyone else in. Willem hadn't done much to protect me outside of the very basics of knife lessons since I'd arrived at Lochfeld, even though his comment was meaningless—no one would enter Laurent's private office right now. I was the only fool brash enough to do so. Still, I appreciated his effort. I was suspicious of his motivation and sudden good will toward me, but then again, Willem had rarely been outwardly hostile except when Laurent had demanded it. Yes, he was probably safe.

One of my candles had flickered out while Willem and I spoke, so I lit another and turned back to the desk. The sheer amount of paperwork on it was overwhelming, but a ledger of the castle finances? Likely in the stack under his seal.

And it was, three books below the journal. I peered inside the front cover, afraid of how complicated the system might be.

Rows and rows of numbers greeted me, some in Laurent's hand, some in another. Not Juliana's neat script, but a blocky hand that didn't look as practiced. An erstwhile steward? Those entries were from at least eight years ago, and as I flipped toward the back, the king's own handwriting became more and more frequent until, finally, as of three years ago, it became the only one.

The accounting form grew less complicated as well: a date, an expense, a monetary amount. There was no running total, but my frequent checks toward the front of the book confirmed Willem's claim—Laurent had certainly cut expenses in recent years.

Or had he?

I ran my finger down the ledger. There were certainly *more* entries five years ago, but none of them were over 500 crowns. Oil, food staples, horse supplies. Firewood, novel vegetable seeds for the castle's test garden. Tithes from both local and farther-flung villages offset them. Incoming candles, yarn, fabric, coins. All made sense. None were suspicious.

But when I skipped forward right to before I'd arrived at Lochfeld . . .

Several entries caught my eyes, each for over 5000 crowns. I tapped my fingertip next to them and focused on the entries in the expense field. All the same word. Laurent had almost scrawled it, as if its very existence offended him.

Horace.

I drew my finger in spirals around the page, trying to think. Large sums, an expense I didn't recognize—it certainly wasn't horse feed, since that was listed just above—and a castle with financial problems.

None of it made any sense.

But then, nothing about Lochfeld made sense. It was home to a map which called to me and illuminated itself to let me know where dangers troubled Meirdre, after all. Odd payments in the royal ledger were nothing compared to the power I'd come into when I'd placed the queen's crown on my head that day. They were certainly nothing compared to the fact that Meirdre was one heartbeat away from having no monarch at all—closer than we'd been in years.

Still, who was *Horace*? And why was Laurent paying him large sums of money?

There was one person who would know.

CHAPTER TWENTY

When I tiptoed into Laurent's room a few hours later, Father Gerritt was gone, and the sun was even lower in the sky outside the closed drapes that still blew in the breeze. The sentry closed the door behind me, and I sank into the chair I'd abandoned earlier. The velvet was too warm in the airlessness of the chamber, and I began to wilt as I stared at the motionless figure in the bed.

What was I supposed to do? Simply sit here and wait until he woke up? It was probably my duty, as were so many other things these days, but it wasn't remotely one I could be happy about resigning myself to. To sit in the darkness and wait for something that might never happen? Surely there were better things I could be doing.

But as my eyes adjusted to the darkness, my heart skipped a beat.

Laurent was sweating.

Heedless of the warmth and the stray hair clinging to my neck, I jumped to my feet and grabbed a few rags, then pulled the covers down, cringing at the rash covering his bare chest. *No time for squeamishness.* As I wiped the sweat away, Laurent shifted, then coughed. My gaze jerked upward, toward—I gasped—toward his open eyes, dark and piercing. The room went absolutely silent. Even the birds outside seemed afraid to sing.

"Riette?" Laurent blinked several times. My name was a coarse growl. "What are you doing here?"

I sank into a curtsy before resuming my place in the chair at his side. He'd never want me attending to him while awake. Would he? I knew I wasn't courageous enough to do it.

"You woke up, sire," I said quietly, clutching the rags. "I didn't think—I thought you'd still be unconscious or sleeping. And I only wanted to make sure—"

"You shouldn't—" He coughed again. "You shouldn't be here. Go away. Now."

I leaned forward. "It's all right. I've had it. And even if I hadn't, most everyone else here is too afraid to do what needs to be done. Someone needs to take care of you." My hand reached toward his forehead, then back into my lap. Yes, it was easier to minister to an unconscious husband than a wakeful king. "Let me get you some water."

Laurent grumbled a bit, but he didn't argue as I poured a glass. He didn't even say anything as I mixed in some ground pulsatilla that Father Gerritt had left next to the pitcher, though his expression was wary as he watched. As though I was desperate enough to poison him. If that had been the case, I'd have done it long ago. Probably after he'd fallen asleep on our wedding night.

I hated to admit I'd have never actually done it. Leaving Meirdre open to Thomas's plans for it would have been worse than leaving Laurent in charge. I knew that now, somewhere deep in my soul.

"How long—how long was I sleeping?" he asked. "It feels like ages."

"I don't know," I replied. His hand shook as he reached for the water, so I held the glass up to his mouth, praying he wouldn't take offense. "You'd have to ask Willem. It's only been a day since you returned to Lochfeld. A few days, perhaps? I would think not quite a week."

"Willem." He said it as if he could barely remember that the captain of his guard existed at all. "I remember him shaking me, and praying, and then having an entire conversation with himself about what would become of Meirdre if the worst happened. I think he thought I was dying, poor man."

I think you might have been.

"It seems he may have underestimated you, sire, and Meirdre is better for it."

It was a cautious, respectful, and perhaps untruthful reply, but I didn't know what else to say. Would Meirdre be better with someone else in charge? Maybe not. I had the immediate realization that if I truly believed that, I wouldn't have agreed to marry him. For who agreed to be a crownkeeper for a man they truly believed was the worst thing for their kingdom?

"How do you feel?" I went on. "I've been especially worried about that fever."

That wasn't true—I'd been much more worried about his lack of consciousness, but one thing I'd learned in Elternow was to never let a patient know how worried you truly were. Worry led to panic, and panic led to . . . all sorts of terrible things. Laurent needed rest now, both physical and mental.

The beginnings of a smile appeared on his face, then faded. I couldn't tell if he'd remembered he hated me, or if he truly felt too weak to complete the motion. To my surprised, I couldn't tell which option frightened me more.

"I think—" He raised a hand and stared at the back of it, then let it fall back to the damp sheets. "If it weren't for this rash, I'd have sworn I was trampled by my own horse. Twice. I can feel every muscle in my body, and I've never had such a fever, even when diphtheria swept through Lochfeld when I was a child."

"I can imagine. You have been rather ill, sire."

"Just imagine?" There was panic in his question. "I thought you said you had the measles."

I sat back and rubbed my eyes. Heavens, his concern was beginning to wear on me. Where had it been the night we'd married?

She blames me for ordering the whipping . . .

I forced the anger down. It wasn't the time or the place—and if his journal was at all honest, Laurent had finally come to understand how desperately he'd hurt me. And it hadn't even taken years for him to do so. It didn't make up for anything, and it didn't make me trust him, not in the least, but it quite possibly meant he wasn't deranged or evil. Could it be he was simply afraid enough to make cruel decisions? Was it the only way he could think of to keep his power, follow through with his immense responsibilities?

Well, justifying his decisions wasn't my problem as long as I didn't follow him down that path. And that, I was confident I would never do.

"Yes, sire, I've had the measles," I said, adjusting my skirts. "I was four. And since then, I've cared for the sick in Elternow with no ill effects, if you're that concerned. But no, I don't remember any details but the headache and constant whining that I wanted to be allowed out of bed and back to climbing trees with—" My breath caught. "With my friends."

With Thomas, I'd almost said.

Thomas, who still languished in the dungeon below us, after conspiring against king and kingdom. He was becoming easier and easier to forget these days, and I hated myself for not remembering him more often. Traitor or not, deserving of his punishment or not, I couldn't forget how horrific my own experience down below was. But Thomas had also betrayed me, betrayed our friendship, the steadfastness we'd shared growing up. The promises we'd made, even if, in the end, I'd planned on keeping them, and he hadn't. Maybe that disloyalty—how poorly he'd treated me before we'd been captured—was the most painful part of it.

Worst, if Laurent ever freed him, he'd immediately make his way to Vassian, and that would certainly spell the end of Meirdre. I understood why Laurent could never let that happen, even though my skin crawled when I let myself focus on Thomas's present situation.

"Good." A sigh of relief. "Good. I wanted to be certain. You need—you need to stay safe. For Meirdre's sake."

I should have taken offense to that—as though I only mattered to him as a tool he could wield—but I couldn't conjure up the feeling, even though he appeared more in control of his senses by the minute. His eyes had drifted closed a few times though, and there wasn't much time to waste. Maybe if he slept, he wouldn't remember what I was about to do.

Because if he did . . .

I took a deep breath before I lost my nerve. "Horace sent a message asking about you, sire. Yes, before I learned how ill you were. He seemed concerned. Should I send a reply?"

Laurent stiffened, fully awake. His body was wracked with a series of deep coughs, then his eyes narrowed in on me, predatory and fierce. But there was something else, as well. Dread?

"That bastard can't know what happened to me—nor what's going on in Harnow. He'll take advantage of my weakness, will—Iraela cannot learn that I'm indisposed," he went on. "Is that understood? Not even my mother can know. She will . . ." He sighed, apparently exhausted.

The kingdom of Iraela?

I set the rag on the table, to keep myself from speaking up and asking questions I shouldn't be asking. Laurent's mother now lived in Iraela—surely, she'd want to know if her son was ill. I would want to know if my child was doing this poorly, and I wasn't even a mother yet.

But—a strange glimpse of the future passed through me at the possibility of a child, Laurent's or not—maybe that's why he'd wanted it kept silent. It was probably humiliating enough for him to accept my assistance. No man, especially no king, would want his mother worrying for him.

But *he*? Who was he?

"All right. Yes. Of course. And they won't," I said soothingly, despite my desire to jump out of the chair and figure out what he was talking about. "Would you like me to stay with you? Call for Father Gerritt?" He'd want to see the priest more than he wanted to see her, that much I knew. "Or allow you to rest?"

"Stay." His brows creased as he reached out for me. "Whatever you put in that water tasted good, my dear. I'm going to sleep some more now, but I'd like you to stay with me. Maybe you can make some more when I wake up again."

"It's simply a tonic." I couldn't help a smile as I leaned toward him. "You have low standards, sire."

"No." He grasped my hand and closed his eyes. "I have high ones."

I squeezed it back, reassured that he hadn't noticed my questioning. He was still delirious after all.

CHAPTER TWENTY-ONE

For the next week, Laurent conducted his business of
ruling Meirdre from his bed, tormenting the servants—who'd
expected a reprieve from their sovereign's demands—with his
drive to recover and bring the rest of the castle along with him.
From the admittedly late seed orders for Lochfeld's summer
gardens to his sudden desire for an inexplicable buildup of a
militia on the western border of Meirdre, nothing and no one
was safe from his need to prove himself healthy and in charge
once again. Once his rash began to fade, Juliana and I took turns
sitting at his bedside, alternately scribbling notes, filling his water
glass, and running off long-winded courtiers or servants who
took too long in agreeing to their duties.

Every so often, after a particularly thorough advisor left, he
glanced my way, his eyes dancing as if with a private joke—only
for solemnity to replace it when he realized it was me and not his
sister sitting there. I tried not to take it personally, but there was
something in that brief expression that even I couldn't ignore.

Happiness. Hope.

A future with a man who might take the chance of loving me.

But could I love him? I wasn't sure.

Ignoring the question for the time being, I watched across Laurent's bed as one of his advisors, Garin Sinclair, rambled on about how the winter hay in his region had been decimated by an unknown fungus. How long had he been speaking? I could scarcely keep track of the words any longer.

". . . won't have enough to sustain the livestock over the winter if the infestation continues. I've already made arrangements to import more from the fields near the Illrus, but if—"

The constant droning on was too much. Sinclair was capable enough, Willem had informed me, so if he'd made arrangements, the issue was taken care of. He was here to air his grievances, nothing more. If the king had been stronger, I might have let him. Besides, he'd hit on something I needed to discuss with Laurent in private—those moldy haystacks, just like the ones Thomas and I had seen when he'd kidnapped me from Lochfeld. The ones he'd sworn had been burnt by Laurent's soldiers.

"Lord Sinclair," I broke in, "I will have a list of villages with a surplus for you in two weeks. You can request from them as you wish. Will that be satisfactory?"

Laurent shifted against his silk pillows.

"Yes, Your Grace." Sinclair stood, looking chagrined, finally. "Sire, my apologies. You surely have more important issues to concern yourself with. Health to you," he added with a bow, then disappeared.

Laurent raised his eyebrows at me as the door closed. "I've never gotten rid of him in under two hours before, and here you have him in and out in less than fifteen minutes. Are you part witch?"

Laurent, joking? Or was he trying to find a way to get rid of me? I gave the requisite laugh and adjusted my skirts. "Juliana told him I had your ear and that he disagreed with me at his own peril." A fool threat, but Sinclair had believed her. "All I had to do was smile."

"Outwitted by my wife and sister." He fell quiet, and I used the opportunity to stretch and open another window. "Not that I don't enjoy every second of it. If this is the price I pay for being unwell, perhaps I'll have to risk my health a little more often."

I stood there for a moment, watching him, then took my place back at his side. His comment, playful as it was, didn't make any sense. He didn't enjoy having me around, and I didn't appreciate the lie.

"Juliana is the crafty one," I replied. "As I said . . . I only had to smile."

"Not so." He reached for my hand, and like a dutiful wife with a convalescing husband, I let him have it. "I've heard who wins at chess," he said, stroking my palm with this thumb.

My heart chose that moment to revolt against me, and I opened my mouth, then shut it again, too much in need of air to speak.

"Only sometimes," I managed to gasp.

"Hm."

It was all he said. Not even a word, only a sound. But the dismissiveness of it—not of me, but of Juliana's chess skill and her very existence in this conversation—shattered me somehow. He'd just made it clear that I was the only one in his world this very moment, and the realization was overwhelming, unwelcome, and the only thing I wanted, all at the same time.

Holding my breath, I leaned forward enough that I could draw his hand toward me, and then lowered my lips to his knuckles. Not as I had the night of our betrothal ball, as his subject in front of a hundred people, but as his wife—someone so starved for affection she'd risk his wrath or, perhaps worse in my situation, indifference. His eyes never left mine, but as his free hand reached for my cheek, I closed mine in a mix of fear and anticipation. One finger stroked my jawline, and I shivered, just as the bed creaked and his touch disappeared.

"Juliana rides for Iraela tomorrow," he said brusquely, shifting against the pillows once more. "I need you to accompany her. My mother is there, as you know, and it's time for our regular visit. I would have liked to accompany Juliana, but"—he waved toward the spots remaining on his exposed skin —"I don't see the need to worry Mother with my appearance. She'd never leave me alone if she knew I'd been so close to death, and I can't have her fleeing to Meirdre. Heaven knows I'm not infectious anymore, but I don't need her husband accusing me of bringing a plague to his kingdom, either. Do you understand?"

"All right." My cheeks were flaming, but if he was going to pretend nothing had happened, so would I, even if the pretense was all but worthless with the way I was shaking. "But what about the map? Iraela is so far away, and if I leave it unwatched . . ."

Laurent chewed on the inside of his cheek as he considered my question, then reached for his glass of water. "You'll be gone a month. As you said, you are not a prisoner here."

"I see."

I didn't, though. It was a drastically different statement than he'd ever made to me before. Directly, at least. What was he planning?

He narrowed his eyes at me. "Remember, your position as a crownkeeper is not something to be bandied about at the Iraelan court. Which is why you need to go, in fact. If my wife is rumored to never leave the castle, people will question why. Rumors and myth will soon become fact, and squashing them as quickly as possible is critical to Meirdre's survival."

But the alleged myth of the crownkeeper *was* fact, and no one knew so more than I. And even I didn't understand what it meant. How was I to do my duty, to protect my country, when I didn't understand how it worked, what the sparkles meant, how to decipher its warnings? I might not want to be a prisoner to the ballroom, but neither did I want to fail, and failure was all I felt now. I didn't understand the magic, and I needed to. What if the warning for Harnow hadn't only been about the measles? What if it had also been telling me Laurent had been in danger?

Fear poured itself over my head and washed the remainder of my desire away.

"Should I be going at all, sire? There seems to be much at stake."

I ground my teeth together. Too late, I realized I'd questioned him twice in five seconds, and questioning Laurent wasn't something anyone at Lochfeld did if they wanted to stay in his good graces.

Laurent didn't so much as flinch, though. "Keep your mouth shut, even around my mother, and you'll be fine."

He wasn't listening. Keeping my mouth shut was fine with me, since I had never been comfortable with anyone knowing my secret. *Secrets*, really, since I had many. Keeping quiet around the former queen of Meirdre would be an easy task. I didn't share Laurent's optimistic change in mood about the map, but it was true it'd been quiet ever since Harnow. The actual truth was that it had only lit a handful of times in our short marriage, and never for anything that would be earth-shattering should I miss it. And Laurent was all but ordering me from Lochfeld, wasn't he?

Yes. He was. And he knew better than anyone what was at stake.

Which meant everything would be fine.

Juliana, it turned out, while pleasant company prowling the castle together, was not proper company in a carriage. Her tendency toward traveling sickness overcame her more than once, and even though she insisted she'd be better once she adjusted to the roughness, I'd already figured out why her personal stallion was hitched with the rest of the team.

"I swear to you, Riette, it's never been this bad before," she said, clutching at her husband's hand. "All right—yes. I don't like how bumpy this is, and I'd prefer to ride, but it's too long for that. Midnight is only here for when I can't stand it anymore and need some fresh air."

"You don't need to apologize to me."

In truth, I wasn't doing much better than she, though indulging in Laurent's opulent carriage took my mind off most everything uncomfortable. The silk upholstery underneath me was just as fine as the silk I wore, the floor polished wood. It brought back memories of the map, and I murmured a prayer that everything remained well in Meirdre.

"She does. Because she's lying, of course." Berend, the Duke of Athnard, spoke for the first time in over two hours, roused from his slumber by his wife's claims. "It's why she's such an excellent horsewoman—anything to avoid the carriage."

Juliana tossed her hair. "You're jealous."

"I am, at that."

He smiled back, no animosity in his response.

Not for the first time, I myself was jealous of their interactions. There were fewer expectations of them than of Laurent and me—though I was certain they'd be happier once the king had an heir or two—and the love between them was obvious. Not forced, not uncut with acerbity, just warm and comfortable and ardent.

"Juliana," I said, reminded of the other member of Laurent's family who was currently in a happy marriage, "tell me more about your mother."

"Oh, Mother." Juliana waved a hand in front of her face. "She might not have loved him, but she appeared devastated when Father died, didn't leave her rooms for almost six months. We all despaired she'd ever be joyful again, and then one day . . ." She frowned. "One day Laurent came riding back with a marriage proposal from Iraela."

"A left-handed marriage proposal, darling," her husband broke in, apparently forgetting I was practically the victim of the same type of marriage. It was clear what the duke thought of that slight —with regards to Laurent's mother, at least. I wouldn't ask if he felt the same about mine and Laurent's. I had learned, over the course of my months at Lochfeld, to not ask questions when I didn't want to hear the answers.

"Yes, well." Juliana's hands fluttered nervously again. "Children weren't an issue, and it seems to have made them happy. You know she never cared much for what court life could give her beyond that. So much that I pray that she precedes him in death and isn't forced back to Lochfeld. The change might kill her."

It was a sharp reminder that Laurent's mother must have been born a commoner, just like me. Did Juliana feel the same around me, despite her kindness?

"The king of Iraela is happy because your brother paid handsomely."

"A dowry is expected," she shot back at him. "Even of a widowed queen."

I raised my brows. Short words between Juliana and her husband? I would never have believed it if I wasn't seeing it with my own two eyes.

"He sold her. If you can't accept—"

"Berend!"

Berend shrugged, leaned against the window, and closed his eyes again. Juliana looked at me, pleading.

"It's not as bad as it sounds," she said. "She once said that Iraela reminds her of her hometown. The palace there overlooks a valley from atop the mountains, and she speaks quite frequently of how she enjoys the views. And her husband is—" She faltered a bit. "He provides for her very well, and that's all I'll say about that. It's not for us to criticize Mother's situation—or even discuss it."

It didn't sound like the love Laurent had told me about the

night of our betrothal ball, but how could he possibly know the entire story? He must have felt secure enough in his mother's future to allow and bless her departure from Meirdre, and that was that. It certainly wasn't any of my business.

"I'm sure he does," I replied, with false assurance. I might have doubted Laurent's motives, but I had no reason to doubt his mother's new husband was anything but sincere.

The duke scoffed at my response. Juliana gave him a baleful look and closed her own eyes, leaving me alone to imagine what Iraela would be like.

CHAPTER TWENTY-TWO

IRAELA'S FOREMOST CASTLE CLUNG TO A CLIFF ON THE NORTH SIDE
of the head of the Cresquet River, and even if it hadn't reminded
Laurent's mother of home, I could see why she'd found happiness
here. Like I'd done when I'd arrived at Lochfeld, I watched it
approach in the distance, though this time I had to stick my head
out the carriage window while Juliana eyed me with disapproval.

"Their guards are staring at you by now, you know."

I didn't so much as swivel my neck. "Let them stare."

For as amazing as Lochfeld still was to me, the home of
Iraela's ruler was beyond anything I could have imagined. I
couldn't tell for sure yet, but it appeared to have been built into
the mountain, for large waterfalls tumbled on each side of the
moss-covered barbican. Above the guardhouse and keep, the
main part of the castle seemed to hang in the air, suspended by
nothing but rock and seeming magic. How could Juliana not
stare like I was?

And I did, for the entire last hour of our journey, while Juliana
fretted over her gown and her husband slept—apparently, the
two inns we'd stayed at had been much too quiet for him to sleep
well at night. Part of me wondered if he simply didn't want to

argue with his wife. Whatever the reason, I didn't care. I only wanted to look at the scenery and worry about how I'd look out of place in a foreign court.

My wariness grew as we rolled through the great gate into the courtyard of the guardhouse. We were all relations to the king's wife—some of us more than others—so a group of soldiers greeted us, all polished in red uniforms and with steel swords. Meirdre had an army, but a small one, and they were rarely seen around Lochfeld. I imagined these men marching toward my home, burning farmland, raiding barns and food stores, torching haystacks—

Torching haystacks.

The hairs on the back of my neck prickled at once. Laurent had so distracted me with his touch the other day that I hadn't told him of my suspicions. That Thomas had blamed the failure of the haystacks outside Haszen on Laurent's troops, even though I thought—like Lord Sinclair had implied—it looked more like mold.

Maybe it didn't matter. I gritted my teeth as Juliana gave me final instructions under her breath—*hold up your head up, don't smile at the soldiers, give Mother a brief curtsy and nothing more, and then wait for her to speak*—and stepped onto the stone courtyard, wobbling a bit as I did. One of the soldiers approached me, and I bit my tongue, determined to make Meirdre proud, no matter how little I cared about Laurent's feelings.

Right. That's why you're thinking about him.

"Your Grace." The man's dialect, so similar to Meirdre's, was clipped. "The queen is waiting for you."

The disapproving tone in his voice made my skin crawl, but perhaps the formality was a custom. No one could control or even predict road conditions, and we'd come from so far . . . surely, she wasn't angry at our arrival time.

Then again, Laurent was her son.

I nodded and followed the soldier through a doorway,

Juliana's footsteps comfortingly on my heels. It was hard to focus on anything but the beauty around me. The waterfalls, it seemed, were so in harmony with the palace that they acted as walls in some places and as pools with sparkling fish and lilies in others. I wanted to reach out and touch the water, but Juliana's reaction to my etiquette violation stopped me. Finally, as I was deciding it was worth risking her anger, the soldier stopped me with a soft tap to my elbow.

He may have introduced me to the woman standing in the parlor we'd entered, but I'd been too distracted to notice. I was not, however, too distracted to notice Laurent's cheekbones and strong chin, though I barely dipped my own as I curtsied.

"You're late, Juliana." Her mother—Elsanne—gave me the briefest of acknowledgements, then swept by me to plant the same brief kiss on each of her daughter's cheeks. "See that it doesn't happen again."

Juliana gave me an apologetic look as we followed Elsanne to the seating area by the window. Water roared somewhere in the distance. I adjusted my skirts as I sat, acutely uncomfortable.

"It's three days by carriage, Mother. Through a desert. You know as well as I do that schedules are fluid while traveling through the Mencote wilderness."

The duke, who'd been silent the entire time—I took that as my cue as well—rolled his eyes sideways at me.

"I wouldn't know." Elsanne reached for a glass a wine. "It's been a long while since I've traversed the waste between Iraela and Meirdre. And I was still practically in mourning when I did."

"Yes"—Juliana's hands fluttered nervously in her lap—"and we all wish you could return for a visit, but—"

"Riette." Her mother's attention swept toward me. "Where is my son?"

"He is—" I straightened, wishing I'd worn the stiff stays that couldn't help but keep me upright. Juliana shot me a cautious look, and my wish that I'd thought about a good lie before now joined my wish of harder stays. "He is quite busy, madam."

"Too busy for his own mother?" Elsanne narrowed her eyes at me. "He'd have never been so blunt as all that."

Laurent, you absolute dog! You could have warned me about her!

"No, madam," I replied. "Of course not—he's not too busy for you. It's simply—springtime is such a busy season at Lochfeld, and he takes his duties very seriously. I'm certain he'll pay you a visit as soon as he can spare the time. And in the meantime, I have a letter from him."

"Hmm. A letter. How decent of His Majesty." Elsanne shrugged and took a sip of wine, peering at me from over her glass. "I heard from Juliana that he refused to crown you."

I let out a breath, not quite a sigh.

"Mother!" Juliana, to her credit, sounded shocked. "The king's decisions are his own, and you certainly don't need to speak of them in front of her."

"Oh, Juliana. You're just upset I betrayed the contents of your letter. Did you expect me to not be curious? It's not the Meirdrean way." Her attention swept to me. "Where are you from, Riette?"

For a moment, I'd already forgotten that the widowed queen had been a commoner as well. Even, possibly, a neighbor of mine from the past. For, of course, the ancient tradition of marrying peasants masked the only chance a Meirdrean monarch had of marrying a crownkeeper—the secret Laurent was desperate to keep.

"Elternow," I said quietly, hoping she'd never been there. I had no desire to speak of the fields that turned gold in the fall, of the poverty that my parents had escaped simply because I'd married well, of the rebels who preferred the small town for its position toward the center of the kingdom. There were simply too many good and bad things to discuss when I was unprepared to do so.

"Hmm," she repeated, sounding disinterested. "I've never heard of it."

I found that strange, since Elternow wasn't so very far from Lochfeld—the first village, in fact, where Captain Willem and his guard had arrived looking for a wife for Laurent. But Elsanne didn't sound like she was hiding anything—she simply seemed like a woman who had one thing on her mind, and currently, that one thing was harping on her daughter's choice of gown and criticizing her son's decision not to accompany me. I couldn't relate to Juliana's mother troubles—my mama was kind and gentle and accepting of almost anything that came along in life—but neither was I much surprised.

And with that dismissive comment toward myself and my history, she left me alone. I half listened to her and Juliana, pretending to be attentive, but my real curiosity was in the fact Laurent's mother had never returned to Meirdre since her wedding.

I lay in bed that night, listening to water rumble somewhere outside. It'd been captivating when I'd first arrived, but now it was an irritation. I wanted my own room at Lochfeld, the moon outside my window, the pattering of Sara's footsteps outside the door, the certain knowledge that Mama and Papa were safe in Elternow. Irrationally annoyed, I crept to the window and squinted out. Was I facing east, toward Meirdre? I had no way of knowing, but a fierce yearning washed over me like the water outside rushed over the rocks below. Was this homesickness? I'd heard Thomas talk about that before—even though his love for Elternow and Meirdre had been a lie—but having never left Elternow before the royal guard had showed up that fateful night, I didn't think I'd ever quite understood the concept.

I did now. To my surprise, I even missed Laurent—and that

cursed map. Nothing here was familiar, from the design on the wool underneath my feet to the chest of drawers that sat to the left of the window. I ran my fingers over the top, desperately wishing for comfort.

And that's when I saw it, scratched in the corner of the lacquer.

Horace.

Horace? I stood there for a moment, staring at the name, then knelt and began to rummage through the drawers that one of Elsanne's servants had already filled with my things. It was odd, I thought, as I sifted through my stays and chemises, to not be allowed to select my own clothing for the trip—Sara had done that—but perhaps it was for the best. She'd always chosen more appropriately than I.

It was unlikely I'd find anything inside the chest, but I kept searching through stocking and silk slippers, hoping the servants who'd brought the chest to this set of rooms in the first place hadn't removed all indications of its past owner. But there was nothing, even when I slid a fingernail under the paper lining each drawer, and I knelt back, my eyes closed. Some hunter I was.

A knock at the door startled me, and before I could climb to my feet—or even look like I belonged there on the floor in front of the chest—Julianna made her way inside and cast me a bemused look.

"I was—I was looking for a gown for tomorrow," I stammered, trying to stand with some semblance of grace, yet failing miserably.

Julianna laughed and strolled to a screen. "Hanging in the closet, of course. But Mother's servants will help you dress—there's no need to find something yourself."

"Of course." I must have flushed, but she was used to my court missteps and didn't say a word as she pretended to look through my dresses. "Julianna—do you know who Horace is?" I pointed at the top of the chest. "His name was etched right here. No one's mentioned a Horace to me since we've arrived, so it seemed odd."

To say the least.

"Horace?" Her delicate eyebrows drew together. "I should say they haven't mentioned him— Iraelan rulers take regnal names. Horace is . . ." She made a face. "That's King Marius's birth name."

My mouth opened; my knees went weak. Laurent was paying King Marius that much money? Why? I clutched at the chest of drawers for balance, unable to ask the question, but unable to think of any valid reason for the numerous payments to a monarch of another kingdom.

Julianna, being who she was, simply attributed my sudden feebleness to traveling fatigue and called a servant, who helped put me to bed.

CHAPTER TWENTY-THREE

I scarcely ate the next morning, even with Juliana's constant prompting. No, I spent all of breakfast trying to convince myself that there was nothing untoward about Laurent sending most of his money to Iraela. A dowry, it must be. I'd have had my own if Laurent hadn't sent his men to my house that night. Nothing large like my own husband was paying his current father-in-law—a few goats, maybe—but I would have had one.

Dowries were a one-time payment, though. Laurent was making two payments a month. Large ones.

Juliana elbowed me in the side once more, and I looked up at King Marius of Iraela—*Horace* before his coronation.

"We do miss Laurent," he said, probably for the second time. "And I wish he could have visited as well. But he did send an acceptable replacement in his stead," he added, lifting his glass.

I gave him a short nod. "It has been an honor to visit Iraela on his behalf, sir."

And now I want to go home.

I swallowed the impolite thought, annoyed at how it'd rushed into my mind, forceful and distinct. We'd hadn't been in Iraela much more than a day, and heavens knew I wasn't desperate to get back to Laurent. But perhaps . . . perhaps I was desperate to get back to Meirdre?

But why? My dreams of leaving Elternow had never been detailed, consumed as I was with the simple activity of survival. Girls like I'd been before the royal guard had shown up that winter night weren't supposed to dream of visiting other kingdoms or meeting foreign kings or eating the roast stag in front of me. Those dreams existed somewhere in my consciousness though, and since I'd married Laurent, they'd only become stronger. I wasn't an explorer, not in the least, but visiting Iraela had become something I hadn't known I'd desired until I was here. Returning to Meirdre should be the last thing I wanted this second.

My hand began to shake, and before I could spill my glass, I set it back on the table and clenched my jaw. Fear, absolute fear, overcame my annoyance at King Marius's continued words, and I knew exactly what had caused it.

The map.

It was calling me. It certainly wasn't homesickness or any desire to create a relationship with my husband. If anything, I'd enjoyed being away from Laurent like I was certain he was enjoying being away from me.

It was the map.

I'd felt the sensation before, now that I thought about it, but last time—when Laurent had condemned me to death and his guards had tried to drag me back to the dungeon—it had been frantic. Now it was simply . . . disappointed?

In any case, it wanted me back.

And that meant—

I wanted to cry, but folded my hands in my lap instead, even as my entire body grew icy.

That meant something was happening to my kingdom.

Marius droned on for what seemed like another two hours, and I held myself together the entire time, though Juliana grasped my hand under the table, a concerned expression on her face. I shook my head each time she tried to elicit a response from me, silent or otherwise. There was no polite way to leave breakfast with a king, even if he wasn't mine, and I was smart enough to not even bother to try. I couldn't tell Juliana the truth, anyway.

But by the time King Marius stood, smiled at us, and headed through a set of doors on the far side of the dining hall, followed by a half dozen servants, I was frantic.

Grabbing Juliana, I pulled her into a private alcove, where water rushed on the other side of the open window, and tried to catch my breath. A lie. I would have to lie to her, since she wasn't, to my knowledge, aware of my status as a crownkeeper.

"Juliana—" Thinking quickly, I came up with the only excuse I could. "The king has called me back to Lochfeld. Immediately. He sent a letter."

"Really?" Her forehead creased. "Laurent wouldn't do that. He knows better. We never cut short our visits to Iraela."

She sounded certain. Too certain. Would she ever believe my lie? She knew Laurent much better than I did, after all.

"Well, he did."

"Did he say why?" Her cheeks grew pale. "He's not ill again, is he? Riette—he seemed to be improving, but if he's taken a turn for the worse—"

"He's not ill—the letter was written in his hand, and the words looked steadier than they have since he recovered." Lying grew easier the more I did it. "But he didn't say why he wanted me back . . . at least, not exactly." Heavens, but she was nosy. "The letter was vague. You know how it is with him. I can scarcely contain my curiosity myself."

Juliana sighed. "I supposed it would have to be, in case the courier became curious as well. Strange, though, I hadn't heard of a Meirdrean courier arriving. They usually arrive near the beginning of the week. Well, if Laurent thinks it's important enough that you return home, I suppose you'll have to. If he receives a message declining his order . . . he might ride for Iraela himself, and we can't have that."

I could have kissed her for falling for my deception. "I'll pack immediately and send a new team for you as soon as I arrive home. It won't delay your return much at all, and if it does, I suppose your mother would be happy to spend a little more time with you. Agreed?"

She nodded, her eyes wide, like she couldn't believe I'd talked her into it—or that I'd rolled right over her desires in my haste to reply to Laurent's falsified summons. And when I waved goodbye from the carriage not two hours later, my trunk packed and attached, she stood in the courtyard with a half-smile, but she didn't wave goodbye in return.

When I arrived at Lochfeld a short two and a half days later, sore and dusty, the castle was even quieter than usual. A few sentries glanced my way and nodded as I padded across the courtyard and then up the stairs to my room, but no one else bothered me until Sara came knocking on my door an hour later. Wordlessly, she helped me out of my dirty gown and into a clean one, then did what she could with my hair. All I wanted was a bath and nap and to check the map, but I knew her ministrations meant something else was on the horizon.

"He's waiting," she said, jabbing another pin toward my scalp. "In the throne room."

"The throne room?" I spun toward her, momentarily wordless.

She nodded.

"But why?" Laurent knew better than to push things so soon after his illness, didn't he? "He's still not well. He should be in bed."

"Yes, well—good luck telling His Majesty that. He'll be back in his bed shortly, I'd imagine, but he informed me that he wanted to see you in the throne room, as soon as possible." Her expression said everything there was to say about my lack of choice in the matter.

Oh, no . . .

"Me specifically?" I pressed my lips closed. "He knows I'm home?"

Sara swiveled me toward the mirror for my approval and nodded. "And I would say that he's most displeased with you. Just a warning, my lady, since I'd never let you walk in there unawares."

My heart sank. I'd come back because something had happened to Meirdre, and Laurent was going to chastise me over it? I supposed that was his right, but that simple fact didn't make my immediate future any easier to accept. I nodded in return and slunk down the corridor, down the stairs, and to the throne room, praying no one else would witness my humiliation.

To my horror, Willem was already there, standing in the center of the room, his arms clasped formally behind his back. He turned when I entered, gave me a short bow—in here, at least, I did have some semblance of power, even if it hadn't been earned on my own—then walked out, his boots tapping on the stone floor.

Laurent raised his chin, and I curtsied, then peeked at him from under my eyelashes as I often did. He didn't look displeased, not exactly, so perhaps his quarrel had been with Willem?

Silly. He's furious with you about something.

"You're back at Lochfeld early, if I'm not mistaken," he began.

"Yes sire, but—"

"You will listen. Not argue."

Oh. Oh, yes. Sara had been right about him being angry.

I didn't apologize for my interruption, but my compliant silence must have been enough, for he continued.

"I thought I made it clear that you were to accompany Juliana. I didn't think I needed to specify that I meant for her entire visit. You have no idea what you've done—the problems you caused. From now on, you will do as I say, no matter how difficult you might find it. Nothing more, nothing less. Is that clear?"

I nodded and began to breathe easy once more. That was it? That was the lecture Sara had felt the need to warn me about? As reprimands went, I'd had much worse from Papa as a child. For that matter, I'd been subjected to Laurent's actual anger during our betrothal, and compared to being thrown in the dungeon and sentenced to hang, this was . . . nothing.

Or was it? Laurent didn't let things go so easily.

"Good. This may still be salvageable. Go back to your room and play with fabric or whatever it is you do. I don't want to see you for at least the next week—make sure it doesn't happen."

My vision clouded as rage descended upon me. He didn't need to warn me about running across him anytime soon; the feeling was certainly mutual. Cheeks hot with fury at his detached dismissal, I turned toward the doors at the opposite end of the throne room, then stopped and twisted back toward him. Laurent had already turned away and picked up a book, apparently secure in the knowledge that I would follow his latest royal command without argument.

"I'll leave you alone after you answer one question for me, sire. Why are you paying King Marius of Iraela 5000 crowns twice a month?"

He froze at my question, then stood and headed slowly toward me, his head cocked at an unnatural angle.

I didn't flinch. Perhaps it was his occasional kindness, but I was starting to realize that his threats towards me—most of them, anyway—were empty.

"How do you know about that?" he asked in an odd tone, too high-pitched for him. "Who told you?

I ground my slippers into the floor. "It was my responsibility to take care of the finances while you were ill."

Since you don't have a steward to handle the responsibility . . . and why not, Laurent? Couldn't you afford him any longer?

"I never asked you to do that."

To my surprise, he didn't blink much at the idea I'd been in his study. Perhaps he'd already assumed I'd been doing some of the financial work while he'd been indisposed. If I was lucky, he wouldn't also consider the fact I might have been reading his journal while I was at it. For an instant, I felt the sting of the whip on my back.

Still, I scoffed, too furious to be afraid. "You were unconscious, sire. You weren't doing much of anything. I did what needed to be done for Lochfeld. So yes, I saw the ledger." My hands began to shake. "I saw all the payments you've made to *Horace*. While I visited Iraela and your mother, I put things together. If you meant to keep it a secret, sire, you shouldn't have ordered me there in the first place. And you shouldn't have assumed I was too stupid to figure out who Horace is."

"It was a dowry," he said through gritted teeth. "Even someone like you should understand that."

"Twice a month?" I ground my slippers in the floor. "Dowries are not recurring in Meirdre. Or Iraela—I asked Juliana."

In a flash, he was only a pace away from me. I supposed he meant it to be threatening, but my heart was not racing from fear. No, it was from the ever-so-masculine stubble along his chin and the memory of the way he'd touched my own that afternoon in his rooms.

Heavens. I truly was a fool.

"It is none of your business," he growled. "Stay out of it."

No. I wouldn't. I couldn't.

"I want to help," I said quietly, my shoulders sagging. "I can help. With—whatever trouble you're in. Please let me help you . . . Laurent."

The throne room was so silent I could hear him breathing as he stared at me. I didn't move, but his eyes flickered back and forth between me and a side door.

"Come upstairs," he said suddenly, gripping me by the elbow.

I protested until he reached the doors at the opposite end of the throne room, then stopped. Was Laurent swooping me off to bed?

No. He was . . . I had no idea what he was doing, truth be told. I flushed as we dashed through the corridors, knowing the servants would assume otherwise. By the time he pushed me inside his sitting room and shut the door behind us, my cheeks were on fire.

"Willem listens in the throne room." He gave my cheeks the briefest look before settling onto the divan by the window and patting beside him. "To everything. It's for my own safety, and I tolerate it as I must, but some things must remain a secret, even from him."

He was acting odd. Too odd. Heavens, the entire situation was odd. Yet I sat, careful to stay far enough away from him, clutching at my gown to keep from touching my face.

"You can't help me." He looked at me as he spoke, but he wasn't seeing me. No, his gaze was distant, off somewhere I couldn't see and wasn't invited. "Please don't offer again. I can't have you involved in this. I won't allow you to become involved."

In what? was the obvious question, but something told me to remain silent.

Laurent glanced out the window and scratched at the back of his neck, then shook his head as if he were arguing internally with himself. Finally, he turned to me and spoke under his breath.

"She's a hostage."

"Who? Who's a hostage?"

His palm closed over my mouth, and my eyes widened in shock before I realized he hadn't hurt me. Nor had he been trying to, came the next abrupt realization. For the look in *his* eyes was nothing but panic and fear and a desperate need for someone to trust.

"Shh." He put a finger over his lips before releasing me. "No one knows except Horace—*Marius*—and me. And now you. Not even my mother is aware of her actual circumstances."

"Your mother? A hostage? Sire, I don't even—"

"She didn't seem like one, did she?" He shot me a wry grin, which faded almost immediately. "That's typical of her. But make no mistake, I worry about her every single day. And if I don't make those payments . . ."

I reached for his hand without knowing why. I didn't love him, certainly didn't want to touch him, but it seemed he needed me, and I couldn't leave him alone right now.

He clung to it, and I chanced the question. "What happened? How did she end up in this situation?"

He frowned at my fingers but didn't let go. "A month after my father died, a courier arrived. I didn't think anything of it at the time. It was an overture toward a more stable peace than we had enjoyed with Iraela in the past, and alliances are never something to dismiss prematurely. So, he and I talked. Then she met *him*. She was happy to leave Lochfeld for Iraela, and I didn't argue much or ask too many questions—I knew she hadn't loved my father, though she mourned his death as the end of an era, and I wanted to see her happy. I thought a change of scenery and someone else to focus on *would* make her happy."

He disentangled his hand and pressed his knuckles into his forehead. "And then the next letter came, demanding money. Not that he needed it, but . . . anyway, I thought it would be a one-time payment, but the demands kept coming. Don't pay, and not only does she die, but his troops arrive on the Meirdrean border that night."

I let out a deep breath. "I'm so sorry."

"Sorry. It's hardly your fault, Riette, dear." Laurent chuckled, a bit darkly. "So you see, you can't help. And you've no doubt angered him by leaving and violating my agreement—I was to send Juliana for regular visits as though nothing was wrong. It keeps suspicion off him. It was a poor agreement, yes, and I wish every day I hadn't made it. But I was rash and inexperienced and determined, and it was what I thought was best for Meirdre and Mother at the time."

Against my will, my heart broke for him. "And that's why you went searching for a wife as you did, wasn't it?"

"It took a few years to realize there was a solution staring me right in the face, but yes." Laurent nodded. "It was insurance against my fool mistake—though I never truly believed I'd be so lucky as to find a crownkeeper. But it doesn't matter. If Marius attempts anything now . . . I'm not sure we're ready."

My heart skipped a beat. He hadn't wanted to hear my excuse for leaving Iraela before, but now . . .

"Sire, I felt something while I was there. At first, I thought it was homesickness, since I'd never left Meirdre before, but—but now I think it was something else."

"What?"

"I—the map, sire. Sometimes it calls to me." I bit my lip. Speaking of this in front of Laurent was painful. It brought back too many memories. "It did the day I saw Harnow for the first time."

He leaned away from me, toward the window, his brow furrowed. "The first time?"

Didn't he remember? Having to remind him was traumatic and humiliating.

I looked away, toward the desk which hadn't been there when I'd left a few days ago. A candle burned on one side, and a familiar stack of books and documents under his seal lay on the other. Laurent was only playing at being recovered then, if he couldn't manage to make his way to the throne room except to reprimand me. Sympathy and anger warred inside me as I took another breath.

"I told you," I began. "I think I did, at least. So much of what happened back then is a vague haze in my mind. It happened when—when you took me to see the map. When I begged you to test me and see if I was truly a crownkeeper. When nothing appeared immediately, and I believed I was going to die, they began to pull me back toward—back toward the dungeon. And it called to me. I told you that much. And for an instant—"

I squeezed my eyes shut. I'd been so certain that had been the end for me.

"For an instant I thought I was simply afraid of dying, but it was the map. It wanted me to stay so I'd see something happening in Harnow."

Laurent cleared his throat, and his fingers touched mine once more.

"And when I looked out the window in my room in Iraela that night, I felt the same. It was calling for me, wondering where I was. And I felt—something like disappointment flowing from it. So that's why I told Juliana I had to leave."

When I opened my eyes, he was staring at me intently, his thumb resting on the back of my hand. "Do you think it will still speak to you?" he asked. "Give you another chance to see what you missed because of my mistake?"

I lifted my shoulders.

"I honestly don't know."

CHAPTER TWENTY-FOUR

My entire body ached from sitting in that chair by the ballroom window, but I hadn't moved from it in almost six hours. Sara had brought me tea and a light supper, and now as the spring air grew cool around me, I shifted in my seat again. Dancing hadn't appealed to me for some reason, but sitting no longer did. The map hadn't sparkled, hadn't glimmered, had just rested there on the ballroom floor looking to me like it looked to everyone else who crossed over its wood insets and borders.

Harnow had flashed white the first time I'd seen it, then white with red the second. I grabbed the journal I'd brought to the ballroom with me ever since I'd returned from Iraela. The colors had to mean something, *had* to, but unless the map spoke to me again, I'd never figure it out.

Unless it spoke to me again, I would never puzzle out its meaning. And if I could not puzzle out its meaning, how could I keep Meirdre safe?

And I hated myself for that. It might have been Laurent's decision to send me away to Iraela—and I supposed I could understand why—but he couldn't fathom the responsibility I felt as crownkeeper. I'd married him to fulfil my duty, all so I could live out my life at Lochfeld and protect Meirdre from the vexatious map that had probably sent the royal guard toward Mama and Papa's house in the first place.

But it wasn't speaking to me tonight. Realizing I'd fall asleep and end up spending the night here if I didn't stand eventually, I found my footing and crept out of the ballroom with one last glance back. In the darkness, with only the single oil lamp, I couldn't see the map, much less any detail. Shadows followed me as I strode to the library, and for the first time since I'd come to Lochfeld, the protection of Willem's men was welcome.

They dropped back as I entered, but the fire was still roaring on the opposite side of the expansive room, and the figure huddled in the chair across from it meant I wouldn't be alone while I searched. With any luck, he'd be able to help.

"Father?" I called, praying I hadn't disturbed a late evening nap.

Father Gerritt shifted around in his chair and waved for me to join him, the dark circles under his eyes more prominent than usual. "You've finally dragged yourself away from the map, I see."

"I shouldn't have, I don't think." I sank into the chair beside him and put my head in my hands. "I missed something while I was in Iraela."

"And that bothers you."

"Of course," I said indignantly. Sometimes his seeming mind-reading was too much.

"You know that's not your fault," he replied. "If he ordered you to go there and leave the map unwatched, he has no one to blame but himself."

I choked out a laugh. Father Gerritt was the only one in Lochfeld to speak that way about Laurent.

"That's not going to matter if whatever I missed harms Meirdre—or it affects me."

"Too true." He swirled a tumbler full of wine, deep red and

syrupy. "Then we need to figure out what you missed and how we can keep it from happening again."

"I never leave Lochfeld, obviously."

Tears welled up before I could stop them. The very idea made me want to throw myself on my bed and sob like a child. I was petulant enough to know that was exactly how I would react if Laurent restricted me to the castle. Instead, I swallowed the peevishness and tried to let the elegance of the place wash over me. What kind of girl complained about being trapped in a castle?

"Nonsense. Queen Silke is known to have traveled the kingdom, after all. This isn't as much as a prison as you might think—you only need to figure out how she managed it."

"Silke." It didn't sound familiar. How many generations back had she lived? Father Gerritt had once mentioned the last crownkeeper had appeared over a hundred and fifty years ago, and it hadn't occurred to me until now that he shouldn't have known that closely guarded secret. "She was another crownkeeper?"

"Yes." He laughed and waved his hand at the shelves of books. "You learn quite a bit when you spend most of your time in the solitude of a chapel and library."

"Father Gerritt!" I jumped to my feet. "You never told me there were books about crownkeepers!"

"Ah, well, you never asked." He stood and wandered toward a locked glass case on our left. "And they aren't books, if we're being technical—they're the late Queen Silke's journals."

"Father!" My gasp was so loud as to be embarrassing. "And you never told me about them?"

"Yes, yes," he replied with a chuckle and glance over his shoulder. "I should have said something before now. But you've had enough of an adjustment to royal life, and you seemed to be doing quite well on the map front on your own. Sara's spoken to me of the chart you keep. Have you noticed a pattern yet?"

I narrowed my eyes. Of course she had.

"No," I replied, shaking my head, "and I'm not sure I ever will, so let's go back to someone who might know. Have you read these journals of Queen Silke?"

He hesitated for a moment, then drew out a stack of hand-stitched papers tied with string. "No. They felt too intimate for someone like me to pry into—but you might have use of them, I think. Just don't tell the king. He'll wonder what has gotten into me, lending you such precious—and private—documents."

"Believe me, I won't." *Especially since I've read his as well.*

Father Gerritt handed them over, and I clutched them against my chest, stifling a sneeze at the dust that wafted up into my face. The writing on the first sheet was neat, with a date so long ago I could barely comprehend it. Only social niceties prevented me from running upstairs and reading page after page.

Or maybe to the ballroom, sitting right in the middle of the map.

"So, there you are." He locked the cabinet once more. "You'll have enough reading to do for weeks on end now, which should make your self-imposed restriction to Lochfeld more palatable." He turned toward me and folded his arms across his chest. "But I suspect something besides missing the map's possible announcement is bothering you so much."

"Oh"—still clinging to the journals, I waved a hand in his direction, then fluttered it about my hairline in what I hoped was not obvious nervousness—"it's nothing."

Nothing I can talk about, anyway.

"Hm." He reached for his glass, took a sip, then set the drink down. "You found out about the payments, didn't you?"

"The—" Resigned to being surprised by his knowledge once more, I shook my head and settled back into my chair. "He said no one else knew."

Father Gerritt chuckled. "He says a lot of things. Some of which aren't entirely accurate—though this was close to the truth, mind you—just Captain Willem and I know the exact terms of the deal. Not even Juliana knows—she's under the impression her mother fairly ran off to Iraela to a new life. Laurent was too afraid she or that useless husband of hers would say something to the wrong person if she knew."

I raised my brows.

"Don't tell me you haven't thought the same thing about him."

Against my better judgment, I laughed out loud. "Perhaps. But, Father, it's a terrible situation. For Laurent's mother, for Meirdre, and for . . . for Laurent. Can nothing be done?"

"Without a war? Unlikely. Marius has a larger army, and more important, he has the desire for more territory. Laurent—Laurent doesn't want what territory he has now."

"But Laurent will protect us, won't he?" I stammered.

"To be sure. He loves Meirdre. But expanding? That's never been his wish. He never wanted a kingdom in the first place."

That was something, at least. I traced my finger along the edge of the table between us.

"But his mother is in danger," I replied. "I don't know how he can live with that."

"So are you, now. So is he." He lifted his hands in an indifferent motion. "He's lived with danger his entire life—it doesn't faze him. Hasn't since he was a child, I would imagine. Pragmatism suits him better, anyway."

I shifted forward and propped my elbows on top of the new reading material in my lap, an unladylike position I'd never consider doing in front of anyone else at Lochfeld. "He *sacrificed* her."

"I doubt she'd mind, even if she knew. She did the same as you, after all—married a man she didn't love."

"But she didn't know the story. She didn't go into her marriage and new position eyes wide open like I did. She didn't get to make that choice." I fell silent. Father Gerritt knew how difficult that decision had been for me. He'd been there in the dungeon, had walked with me to my almost-death. "That time around or this one."

"Not to sound unsympathetic," he replied gently, "but it's a little late to be worried about what may as well be ancient history. And don't forget what happens if Laurent doesn't fulfill his part of the bargain."

"I don't see any reason she'd make the same decision I did." I chewed on my lip. "But she needs to *know*."

With an odd look, he polished off his glass and stood to rummage through a drawer. "It is not my place to talk you out of this, Your Grace." He pulled out a quill and a blank sheet of paper, then said with a sparkle in his eye, "And you know, it's been a long time since I've participated in any rabble-rousing. Just don't"—he winked as he handed the supplies over and I added them to my stack—"tell Queen Elsanne I was involved."

Silke's journals were smudged, faded, and written in a style I could scarcely read. Even so, I lit one more candle as I hunched over the first book, my eyes dry and painful. There hadn't been much about the map yet, but her life had become real in the past hour. More than that, her very existence, the one of a merchant's daughter turned queen long before I'd been born, validated my own. Silke had been less thrilled than I had been with leaving her family and her own betrothed, but still, she'd come to Lochfeld for reasons I hadn't quite discovered.

The castle is cold and dark, with a certain lack of charm.

I had to laugh. Lochfeld hadn't been exactly warm over the past season, but somehow, I suspected Silke hadn't spent her first days here in the icy dungeon like I had. And lack of charm? I glanced at the tapestry that still hung on my wall even though the fireplaces kept the room warm in winter. There was charm here, from the oil lamps that smoked in some of the more closed-off corridors, to the false stained-glass windows in the library, to the stables where one of my few friends—however equine—lived. No, unless Lochfeld had been drastically renovated over the years, Silke was wrong about the lack of charm.

And this dreaded map. All the secrets surrounding it. The king believes it's some sort of magic, and perhaps it's that, but it's not as esoteric as he supposes. Can you believe the man asked me what happens when another village is built? As though if a new settlement wasn't installed on the original map, the magic doesn't work. Trust him to not realize any part of the floor can glow, not only those parts with existing villages—though I sometimes wonder if his dullness is a benefit to Meirdre. A dim-witted king can easily be controlled by others, and he is, thank the heavens, surrounded by competent advisors.

All that said, he's not the worst man to spend my nights with.

I slammed the book shut, blushing. *That* was too personal, especially when Laurent and I had never spent a night together. Not like that.

Maybe this was a terrible idea. I hadn't learned anything I wanted to know about Laurent by snooping through his writings, after all. Only that he still tried to justify his decisions regarding my treatment, still didn't understand why I could never trust him as my king or my husband.

Yet I couldn't help but wonder if things could ever be different. Juliana and Skylark made good company, yes, but they didn't take the place of a husband. Someone to console me when I cried of loneliness at night—someone who needed me to console him when things went wrong. Like I'd done, even if he hadn't known it, when they'd brought him back to Lochfeld, feverish and near death. Would he have let me sit by his bedside had he been aware?

And there were more practical issues at hand. Laurent would need heirs someday—sooner rather than later, I supposed—but there was no talk in the castle yet, and Laurent himself hadn't said a word. Perhaps he depended on Juliana to eventually fulfil that expectation with her husband, but how long could that last until the gossip began?

Beautiful as you are, I won't take what you're not willing to give without reservation. When you feel differently, you may ask for an audience and inform me, he'd said the night of our wedding. I hadn't felt differently since then—at least, not differently enough to acquiesce to his presumptuous demand and tell him.

With a sigh, I set Silke's journals aside and picked up the pen and paper Father Gerritt had given me. There was no use dwelling on Laurent when I needed to save his mother.

CHAPTER TWENTY-FIVE

THE LETTER THAT I'D HANDED OFF TO THE COURIER HEADED FOR Iraela was at the forefront of my mind as Skylark and I ambled along the forest path next to Laurent astride Foxfire. Most of me was unwilling to be on the trail so early in the day, yes, but Laurent hadn't exactly given me a choice when he'd knocked on my door that morning.

The servants are becoming suspicious of our lack of relationship, he'd said. *We need to be seen going off somewhere together.*

Dutiful as always, I'd called for Sara, who'd been nearly beside herself with joy that I was accompanying the king out of the castle, *alone.* I was less thrilled at the stays and gown she'd selected, both too elaborate for a morning of riding. Did she suspect something was wrong between us, as Laurent believed, or was she simply dressing her mistress as her station required?

Shaking off the question, I glanced sideways. Laurent was staring forward at the hanging vines like I didn't exist, so I stared at him in return, trying to figure out what kind of man could exchange his own mother's life for the safety of his kingdom. A cruel one? A desperate one? Desperate was probably better than cruel, but did it matter in the end? Did the ends justify the means?

Maybe they did. Maybe they didn't.

At that very moment, the answer to the question people had asked for centuries became even more impossible to answer, because the way the light reflected off Laurent's face caught my attention. A sculpted chin—though not arrogant-looking, unless you knew him—a relaxed jawline, and hair that was interspersed with gray despite his youth. Though it hadn't left any lasting physical scars, his bout with measles had not been kind to him in some regards. Like on the night of our betrothal ball, I suddenly saw him as a man—not a king—and it was a swift and not unwelcome reminder that he was also my husband. A husband who knew all the terrible things he'd done.

"I should feel flattered"—I jumped at his voice—"that my own wife is staring at me once more. I wonder if I should dare ask how many times you've done it, and I haven't caught you."

"Don't flatter yourself," I replied, gripping the reins so tightly my knuckles went white. "There was an owl over your shoulder, sitting in a tree. I'd never seen anything like it before."

Laurent's brows rose. "You've never seen anything like an owl sitting in a tree? I hadn't thought Elternow, with all its faults, could possibly be as constrained as all that, my dear."

Miscreant. I was about to snap at his less than flattering comment about my hometown, but—was that a grin on his face? I looked away, lest I react in kind. Skylark tossed her head, displeased with my less-than-graceful control.

"Elternow is certainly not Lochfeld," I replied, guiding her farther from Laurent. "I would have thought that was understood, sire."

And a morning ride was a horrible, horrible idea. I should have pretended to be asleep when he knocked. Or sick. Or perhaps even dead.

"Indeed. But you don't dread waking up here every morning very much, do you?"

At first, I thought he was accusing me of enjoying the periphery of his wealth and power more than I should, but at the true concern in his question, I twisted back toward him with a frown.

"Of course I don't mind, especially now. Please don't take this the wrong way, but I hadn't realized how content I was here until I came back from Iraela. I think I needed that time away to see it."

"No offense taken. Sometimes we need to lose something—even temporarily—to realize how good it was." He cleared his throat and gestured forward with a slight tip of his chin. "Up ahead is the clearing I've been wanting to show you since that day you ran out on me."

I flushed deeper and urged Skylark into a quick gait, past Laurent and his prying eyes. It was one thing to have run out on him that day but quite another to have him bring it up. Of course, he probably wasn't used to his speech being curtailed. Anything he thought, he said—as long as it benefited him.

But how did *this* conversation benefit him? I cringed to think of the possibilities as the narrow trail opened into a clearing, golden and warm, with a small spring on the opposite side. It was clear why the trail stopped here; the horses would be unable to make their way past the boulders and rock wall behind where the water left the earth. It was crystal clear as it bubbled into a small creek, and I suddenly felt very thirsty.

"This was worth riding with me now, wasn't it?" Laurent came to a stop next to me and hopped off Foxfire in one swift movement.

I nodded, wondering if he planned to help me down, or if I could escape from the opposite side of Skylark before he touched me. I'd ridden sidesaddle today though, and he'd trapped me neatly. With more patience than I felt, I waited for him to present his hand and then slid to the rocky ground with his assistance, my left foot landing squarely on a primrose as I did.

"I suppose I'd have never come all this way by myself," I replied. "Not for a while, at least."

Not after you ordered me back to the castle last time I tried.

"I was wrong, you know." He plucked a fresh primrose from the ground and handed it to me. "To insist you either go back to Lochfeld that day or come here with me. And I am sorry about that. You won't be happy if I keep you inside."

What do you care if I'm happy?

I stuck my nose in the bloom in an instinctive reaction, though perhaps it was to avoid looking at him and apologizing as well. The words were on the tip of my tongue, but it was he who'd wronged me. I wouldn't apologize for something I hadn't done.

Laurent sighed at my silence and pulled another flower from the earth, this one a pale violet that shone in the morning sun. He considered it for a moment, then took a step toward me as I ground my toes into the dirt. His closeness made me want to flee, but before I could argue my own intentions, he'd tucked the flower behind my ear.

A long shiver ran along my back as his fingers drifted from my ear down my jawline. This was—

Silly girl.

This simple touch was better than kissing Thomas had ever been.

"What do you want from me, Riette?" Laurent asked under his breath. "Anything. Just tell me."

I shook my head as his fingers settled under my chin, the meadow still spinning about me. I yearned for him, as most wives would for their husbands, but fury was somewhere in there, for I knew his pretense at courting me had been for one reason only, but something kept me rooted in place, like the trees around us moved for nothing. But above my anger, floating and distant, was something I didn't want to accept.

"Nothing," I managed to whisper, though it was a lie. I wanted his companionship, his love, his respect, even though he'd sealed that fate months ago. "I don't want anything from you."

"I don't believe you. Everyone wants something from the people in their lives."

My breath caught. "Then you tell me first, sire. What do you want from me?"

Laurent was silent for a moment, then pulled away and wandered through the grass toward the spring. His disappearance left me cold, though the sun was warm on my skin, and for a second, I could only stand there and watch his back as he retreated. Grass swished about my ankles as I darted toward him, though I stopped myself short of catching him by the arm. He turned as I approached and, pointing at the water, smiled at me like our conversation hadn't ever happened.

"I used to play here as a boy. I would imagine the spring was the ocean, and dragons of old had returned, and I fought them, only for them to trap me at the edge of the world—just me and a sword."

I inched up to the edge next to him, wavering on the uneven rocks that surrounded the small pool. Laurent hesitated, then reached out. I wiped my palm on my gown, more to delay the inevitable than to dry my hands, then took his hand in mine. *Practical.* It was a practical move and nothing more. If I tripped, he'd have to carry me back to Skylark, and I'd die before that happened.

"And then what?" I asked. I didn't care much, but I had to distract myself from his touch, because the thoughts running through my head were definitely *not* practical ones. "After the dragons trapped you here."

"Sometimes I slew them. But most of the time—" He looked up toward the high trees above us, as if I weren't right there next to him. "Most of the time they slaughtered me, then laid waste to Meirdre."

I held my breath.

"You ask me what I want?" Laurent turned to me. "That's what I don't want. A childish nightmare that I can't shake, no matter how hard I try. What I do want comes second to that—always has. Always will."

"But if there were no . . . dragons? Ever?"

He scoffed. "There will always be dragons, whether they breathe fire or not. Meirdrean insurgents, foreign rulers bent on expanding their own kingdoms, pirates who steal the lives and catches of our fisherman."

I sank to the ground as gracefully as I could and tugged at a piece of grass. "You can have a life outside of your duty. Maybe not like others, but I think there's hope. Even happiness." Laurent stared down at me as if I'd just informed him that he'd grown another head, and I shrugged. "So? What do you want?"

He collapsed beside me and reclaimed my hand. "Something I can never have."

My heart skipped a beat. And that water next to us—when his fingers touched mine, I could have been drowning in it, for as well as I couldn't breathe.

"You have no way of knowing what's in your future," I replied. "Even I can only tell some things, and that's an enchantment most don't have. I think you presume too much, sire."

"Do I?" A laugh, but it was dark, especially in this breezy meadow. "I doubt that. But I'll tell you what I want, since you're so insistent. There's so much. I want you to call me Laurent. I want you to trust me, and to love me, and to hold my children during the day and me at night." He rubbed his forehead with the heel of his palm and sighed. "I want—" His voice cracked. "I want you to forgive me."

His honesty hit me like a rock, though it shouldn't have, with as hard as I'd been pressing him—a strength which seemed wrong now.

"Forgive you for what?" I asked, my voice breaking. "I want to hear you say it."

I expected him to hedge, but he merely took a deep breath. "For not valuing you immediately, crownkeeper or not. For not trusting you, for accusing you of lying—and worse, for sending you to the dungeon, for having you whipped, for treating you as though you were something unwanted."

I hadn't expected him to answer my question, and as the breeze tugged my hair from its plait, I couldn't do anything, couldn't even say anything. I could only grab the loose strands while I stared at him.

"Can you?" he added, as I sat there frozen. "Forgive me?"

"I think so," was my cautious reply, and to my surprise, I meant it. "In time."

Laurent's shoulders sagged in apparent relief. "In time is . . . more than I could have ever asked for. And I will do everything within my power to give you a reason to do so."

"Is that why you brought me here today?" I licked my lips. "To apologize?"

"Riette, dear. You're giving me too much credit on my planning ability." His eyes shone as he looked down at me. "I only wanted to ease the servants' suspicions—but this will do as well, as long as we can sit here a while without any other responsibilities."

Without another word, I shifted my weight to the side and leaned against him. A heartbeat passed—the longest heartbeat ever—then his arm wound around my back, drawing me even closer to him. We sat there for almost an hour, my head on his shoulder, listening to the water splash and the birds singing their melodies of spring. The meadow cooled as the sun traversed the sky, then disappeared behind a cluster of particularly tall trees, but it didn't matter. With Laurent next to me, I felt warm. Safe. Almost—almost loved.

And then we heard the shouts.

CHAPTER TWENTY-SIX

I DIDN'T KNOW THE NAMES OF THE ROYAL GUARDSMEN WHO RODE behind and next to us, but Captain Willem hadn't arrived with them—though no one told me what made our ride so urgent. My heart thumped as Skylark flew down the path through the open meadow atop the cliffs. Anyone could see us riding back to the castle out here, but the guard wouldn't have ridden for Laurent and me in the first place if it wasn't safe, would they?

More men than usual prowled atop the walkways. Someone must have called them from the nearest village, and even though my soul screamed that their presence meant danger, we ran on. In front of me, Laurent shouted back and forth with one of his guardsmen. We were safe enough, for now.

When I arrived in the back gate of Lochfeld, sore and wind-blown, I was pulled from Skylark before I could recognize the person doing the pulling or see where Laurent had disappeared. I yanked my arm away, prepared to shout at whoever was in my way, then stopped.

The man who'd pulled me from my horse wore the uniform of the Meirdrean army.

I backed against Skylark in shock and more than a little fear.

Meirdrean soldiers patrolled the border for protection and deterrence, or, if the unthinkable happened, for war. They didn't appear anywhere else, even at Lochfeld.

Was this—was this war?

"You need to come inside, Your Grace," he said. My eyes darted from the sword at his side to the group of soldiers beside him. "It's not safe for you out here."

I tried to spit back some argument, but our dash from the springs had stolen both my breath and desire to squabble. Instead I nodded, and he followed me inside, my riding clothing a stark contrast to his deep blue jacket. Brushing the dirt and grass from my skirts didn't make me anymore presentable, so I lifted my chin and pretended I didn't care what any of them thought. That performance became more difficult when he escorted me to a small room in the old keep, and Sara sprang from a chair in the corner.

"Oh, there you are!" She circled around me, her hands fluttering until they finally landed on my disheveled hair. She swept away a few leaves, then stood back and examined me. "Are you all right? Did anything happen?"

"I'm fine." I swatted her hand away as the soldier nodded and shut us inside. "It was a pleasant ride until we were interrupted—not that I'm all too surprised about that, I suppose." To tell the truth, I was a bit irked about my day with Laurent being taken away. "But what's going on?"

Sara exhaled, then circled about the room, her eyes darting from me to the floor to the door. I watched her pace, my forehead drawn. Sara was frequently anxious, but not like this.

"They came a few hours after you left," she said, fussing with the pins in my hair. "Overcame the guard and headed for the dungeon."

The dungeon.

"They? Who's *they*?" An odd feeling welled up in my gut. Edgy, twitchy, a combination of wrath and dread. "They came for Thomas. Didn't they?"

"That's what they told me. The soldiers, I mean, and I think they're the only ones who know what's going on at this point. Willem sent for them before—" She pulled a pin from my hair and fell silent.

"Before what? Before what, Sara?"

Sara twisted the pins around between her fingers.

"Before they killed him."

I had no idea what was going on in the rest of the castle. Male voices echoed in the hallways, but none belonged to the servants I was used to hearing. My temporary shelter must have been hastily planned, for besides the chair Sara had relinquished to me, there was no furniture, and she'd grabbed no embroidery to pass the time. I alternately sat and paced, and, at one point, when the sun disappeared under the high window, stuck my head outside the door.

The soldiers standing guard simply told me to go back inside.

I agreed with no argument, but I was screaming internally. I needed to see the map. Didn't they understand that? Of course they didn't, but once more, I'd left the castle and missed something.

Or had I? Would the map have shown the attack on Lochfeld, the assault on the dungeon, Willem's murder?

Of course it would have. All those things affected the security of Meirdre, didn't they?

Yes.

In the worst way.

And it was my responsibility.

By the time a knock sounded on the door hours later, I was beyond caring that the floor hadn't seen a mop in fifty years. It was more comfortable than the chair, and Sara agreed, so we sat on the hard stone while she tried to make me somewhat presentable, for no other reason but to make time pass faster. I'd hoped, simply because she'd failed in that regard, that the knock wasn't Laurent, but when the door opened, he stood there, looking quite possibly more unkempt than myself.

I sprang to my feet and curtsied. "Sire—"

He gestured Sara out, and it looked like she couldn't escape fast enough. Did she know something I didn't? She regularly left to bring me my meals, after all.

The door closed, and Laurent spoke.

"You did this," he said. "You allowed them in."

"I *what?*" He'd sent me up to the keep for my own protection, yes, but the dungeon where I'd spent too many days suddenly seemed so close. So dark. So cold. "You think I—you think helped them break into Lochfeld and free Thomas?"

"It only makes sense." Laurent folded his arms and began to pace the chamber, stopping only to lean against the door. "You agreed so easily to our ride this morning. You flattered me. Stalled. Knew the guards would be with us, and not at Lochfeld. Told me things I wanted to hear and things you knew would keep me in that meadow until it was all over."

My mouth went dry. He couldn't honestly believe—

But it all made sense. Call it fate, call it bad timing, but he was right. My easy agreement made sense through his eyes. And I *had* enjoyed our ride, enough to stretch it out and spend time learning more about this man I'd agreed to marry. Had I'd known my vulnerability and forgiveness would have proven suspicious just hours later . . .

"Don't try to convince me otherwise. I can't believe a word you say anymore." He cracked open the door and slid outside to address the guard. "She's not to leave. At all."

My skin heated, becoming raw when I brushed my fingers together.

"But what about the map?" My panic should have been obvious—how could it not be? "You know I have to be allowed downstairs to see the map!"

"You missed it once." His expression was cold, dead—the exact opposite of that day in the clearing. "Maybe more than that, for all I know. Missing it again won't be the end of the world."

With that, he slammed the door shut, and his footsteps down the corridor were the only thing I could hear.

The chamber in the keep's upper floors wasn't as dirty and cold as the dungeon I was so familiar with, but neither was it the comfortable room I'd grown so used to. The soldiers had brought me a blanket, but I couldn't ask them to bring Silke's journals, and the very idea that Laurent could stumble upon them while searching my room for evidence of my *alleged* collusion with Thomas was disconcerting. It wasn't as though there was anything in them unfit for his eyes—*I hoped*—but my curiosity in them felt too intimate. He had no right, anymore, to know what interested me, even if it was nothing more than the scribblings of a long-dead queen.

The soldiers protecting Lochfeld thought they knew what interested me, though. Laurent, out of compassion or some sense of guilt—or perhaps more likely, vanity—had allowed Sara to bring me a few gowns, and the change in my appearance seemed to change the soldiers' behavior toward me . . . which on second thought, might have been why he'd permitted it.

A few days after Laurent had locked me away, one of them, a lieutenant almost as young as I, knocked on the door. I was certain he hadn't expected me to be dressed in silk.

"Your Grace, the king has commanded me to escort you to the ballroom and . . ." The lieutenant's brow creased. "To wait with you."

Well, at least Laurent had listened to me, though I was fraught with rage that he wanted me to watch the map even while once again accusing me of treason. And while lying about my ability and placing the continued secrecy on me, no less.

I shouldn't have been surprised. He was mourning the deaths of his personal guards and Willem, in particular, but with them gone, only a handful of people at Lochfeld knew of my power—if any. This young lieutenant—I gathered from his wording —did not.

"It was kind of him to allow me to stretch my legs," I replied, standing shakily. What I really wanted to say was *why* Laurent *actually* wanted me in the ballroom. But hadn't my mouth gotten me into trouble before? I could always tell him later, but I couldn't take it back if I mentioned it now. "May I know who's escorting me?"

The lieutenant gave me a cautious smile, and I almost laughed.

"Jonas," he said, the smile turning to a frown. "Jonas Vahl."

Perhaps realizing he'd been too familiar with the king's wife turned prisoner-or-whatever-I-was, he cleared his throat and gestured down the corridor. The keep had warmed over the past few days, and I breathed a sigh of relief as we entered the ball-room, cool as always. Those thick stone walls of Lochfeld had more than one use, I was discovering.

I ignored the chair next to the window—I'd done all too much sitting lately—and gave the map a cursory glance as I circled the ballroom. My pacing probably made Lieutenant Vahl uncomfort-able, but I didn't care—I was more concerned with the map. I hadn't felt it calling to me while I'd been trapped upstairs, so it was unlikely it would speak to me today. Then again, maybe it sensed I was nearby and checking on it. Unlikely . . . but not impossible. I'd just have to wait and see.

Sensing everything in Meirdre was calm enough for the moment, I turned back to Lieutenant Vahl.

"Lieutenant, there are some journals in my room. On the desk underneath the window. Would it be possible—"

"The king said you weren't allowed anything from your room besides some clothes." He cleared his throat again and glanced out the window, clearly trying to end the conversation.

"Yes, but what if you were curious about what you might see in there? What if you suspected I truly was collaborating with Thomas Wennink, and that there might be information in those journals that would prove it?"

He shot me a sharp look. "Were you collaborating?"

"Maybe you should check and find out." I stood and meandered toward the center of the ballroom. Something was flickering there, but it was probably just the afternoon sun. At least, that was what I tried to convince myself as I rubbed my eyes and tried to ignore Vahl.

"I don't appreciate being forced to guard wily women, Your Grace," he added.

A choked laugh rose in my throat. Yes, I may have acted as a lookout for Thomas a few times, but *wily*? No one who'd known me for more than ten minutes would ever describe me as *wily*. Not even Laurent.

My amusement died almost immediately. If Vahl thought I was devious, he'd never take his eyes off me. But did it matter? What was I thinking? That I'd escape Lochfeld, and . . . and then what? My loyalty was to Meirdre and Laurent, even if he refused to believe me.

"I doubt you know anything about women." My argument was weak, but anything else would be a confession. "But I'm certain you know about following orders."

"I know that a loyal Meirdrean subject, fairer sex or not, shouldn't joke about treason. I also believe the king's wife shouldn't joke about anything."

He had no idea. I waved him off and focused on the glittering that coalesced on the floor. It was a royal blue this time, interspersed with gold flecks that shimmered every time I blinked. I rubbed my eyes and tried to focus while Vahl continued his reprimand. The shimmering curtain waved and stirred, moving from the Galvan Sea west toward—

"Riette?"

Rapid blue flashes turned to a deep green. My heart raced as the curtain became thicker and more opaque, narrowing in on . . . on Lochfeld?

No. It couldn't be.

But Thomas had escaped, hadn't he? The map warning me of danger to the castle wasn't beyond the realm of possibility. I ground my palms into my temples, praying the map would change, that the sign would move somewhere far away, out to the desert, perhaps, signaling a dust storm that wouldn't affect anyone. But the splendor of the magic hovered over Lochfeld, then settled into the mahogany castle inset in the floor.

I cried out, though it was a weak sound I doubted anyone could hear.

"Riette, what's wrong?"

"Nothing's wrong," I snapped. I wasn't much given to any kind of royal protocol, but Vahl using my given name was a line I wouldn't allow him to cross, if only because it would infuriate Laurent, and there was already enough trouble. Plus, his voice was adding to the headache that sometimes appeared when the map was revealing its power. "Please stop talking."

"I simply came to check on you." The voice shifted into a familiar tenor. "But if you'd rather I go away, I could do that."

Frowning, I tore my attention from the map, only to see Father Gerritt standing there. Vahl stood behind him, his arms crossed.

"No." I turned toward the glittering version of Lochfeld once more, then back to him. "I thought you were someone else."

"Let's talk, then. Somewhere else." He made to guide me away from Vahl, but the lieutenant closed in on both of us.

"Father, I'm sorry, but she's not to speak with anyone alone."

Father Gerritt gave him a single look and practically dragged me to a far window. I protested his ignorance of whatever rule Laurent had placed upon me, but he glanced backward once to Vahl—standing there with his hands on his hips right over where Lochfeld shimmered—and raised one eyebrow.

"If you give in that easily, you're not the person I thought you were," he said. "Unless it's true, as he said, that you were responsible for Thomas Wennink's escape."

"Oh, please." The rude reply tumbled out, before I realized that no one except Laurent and I knew what had transpired between us at the spring. "I had nothing to do with it. Why would I? I might not want Thomas dead, but I certainly want nothing to do with his plans or him personally. I'm Meirdrean, and I won't let him get away with what he wants to do to our kingdom. Besides, I think—"

I think I'm falling in love with my own husband.

The ballroom began to spin around me, but that time, it wasn't the power of the magic, although a quick glance over Father Gerritt's shoulder showed Lochfeld still shimmering, invisible to everyone in the castle but me. No, the spinning was my own emotions, both overwhelming and so welcome I could comprehend the combination.

Because I *couldn't* love Laurent.

It wasn't possible, and it wasn't the intelligent thing to do, and it wasn't like me. I wasn't given to forgiveness—at least, I didn't forget—and I certainly shouldn't choose to tie myself to a man who had the power and opportunity to hurt me. Laurent was an arrangement. A contract. He financially supported my parents, so I married him. For heirs, yes, but more importantly, so he'd have a chance of acquiring a crownkeeper as a wife. We'd both been lucky in that regard, but even after our conversation about dragons and forgiveness, that was all it was now—an agreement.

Or was it?

"You think what?" Father Gerritt asked.

I shook my head, my mouth gaping. This was too intimate for even him to hear. Once again, Laurent had betrayed me, and so my loyalty now should have been to Meirdre and Meirdre only. Only it wasn't.

"Nothing. I just—"

"Has the map spoken?"

"Right now," I said, pointing before I remembered he couldn't see it. My feelings about Laurent had to wait until I could process them alone. Even without Sara. "I need to talk to the king."

"About what?"

I swiveled at Vahl's question.

"About—" I looked at Father Gerritt, but he only shrugged his contempt of Vahl's curiosity. "That's not your business. But I must see him." Because *Lochfeld* was in danger this time. Laurent would want to know, no matter how furious he was at me, no matter how much he distrusted me. "You have to let me talk to him!"

Vahl blew out a deep breath. "He gave orders, Your Grace. He doesn't want to see you. Besides, it's time to go back upstairs. You were given an hour, and you've had almost that."

Laurent didn't want to see me? Even with news of the map? Then what was the point of letting me see it—or of keeping me alive? Father Gerritt looked like he didn't have the answers to those questions either, so I gave in and let Vahl escort me back to my prison—mostly so neither of them could see my tears.

CHAPTER TWENTY-SEVEN

Sara set the pen and paper down in front of me and frowned.

"If you don't feel like writing to your parents, I'm sure they'll understand," she said.

"It's been months since I sent a letter." I drew the paper toward me. Laurent had allowed me a small table for just this purpose—I suspect he was hoping I might feel guilty enough for a written confession—but it was an awkward height for writing. "And they'll begin to worry if they don't receive one soon."

She eyed me sideways as she hustled around the almost-empty room, pretending to tidy it. "Do you miss them, Your Grace?"

The pen skipped as I began the first stroke of the salutation, so I set it down and sighed. "Of course. But it's not as though I can visit." A sudden thought occurred to me, and I glanced her way. "Do you see yours often?"

"My mother"—her hands fluttered as she tried to smooth the wrinkles from my spare gown—"I haven't seen her in five years."

I scratched a brief greeting to Mama and Papa, then set down the pen. "But why not? If you need time—"

"Oh, it's not that." Sara pressed her lips together. "It's not important."

I blinked at her, then shut my mouth. In another world, I'd have pried the information out of her, but trusting Laurent's wife with an obvious secret? I couldn't ask that of her. It was an isolating realization, even as I gave the gold pen another glance.

"I'm sorry," I said, simply. "And I hope that changes soon."

"I'm sure it will." I could tell it was a lie. "But you—you could visit yours, if he allows."

A broken laugh burst forth. "He has me locked in the keep because he thinks I'm responsible for Thomas's escape. A visit to Elternow is hardly in his plans for me anytime soon."

She settled on the floor, against the wall, and adjusted her skirts. "If that was truly the case, you'd be in the dungeon."

I fought to hide a shudder. Sara didn't know I'd already spent time there. But did she have a point? Laurent had already proven he had no qualms about accusing me of treason . . . though I supposed I'd confessed the first time around.

"Perhaps you're right." I managed to keep my voice steady. "But he doesn't seem to believe anything I say right now."

Sara made a noise of assent.

"Do you believe me?" I asked.

"Of course!" Her brow creased. "I've seen the way you look at him. Why would you risk that for a love affair with a rebel?"

"The way I look at him?"

Did I look at Laurent like that? My blazing cheeks didn't lie, but they did catch me off guard. I hadn't realized I'd begun looking at him with anything but disdain . . . nor that anyone had noticed the change.

"We've all noticed," Sara said in reply to my unstated realization. "And yes, he might not believe you now, but he will. He has to. Now finish that letter, Your Grace, and I'll have a rider send it out. You likely have time before he sends for you again."

Still, as the soldiers escorted me downstairs almost a week after the progress Laurent and I had made in our relationship had been shattered, I realized he couldn't avoid me forever. Whether I next saw him as his wife or semi-prisoner remained to be seen. Even more confusing were my allowed visits to the ballroom—if Laurent didn't want to hear from me, why was he bothering to allow me to view the map at all?

I asked myself the question over and over as we descended the stairs, but when we turned away from the ballroom and toward the rear courtyard, I protested. The soldiers weren't taking me to the dungeon, that much was clear, but neither were we headed for the ballroom and my daily check of the map. Perhaps Laurent's secrecy had backfired. The soldiers, especially Vahl, didn't know of the reason behind my visits there, and if they'd decided to change up the routine and take me outside out of some misguided sense of compassion . . .

Laurent would be furious, and I didn't want to deal with that, either.

"This isn't the way to the ballroom," I said.

"As though you ever dance while you're there, anyway. I'm starting to believe you don't know how." Vahl shrugged. "But you're right—we're not going to the ballroom today. You should be grateful for the longer walk."

He thought Laurent was allowing me to visit the ballroom so I could practice dancing? I could have laughed, but the sheer number of strangers passing us in Lochfeld's corridors, soldiers and mercenaries both, brought a sense of dread to my very soul. And Laurent's vague intentions for me today had already worn on my nerves. Was Vahl taking me to see him?

"I don't dance with others watching," I replied.

"Well, since you're going to be watched, I guess you don't need to be in there."

He motioned toward an iron door I'd never given much attention to. Probably just another cold storage vault. Not for the first time, I wished Juliana and I had explored more, but after my time in the dungeon, I preferred to stay in the more updated parts of the castle. Anything to keep from being reminded of Lochfeld's original purpose as a fortress, and the horrid things that had—and still happened—here.

"What is this?" I asked as Vahl pried open the door.

"The war room," he replied.

War room?

It took a moment for my eyes to adjust, even though a dozen oil lamps illuminated the octagonal room. If the keep was secure, this room, windowless and cool, was a fortress.

And there Laurent was, leaning over a large table in the center of the room. A map of the entire region covered it, though unlike the one in the ballroom, it was stone, and I assumed it wasn't magic. A dozen miniature men, painted dark blue like Vahl's uniform, were spread across Meirdre, tiny beacons of protection.

Laurent waved Vahl away, and I flinched as the heavy door clanged shut, trapping me with him. I didn't curtsy, and he didn't say anything about that—maybe because I'd shivered at the same time, from both the chill in the room and the heartbreaking expression on his face.

"They killed him," was how he greeted me instead. "Killed him and left his head in front of the throne. Like he was something to throw away, someone whose sole purpose was to send me a message."

My knees went weak. Laurent didn't sound angry, even at the ones who'd done this. Grieving, yes, he sounded like that. When he looked at me, his stare was distant, not furious as it'd been when I'd last seen him. He was dressed as suitably as ever, though an empty scabbard hung at his side—unusual for him—but the usual arrogant manner with which he wore silk had vanished since I'd last seen him. He was acting now—as a king, as someone who had everything together, as a man who still had control over his life. The reality was, he was devastated.

"Captain Willem?" I asked, though I didn't need to.

"And six of his men." Laurent nodded as he approached me. "Fifteen years of service, all taken in the blink of an eye, all because I was careless."

"Careless how, sire?" He stopped and considered the floor when I spoke, and I realized he had absolutely no idea how to answer that question—and that he'd somehow learned I had nothing to do with Thomas's escape. "Because you allowed yourself to be happy for five minutes?"

His chin jerked up. "They did not need to lose their lives because I was off courting a woman."

"Not a woman. Your wife." Laurent's eyes flared at my impertinence, and I went on, quickly. "And forgive me for saying so, sire, but you are not trained in war—at least, not like Captain Willem and the rest. If you were so trained, if you were so confident in your ability to take on the enemy alone, you wouldn't have soldiers here now. If you'd been inside the castle that day, who knows how things might have ended? You dead. Meirdre lost."

"I have fought. Maybe not in all-out war, but I'm hardly inexperienced." His forehead creased. His stance grew rigid as he waved back at the table and map. "Who do you think helped force the Nantoisens back across at the border at Vistel over the winter?"

"I know you did." It seemed different to me, though I knew it didn't seem so for him—maybe dragons really were dragons, even if some were more dangerous than others. "And I am sorry he's gone. I'm sorry Lochfeld feels less like a sanctuary for you than it did. And I'm sorry you blame yourself for what happened."

"But not you."

"I'm sorry, sire?"

"I don't blame you, and I was wrong to do so." Laurent sighed and glanced up at the ceiling. "We captured one of Wennink's rebels yesterday. He confessed to everything—that Damir of Vassian had set things up, that he'd requested they raid Lochfeld and attempt to rescue Wennink. He was paid handsomely by Damir, from what I understand, though he didn't live long enough to enjoy that new wealth."

For a long time, I didn't know what to say. Thomas had made a deal with Damir at least a year ago: once Laurent was dead and Meirdre thrown into disarray, Vassian would use its armies to take over our kingdom. But Thomas's continued survival was key there. Damir wouldn't make a move until Thomas appeared in Vassian to assure him there would be no protracted war over Meirdre.

That plot was one of the biggest reasons I'd agreed to marry Laurent.

I didn't want to be the one to point out that Laurent would have gone on believing I was involved had they not been lucky enough to capture one of Thomas's men. The trust between us was already splintered, and the king of Meirdre had a more urgent problem, made evident by our current location and the army movements playing out on the map between us.

The Kingdom of Vassian wanted Meirdre.

And they were ready to make their move.

CHAPTER TWENTY-EIGHT

Though the door was solid, I swore I could hear the boots of the soldiers, and I shivered again. It was Thomas himself who'd said Damir didn't want a war, that he wouldn't move on Meirdre until Laurent was dead and our people amenable to foreign rule. Had he become impatient? Did he believe Laurent had turned weak in the wake of his bout with the measles? Had he found out about the payments Laurent was making to Iraela and believed he could manipulate Laurent just as easily?

"I am sorry for what I accused you of," Laurent continued, apparently unconcerned by my fears of an invasion. "I was a fool to even think it, much less treat you like—well, like I did. I was emotional. And I listened to the wrong people, people who don't know you and don't know our history. That won't happen again. Please believe me."

"I won't lie." I began to pace in a circle around the octagon. "That forgiveness you seek? It's further away now than it was."

He held out his hand as I stopped a suitable distance away. I bit my lip and looked up, unsure of what he wanted from me. Before, I'd knelt and kissed the back of his hand, but something told me that kind of formality was the last thing on his mind right now.

"Come here."

I stepped toward him, then stopped.

"You've been spending so much time dancing in that ballroom," he added, his voice rough. "And because of my foolish pride, I haven't been able to partake in your new skills. Before what's coming makes its way to Lochfeld . . . I'd like to."

Dance? Not the map? He wanted to dance with me here? Cautiously, I took his hand, and he pulled me toward him, his other hand sliding to my waist. My heart skipped a beat as it did, but before I could dwell on the consequences of that feeling, Laurent was dancing, sweeping me along with him in precise and sensuous motion. The stone floor of the war room wasn't the smooth mahogany of the ballroom, but I followed his lead as if it were. At that very moment, I would have danced with him anywhere. My brain screamed at me to walk away, but my soul . . . my soul wouldn't let me.

"I should have done this a long time ago," he whispered in my ear as we circled the table for the third time. "You deserved it— and so much more."

Too broken to resist whatever warped sense of kindness he'd finally managed to conjure up, I lay my head against his chest. The formality of the waltz was shattered then. One of his hands drew me against him, the other sat gently on the back of my head as I sobbed.

"I never wanted to make you unhappy." He whispered the claim in my ear, sending goosebumps shooting down my arms. "Ever. Please believe me."

"You did a fine job of it," I murmured against his chest. He wasn't getting away with that kind of tepid apology, not now. "More than once."

"I know I did. And fool that I am, I'll probably make you unhappy again." He wiped my tears with his thumb. "Though, in less severe means from now on—by snoring in your ear, perhaps. Or not praising your newest gown enough. Do you think you could love me anyway?"

Maybe we were both fools, because I didn't hesitate that time.

"As long as you keep trying."

I wanted to dance with him again, but a lamp flickered out, and we both turned toward it. The new darkness sent waves of shadows across the battlefield map, and Laurent released me to relight the oil. Without him holding me, I felt cold, and alone, and silly. Who cared about love when an invasion was about to destroy everything? Was that—the possibility of his death—why I suddenly felt this way about him?

"I think you should leave Lochfeld," he said, as I stared at the figurines. Maybe they were enough proof. "Go to Iraela, perhaps. Damir can't reach you there, not with that army of Marius's, and my mother wouldn't be displeased to see you. Neither would Juliana." His tone was dry, but there was an underlying emotion I couldn't identify. Concern?

"I can't read the map there. If I stay here, I can tell you when war is imminent."

Well, that wasn't quite true. I could tell if something was happening on the border. Timing? Hardly.

"Does the map matter now?" Laurent began to pace around the center table, touching the heads of the two figurines west of Brannitz and north of the Illrus River which separated Meirdre from Vassian—then slid the man at Brannitz south, toward where the river curved. "Along with Wennink's freedom comes an invasion. It's only a matter of time. When the snowmelt subsides and the river is passable once more . . . that's when they'll make their move."

Only once you're dead. Hadn't Laurent realized being at the spring with me had probably saved his life? He seemed too caught up in his new strategy to appreciate that was the case.

I edged toward the table and studied the figurines. He'd

moved so many from the border of Nantoise that I had to wonder if he remembered the skirmish near Vistel the night of our betrothal ball. But Laurent had spies throughout the kingdom, and probably outside Meirdre, too. He knew what he was doing—didn't he?

"Sire, I don't want to be the one to remind you, but an assassination attempt would come first, and—"

"Yes." His reply was curt, but then again, how could it not have been? I'd just reminded him of his unwelcome mortality. "But the army is here now, and I can take care of myself. Vassian will not take Lochfeld without encountering more resistance than they can possibly imagine."

"Yes, but—"

"Riette, dear"—Laurent's lips curled into a half smile—"are you worried about me?"

I scoffed. A very unladylike sound, true, but he had me figured out, and I didn't like it. I didn't like that I *was* worried about him, or that he knew it.

"As you said, sire," I replied, lifting my chin and looking him straight in the eyes, "you can handle yourself. Please make sure you do."

"I thought as much." He grinned, but it immediately fell. "Willem's burial is this evening. I would like you by my side."

I wanted to hold him, to kiss his cheek, to bring Captain Willem back, to do anything to take away his pain, but I simply nodded.

"It would be an honor."

A warm breeze ruffled my skirts as I stood next to Laurent in Lochfeld's royal graveyard. Transporting Willem's body to his hometown was out of the question with Thomas out there somewhere, and as Laurent rightly pointed out, it would have been his own body in the cool ground otherwise. I'd never argue with that.

Father Gerritt finished his prayer and nodded to the undertaker. I flinched as the first dirt hit the casket, but neither Father Gerritt nor Laurent showed any indication they'd heard the finality of the sound. With a slight touch at my elbow, Laurent nodded me inside, then stopped me next to an alcove.

"I want you to know," he began, "that—"

"Sire!" A shout interrupted him, followed by the dash of boots on the marble floor. "There's a rider approaching. Perhaps another hour at his current speed. We'll have to be fast."

Laurent moved to push me farther into the alcove, but he was wasting his energy. I was already hiding from the commotion approaching us, the stone cold even through my clothing.

"Your men are prepared?" he asked.

The soldier handed over a sword. "Waiting on your word, sire."

I tried to slide around Laurent and the group of men who'd gathered, but Laurent slid the sword into his scabbard and nodded at me.

"Go with the lieutenant," he said, smoothing his sleeves. "He'll make sure you're safe."

"From one rider, I should hope so!" I'd never crossed Laurent, especially in front of anyone else, but my nerves were raw.

"Just go with him," he said through gritted teeth. "I have to see to this."

"You think it's Thomas?" Suddenly, a single rider seemed more of a threat than it did thirty seconds ago.

"It could be." Laurent's hand caressed the pommel of his sword. "And if it is, he won't be alone—this is a diversion if it's anything. But he's expecting a decimated royal guard, not a full company of soldiers. He'll be sorely disappointed when he finds out how well-guarded Lochfeld is now."

My heart thumped. Going with this soldier I'd never met

before seemed the best idea. The safest. If Thomas had already returned, bringing an army of his own, I couldn't be found standing just inside a door that led outdoors. Still . . .

"I'd rather stay with you, sire. Please."

"I'd rather have the same thing. But this isn't your battle, and I need you safe. Please don't distract me by insisting otherwise."

I drew myself up. "Protecting Meirdre is my battle. If I can't stay with you—" I glanced around at the soldiers, then turned sideways and spoke under my breath. "Let me at least visit the ballroom first. I want to . . . check on things."

"Do you know something?" he asked. I shook my head, but Laurent's stance relaxed anyway. "Yes. Go. But they're going to accompany you, and the first sign something's wrong, you head to the keep."

"Agreed." I'd seen something happening to Lochfeld after all, but was this it? A single rider?

He nodded, kissed my hand, then disappeared into a throng of men, leaving me standing in the alcove. Able to breathe at last, I shook off the two soldiers at my sides and darted toward the ballroom with them at my heels. The room's oil lamps had been extinguished in preparation for an attack, but that would only make it easier for the map to speak to me.

Which it wasn't doing.

The space was dark, cold, and empty as I tiptoed inside. I couldn't see any of the inlays, so shrouded was the floor in shadows. That was good, wasn't it? But I'd seen the blue and gold sparkles over Lochfeld before. Why hadn't I finished Silke's journals when I had the chance? The answer didn't necessarily lie there, but if it was anywhere, it was in the writings of a woman who'd been a crownkeeper for much longer than myself.

"Your Grace, really," one of the men behind me said. "You must get somewhere safe."

I sighed.

"My room," I said. "Take me to my room."

One of the soldiers waited in the doorway while the other paced in circles around my room. Sara waited, wide-eyed, as I dug through the papers. It would have been easier to have her help, but she didn't know the secret of the map, and I wasn't going to be the one to tell her—though after I'd made such a fuss about seeing the journals tonight, Father Gerritt was going to have to lock them up again once I finished.

"Your Grace, I'm not sure . . ."

Her protests disappeared as I flung myself in a chair and skimmed Silke's later writings. Complaints about summer's ice storage failing. Fears of her children never growing up. Wonders about how much it'd snowed, this close to the coast.

Nothing about the map.

How was that possible? I had a chart of colors and disasters, though it hadn't meant anything up until now. Didn't this ancestor of Laurent's, who appeared much more skilled at her responsibility as crownkeeper than I, have something similar?

Maybe she didn't need a chart. Maybe the answer was so obvious she didn't even bother writing about it.

It was a disheartening thought. I flipped faster, looking for any mentions of blue sparkles.

Blue sky, blue silk, the blue of the ocean in the fall. Silke *really* liked to write about blue things.

Not helpful.

A shadow crossed my vision, and I looked up at the soldier who'd blocked the illumination of the one oil lamp allowed in the room.

"We need to leave, Your Grace. Now."

I blew out a deep breath and held up a hand. "Five more minutes."

He threw his hands in the air in reply, and I went back to the journal.

The floods in the Illrus river valley have been ghastly this spring. Dozens of Meirdreans dead already, so many crops lost. I suppose, if the pattern follows, that must have been why the map was blue a few months ago. A deep blue with gold sparkles, almost like the night sky. It's a relief to have my suspicions confirmed, but waiting months for the event the map predicts makes my soul uneasy. If I should see the same again, I'll take to my bed and not emerge until the crisis is over.

Shaky laughter escaped me.

I'd found it.

The colors had nothing to do with the type of crisis, even if my mind had been locked on the idea for months. They gave the crownkeeper—at least, one smart enough to figure it out—an idea of when they could expect trouble to occur. It seemed so obvious in hindsight, but I knew I'd have never figured it out without Silke's help.

But my relieved laughter had another cause—I hadn't seen anything lately besides the blue and gold, and if Silke was correct about the meaning, that meant the next attack on Meirdre was months away. I'd suspected nothing would happen until after the spring thaw and, heaven forbid, Laurent's death, but Silke had just confirmed it for me. How many months, I couldn't exactly predict, but that didn't matter now. For the moment, Lochfeld was safe, and I could say that with near certainty. Elation filled me, and then something akin to resignation, though much more joyful.

I could become a capable crownkeeper, invaluable to my people—if I so chose.

But right now there were soldiers on the ramparts above me, ready to fire on the rider approaching Lochfeld. The rider who was no threat. Not to Meirdre, at least, and Laurent *was* Meirdre. Though there was no doubt an attempt on his life was coming, this particular event was no assassination attempt. The map would have shown it, otherwise—and it had only called to me once when I'd missed it. That had been Thomas's rescue and Willem's murder, no doubt.

I sprang to my feet and darted past Sara and the soldiers. The latter ran after me, right on my heels, but none of the men would risk grabbing me. I was out of breath by the time I found the stairwell leading up to the rampart where I was sure Laurent had gone, and the threats from the soldiers had become a little louder and harsher, but I wouldn't let them kill an innocent person.

The night breeze ruffled my hair as I slowed my dash to tiptoe along the wall, behind the musketeers and crossbowmen who scarcely moved at my presence. I couldn't imagine being that well-trained—or silent—for anything, especially an impending attack. I could see Laurent's figure through the shadows, just around the corner. The soldiers must have given up on stopping me, because I stormed up to him without being stopped. He swiveled toward me, shock and annoyance on his face, but I spoke before he could say anything.

"Sire, it's not Thomas coming." Laurent narrowed his eyes at me, and I hurried on, all too sure he'd send me back downstairs if he had half the chance. "I can't tell you how I know. Not right here and now. But this isn't an invasion, and it's not an assassination. Please, you can't fire on that rider!"

Laurent spun away from me instead of replying. "Who let her up here?" he hollered toward no one in particular. No one seemed to come to his rescue, and he took a step toward me.

"What do you really want? You know you shouldn't be up here, Riette. It's not safe, and I won't have it."

"Sire, please—I don't know who it is, and you know I can't tell you why. I'm just saying, please make entirely sure who you're shooting at!"

He folded his arms. "Well, if it's not the prelude to an invasion, what is it?" he asked, as my ineffectual guards finally caught up. "You can't just barge up here and tell me this without giving me some sort of information."

"I don't know." I shrugged. "I wish I could tell you more, but I can't."

Bad idea . . .

"Wait a minute, sire." The soldier next to Laurent lowered his spyglass and frowned at us both. "Unless you think Thomas Wennink sent a woman of, uh, advanced years, to do his work, I'd say that this isn't an attack."

CHAPTER TWENTY-NINE

T HE AGING WOMAN, AS THE SOLDIER HAD REFERRED TO HER, alternated her glare between Laurent and me as we stood in the gallery off the ballroom like children caught stealing milk from cold storage. I could tell Laurent would have rather been subjected to our reprimand in the comfortable formality of the throne room—where he could exert a little more control over the situation—but I also knew it would be a long time before he could set foot inside again. I simply wanted to flee before my part in the situation came to light, but Laurent had made it clear hiding wasn't an option. I'd turned into his protection, somehow.

"You almost killed me," the dowager queen said. "Your own mother!"

Laurent cleared his throat. "There was—"

"I don't care if you thought I had an entire army behind me! What were you thinking, preparing to fire at an unknown target? Of all the stupid, reckless ideas!"

"You were on a horse. By yourself. Not a carriage, not with a—"

"It's been three days on the road since Iraela, no servants, no guards. I left that sorry team and carriage in Haszen and borrowed a horse to make it the rest of the way. I didn't expect to be greeted by half an army waiting to take off my head!"

I shifted as Elsanne's tone grew more and more strident as her protests wore on. There was only one reason she was here, away from the control of her new husband, and when Laurent found out what I'd done, he would—

Oh, heavens, I didn't want to know what he'd do. I tried to slink backward, but Laurent took a breath and straightened, grabbing me by the wrist at the same time.

"You forget your place, Mother," he said, transforming from a scolded child into the king of Meirdre once more. "You are always welcome at Lochfeld, but while you are here, you will treat me with the respect I am entitled to."

Elsanne blinked at him. I turned toward him and stared, though even as I did, I doubted the intelligence of questioning his authority, however subtly.

"Now"—having suitably frozen me with his reprimand, he let go of my wrist, though he didn't flinch at our reactions—"why don't we start over? Properly, if you would."

Elsanne swallowed, and I could tell she was debating how far to push him. I knew, because it was probably the same look I usually had on my face when I spoke with him in private.

"If you so insist, sire." Her annoyance turned swiftly to pride, and she dropped into a small curtsy. "It is so wonderful to see you again. It's been altogether too long."

Laurent glanced at me, like he expected me to intervene for some reason, but I stood motionless, my eyes flickering between the two of them. "It certainly is an honor to see you back at Lochfeld, Mother," he replied. "It has been a long time. May I ask what the occasion is?"

"You may not." Elsanne turned toward me, and even though she smelled like horse and I was properly attired and coiffed for a funeral, I felt like I was an inch tall. "You can ask your wife, if you're so curious."

Laurent didn't just glance at me that time. He turned and faced me, his brows raised. "Riette, dear? What in the heavens is my mother talking about?"

"She . . ." I sank to the stone bench behind me, heedless of how the motion would offend either of them. "I don't know."

"Of course you do." Elsanne pulled a piece of paper from somewhere in her skirts and stuck it in Laurent's face. "She wrote me a letter, Laurent."

"A letter." Laurent glanced from the paper in his hand to me.

"A rather fascinating one in which she informed me that Marius is holding me hostage."

"Hostage. I—I see." Laurent had gone pale—with rage, I suspected. And that rage was likely not directed at his mother. It probably wasn't even directed at the king of Iraela.

"Well?" She fluttered it in front of him. "Are you going to do something about it?"

"Do—do something?"

Beginning to wonder if he'd developed a permanent stutter, I looked up.

"Your wife has overstepped her boundaries, and I won't stand for it!"

"She . . . ah . . . that's what you're upset about?"

"I love Marius. And don't give me that look," she said, as Laurent grimaced and I glanced at the floor. "You've known that for a long time."

"Mother, it doesn't matter how you feel about him. He doesn't love you. I don't know what Riette told you in the letter, but the plain truth is, not only has he threatened to kill you if I don't keep paying him, but he has threatened to invade Meirdre! He's been blackmailing me since before you were married, Mother, and I've been paying him. It was a terrible idea, but I couldn't find a way out. But I will. I promise I will."

"Sire, if I could—" I began.

With a huff, Elsanne ignored me. "Do not presume to tell me what my husband feels for me."

"Mother, he might love you, but he loves the money I send more. I don't know what Riette told you, but—but she was probably right. She usually is. Well, always, actually."

Always? Had he finally lost his mind? Or his memory, at the very least? Or had he, at long last, truly admitted to himself that I'd had no involvement in Thomas's first attempt to overthrow the king?

What if everything he'd said in the clearing that day had been true?

"But you tried to sell me out for the protection of the kingdom? And you thought I'd never find out? I should think you'd know better than that."

I stood, too caught up in the possibility of an actual future with him to think rationally. "Sire, I—"

"We'll discuss *your* part in this later." His expression turned soft, for just a moment, then he folded his arms and turned back to his mother. "I made a mistake, Mother. And I will set it right, even if it means I have to protect Meirdre from an attack on both sides."

"You won't do anything of the sort." Elsanne snatched the letter back, shoved it back from wherever she'd produced it, and gave him a sly smile. "And you've already proven to me that you can't handle the situation, so I'm taking you out of it."

"He will kill you if you challenge him," Laurent ground out. "I will not allow that."

"Hardly. You'll forgive me, darling, if I don't trust your judgment about such things any longer. Now, if you don't mind, I need to make my way back to Iraela and discuss this new information with my husband. I'm sure with time and dialog that the three of us can come to a mutually beneficial agreement. One which needn't include you sending half your coinage outside of the kingdom." She glanced around, evidently at the almost-empty castle. "Heaven knows Lochfeld could use it."

Laurent's mouth fell open. "You cannot leave Lochfeld! Not in the middle of the night. Not for that man. You are not returning to Iraela now. Or ever. I forbid it, do you understand?"

"Forbid it?" Elsanne took a step forward, kissed his cheek, and laughed. "Dear boy, if Marius doesn't have the power over me that he thinks he does, what makes you think you do?"

"I have every authority over you." Laurent squared his shoulders. "You are still Meirdrean."

"Not," she replied, "since I married Marius."

His lips curled upward in a broad grin that was completely out of place in the conversation. I slid a little closer, as though my presence would cure him of the madness which seemed to have overtaken him.

"You think the left-handed marriage was his idea, didn't you?" he asked lightly.

"Of course." Elsanne blinked in confusion. "And I was happy to marry him all the same, even under that condition."

My breath caught.

Laurent wasn't as naïve as I'd thought, no, not even close. He'd succumbed to the king of Iraela's blackmail, yes, but he'd given Elsanne protection in the form of the only thing he could—recognition that as long as her marriage remained uneven, she remained a Meirdrean subject. Had even King Marius realized the drawback of the deal he'd made?

"Well, it wasn't his. It was mine." Then, brushing his fingertips against mine, he shouted down the corridor. "Lieutenant!"

Elsanne's eyes grew wide as the nearest soldier hurried toward us, questions in his own. I simply stared, the sensation of his touch hanging about me like a cloud. Laurent was standing up to her? He was siding with me? He—he had manipulated the king of Iraela like this?

"Find my mother a suitable suite for the next few weeks," he told the lieutenant. "And I want someone outside her to door to make sure she's safe."

"You're locking me in?" she all but screeched at him.

"Not exactly." Laurent's easy smile didn't falter. "But in case you hadn't noticed, Mother, war is on the horizon. What kind of a king—or son—would I be if I let harm come to you?"

The corridor fell silent except for the muted conversations of soldiers and servants somewhere in the distance. Laurent's fingertips found mine once more, and my heart thumped wildly as I pressed my lips closed and waited for Elsanne's reply.

"And what of Juliana?" she demanded.

"What of her?" He ran his thumb across the palm of my hand, and I sucked in a breath. "If Marius loves you as much as you claim, he'd dare not hurt her. Or were you misleading me about his feelings for you? Speak carefully—I do hate being lied to."

Her jaw dropped, as if she couldn't believe he'd reprimanded her, then she lifted her chin.

"She'll be fine."

"Good. Then we can carry out a friendly exchange sometime in the future, yes?"

"If you so will it, sire." She tossed her hair and turned to the lieutenant. "I have my own rooms. You may follow me."

And then, without even a curtsy or nod in Laurent's direction, she disappeared.

The soldiers still patrolled the corridors when I finally made my way to my room, but Sara was more than happy to act like nothing untoward had happened today, or even the past week, for that matter. Nothing was said of Thomas's escape, nor of the soldiers outside, nor of Elsanne's unexpected visit.

"They say the spring rains will end soon," she said, pulling a chemise over my head. "It will be a nice change from this dreary weather, don't you think?"

I didn't think. Lack of rains plus the end of the snowmelt floods meant the armies of Vassian could cross the river.

"Yes," I lied, praying she'd finish quickly and go away. "It will be nice to see the sun."

"You have been looking a bit pale. I think—"

A knock sounded on the door, interrupting what she thought I needed. Sara rushed to open it, only to reveal Laurent standing there. I couldn't tell which one of us was more surprised to see him. Probably me, since Sara curtsied and hurried out in the same amount of time it took me to stand.

"I didn't want to interrupt," he said, closing the door.

"You didn't." I glanced at the fireplace. A single ember glowed, and for some reason, I felt as though I'd failed in preparing for his unexpected visit. "Though I should have had her relight the fire."

"No need." Laurent strode quickly across my room and knelt before the hearth to fan the flames back to life. "This is my duty, not hers."

His? In his entire life, had Laurent ever lit his own fire? I wanted to laugh at the stark inaccuracy of his comment, but after the fire caught and he stood and turned toward me, his expression was somber.

"We ought to discuss the letter," he said.

"I will not apologize for that." My bravery, reckless as it was, surprised me, though it didn't look like I'd surprised Laurent. "Ever."

"I didn't expect you would." He rubbed the back of his neck, a startlingly vulnerable movement. "And I would never ask it of you. I'm beginning to understand that it would be a waste of breath, anyway."

"I had only good intentions. She had to know. What you subjected her to was unfair, and very unlike you, sire."

In fact, it was exactly like the Laurent I'd first met, but what had Father Gerritt once said about tipping the sum of Laurent's works toward good? He was responsible for that outrageous agreement with Iraela, but my cautious lie could easily tip him in the opposite direction, especially if he thought changing his mind was his own idea.

"And she may well work herself out of the predicament I put her in. I do worry more about Marius than her." Laurent sighed and fell onto my settee by the window. "And yet, I cannot have you undermining my authority in that matter or any other."

My entire body grew hot, and it wasn't from the flames. Why had he restarted the fire if he was going to lecture me? Or worse —punish me like he'd ordered before? We couldn't keep starting over time after time. If he wanted me to forgive him, then we needed to move on. As husband and wife.

"I never meant—" I began.

"You think this is about my ego, don't you?" He sprawled then, an arm draped over the back of the seat, and I frowned at his casualness. "I wouldn't blame you for thinking that, though you'd be wrong."

"How so?"

He grinned, an odd reaction for such a serious conversation. "You will be in charge of Lochfeld when I leave for the Vassian border."

"What?" The question spilled out in a frantic rush as I dashed toward him. He stood, stopping me in his arms. "You can't do that," I said to his shoulder. "You know what will happen."

"Your flattering concern for me is duly noted, Riette." He tilted my chin upward, and his tone grew grim. "They must not be allowed to take the heart of Meirdre. Our access to the coast. Never. We will meet them in the south and prevent that."

"And what if you don't?" I whispered. "What if—"

"They kill me first?" Laurent kissed my forehead and then my cheek. "Then I suppose I shall die thinking of you."

My knees went weak. "How can you joke about this?"

"It's either joke about it or fall apart." He leaned his cheek against mine. "And what would Meirdre think of me if that happened?"

"That was rhetorical," I replied with no small amount of acerbity. "And another inappropriate joke."

"Well, now you have an answer to a question that would have bothered you until I left." He backed toward the settee, dragging me along by the hands, then collapsed with a laugh, pulling me onto his lap. I let out a yelp as I fell, and he drew me against him, his mouth against my ear. "And now I need an answer from you."

"Yes," I stammered. "I'll protect Lochfeld. As I was meant to. Even if—even if it means I never leave the castle grounds again." My stomach flipped a bit at my vow, but Laurent's touch drove away any remaining indecision. He needed me, not for him, not for Meirdre, but for both. I'd always felt it, but now there was a certain amount of power in *knowing*.

"If that's the sacrifice you feel you need to make, then I'll make certain it's not in vain. I swear to you." A hand drifted downward, resting on the small of my back. "But I wasn't speaking of the map, Riette."

His lips crept down my jaw, lingering at the corner of my own. I closed my eyes, too afraid of what I was about to do—and much too desperate. Laurent's hand found a smattering of hair pins as I clung to him, achingly incomplete, and by the time I pulled away to gasp for air, my hair was undone, his tunic askew.

"Now, no more talk of war," he said, his voice thick. "We've other things to sort out right now."

"For how long?" I asked his neck. War was coming, and I needed to know how long I had with the man I was falling in love with.

"Hmm. Let's say for tonight, for a start. And after that?" He leaned back and studied me, his eyes sparkling like I'd never seen before. "As long as you'll have me."

Part 3

Queen's Crown

CHAPTER THIRTY

LAURENT

MEIRDRE HAD ENDURED WAR BEFORE, BUT LAURENT WAS TOO young to know it. So too had been his father and grandfather. The stories of battles and bodies and sobbing women? They haunted him, yes, but that was all they were to him—stories from decades upon decades ago, before he had so much as existed.

Yes, wars were bedtime tales like the ones his nurse had tried to frighten him with as soon as she'd deemed him an appropriate age to hear. Or fiction, like the myths of dragons roaming his kingdom, long before such accounts were written. Legend had it, at least among his ancestors, that the enchanted map in the ball-room of Lochfeld Castle had been created in a desperate attempt to protect Meirdre from the winged beasts which had once turned the countryside to ashes every few years. That wasn't true —the timeline didn't even make sense—but no one could blame the royal family for coming up with such a story. Even magic could be turned into something mundane when ignored for so many years, and Riette was the first Meirdrean crownkeeper in a long while.

And now, as he'd told her last night, the dragons were coming again. Flesh and bone humans they might be, but did that matter in the end? The Kingdom of Vassian could do as much damage as a pair of dragons. Maybe more, for even dragons satiated themselves eventually, a constraint to which the Vassian king—Damir—didn't seem willing to subject himself.

Laurent glanced behind him, at the soldiers breaking camp in the meadow outside Lochfeld. They weren't ready for all-out war, having spent his entire reign patrolling the kingdom, running off pirates, protecting the borders. Dew lingered on the grass as the soldiers prowled about, and his fingers cramped in the chill as he fastened his scabbard around his belt and slid his sword inside. He'd spent the night here on the hard ground with the soldiers who would ride off to the Vassian border, loyal to their own deaths.

Well, most of the night.

The scent of Riette's rose perfume clung to his shirt, and he hadn't the heart to exchange it for a clean one. No one said anything within ear shot about the king wearing a dirty shirt that smelled of his wife, though had Willem been here, he'd have subjected him to a good-natured jibe—but naturally, if Willem had been here, there'd be no cause to ride to war. Not as much cause, at least.

The camp grew louder as he wandered to the edge and stared south, past the castle. Laurent wanted to draw the sword and practice, but that might show fear, anxiety, apprehension—and that, he would never do. Not even when his soldiers were preoccupied with wagons and stallions and muskets and tents.

He went through a few motions in his head, deliberately not looking up toward the windows of the sprawling fortress in front of him. Riette would be watching, and if he saw her, he might lose his nerve, run back inside the castle, sweep her into his arms, carry her back to his bed . . .

No. He'd never abandon his duty to Meirdre and Riette herself, even if his very soul cried out for her and whatever magic she'd bewitched him with. When—*if*—he came home, he'd do that. But if he thought about that now, he would keep thinking of her instead of keeping his mind on strategy, and he would not betray his duty.

Someone hollered behind him, and he turned to see one of the captains hurrying toward him, Foxfire's reins in his hand. The stallion was fairly glistening with the shine of a recent brushing—that was Riette's doing as well—but he was nervous, that much was clear in his sidestep and the way he tossed his head upon seeing his master.

Skidding to a halt, the captain said, "They're ready, Your Majesty." He gave a brief bow, but it was difficult to tell if he or the horse was more anxious. "Waiting on your word."

Laurent nodded. "Cadaval, is it?"

"Yes, sire. Third Company. Out of Brannitz."

Their route to the Vassian border would take them straight through there—for a night only. "Going home, then."

"Passing through, sire, yes." Firefox reared, and Cadaval gripped the reins harder, then lifted them in an offering—or perhaps a plea. The stallion had that effect on people. "He wants to run."

Foxfire always did. Laurent patted him on the flank, then turned back to Cadaval.

"I need someone at my side," he said. "But I will not order it of you."

Not after what happened before.

Cadaval lowered his head. "I would be honored, sire."

"So quickly you agree." His brows rose. Impetuousness from a senior leader would not serve him well. "You're not aware of what happened to your predecessor, then?"

Laurent still had nightmares about Willem's headless body lying in front of the throne inside Lochfeld. The blood, the violation of someone not only entering the castle, but taking his most trusted guard's life. Did a man ever forget something like that? He wasn't sure he could. Or should.

Cadaval's stance grew straighter and, if possible, more sober. "I am."

Laurent focused on the ground, as if it could suggest a suitable reply for him.

"Well." Shouldn't ordering a loyal man to almost certain death make him *feel* something more? Instead, he only wanted everything over with, however it was to end. Like Foxfire, he was suddenly ready to be underway. "Then let's be off, shall we? Inform the men."

Cadaval saluted him before departing. The gesture made Laurent strangely uncomfortable after his more informal relationship with Willem, but the captain would learn what it meant to serve him—if he survived long enough.

"Sire!"

Laurent twisted around at Father Gerritt's voice and forced a half-smile. He'd spent the morning avoiding the priest and his bottle of oil, convinced of the futility of its meaning. Besides, didn't accepting last rites, as many of the soldiers had, imply certain defeat? He wasn't an optimist, especially now, but there was certainty, and then there was *certainty*.

"You found me at last, Father." He raised his arms to his sides in surrender. "Congratulations."

"So I did." Gerritt's lips twisted in amusement. "Much as you've been attempting to dodge me all morning."

"I've been busy. So much to do. You know that." The reply was too short, and his shoulders sagged. Gerritt wasn't someone he could brush off—ever. "But I am glad to see you before we leave."

"As am I—and never fear, I won't subject you to any long lectures about war and death and life."

Laurent burst into laughter, something he'd only ever done among a handful of men. Still, it must be anxiety now. Who laughed before riding off for war?

"No? Then I *am* curious about what's so important for you to spend hours tracking me down, Father."

"Riette."

"Ah." Her very name pierced his heart. "Riette. How is she?"

"Holding up. She knows her duty, and she'll fulfill it if it's the last thing she does."

"Good," Laurent breathed out. He wanted happiness for her, but duty would have to do for now. "Good."

"But what she doesn't know," Gerritt went on casually, "and what I suspect you're not aware of either, is that more magic than the map enchants Meirdre. All related, of course."

Laurent glanced to the side, at the soldiers and horses surrounding them, certain he'd misheard given the din of a departing military camp. He'd had wine last night, yes, but . . . *more* magic?

"I'm—I'm sorry?" Confusion laced his words. "I don't understand."

Gerritt folded his arms and smiled, smug as always. "Because you rarely accept my offers to explore Lochfeld's library, sire."

Irritation swelled over the confusion. "Yes, yes. I neglected my education, but it's a bit late to be lecturing me about that now. Speak and speak quickly."

So Gerritt did, and Laurent listened. And when the priest was done, Laurent let him apply the oil before saying goodbye, even though it seemed more meaningless now than before. Heaving himself up upon Foxfire, he dug in his heels and focused on the trail in front of him, ignoring how Lochfeld was fading in the distance behind him, Riette along with it.

The future of Meirdre was in his hands now.

The future of Lochfeld?

In Riette's.

On second thought, he realized, as the trail descended the cliff and Foxfire's stride grew more intentional . . .

Maybe Riette would save both.

CHAPTER THIRTY-ONE

no dust, thanks to last night's rain, only a field of mud where short, spring grass had grown only ten days before. It would harden soon enough—that much I knew from the sun that warmed my face and mocked the chill in the rest of my body. Laurent was gone, and heavens, but I wanted his arms around me still.

Bottles rattled behind me. Sara was arranging the things on top of my chest, not-so-surreptitiously waiting for me to choose a gown for the day. I needed to, since the map was waiting, but pretty fabric seemed frivolous. As frivolous as I'd thought it when I had first come to Lochfeld.

Then again, I realized, as I shook off the memory of Laurent's arms, Lochfeld was mine to care for now, and that meant acting the part. Servants and soldiers who prowled the corridors—they needed that from me as well, didn't they? I truly had no idea. I was wholly unprepared for this kind of responsibility.

A bottle crashed to the floor, and I turned.

"I'm so sorry, Your Grace." Sara knelt to gather the shards, but I waved her off.

"Leave it." I sighed and picked at the skirt of my nightclothes. "You're right—I need to get dressed."

Sara sprang to her feet all too willingly and yanked a deep blue gown from my wardrobe. Feigning interest and marveling at how she could pretend today was just another day, I raised my arms over my head and allowed her to dress me. Maybe pretending was the only thing that kept her sane. If that was the case, I could do it as well.

I kept pretending as I wandered downstairs toward the ballroom, footsteps of strangers behind me. The royal guard had always been uninvolved in my security by my request. But Laurent had ordered both them and the soldiers to keep a close watch on me after he departed, and so far, they'd listened. That would have to change—it was already suffocating—but for now I'd pretend that didn't bother me, either.

Shadows crumpled in the corners as a servant lit the oil lamps behind me. Light didn't matter since I could read the map in pitch blackness, but I suspected they thought I was addled enough as it was, so I didn't argue. The provisional mistress of Lochfeld couldn't be seen sitting alone in a dark room. That was how rumors began and reigns ended, however temporary both might be.

I sat by the narrow window, letting the sliver of light from outside try to warm me once more. Normally I practiced a waltz, a minuet, or even one of the Elternow folk dances I'd learned in childhood, but I'd already used up my desire for subterfuge in simply getting dressed.

Heavens, Laurent would be aghast by my moping if he could see me now.

Grumbling to myself, I stood and circled the map inlaid on the floor. Harnow, thankfully, was quiet. So too was Lochfeld, Elternow, and the Vassian border. That was something, at least. Though Laurent was confident of the tiny Meirdrean army's ability to defend the kingdom, they were spread much too thin already. Would I be able to order the soldiers who remained at Lochfeld away if they became needed elsewhere? The woman who Laurent had trusted with his castle said yes. The terrified child in me said no.

Then again, as Lieutenant Julian Vahl cleared his throat behind me, I decided that war might be worth it if only to force him to leave Lochfeld for good. I pinned on a smile before greeting the one person who still seemed to doubt my innocence in this entire mess.

"Good morning, Lieutenant. Come to make certain I haven't absconded with yet another traitor?"

Vahl folded his hands behind his back. "They sent me to fetch you. For a meeting."

"They? A meeting?" My forehead creased.

He gestured out the door with his chin, and I followed beside him through hallways that were too quiet for late morning. Lochfeld was quiet on the best of the days, what with Laurent's lack of a full court, but there was something about her sovereign being gone that gave an eerie ambience to the place that had finally become my home.

By the time Vahl ushered me into the war room, my mind was racing with possibilities. Part of my soul wondered if Laurent was inside, but that was foolish, and if I'd learned anything since he'd ridden off for the Vassian border earlier this morning, it was that fool hope was the last refuge of . . . well, fools. The Riette who'd left Elternow on that snowy winter's night believed in such things. The Riette who stepped inside the octagonal chamber did not.

Every oil lamp was lit, casting sharp shadows on the center table and the tiny soldiers standing there. Most had been moved south, toward Vassian, leaving a single figure remaining on top of Lochfeld and a few others scattered toward the north. I wanted to rearrange them, to move several of the southern ones back up to where I stood, but I steadied myself and looked toward the highest-ranking man in the room, a captain in a pristine uniform like Vahl's but with the tall boots of a cavalry officer.

"Yes?" I asked, leveling my shoulders and attempting to fake a modicum of authority. "Has something happened?"

Has something happened?

How naïve could I sound? Laurent had just left. Of course nothing had happened.

"No, Your Grace." The captain bowed quickly, then meandered around the table toward me. "Tobias Erstad. I only wanted to introduce myself and fill you in on the plans for protecting Lochfeld."

I took a breath. Laurent had said as much, and I'd been ready to fulfill the duties his departure had imposed upon me. But hearing it now, like this . . . that was a reminder that I wasn't ready for.

Still, I nodded. "Which are?"

Erstad elaborated as he pointed at the map every so often and asked for clarification from one soldier or another in the room. I tried to keep up with his explanation, which I suspected he was simplifying for my benefit, but the only strategy I understood was leaving a cadre of soldiers here to patrol. I couldn't argue against that, as much as I hated the castle being turned into a place of war.

Biting the inside of my cheek, I glanced at the thick stone wall next to me. Lochfeld had always been a place of war, splintered by slender arrows of peace. When would I learn? Never, it seemed.

"And Laur—the king?"

"It's several weeks to the Illrus River." Erstad pointed casually, not calling attention to my lack of geographical awareness. "Scouts are following behind, but I wouldn't expect any kind of news for a long while."

"So we are safe at Lochfeld."

"For now," he replied.

For now.

The stone walls seemed to cave in around me, and I sucked in a breath.

"And Lochfeld is . . ." What was that word he'd used? "Defensible? We are prepared for a long siege?"

Food, water, medicinal supplies—I ran through a list in my head. If Laurent hadn't stored enough in the castle, I wasn't sure what I would do. Taking more from the subjects around Lochfeld would be impossible.

"Without a doubt, Your Grace. It's stood through worse than the Kingdom of Vassian can bring."

Laurent hadn't sounded so certain, and I knew Erstad was afraid I'd panic if he told me the truth. I nodded again, like I'd probably done throughout his entire update.

"All right, then." I bit my lip. "And how long until—until we can expect something to happen here?"

He shrugged. "Weeks, certainly. If there's anywhere you want to visit, anyone you need to see beforehand . . . you'd best do it soon. Even if you only want to explore the countryside."

I pressed my lips together. Explore the countryside? Didn't he know I couldn't leave Lochfeld?

But Queen Silke had.

Somehow, she had. She'd found a way to travel the kingdom and still watch the map. Free from Lochfeld, she'd still been able to protect Meirdre. I just needed to figure out how.

And even if I couldn't . . . if war was coming, I knew exactly where I needed to go first.

CHAPTER THIRTY-TWO

MOONLIGHT GLISTENED OVER THE MOORS, CASTING SHADOWS across the rolling hills. Below us, in what passed for a valley, Elternow sat, scarcely more than a cluster of homes. I hadn't seen it in months, and then it had been covered in snow. Tonight, though, the spring breeze whipped my loose hair about me as I urged Skylark closer.

It hadn't been my idea, not exactly. Well, riding all this way had—though a carriage followed with my things, doubling as shelter during the night. Laurent would be furious if he knew I'd left Lochfeld, and to tell the truth, I was already second-guessing my decision. But the map had been clear that no harm would befall Meirdre soon.

At least from the south, from Vassian's army. The rest? I hated to admit I didn't know.

"It's hardly even a village." Erstad edged beside me on his horse as we headed down the hill. "Do you miss it?"

"There's hardly anything to miss." I stared off into the distance, searching for Mama and Papa's house. The lights were too difficult to see from all this way, so I turned my attention back to him. "Just some horses and small homes."

And Mama, Papa, apple trees, clean snow in the winter, the bright smell of a new calf in spring, and . . .

Even that crack in the window of the cottage where I'd grown up.

Well, what did it matter? I was only visiting one last time, then I would head back to Lochfeld and whatever disaster the future held for it. Once I returned to the castle and the two fireplaces that had kept my room warm for the remainder of last winter, I would laugh at the fact I'd missed that drafty room where the royal guard had stood that night. It seemed like so long ago.

"And hay, it appears." Erstad pointed toward town, toward a stack in the distance. "Odd it's sitting out right now."

Odd indeed. Even the poorest farmers in Elternow had shared barns for wintering their crops. Feeding the livestock was just that important where I'd grown up. And for it to be left in the fields . . .

Soldiers burned them. Thomas's voice echoed in my mind, as clearly as it had when we'd played as children, when Laurent had condemned us both to death. *As they were stacked.*

Ice slunk down my spine. Soldiers, like the man who rode with me now? Like the four others trailing behind us? Had I allowed myself to be escorted by criminals?

Silly.

I hadn't been afraid of Captain Erstad back at Lochfeld, and Laurent had trusted him enough to leave him in charge of the castle's security—and mine. But Thomas's claim was so hard to dismiss, though I'd tried as we'd ridden through the fields west of the Arsele, but he'd slammed me down. It was arson, and the Meirdrean Army was responsible, he'd insisted. Wouldn't hear anything else about it.

But now . . . now Thomas had proven himself a traitor by selling Laurent and Meirdre out to Vassian. By using me, heedless of the fact it had almost cost me my life in the Lochfeld's dungeon. By murdering Willem in Lochfeld itself. He wasn't just a rebel anymore, for I could understand that kind of motivation. I didn't agree with it, now that I knew why Laurent's coffers were in the shape they were in, but I could understand it.

But murder? And the things he'd done to me?

Maybe Thomas was wrong about the destruction of the haystacks, too. Erstad had commented on them, after all. He wouldn't have called attention to them if the army had been responsible.

I sighed and tightened my grip on Skylark's reins.

"It's just mold," I replied. "Life is hard in Elternow."

Candlelight flickered in that cracked window as I pulled Skylark to a stop outside Mama and Papa's house. Late it might be, but surely she was still working on her mending. It wouldn't be Papa, since I could see two figures moving around inside the open barn, the hired boy that Laurent's money allowed for, along with Papa himself. Most of me wondered why he was working at all—his fingers were much too twisted with gout to handle that kind of labor, but that was Papa. *Roland is help*, his last letter had said. *Not someone to do everything for me.*

The door opened as I tossed the reins over Skylark's back and let one of the soldiers lead her toward the barn. Mama stuck her head outside, and I flew to her, burying my head on her shoulder.

"Riette, what in the heavens are you doing here?"

She patted my head, and through my emotion, I realized she was concerned. How had I not appreciated how my arrival would look to her?

"Just visiting. I missed you, and—" I pried myself away and forced a weary smile. Laurent hadn't specifically said not to talk about it, and although I was sure rumors of the army headed south had made it to Elternow, somehow speaking of war now seemed wrong. "It was the right time."

"But on a horse! Riette!"

"There's a carriage trailing us." I waved behind me, though I doubted she could see it in the dark. "I wanted to ride—and when you meet Skylark, you'll understand why."

"Well—" Her hands fluttered in front of her. "Come in, then. There's not much to eat, not prepared at least, but perhaps I can find something."

Before I could protest that we'd brought our own food, she darted inside, her mumblings trailing away. I followed her, wordless. Perhaps she didn't want more charity. Erstad had disappeared with his own horse, but I thought I heard his voice somewhere out toward the barn. For a moment, I thought about going out and rescuing Papa from that awkward introduction, but when Mama placed a hot cup of apple water in my hands, I stopped.

"This smells wonderful." I greedily inhaled the scent of my childhood. Too poor for actual tea back then, dried bits of apple in water had made an acceptable substitute—or so I'd thought before I'd known better. Still, it was comforting. "But you didn't have to waste your provisions on me."

"Nonsense." Mama settled into her chair, her eyes glinting with some sort of joke. "I'm saving the tea you sent for myself."

I burst into laughter as I sat across from her, spilling some of the water across my wrist. "I'm glad. And even gladder Papa seems healthier. That's him in the barn, isn't it?"

"It is." She nodded. "He rubs that medication into his hands every morning, and—Riette, you wouldn't believe the change in him. It's an absolute miracle. And if you hadn't—"

"I was happy to do it," I whispered. I hadn't been that night, but what other option had I had? Leave them to poverty when I'd had a chance to save them?

Mama leaned forward. "But are you happy now?"

I raised the cup to my lips, wished it was Laurent's lips instead, then lowered it.

"I was. But now he's gone, and I—" *Stupid tears.* "Some—some things have happened. I was happy. And now I'm not."

"We heard of the army headed toward the Vassian border," Mama replied. "He was leading them?"

I nodded, miserably.

"And you love him?"

Again, I nodded. It felt like I was confessing to a crime.

"Well—" Her expression grew comforting. "I suppose I see why you're here now. How long do you intend to stay?"

I clutched at the apple water. The map hadn't called to me like it had when I'd been visiting Laurent's mother in Iraela, but that didn't mean it was completely quiet. Did it? Or was that how Silke reined in its power? Did she simply rush home when it bid her to? That seemed too simple.

"Not long," I replied. "Likely just long enough to recover from the trip. While the king is away, Lochfeld is my responsibility, and . . ."

"I understand." Her smile grew tight, as if she'd realized my position, windfall as it was to her and Papa, had put me in danger. "Then we'll enjoy every minute we have together, won't we?"

I nodded as the door swung open again.

"Nice horse you have," Papa's voice boomed. He shoved his hands in his pockets before I could confirm what Mama had said about his fingers.

He hadn't sounded that strong in years, and I sprang from my chair to embrace him. He smelled like horse and sweat, but then again, so did I.

"She's lovely, Papa." He'd never been given much to emotion, so horse talk it was. "And she's taught me brilliantly."

"Nice horses the soldiers have, too."

I sighed and backed away.

"Yes—well. I'm sure you've heard about the attack on Lochfeld. What's left of the royal guard must stay with the king. He spared a few soldiers to protect Lochfeld."

Wherever he is.

"And its queen?"

"Well, yes. Me, too."

Papa made an ambiguous sound in his throat.

"At least they brought their own hay," he replied. "Since they destroyed the rest, we're a little scarce on feed."

Not this again. But Papa, at least, was more trustworthy than Thomas. Maybe I could get an answer out of him.

"How did they do that?"

"It molded."

"Not burned?"

He laughed, though it didn't sound humorous. "The stacks are still standing, aren't they? If you burn them, they'd be nothing more than a flat pile of burned grass on the ground. Transfer mold spores from somewhere else, though, and add some water —you've just destroyed any chance a farmer has at feeding his livestock in the winter."

"But—" I slammed my mouth closed. Thomas had lied, and I felt like an idiot for believing him.

"Ah, it doesn't matter." Papa waved a hand toward the fields. "If they try anything again, we'll know just who did it. And they won't get away with it this time."

CHAPTER THIRTY-THREE

Mornings in Elternow were always cool in the spring, and as I dressed myself for the first time in months, I couldn't keep the haystacks out of my mind. All night I'd tossed and turned in my old bed, lumpy and creaky, wondering what motivation Thomas had for lying to me. Why had I fallen for it?

At heart, I was a peasant girl, after all, though one who'd never seen a haystack torched, naturally. I grumbled at that as I pulled an untailored muslin gown over my head. How could I have been such a . . . girl? But to my relief, nothing more was said of the haystacks and soldiers when I stepped into the main room, and Mama simply smiled and handed me a cup of tea.

"From Brannitz," she said. "Can you believe it? They buy the tea from a plantation somewhere across the sea, then dry and make it in Meirdre. I never thought such a thing was possible."

It was something that was part of my life now, but I smiled as I took it. "You're sharing now, Mama—but you truly don't need to."

She pointed toward the cellar underneath the cottage. "They brought food. Unloaded it after you went to sleep. You must have been exhausted, because you slept through all the commotion."

I hadn't even realized I'd slept more than five minutes at a time last night, much less through soldiers tromping through the house. I gulped down some of the tea, glanced down the ladder into the shadows of the cellar, then hesitated.

"Papa is outside?"

"Feeding the cows. Roland wasn't feeling so well this morning. His sister sent word." Mama wiped her hands on her skirts. "I was just about to start breakfast for you and your escorts, but it appears they have their own food and no problems cooking it themselves. So—what would you like?"

"An apple?" I asked. Truthfully, I wasn't very hungry, and I wanted to explore, like I hadn't done much of at all since Laurent had departed. And gallivanting around Elternow on a warm spring day had a definite appeal.

"Only dried ones right now."

Mama pointed at the basket, and I grabbed a handful of slices, my mouth watering. Dried and a season old or not, I could hardly wait to shove them in my mouth. With a wave, I headed out toward the barn, chomping on my breakfast, thankful, for the first time, that Laurent couldn't see me. I was still laughing at the way he would have looked at the way I was eating when Papa came out of the barn, hefting a bag of grain.

"Let me get that," I said, shoving the slices in my pocket and darting toward him. "You should have woken me up to help."

"Riette." His brows rose as he dropped the bag on the ground and eyed the brown damask I wore. "The king's wife, helping with livestock? What would people think?"

"Papa, I didn't come here to be waited on."

My hurt must have been obvious, for he sighed.

"I know you didn't. And yet—we're fine. Roland has been a great help to us, and I could have waited for his return, yes, but—"

"But you needed something to do."

"If you'd perhaps sent word—"

"Security." My response was clipped. "Even a letter might have been . . . unwise."

Papa exhaled again. "I understand."

"The bag?"

"Is too heavy for you to lift." He hefted it over his shoulder once more and tromped to the pen behind me. "Though I appreciate the offer."

I followed, my skirts trailing along in the dust. The pen was new since my departure, and when I looked inside, dark eyes over a pink snout stared back at me.

"You have a hog!" I said as the creature ambled toward me.

Papa dumped the feed to the ground once more and placed his hands on his hips. "She'll fill the cellar nicely next winter, won't she?"

"Indeed." I reached down and ran my fingers along the top of her head. "Or produce babies to fill the cellar later."

"Riette! For heaven's sake."

"You sound like Mama." I rolled my eyes and sidestepped a roaming chicken. "It's not as though I've never helped you deliver a calf."

"Well, that is accurate enough. But you're a different person now, and the king wouldn't approve of such talk." He stood there, regarding me. "Now off with you. I have work to do, and I assume you're not here to do farm chores."

I sighed. There was no arguing with Papa sometimes.

"Are the apple trees blooming yet?" I asked.

"In the Caballero's orchard." Papa pointed, then laughed. "But don't let the owners see you—unless you feel like playing their idea of a princess."

Hoary petals drifted through the air like silk as I strolled through the orchard edging the Caballero farm, smiling at Papa's warning. I'd wondered what the rest of Elternow thought of me since I'd left to marry Laurent, and now I knew—if only *they* knew how little I'd changed. Especially with the way I was eyeing the tree at the perimeter of the orchard, an enormous thing with gnarly, twisted branches that reached toward the sky.

The tree I'd used to sit in and watch for the king's men coming up the trail through the nearby thicket.

The bark was rough under my hand as I ran my palm down it, acutely aware of how the king's wife shouldn't be climbing trees. But I was also acutely aware that the orchard was empty. Even Captain Erstad was back at the barn doing whatever it was soldiers did in the mornings, which meant I was freer than I'd been in months.

With one last glance around, I placed my foot on the trunk and hoisted myself into the bottom cleft. The tree didn't so much as wobble under my weight, and I lifted my skirts around my knees to better climb to my former spot. Laurent would have a stroke if he could see me now.

But as Father Gerritt had once told him, I needed contact with the land for my gift to work, and he didn't just mean the ground itself. So I climbed upward, shaking apple blossoms from my hair and feeling for just the right handholds, until I reached that spot I'd loved so much. The ground was far below me, but the tree was sturdy enough that I had no fear of falling. Pale green leaves that were finally replacing the flowers concealed my presence, and I leaned against the trunk, my eyes closed. Was there anything like the scent of an apple orchard in spring?

The sound of hooves rustled me from the daze I was slipping into, and I sat forward, gripping with one hand the branch that held me. It was a natural movement, for though I could see through the trees on the other side of the low fence, the angle of the sunlight meant no one on the dappled path could see me. That would change this afternoon, but for now, I could be nosy.

Though there was really no need. Thomas and his men were

long gone, escaped deep into Vassian, and the Meirdrean army was now, as far as I was concerned, on my side. Perhaps I only wanted to see if there was any of that girl I used to be left. I was up in a tree, yes, but Laurent should have expected that much of me.

The horses drew closer in the dense thicket. It wasn't the principal route to anywhere, but it was one of the few stands of dense trees here in the moors, and that was why Thomas's resistance group had always used it to bypass the village. Merchants certainly didn't come through here—the trail was too narrow for all but the narrowest of carts, especially when they could take the main road through the grasslands. We occasionally saw local farmers, yes, but this time of year, few had reason to be on the edge of the Caballero's farm.

I bit my lip. Yes, I'd walked by a few newly planted saplings on my way here, and Elternow was still poor enough that thievery was an ever-present problem. Even of young trees.

The tree cooperated with its silence as I climbed one branch higher, anxious at the idea of a bandit seeing me up here. For the first time, I regretted not telling Captain Erstad where I'd disappeared to. I tucked my knees under myself and leaned back, easing myself against the branch and in line with a hole in the leaves and blossoms. From this position, I could see the bare dirt of the trail, though the horses were far enough away that I still couldn't see them—or their riders.

But I could hear them.

And they were trotting.

A spark of dread ignited in me, though I couldn't understand why. Even Skylark could trot if forced, through Meirdrean horses preferred the gaited amble of their ancestors, brought across the Galvan Ocean by Laurent's ancestors long ago. It was so ingrained in my mind as the proper and *natural* manner of a horse that I knew nothing else.

Don't let her trot, had been Papa's first instructions when I'd sat on his mare for the first time, my short legs dangling against her sides. *That's something only* foreign *horses do.*

Still, *foreign* could mean anything. Iraela was friendly enough —besides to the king himself—and it wasn't uncommon to see their traders traveling by. I was only afraid of shadows.

A whistle cut through the orchard, and the hooves stopped. My palms grew damp, pressed against the branches. Had they seen me? Brown though it was, my dress would be noticeable from a distance, but the limbs had to be breaking up the outline of my figure. The fence that marked the edge of the Caballero's property sat in the middle of a belt of grass, filled with wildflowers, between the end of the orchard and the beginning of the thicket, but was it enough distance to hide me?

One of the horses whinnied, and leather slapped against leather. I sat there, my breath ragged. Someone called the group to a halt, and they dismounted and tossed the reins over their saddles. I glanced toward the Caballero's cottage, but at this distance it was a scarcely noticeable speck in the distance. No help would come from that direction.

Boots thudded in the dirt, louder by the second, and I risked a glance through the apple tree. The man who appeared from between the trees was slight, almost willowy. His shoulder-length hair, bleached by the sun, was loose and disheveled.

I recognized him at once.

Thomas.

CHAPTER THIRTY-FOUR

I HELD MY BREATH AS THOMAS STEPPED INTO THE OPEN, HIS PALM flat on the pommel of his sword. He glanced upward, and I went as still as a deer cornered by a hunter, frozen in the complete certainty of my impending death. How had I been so thoughtless as to come here alone? It seemed the dozenth time that very reprimand had flitted into my mind since I'd climbed up here, and I bit my cheek. Berating myself would do no good with him this close. I needed to think before he found me, not waste time on pointless admonishments.

But no. As I silently berated myself, Thomas turned back to the thicket and the trail, and then I realized—

He was *remembering*.

He knew this tree, recognized it just as easily as I had. And he —he had cared enough to stop and look at it once more? I hated seeing that humanity in him.

Or was he plotting his revenge?

With a whistle, the horses moved once more, and I sank against my branch, trembling like the very leaves above me. I needed to run back to Mama and Papa's house, needed to alert Captain Erstad about what I'd seen, but my body wouldn't let me move, much less climb down. I sat there for a moment, my breath heavy. By the time the sound of hooves was replaced by the lone wind in the orchard, my heart had returned to normal, and I slid down the tree.

My feet hit the ground, soft underneath me, but before I could walk back toward the cottage, an unyielding hand seized my forearm. My heart thumped widely, whipping away the calm I'd found when I'd climbed down. I opened my mouth to scream, and a hand slammed over my lips.

"They're returning. Back up the tree and do not come down."

Papa's voice was soft in my ear. Soft but firm, with no room for argument. I nodded, then put a hand on the trunk. It seemed to waver in front of me, and I closed my eyes.

"Now!" he whispered, giving me a shove.

I clambered upward as the whinny of a horse filled my ears. They'd approached silently this time, and fool that I was, I hadn't been paying any attention. I glanced down. Papa bustled around the base of a tree farther down the row, yanking out weeds and tossing them into a pile. He looked so comfortable at work that I wondered if he'd been working at the Caballero's for a while now.

"Master Kaleveld!"

Thomas's voice echoed through the orchard, and Papa straightened.

"Hello, Thomas." His greeting was oddly normal. "It's been a long while."

I didn't want to move, certain Thomas would notice me if I did, but I needed a better view. Carefully, I shifted against the branch, sending a shower of petals to the ground. Papa and Thomas were only a few paces apart, and though Thomas's hand was no longer on his sword, he'd lost my trust a long time ago.

"Almost a year, I should think. What're you doing in the Caballero orchard?" He glanced at Papa's hands, the now-nimble fingers no longer red with inflammation. "I'm surprised you can handle manual labor."

Papa grunted and turned away, heaving an empty apple crate to the other side of the tree. "Found some medicine that worked."

"Ah." Thomas sauntered toward him, his back to me now. "Miracle, that. In Elternow, of all places."

"Traders come through," Papa replied. "Even through Elternow."

"Then you're doing better. I'm happy to hear it."

The flat edge of his sword struck Papa's stomach. I hadn't even seen his hand move. Had I blinked? Was it the sudden tears that had hid his movement? Clinging to the branch, I choked down a scream. Letting go would be so easy. Falling to the ground and punching his face would be delightful—but it didn't look like he was bluffing with that sword.

"You don't have to rob me, Thomas." Papa lifted his hands to his sides. "If you need help—"

"Where is she?"

Papa's forehead creased. "Back at the cottage, of course. The spring onions are ready for harvest."

"Don't play stupid." Thomas took another step forward.

"If you're asking about Riette, she left a long time ago. You've seen her more often than we have, I hear. We get letters, some-times—not nearly as many as I'd like. That's it."

Thomas's head swiveled behind him, toward the horses and who knew how many other rebels still hidden in the thicket. Did Papa actually think he was fooling him? I didn't know. Perhaps Thomas would believe him, since the soldiers and horses were still back at the house. The only thing I was sure of was that holding my breath was making me dizzy, so I took a few slow, deep ones, praying the breeze hid the sound.

When I looked down again, two other men had joined Thomas. Both too solidly built for anyone in Elternow, both with swords far beyond what I'd ever seen outside of Lochfeld. They hadn't drawn them yet, but when Thomas murmured under his breath and they darted back toward the horses, my stomach grew even tighter. Instructions, certainly, but for what? I twisted toward the thicket, trying to count how many had just ridden off again.

A grunt echoed through my tree. Thomas cleared the fence in one jump and disappeared into the thicket. I couldn't see his horse, but dirt flew into the air as it galloped down the road after its companions. Once it settled on the ground, I decided they were far enough down the road that I could descend, and I scrambled down the trunk, shaking.

"Riette?"

Papa sounded weak, shocked, laying on his side under the apple tree where he'd been pretending to work. For a moment I thought Thomas had shoved him, or that he'd fallen, but as I knelt to help him sit up, a red stain appeared on his shirt.

My stomach lurched.

"Lay back," I said, ripping open his shirt. The wound didn't look deep, but I couldn't go digging around in it, not after climbing a tree. "I'll get help."

I had no idea how. Mama and the safety of the cottage were all the way on the other side of the farm. Skylark wasn't here. And there was so much blood . . .

"I—I can walk."

He tried to sit, and I gently pushed him back down, then stood.

"No. I'll get a horse."

Without looking back, I darted through the orchard, stumbling over the odd rock and fallen branch. A band of smoke drifted through, lifting the falling petals into the air, and I wrinkled my nose. If the Caballeros were burning something, though I couldn't imagine what they'd be burning on a spring morning, they'd be closer than Mama.

"Master Caballero?" I yelled. "Is that you?"

Fresh earth joined the scent of smoke and apple blossoms. I ducked behind a tree as a horse—no, two horses—appeared at the end of the orchard. If Thomas and his men had circled around to trap us—there would be no way out for Papa or me.

I swallowed, hard. I'd made noise. I'd told them exactly where to find me.

The hooves grew louder in the uneven dirt. I couldn't stay here, pressed against this tree, but I couldn't move forward, either. The smoke grew thicker, not a band now, but a haze that filled the orchard.

And then, too close, the whinny of a horse.

Skylark.

I dashed toward her and grabbed her reins, too surprised to care who might be on the second. But it was Captain Erstad who stared down at me, his own sword drawn.

"Your parents' house is on fire," he said, half out of breath. "And no one could find you."

"Mama?"

"Safe, for now." His horse did an odd side-step. "But the house isn't."

"Thomas Wennink did it. Or his men." I looked down the row of trees and coughed. "And Papa—you have to help him!"

Erstad disappeared toward fresher air without asking questions, and I led Skylark toward him and Papa, unable to move enough to ride her. Papa had somehow managed to lean himself against a tree, though his hands were covered in blood, and I held back as the captain gave him a brief examination.

"How is he?" I asked, gripping Skylark's reins. "Will he—"

"Could be worse." Erstad hefted him up and onto the back of his own horse. "We'll get him to . . ." He trailed off, likely realizing if there *was* a doctor in Elternow, he certainly wouldn't be visiting Mama and Papa's house any longer.

"There's an inn." I tried to mount Skylark and succeeded that time. Obliging as she was, she didn't react to my less-than-graceful motion. "Small, but they won't be looking for us there—at least for a while. And it's not far if we take the forest path."

Erstad shook his head and pointed back through the orchard where the thick smoke was settling to the ground.

"They might be waiting for us in the woods. We'll take the long way."

I wanted to argue that Papa wouldn't last that long, but Erstad was right. So I clicked my tongue at Skylark, and we set off as the smoke grew thicker around us.

CHAPTER THIRTY-FIVE

THE INN AT ELTERNOW WAS NOTHING LIKE THE LUXURIOUS INNS Juliana and I had stayed at on our way to Iraela not so long ago. Only one fireplace illuminated the roughspun linens on the narrow bed in our room, so after I heated some water, I settled in a corner and watched the midwife work. A doctor, as Erstad had likely guessed, was as common in Elternow as gold coins. But it seemed her services might be enough, for Papa had been conscious enough to order Mama downstairs, saying her pacing was making everything worse.

I put my head in my hands and closed my eyes. I smelled like a smoldering grass fire—we all smelled the same—but bathing was the last thing on my mind. Even though the wound had turned out to be superficial, a warning slash instead of a fatal stab, infection was always a worry. The scent of balsam from the midwife's poultice overtook the smoke, and I shifted.

"He'll be fine, though in pain for a while." The midwife stood, wiping bloody hands on her white over-apron. "No farm work. And no rebuilding."

Papa opened his mouth, and I hurried to his side before he could argue.

"We'll figure out what to do about the house," I said, my hand hovering over the bandage on his stomach. Shirtless, his injury looked far worse than the midwife claimed. "If nothing else, you can come to Lochfeld."

I hadn't visited the cottage since the fire, but Erstad had seen it with his own eyes. *A smoky pile of wood and thatch,* he'd said. Even the barn was gone, though the soldiers had released the horses before dashing after the arsonist—who'd escaped once they'd returned in an attempt to douse the fire. No one had been injured, not even Papa's prized sow, but the message Thomas's men had left was clear.

We will destroy anything King Laurent has paid for.

"I won't." Papa's eyes steeled. "I won't go there."

"You'll be safer."

"Safe," he scoffed, wincing. "Thomas has done what he wanted in Elternow. He'll head for Lochfeld next."

I knew he was right, but that didn't make leaving any easier. I sank to the bed next to him and grabbed his hand.

"You know I have to return. And I—" A tear landed on his hand, and I brushed it away. "I've missed you. I need to know you're safe."

"We will be." Papa winced as he shifted. "I swear to you. If that means leaving Elternow, we will find somewhere. Your mother has relatives outside of Harnow who might be willing."

Erstad cleared his throat before I could object to a wagon ride all the way to Harnow. "If that's the case," he said, "we must ride for Lochfeld immediately, Your Grace. Master Kaleveld is correct —once you're gone, Wennink will have no reason to return to Elternow."

"And once we return?" I asked, gripping Papa's hand like I'd never let it go. "Won't he be there?"

"He broke through the castle's defenses once. That will not happen again." Only a hint of disdain dripped from his voice. "We are better prepared this time, with much greater reinforcements.

But Wennink and his men were headed south as we pursued them, likely back to Vassian. Even if they turn around, they won't make it to Lochfeld before we do—which is why we must leave at once."

"Can I see Mama first?" There was no way I could leave without saying goodbye, not after she'd lost her home and almost Papa.

"I'm sorry, Your Grace, but we must ride. Your mare is outside and waiting."

I sighed as I nodded and stood. Duty was . . . it was heartbreaking, sometimes. Since I'd married Laurent, duty had seemed dull, sometimes frightening, but I'd never expected it to involve this kind of emotion. Even watching the map had involved dancing, and therefore a tiny of joy.

But this—somehow it was worse than when I'd walked out of their house that winter's night. I'd hope then that I would see them again. Hadn't been certain, though I'd hoped. But now?

It didn't matter. There was only one thing left to do. And so before I could cling to him like a child and refuse to leave, I kissed Papa's cheek and walked out.

The acrid smell of smoke hung about me for the first few hours. After that, I could only smell my own sweat. Erstad had wanted to push the horses at first, to put as much distance between us and Elternow as possible, and by the time we stopped at a pond for rest and water, I could scarcely stand, either.

Knowing I would waste too much time floating aimlessly in the water if I went all the way in, I splashed a bit on my face. On the other side of the pond, the soldiers were filling water bags— probably a more efficient use of our time, but I couldn't help my vanity. As my legs stiffened, I eased myself to the ground and looked up at the sky, crisscrossed with feathery clouds. It was hardly a ladylike position, but the reeds block me from the soldiers' view, and I needed the break.

A piece of hay hit my nose, carried on the breeze from some farm or another, and I twisted backward, trying to find the source. On the other side of a narrow creek, one that could scarcely be called a ditch, lay a fallow field. Odd for spring in an area of the kingdom where empty fields meant empty bellies. Risky, yes, but we did what we had to in Meirdre.

I pushed myself up and meandered toward the open area, crossing a creek on a few large stones. When I'd brushed off Erstad's questions about the haystacks earlier, I hadn't actually let it go—but the fire and Thomas's attack on Papa had distracted me too much to worry about it until now.

There were no stacks in this field, however, and feeling fool-ish, I turned back toward the pond and prepared myself for another few hours of pretending I was comfortable on Skylark's back. Erstad waved at me from across the pond, and I picked up my damp skirts so I could hurry back.

It was then I noticed the hay. Not piled up, no, but enough was scattered on the ground that I knelt down and examined it. Black streaks ran along the length, confirming the suspicion of mold. I sniffed at it. It didn't smell like smoke, but then again, I could hardly tell if anything did, grimy as I was. Erstad waved at me again, so I grabbed a handful and made my way back.

"Does this look burned to you?" I asked, brandishing the hay in front of him.

"I—" His nose wrinkled. "No, Your Grace. Should it?"

I scanned his face, but there was no deception there—only confusion. But it wasn't as though every soldier in Meirdre would be party to such a thing, would it? Maybe Erstad truly didn't know. It didn't exonerate the army. It didn't make Thomas's accusation false.

"Yes." My hands shook, and I shoved the hay closer to his face. Perhaps catching him off guard would force him to confess.

"You've been burning hay stores all over the kingdom, haven't you?"

"Your Grace—" Erstad grabbed the straw from my hands. "This is stem rot."

"Stem rot?"

"A fungus, specific to alfalfa and ryegrass. It'll absolutely destroy crops if it becomes established, haystacks especially. We've fought to keep it out of Meirdre for centuries. Thankfully, it's too heavy to be carried on air currents on like regular mold."

"Keep it out?" The spring afternoon chilled. "Where's it from originally?"

His eyes narrowed. "Vassian, of course."

CHAPTER THIRTY-SIX

So, it was Thomas—or, at least someone he knew—who'd seeded the haystacks with stem rot then lied about it, blaming his own crime on the soldiers. Based on his hostile reaction to my question so long ago, I should have known, and yet something had kept me from fully believing my own eyes. Now though . . . I believed. I believed every terrible thing I'd once suspected about him.

Well trained as she was, Skylark tossed her head in displeasure as I stared off into the distant sunset, Laurent's face at the front of my mind. How had he ever forgiven me for mistrusting him so deeply? I'd accused him of the most heinous things, if only to myself, had run off with a man who'd wanted to kill him, and yet—he'd shown me mercy, though I'd thought otherwise at the time. And Lochfeld had become my home.

We had another day of riding in the morning, so I couldn't see the castle up ahead, but it tugged at me from the northeast, enough that I could tell the road would soon curve to the right. I closed my eyes and let Skylark continue on one of her infrequent trots. She knew where she was going, just like I did. And oh, how I wanted to be there again, too.

A rush of wind blew across my face, and my eyes flew open. I hadn't been homesick for Lochfeld since we'd left. I missed Laurent, yes, and it was painful much of the time, but . . . but Lochfeld?

My breath grew short.

It wasn't the same feeling I'd sensed at the castle in Iraela. Not exactly, at least. Still, I was quite sure it was the map—a gnawing hunger, an emptiness that even Laurent's absence couldn't match.

It was calling to me.

I wanted to scream at it, to tell it that I wasn't at Lochfeld, and it just needed to *hold on for another day*. I bit my lip instead, hiding my panic as Erstad let his horse drop back beside me.

"Last chance to stop for the night while the ground is still comfortable," he said, retying dark curls at the base of his neck. "If you're willing."

My eyes unfocused as I looked up the road. I wasn't willing. I wanted nothing more than to continue on and reach the map as soon as possible, but none of the horses were capable of that. And Erstad was correct—soon the ground would grow rocky as we approached the cliffs which protected Lochfeld, and that would mean no sleep for me and less grazing for the horses.

The pull grew weaker, and I blinked. Was the map telling me it was all right to stop?

"Yes," I replied. "Here seems sufficient."

He nodded and rode off, giving orders to his men. I eased Skylark off the trail and slumped in my saddle. How was I supposed to sleep tonight? Still, as the carriage appeared behind me and I grudgingly climbed inside, I couldn't deny that my exhaustion was warring with the map's pull. I lay back on the seats, fully clothed, and stared at the ceiling.

Silke had traveled. She *had*. Her journals attested to it, over and over. But she'd never said *how* she managed to explore Meirdre and watch the map at the same time. Was it possible it was so obvious that she never thought to write it down? Or was it that secret?

I yawned and rolled to my side. The flickers of a fire reflected in the carriage, and the encroaching darkness didn't help my mood. How I wanted to be outside, at the edge of the moors I loved so much. But that would not do for the king's wife, even if —even if she needed the land.

Cautiously, I slid to the other side of the carriage and unlatched the door. A soldier paced somewhere in the distance, and I waited until he wandered off to relieve himself before sliding the door open and creeping out to the back of the carriage.

The pull here was even stronger. Not a surprise, since my feet were sinking into the loose soil that Skylark had no difficulty with. Could that be the key? Father Gerritt had said that I needed contact with the land for the map to speak to me, and out here in the moors, with the moonlight spilling across the carriage, I was closer than ever. Short of having dug through the frozen dirt for rotten potatoes as a child, that was.

Or had Silke simple not cared what happened to Meirdre? Maybe she'd convinced her husband she could read the map while away from Lochfeld, and he'd simply been fool enough to believe her. She hadn't seemed too enamored with her king, and maybe that disinterest extended to Meirdre itself. Maybe there'd been more threats during his reign than she'd written about, and she'd ignored most of them.

I leaned against the carriage, my jaw tight. Perhaps Silke had been wrong. I'd meant it when I'd told Laurent that if staying at Lochfeld forever was what I needed to do, then I would. Yet I'd already broken that vow, was stranded over six hours away from the castle and that vexing map, which was calling for me once more. Yes, it had glowed blue and gold before, showing the next disaster was a few months away, but what if I'd missed something prior to that? I'd assumed seeing the prediction meant things would be safe for a while, but I'd missed something when I was in Iraela, after all. When would *that* disaster happen? Before or after the Vassian invasion?

Silly girl. You have no idea.

The shouts around the campfire grew louder, spurred on, I assumed, by liquor. I wandered away from the carriage as they did, easing my muscles into a painless stroll. The moon bestowed a shimmering path as I drew farther and farther away, until the crackle of the fire and gleeful roars were drowned out by the wind of the moor. Here, at the edge of the grasslands, the land had become rocky, and soon I found myself scrambling over the top of a small rise in the moonlight, the pull of the map too strong to resist. Stars flickered above me, thrown there at the beginning of time, innumerable and eternal. And—and something brighter ahead of me?

Another campfire.

I sank to the ground, too conscious that the moon's radiance illuminated everything between here and Lochfeld itself. But that was fine—it also meant I could see the horses down below, grazing while their riders hurried about. Merchants? Tradesmen? I couldn't tell from up here, and their voices were hidden in the soft whispers of the night breeze.

For almost an hour I sat there, waiting for Erstad to realize I was missing, waiting for the travelers down below to go to sleep. Perhaps something told me they wouldn't, even as I shivered in the cooling air. The horses, far from as exhausted as I suspected Skylark was, became increasingly agitated, pawing and circling around, until the figures below saddled them.

I held my breath. Who traveled the moors at night, when bandits roamed and the slightest misstep could be fatal?

Even as I asked myself the question, I knew the answer.

Scrambling back down the hill, I considered my options. Waiting was not among them. Neither was telling Captain Erstad, for a reason I couldn't articulate. Probably because he would doubt me, question me, and by the time he *believed* me, Thomas and his men would be long gone toward Lochfeld. I couldn't let that happen.

I skulked back toward the carriage in the moonlight. Skylark had rested for quite a while now—a few hours, if memory served. She couldn't run all night, especially across the rocky terrain, but she could get me closer than we'd be if we slept all night and then rode. That would have to be enough.

Skylark nuzzled my hand as I whispered in her ear. Her ears pricked, attracting the attention of the horse next to her, but I gave him a pat on the haunch, and he quieted down. Skylark had no such anxiety as I slid into her back and circled her around the group, debating how I could disappear without being seen—or pursued. The soldiers would give chase if one of their horses vanished down the road, wouldn't they?

"Your Grace!"

I twisted around at Erstad's voice and brought Skylark's impatient saunter to a stop, the lie coming easily to my tongue. "Captain. There's a pond just up the road. Not more than a five-minute ride. I need—I need some time alone. To bathe. Change into something fresh."

He caught Skylark's reins and frowned at me. "Your Grace, it's late."

"Dark," I replied. "Not late. Not especially. And I can't sleep, filthy like this. All I can smell is smoke in that carriage."

He stared up at me, as if he suspected a trap, then his shoulders relaxed. "If you're not back in half an hour, I'm sending someone for you."

I nodded and forced my most demure smile. Skylark reacted at once to a click of my tongue, eager for an evening walk, and we set off down the road, alone and unpursued. The moon rose as we did, and for what might be the last time in a while, I let myself believe I was home in Elternow, going for an evening stroll, secure in the knowledge that a bed awaited me in the morning.

It wasn't until I was twenty minutes away that I realized how fortunate it was that he hadn't realized I had nothing clean to change into.

CHAPTER 37

I'd drifted off to sleep several times on Skylark's back, but she was steady enough—or perhaps used enough to my poor riding—that it hadn't seemed to affect her at all. For when Lochfeld came into view atop the cliffs and I yawned once more, she continued as though nothing untoward had happened the night before.

And perhaps for her, it hadn't. She hadn't seen the men down below, preparing for an evening ride, and we hadn't encountered them on the road, either—which meant they'd stayed far away from any potential traffic. Erstad's men hadn't found us either, likely too consumed with finding the non-existent pond to even begin to close in on me.

Skylar and I pulled off the road and into a stand of trees for two horses and a carriage, but they'd turned out to be brazen merchants, likely headed to Haszen, taking advantage of the moonlight to further their journey and avoid overnighting in the Arsele Forest. We were mostly too enlightened in Meirdre to believe in such things as ghouls, but there was enough of a question that merchants and everyone else avoided it at all costs.

The morning sun grew hot on the right side of my face as Skylark ambled on, and I couldn't help but be grateful that Laurent wouldn't see the freckles that would no doubt appear shortly. In love with him, yes, I was that, but I hadn't forgotten, and probably wouldn't ever, how particular he could be. And the king's wife couldn't be seen with *freckles*.

I laughed out loud at the idea of Laurent's reaction to freckles just as the sound of hooves echoed somewhere in front of me.

With a gentle tug of the reins, I backed Skylark into the woods once more and held my breath. We were hardly hidden here, but I was counting on the branch in front of my face and the fact that this interloper, like all the rest, was simply traveling Meirdre like anyone would do.

But as I squinted into the sun, the figure turned familiar.

"Lieutenant Vahl!" I shouted.

He brought his horse to a halt as I rode out of the woods, shame-faced at having arrived without my entourage and in a dress that probably smelled like I'd set myself on fire. But somehow, he didn't look startled to see me—not a surprise, I supposed, for a man who'd first met me when Laurent had locked me up for treason.

"Your Grace." He glanced around and conspicuously behind me. "What are you—"

"I had to get back," I replied. Now that I was close to Lochfeld and no one could stop me, I could tell him what I'd seen. "I saw— there was a group of men and horses, off the road, preparing the ride through the night. And I knew Captain Erstad would never believe me, or at least not take me seriously enough to do anything about it, so I snuck away and rode through the night to get here." He frowned, and I added, even though he wouldn't understand completely, "I had to warn Lochfeld, someone, anyone!"

"But how do you know they were headed for Lochfeld?" His brow furrowed. "They could have been anyone."

"I—"

Oh, heavens. How had I known? Why had I thought the people I'd seen could have possibly included Thomas? Out in the moors in the moonlight, it had made sense, but now, with the castle towering over us in the morning sun, I was less sure. Not certain at all, if I was being honest with myself. Hadn't I passed benign travelers on the road, after all?

"I don't know." I slumped in my saddle. From here I couldn't even see the soldiers patrolling the top of the castle, and the entire situation seemed a dream. "They seemed—threatening."

"Well . . ." His brows raised, and I felt like an idiot. "Then we shouldn't be standing here on the road, should we?"

I shook my head, and then we were off.

Lochfeld was quiet when we arrived at the stables. My muscles protesting my foolishness more than Vahl ever could, I slid off Skylark and glanced around. No stable boy arrived to take the horses, but then again, it was still early in the morning, and Vahl was obviously under the impression I wouldn't reprimand him for allowing such an oversight. I'd disappeared to Elternow, had abandoned my position without so much as a second thought, so I couldn't blame him for that. Perhaps he'd run off to visit his own family, so I gave Skylark a perfunctory cool down on my own.

Still irritated at the oversight, I climbed the stairs to my room. Vahl knew enough to alert the soldiers before I could tell the rest of the story, and I was vain enough to refuse to tell it while smelling like smoke and horse.

But Sara was also missing. I yanked off my gown and pulled on another, grumbling over my lack of a bath. My hair? I ran my fingers through it, and then a brush, and then gave up. Laurent wasn't here, anyway. Who was I trying to impress?

Even Laurent's mother seemed to be gone, though she was probably on one of her early morning rides. Elsanne was prone to those ever since she'd arrived, and most of the time I suspected she was trying to see how far she got from Lochfeld before the soldiers found her and begged her to return home. I'd always laughed when they did, for it was obvious they were more afraid of her reaction to being caught than failing to follow Laurent's orders regarding her. Eventually she would outrun them or perhaps even out-sly them, and then she'd be back in Iraela before they could do a thing about it.

And then—and then the king of Iraela would have to decide. Continue coercing Laurent into paying a never-ending dowry, or drop the blackmail and fall back into the distance, enjoying the last years of his life with the wife who now knew she was a pawn —yet somehow loved him anyway.

Not that it any of was my business. Not anymore, at least. I'd done everything I could.

Laughing over Elsanne's continual insistence that she belonged in Iraela, I made my way to the octagonal war room on knees that wouldn't stop shaking from fatigue. It was the longest ride I'd been on in a while, and had I known I'd be in so much discomfort at the end, I might have made a different decision. But it was done now, and I could deal with Erstad's fury later. Well, soon, for there was no doubt he was closing in on Lochfeld soon.

Clenching my teeth, I pushed open the heavy door. Darkness greeted me, so I lit one of the oil lamps and took a breath. No one was here, preparing for what was to come? It made sense, I supposed. I hadn't seen the soldiers up top when Vahl and I had ridden up the cliff trail, just like I hadn't seen them from the ground below, but they had to be up there somewhere. Actually doing something. Not just planning and hiding inside.

Fool.

The word had scarcely dissipated in my mind when the war room blurred around me, a haze of gold sparkles. I cursed under my breath—of course I hadn't thought to bring any water on my night ride through the moors, and unlike Skylark, I hadn't been able to take a five-second break to slurp water from a puddle. Or was it the map calling to me in some peculiar fashion?

Nonsense. It hadn't acted like this since Juliana had first set the crown on my head.

"There you are." Vahl stuck his head inside, a fuzzy shape

surrounded by that same gold effervescence. "Captain Erstad just arrived," he said, gesturing me out. "He's in the throne room waiting on your arrival, and—and he's most displeased with your disappearance last night, Your Grace."

"Oh." Through the pain in my head and my declining vision, I was a child once more, though I couldn't decide if it was my impending chastisement or my complete and utter discomfort with holding an audience in Laurent's seat of power. "Of course."

Vahl trailed behind me as I made my way down the glittering corridor, pretending I didn't care what sort of tongue-lashing I was in for. I'd made it back to Lochfeld, had warned someone of Thomas's approach, hadn't I? Erstad might think he was in charge, but he would have ignored my warning, just like Vahl had at first. I couldn't have that.

Vahl pulled open the door, and I wet my lips with my tongue, preparing to speak first, before Erstad could make a fool of himself, say something that Laurent would never allow of one of his soldiers.

Or at least, I tried.

Because wasn't Erstad standing there in front of the throne, ready to tear into me for my foolishness last night. In fact, it wasn't a soldier at all.

It was Laurent.

Kneeling.

Kneeling?

And—

And Thomas was beside him, a sword at his throat.

CHAPTER THIRTY-SEVEN

For a moment I could do nothing but stare, praying whatever magic that had overtaken me in the war room was responsible for this new vision as well. For I couldn't be seeing what I was seeing. It was a dream, a nightmare, some trick of the map that showed me the future. But even when I'd worn the crown, even when the crownkeeper gift had been bestowed upon me prematurely, I'd been in control of my senses. Confused, yes, but I hadn't suffered from delusions.

Just like I wasn't suffering from them now.

A cry arose in my throat, and Laurent looked up at the sound. The golden sparkles disappeared in an instant, and my stomach clamped down on itself as I stared at him. His right eye was purple and swollen, his wrists chained in front of him. By the look of the bruises, they'd been that way for a while, which meant —it meant something, but when the shimmering magic had fled, so had my ability to think.

Undaunted by Thomas's sword, I rushed toward Laurent and dropped to the floor in front of him. His harsh inhalations grew steady as my fingers touched his skin, but he didn't move, didn't speak, just watched with weary eyes as my hands ran across his shoulders, his chest, his back. Finding no serious injuries, I lay my forehead against his and wept, my palms against his temples.

"Move away from him, Riette."

I froze at the irritation in Thomas's voice.

"No," I replied, squeezing my eyes shut as the tip of his sword tapped against my collarbone. What else could go wrong if I refused? "I won't."

"Then you will die beside him." The sword tapped again. "A fitting end, perhaps, though I once wished for another."

Bile rose in my throat, and it wasn't from the metal there.

"If you wanted to kill us, you'd have done it already."

"Riette, stop."

Laurent's voice was soft as he reached for me. The chains were too short, so I grabbed his hands and clung to them. They were still smooth, minus a few new blisters from riding, and I ran my fingers over his knuckles, knowing and not caring how much it would infuriate Thomas. But somehow, the order made its way into my heart, and I pressed my lips closed.

"That's all it takes for you to do what you're told? A simple order from a despot?" Thomas laughed. "You really have changed."

I glanced up at him, trying to find the boy he'd once been. The one who had climbed apple trees with me before feeding the apples to the neighbor's horses and skipping home for supper. The one who'd once stood between me and a charging bull. Instead, I found nothing but a hardened expression, the deep lines in the skin of a man who'd traded gentle smiles for frowns and hate.

"So have you, Thomas." I glanced around the throne room. Besides Vahl, the duplicitous bastard, there were no other soldiers around, not that their absence comforted me. If they weren't on Vahl's side, they were no doubt dead. Thomas had enough of his own men positioned around the edges of the room to have seen to that. "And somehow, even after everything, I'm still surprised you could lower yourself to this."

"You always were naïve." The sword slid away from Laurent and me, but Thomas didn't sheath it. "What did you think would happen? That you'd marry a king and live happily at Lochfeld forever? Forsake those you grew up with it? Your family?"

Laurent's breath caught. My tears fell again, and that time, he managed to wipe just one finger across my jaw.

"You did, didn't you?" Thomas chuckled. "Well. Let me tell you how it'll actually end. King Damir wants to see him executed as a common criminal, devoid of any dignity. Just think of it, Riette. Dying far from Meirdre, his power usurped, away from any battle which might have preserved his honor in death. And you—"

I tore my gaze from Laurent's anguished stare and met Thomas's.

"You." He tapped his sword on my shoulder. "I would so dearly love to see your blood spilled besides him, but"—glee sprang into his tone—"I'm told you have a gift that might still be considerably useful."

The throne room spun about me once more, but it was a gray haze that had taken over my vision this time. My own terror flowed through me, not a belated enchantment. If I hadn't already been kneeling, I would have collapsed on the floor from the fear and anger and betrayal that seized me, for it was obvious how Thomas had figured that out. I met Laurent's gaze, and he nodded, just enough.

"They were going to—if they found you—" he began. "I had to tell them. Please—please forgive me—"

"He saved your life, Riette," Thomas interrupted, "by telling me your secret. Even as he was condemning his own."

I leaned my forehead against Laurent's once more and tried to steady my voice. What I was about to say would earn me my death, but I didn't want to live anymore. Not without him.

"So what?" I gripped his hands tighter as I spoke. "I don't see what that has to do with you, what you think my power will gain you. It protects Meirdre and her sovereign, no other kingdom, no other person."

"It certainly didn't do a satisfactory job this time." Thomas's lip curled in a sardonic smile. "But regardless, and fortunately for you, King Damir disagrees with your assessment of your inadequacy. He finds your gift . . . rather fascinating."

I swayed as he spoke, certain I would crumple to that luxurious stone floor. It was Laurent who clutched at my hands now, whispering something consolatory in my ear, though the words no longer had any meaning. Not so long ago, I'd knelt in this exact spot, that night Laurent had sentenced me to death—and as horrified as I'd been, being sentenced to life was worse. There had been a pang of regret in Laurent's expression then, even as he'd pronounced the words that would end my very being.

But Thomas displayed no such remorse.

"It only works here." I could scarcely draw a breath. "Only at Lochfeld. If you take us to Vassian, the gift won't follow."

"Is that so?" Thomas snapped his fingers, and Vahl yanked me to my feet. "Then I suppose we'll find out, won't we? Hope you enjoy the voyage."

CHAPTER THIRTY-EIGHT

I HAD NEVER HAD THE MISFORTUNE OF TRAVELING ON A SHIP before. Laurent, I was certain, had. Nonetheless, almost immediately after they shoved us in a dark hold, he'd become ill, and I'd spent the next few weeks tending to him. No matter how much I tried to cajole Thomas's men for the slightest comfort, they'd refused to anything more than give me a few buckets to relieve ourselves in and a basket of salty, dried fish. That was reassuring, in an odd way, for it meant we wouldn't be aboard this creaking hulk for long.

Not that I truly had to wonder. Too weak to give details, Laurent had been vague about how he'd ended up back at Lochfeld after heading to the Vassian border, but I knew the army of Meirdre would have spread throughout the kingdom looking for him by now. Taking us to Vassian by sea, sailing down the coast and past our borders, avoiding our army, was the safest route for Thomas.

I soaked a piece of cloth in what little condensation I could find on the wood above my head, then lay it over Laurent's head. He'd curled up in the corner of the hold a few hours ago, and although he'd refused the fish, his stomach seemed to have settled. Perhaps the waves had subsided as well, but I wouldn't let myself think of what that meant.

"I will never forgive myself," he whispered, as I leaned against him, "for not being the one to take care of you."

I forced a laugh. "I'm happy to be healthy enough to be able to do it. We needed a bit of luck."

"I wouldn't call this luck, Riette, dear."

"I suppose not." His forehead was warm under my palm, even though the rag was cool. "But I'm still glad I'm with you."

Laurent pressed his lips together. "I am not."

"I know. But—" He didn't ask for clarification of my lingering silence, and my eyes grew wet. "But I couldn't have stood it if you'd disappeared and I had no idea of what happened to you."

"I don't think you want to find out what happens to me now."

I didn't. I couldn't even bear to think of it. Shifting on the hard wood behind my back, I squeezed his hand.

"The map never warned me of this," I said. Was the magic gone? Had it abandoned me? Or was it true, like I'd said to Thomas, that it didn't work outside the borders of Meirdre? "Perhaps—"

Metal clanging above interrupted my thoughts. A shaft of light fell across my grimy dress as the trapdoor slid to the side and a man dropped a rope ladder to the floor.

"He wants to talk to you." He pointed down at me, his Vassian accent strident and authoritative. "Up."

Laurent made a noise of disapproval, but I didn't look at him as I stood. If I did, I would cling to him, and while I wanted to do that, I wanted to know what *he*—likely Thomas—wanted to talk to me about. So raising my chin, I lifted my skirts, and climbed the ladder as gracefully as I could.

The warm breeze caught my hair almost immediately, carrying with it the briny scent of the ocean. Over the edge of the deck, the faint darkness on the horizon signaled land—but then again, we wouldn't have had to sail very far east to sail down the coast unnoticed. But the recent serenity of the waves and Thomas's summons didn't lie, and I was certain we were almost to Vassian, if not within its waters already. If only my knowledge of maps went deeper than the one on the floor of the ballroom at Lochfeld.

The man motioned me through a doorway in the center of the ship, a shadowy and cool compartment, lined with windows. The wool carpet was soft under my feet, the exact color of the glassy ocean outside, and a rich silk printed with sea dragons lined the slender walls which remained in between the glass. It was a bit of royalty, right here in the middle of the sea.

But instead of the ship's captain, who doubtless occupied this space in normal times, Thomas was sprawled in a velvet chair against the far window, a grin on his face and his boots propped up on the desk in front of him. He hadn't bothered to move the charts underneath his feet, and I couldn't help but wonder if the captain knew. Thomas's shoulder-length hair was cleaner than I suspected it had been for some time, and I hated him even more for being clean when I was not.

"You don't look well, Riette," he greeted me. "It's amazing what such an extensive lack of sunlight does to a person."

"You deserved it," I spat at him. "And more. But I fought for your life anyway, and this—this is how you repaid me for that mercy? Repaid him?"

"Mercy?" His tone was sharp as he sat forward. "What would you know of mercy? What would you know of a dungeon under that castle? Of scarcely being able to sit, so restricting was your confinement? Of being so thirsty you could hardly speak?"

I wanted to retort that Thomas being hardly able to speak was likely a boon to everyone in Lochfeld's dungeon, prisoner and jailer alike, but I held my tongue.

"No," he went on, as I stood there, my jaw tight. "I don't suppose you know anything about mercy. And so I shall show him none."

My heart disappeared somewhere I couldn't feel it any longer. I knew beyond a doubt that Laurent's future was short, and likely painful, but accepting it? I couldn't accept it. Yes, his decision to not release Thomas was cruel, and from time to time I still had nightmares about the moans I'd heard in that cell when I'd left the dungeon myself, but . . . there was mercy there, too. For Thomas *was* a traitor. And he'd deserved death, just as I had, I suppose. Had worked to overthrow Meirdre, and Laurent had done what he'd done to save it. Even to save me and Thomas and ourselves, for weren't we part of Meirdre?

"I won't plead with you," I replied. I wanted to. Oh, heavens, I wanted to. Pleading my own life, no, that I would never do. But pleading for Laurent's? Yes, I would have done that if I'd thought it would make one bit of difference. "If that's what you're looking for, then you've called me here for nothing at all."

"I wouldn't go that far." He reclined once more, lifting his boots back onto the desk. "I want to talk to you."

"About what?" I ground out, clenching my hands behind my back. It occurred to me that it was the same way I used to stand before Laurent. I'd always thought it was fear, but now I realized it was anger.

Thomas folded his hands behind his head and regarded me.

"About your future."

My eyes burned, but I blinked away the tears. It occurred to me, for the first time since I'd entered, that I was still standing just inside the cabin like a fool, frozen. Like a deer who'd caught the scent of a hunter in the small stands of trees around Elternow.

"What about it?" I asked, stepping forward. "I was led to believe I didn't have one."

He cocked his head. "That depends, of course."

Of course.

If Lochfeld's magic worked for the king of Vassian, I would be a slave, doomed to spend a lonely existence in exile, away from the castle I'd grown to appreciate, far from my parents, unable to mourn the husband I never thought I'd love. Lonely, confined, captive to a foreign king who hated me and everything I cared about.

Or would it be so lonely?

My blood ran cold, even though the ocean breeze through the open door was warm, and sun spilled through the countless windows.

"Depends on what?" I asked.

Thomas's lips curved, revealing teeth stained with tobacco. I'd smelled it when I stepped inside, and it hadn't bothered me then, but that was back when I'd imagined a kindly sea captain smoking a pipe and staring at maps.

"You shouldn't worry about what's coming," he said, examining his nails. "Yes, it's true that if you turn out to be of use to Vassian, you will have to remain there for the rest of your life—but that life needn't be excruciating. I would be willing to shield you, shall we say, from some of the worst parts of your captivity. It's the least I can do as an old friend, someone who you once cared for. Though, naturally," he went on, "that depends on your ability to help His Majesty. If, as you claim, the magic is limited to Lochfeld, there's nothing even I can argue that would save you."

"I don't want anything from you."

His sharp gaze focused on me. "That's rather short-sighted, don't you think?"

I shook my head and glanced out the window. A gull floated there, hovering on the breeze. Past it, the horizon darkened, darkening my soul at the same time. Without saying goodbye to Thomas—without even acknowledging him—I turned and strode out of the captain's cabin. No one stopped me, not even the man who'd ordered me up from the hold, so I wandered to the side and looked over the edge.

The sea was shallow here, clear and vibrant with fish and

colored rock. I could see all the way to the sandy bottom, covered in the shells, the remains of sea creatures that had been smashed upon the waves. They hadn't wanted to die either, but nature was cruel. Human nature—or at least the men who had control of mine now—was even crueler.

And shallow or not, my feet would never reach the bottom. Jumping would be so easy. They might come after me, but I could fight them off—or at least use their own weight in my favor. I wouldn't have to see Laurent murdered, I wouldn't have to stand there and be tested by a man I feared and despised, I wouldn't have to toil for him for the rest of my life, betraying and annihilating my kingdom.

A shadow fell across my hands as they gripped the side, feeling the splinters where the wood had been abraded by whatever work sailors did on a ship. I shoved my palm against one of the larger splinters, flinching as it plunged into my skin. Rash, yes, but just like when I'd almost destroyed my fingers trying to undo the shackles in Lochfeld's dungeons, it wouldn't matter soon. I wouldn't live long enough to die of infection.

"Riette." Thomas spoke too close, too plaintively, though he didn't touch me. "Come back inside."

I shook my head and braced myself.

Please forgive me.

I lifted my right foot, but before I could place it against the railing, the calm sea of five minutes ago disappeared in an unnatural rush of whitecaps, sending the ship rolling sideways and propelling me backward a step. My face damp with sea spray, I ground my feet into the deck and sprang for the railing once more, but the ship rolled to the left, and I tumbled sideways, straight into Thomas's arms. He grabbed my wrist as I tried to yank it away, then jerked my arm behind me.

"Dammit, Riette, don't be stupid!"

I shrieked at him to let me go, but he clung to me as I kicked at him, fighting to reach the side once more. His grip grew tighter as he dragged me to the center of the deck, and for a moment I heard actual fear in his voice. In confusion, I stopped. The ship swayed backward, and smooth glass replaced the waves that had been there just a moment before. I let myself sag in his grip, heavy reality overcoming my desperate desire to flee.

What would jumping accomplish? Laurent's fate was certain, yes, but—but I couldn't leave him to it alone. I couldn't betray him like that. I wouldn't allow him to die alone, especially if that was what Thomas and the king of Vassian wanted. I shoved my elbow into Thomas's side, and that time he stepped away, but not before giving me a wary look.

"Take me back to him," I ordered. "Now."

"Riette, look, it doesn't have to be this way. You can—"

"I will not abandon him." My voice shook as I interrupted him, turning toward the hatch that led to the hold. "Not now."

Not ever.

CHAPTER THIRTY-NINE

There was no roof on the cart that drew us through the streets of the seaport village where we'd landed to the minor castle on the cliffs above. Soldiers in brilliant red uniforms, gaudier than anything anyone in Meirdre would ever consider wearing, rode alongside us. They were ostensibly to protect us from the residents who'd gathered to see the condemned king of Meirdre hauled to his death, but protecting our lives was all they appeared to be doing. They certainly weren't doing much to deflect the rotten vegetables and small stones being hurled at the cart.

Laurent drew me against him as another rock landed by my feet. It bounced off the shoes I'd been given, but I was lucky—Laurent's exposed skin showed bruises. Some of his former strength seemed to have appeared since we'd disembarked at the wharf, though he still looked pale and drawn. The shackles around his wrists ground against the back of my neck as he held me, but I didn't complain. King or prisoner—or both, I supposed—I felt safe with his arms around me, even in such a place.

"I love you," he murmured against my hair. "I am furious you're here, but heavens, sometimes it seems a miracle at the same time." He sucked in a breath, then pushed my face against his chest, a hand on the back of my head.

"What happened?" I mumbled. "Let me see!"

"Just a rock." I strained to free myself to check on his injuries, but he held me tight and ran his fingers through my hair. "There will be more. Don't trouble yourself with a bit of blood, my dear."

"They can't do this." I'd been saying it since we left the wharf, but I'd say it once more, like it could change something. "They can't."

"Damir has been wanting Meirdre for years. At least a decade." He took another breath, but that time I didn't fight to see what had happened. "We stand in the way of his movement toward Nantoise and beyond, always have. But I will not surrender our access to the sea by retreating to the west like my father always spoke of doing."

"He did?" I chewed on my lip. West of the Tourmel Mountains, Meirdre sprawled for days, but Laurent was right—access to the ocean was too important to concede. The castle above Windersay, where the cart was now dragging us, was enough proof of that—Vassian's own watch of the coast. And how could I forget that Elternow sat right where Damir would march on his way north? Lochfeld, as well. Had my parents made it somewhere safe? Would Thomas find them if Vassian took our kingdom? They would have to become almost invisible to hide from his retribution.

"Damir spoke of a treaty, some years ago. Give up the kingdom east of the mountains, and all threats of war cease." Laurent sighed and loosened his grip so I could see the fortress ahead of us.

It menaced above us on the hill, ever so close now, stone and cannons and a flag I'd never seen before. It took my breath away, and I had to remind myself that this wasn't even the principal castle of King Damir—just an old garrison turned royal abode a century ago, kept for its view of the sea. From there, his soldiers could see—and repel—any invasion from the east.

"But I refused to order my people to emigrate," he continued, "to leave their homes to be burned and eventually taken by the enemy. I assumed if I put up a strong enough fight at the beginning, the threats would cease."

I didn't bother mentioning his deal with Iraela that had plunged Lochfeld into near-poverty and nearly destroyed our fledgling marriage. Or that it was, technically, still in place. Maybe it had seemed a lesser evil to a king threatened with invasion on all sides.

"Is there still a chance? For a treaty, I mean?"

He was silent for a while, and I hated it, because it made the shouts of the villagers impossible to ignore.

"No," he replied at long last. "The time for talking, for agreements, for peace, is past. I have infuriated him with my refusals, clearly"—this with an intentional rattle of the shackles—"and he will not stop until he sees all of Meirdre burned to the ground, her people destroyed. I'm only the first of many, Riette."

"But what about me?" I whispered. It was childish and selfish, but he had to make everything better. He had to. I still trusted him that much, even after everything. Because if he loved me, if he wanted forgiveness, he would make everything right, wouldn't he? "What's going to happen to me? Why did you tell him about the map?"

"You would have been right there beside me, otherwise, a sword at the back of your head." Laurent shifted on the hard bench as the shouts grew quieter once more. "I had no choice. If I couldn't save Meirdre, at least I could save you. And then perhaps one day, you can fight to get her back."

"That's ridiculous." I choked out a bitter laugh. "You don't know what you're talking about."

"You dare call your sovereign's wish ridiculous?" If my statement had been harsh, his reply was castigatory. For the briefest moment I wasn't in the cart, clinging to him like a child, but in front of him in the throne room at Lochfeld, a peasant girl, a subject, his to order about as he pleased. "You will do what I ask of you, you will do it immediately, and you will not question it."

I pulled away and stared at him, heedless of the moldy apple that had fallen to the bench beside me. Protecting me had come at a cost. Blood oozed from a cut on his jawline, and a bruise was forming on his left cheekbone, but that wasn't what kept me frozen with fear.

It was his eyes.

They weren't dull with inevitability, like I suspected mine were. They were full of . . . well, not hate, not exactly. Laurent had never let such banal things as hate color his view of the world. Fury, yes. Maybe. I couldn't deny that I felt the same. But there was something more than that, even. Hard—they were simply hard. Not with fear, but with arrogance.

My heart sank. This wasn't the man I'd fallen in love with. It was the king I'd feared when I first met him, who'd laughed at me when I'd stood up to him and ordered me whipped when I'd betrayed his trust. And I knew then—this was the only way he could die with his dignity intact. And if he needed to pretend, then I would as well. I owed him that much, and he deserved that much.

I lifted my head as the horses slowed to pass under the portcullis. The bailey was filled more soldiers than I could count, and when the cart stopped, I slid away from him and gripped the edges of the bench.

"What else would you order of me, sire?" I asked.

It felt like I was questioning a stranger. Perhaps I was. Maybe I'd never really known him, and the brief emotion I'd felt toward him had been nothing more than my imagination. Wishful thinking. The pretending of a girl who knew the world was against her and tried anyway.

Laurent stared off into the distance, over the battlements and into the woods that surrounded them. Fog hung in the trees, shrouding the rear of the structure in mist. I imagined it was a good defense—on cooler days, the castle probably disappeared into the fog, invisible to invading ships until it was too late. The cannons above us certainly saw to that.

"Whatever they ask of you," he replied finally.

Even as I climbed the low, stone stairs in the keep, soldiers in front of and behind me, I wondered why they'd brought us here, instead of to Damir's main castle, far to the south in the capital of Vassian. Was this simply a stop, a place convenient to the sea where they could regroup, pack supplies, and continue the journey later? Or was it to end here? The shadows cast by the oil lamps seemed to imply a dark future, one I still couldn't accept.

Laurent was no longer with me. The soldiers had dragged him away as soon as I'd scrambled from the cart, and he hadn't fought them. I had tried to fight my escorts, but no sooner had I jerked my elbow away from the nearest soldier than Laurent's words echoed in my mind.

Whatever they ask of you.

I still wasn't entirely sure I agreed with this command, but asking me to scale a few flights of stairs seemed harmless compared to everything else that had and would happen, so I let myself be ushered into the tower, and now, toward the top. The overwhelming constraint of the structure and lack of windows made my physical situation even clearer than before. Seawater soaked the bottom of my gown, and the rest hadn't fared much better. I couldn't decide whether it was the slime I'd acquired in the ship's hold or the rotten fruit which stuck to the fabric, but I smelled worse than I ever had as a farmer's daughter. Even cow manure had a certain sweetness to it that I now lacked.

I was to face Damir like this, certainly. Maybe that was a

blessing in disguise, for what man would believe a woman who looked anything like I did would be capable of any kind of magic? But then, if I lied . . . I forfeited my life.

My breath grew short as my guards knocked on the door on a small landing. They swung it open without invitation, and sunlight streamed across my face. In the dark of the stairwell, I'd already forgotten such a thing as the sun existed, and for a moment I could only blink in the brightness, a headache sparking through my brain. It was a window across the tower room that was responsible for the sudden illumination, and I focused on the sea in the distance.

Freedom.

"You didn't have a pleasant voyage."

The voice, low and accented, shrouded in the shadows beyond a stone column, caught me by surprise. He added a few words, a little louder, in his native language, and the soldiers disappeared.

"I imagine sailing could be undertaken in a more pleasant manner, yes," I replied. I moved to smooth my skirts as the door thudded shut, then stopped. What did it matter? He could already see how dreadful I looked.

"Indeed."

Damir moved into the light then, and I caught my first real glimpse of him. He was certainly older than Laurent, with cropped gray hair above a leathery face. I hated him immediately, more for his age than anything else. How dare he deny Laurent the time that he had enjoyed for so long?

"But such things are unfortunately necessary sometimes," he went on. "Especially when the future of Vassian is at stake."

"I have no real worry for the future of Vassian," I retorted.

"No, you wouldn't." He chuckled. "Nonetheless, I do, and you appear to be the answer to some of my prayers."

Whatever they ask of you.

"And I'm here for you to test me." I wandered toward the

stone bench under the window and sat, inhaling the sea breeze. It was a risk to do something so casual in front of a king, but he wasn't *my* king, and I needed to catch my breath. How much longer would I be allowed something as mundane as fresh air? "To see if the rumors are true."

"I don't need to test you. You are a crownkeeper." He held up a hand as I opened my lips, questioning. "Oh, yes, even in Vassian, we've heard of the legends. But some of us believe more than most. Have seen things, even, things that make testing you irrelevant. I know you have a gift."

"How?" My mouth was dry. I'd hoped he would have dismissed me as a charlatan.

"Legends and myths all have some basis in reality—even such things as dragons. And your husband was insistent enough that you could be of use to me. It's not something you could feign for very long, if at all, so I have to believe his claim is true."

"I told Thomas. The magic only works at Lochfeld."

"So he said. But I don't believe that's the truth."

The breeze caught my hair, and even though the spring morning was cool, I was suddenly hot. The sudden waves that had appeared when I'd tried to jump over the side of the ship— had that been the magic? I should have been relieved at the idea of the map protecting me, even from myself, but instead, I felt trapped. More trapped than I'd ever felt at Lochfeld, wondering if I'd ever be able to leave again.

Damir fell to the bench across from me, and though I could feel his stare, I could only focus on my feet and the smell of salt that filled the tower room. Maybe that was the answer to Silke's freedom, so long ago. Perhaps it so was obvious, like I'd once wondered, that she hadn't bothered writing about it. Because if the magic worked at sea, surely it could reach me away from the ballroom. The Creator wasn't limited to Lochfeld, after all.

They can feel when Meirdre is in danger, can warn of wildfires, border raids, epidemics. And the map speaks to them, shows them where misfortune is happening.

My heart skipped a beat.

Father Gerritt. He'd given me the answer back then, when he'd first told me about crownkeepers, and he hadn't even realized it.

Oh, heavens.

No, that wasn't right. This was Father Gerritt I was talking about. His wording was no mistake—it never was with him. Of course he'd realized it. He had *definitely* known exactly what he had said to me.

They can feel when Meirdre is in danger . . .

Could it be—could it be that it wasn't the map calling to me at all? Could the intense pull I'd experienced have been the magic itself, not calling me back to Lochfeld, necessarily, but simply warning me? The map helped, yes, there was no doubt about that, but I was starting to wonder if it was only one tool in a crownkeeper's armory. Perhaps a more experienced crownkeeper would have a better grip on things, could determine what the *feelings*, as Father Gerritt had called them, meant.

"It is the truth," I gasped, too conscious of Damir's attention on what must be my terrified expression. "The map—it's the only way my gift works."

The sensation of disappointment that flowed over me was immediate. Not from the king, for he merely raised a suspicious eyebrow, but from somewhere else, out past the Galvan Ocean that stretched further than I could imagine, west of Iraela and its palace were Elsanne was doubtless now cavorting with her scheming husband, north of Lochfeld and its map that had introduced me to such power.

I clutched at my chest, not caring what Damir thought. If he thought I was terrified, so be it—for I was that too, in all honestly. But there was also hope, for if I didn't need the map, I could protect Meirdre even as cut off from Lochfeld as I was. But that also meant Damir had a greater chance of using my gift for the glory of Vassian, and I would not allow that. No matter what Laurent had ordered of me.

"If that's so—" He stood and called for the soldiers in that odd language of Vassian. "Then we shall proceed without delay. I do wish things had gone differently, Your Majesty."

I sank against the stone as he disappeared, too devastated to correct him. And in my heart, I knew I could never agree to what Laurent had ordered me to do.

CHAPTER FORTY

REGARDLESS OF WHAT DAMIR HAD SAID, I KNEW HE HADN'T believed my claim. Why would he, when Thomas and Laurent had both suggested the opposite? I struggled with his calm acceptance for hours as the sun circled the tower, leaving my stone bench shrouded in shadows that hadn't been there when the soldiers had locked the door behind the departing king.

The earlier warmth had departed too, and I shivered in my still-damp gown as the breeze through the window cooled. By the time Thomas entered, a hunk of bread in one hand and a flask of water in another, I would have done anything for a blanket and dry shoes. Instead, he took a white dress from a soldier outside and handed that to me as well.

"You expect me to wear this?" I asked.

He closed the door, leaned against it, and nodded toward the dress with his chin. "King Damir wishes you to be suitably attired for the execution."

I dropped the gown to the floor and stared at the shadows swimming in the folds of the silk. White, naturally, and the reason for Damir's choice of the celebratory color was apparent. I was forbidden from mourning. Become a maiden again, as if

Laurent had never existed in the first place. And Thomas himself, always one to appreciate the dramatic, was reminding me of what Laurent himself had forced me to wear in the dungeon at Lochfeld.

"I would rather wear what I have on, thank you."

"That is not your choice." In the shadows, his eyes flashed. "You are allowed no preferences anymore—or were your circumstances not clear enough?"

"Thomas." Stepping over the fabric, I held out my hands. "I don't want any food. Or the dress. Or any of this. Please. You can still fix this. If you ever cared one bit for me—please help me. Help us."

He scoffed, and the sound was a dagger through my heart.

"Put it on."

Without releasing his gaze, I picked it up and crept behind a column to change in almost-dark privacy. That was something, and so was the cleanliness of my new garment, even if my stays were filthy. How long had it been since I'd picked them out in my room at Lochfeld? Time had so little meaning anymore.

Thomas gave me—or perhaps the gown—an approving nod when I ventured from behind the stone once more, having disposed of the wet shoes as well. Without a word, he opened the door and motioned me out onto the landing, where six soldiers waited. I stumbled on the threshold, and when I looked up, all seven of them were staring at me with no expression whatsoever.

Any warmth I might have felt upon discarding my wet clothes vanished as I crept down the stairs, surrounded by this group who hated me more than I could comprehend. It wasn't the chill of the evening though, just a desperate, ill feeling. Part of me knew what was waiting for me at the bottom, but part of me refused to imagine the horrors. That refusal, protective as it was, didn't last long enough. Shoved out of the tower and into the bailey, I stumbled in the dirt.

When I looked up, I was thankful I'd declined the bread—and

even the water—for Laurent stood in the same wagon that had brought us here, shirtless and calm, his hair blowing in the breeze and hands tied behind his back.

And a rope around his neck.

Like he had ordered of Thomas.

The courtyard spun around me, a blur of oil lamps and darkness and stars. My scream must have surprised Thomas as much as it surprised me, for he didn't flinch until my nails had drawn a long line of blood down his cheek. He grabbed my wrist as I tried once more, but the pain was merely a flash compared to the agony in my soul.

"You bastard." I doubted he could understand my slurred words. "You couldn't just let him die. You had to make a point!"

"I told you at Lochfeld," he said, yanking me against him. "So this should come as no surprise. He will die as a criminal. If it so happens that I can arrange his death as he would have had mine, so much the better. The manner of his death was one of the few favors I asked of King Damir for my service."

"The money wasn't enough?" Dizzy, I sucked in a breath. Behind me, a horse whinnied, and I thought of Skylark, of running through the meadow north of Lochfeld with Laurent by my side. We had been so happy, and I hadn't even realized it. I hadn't appreciated everything he'd given me—not the money, not the luxury, but the gift of his love.

"The money is never enough, Riette. It wasn't for me, and it wasn't for Vahl—though unlike him, I won't be taking my payment and heading for the islands quite yet." Thomas spun me around to face Laurent once more as the gravity of Vahl's betrayal sank in. What a fool I had been to trust someone I'd never really trusted. "You'll walk behind the cart," he whispered in my ear. "Next to King Damir. You will not cry, you will not speak, you will not stall."

Whatever they ask of you.

In a heartbeat, Laurent's order went from foolish to comforting. I tried to wrap my grieving heart around the change, but the horses drawing the carriage began to move, and Thomas shoved me forward. Damir, naturally, did not walk next to me, but rode a stallion, so tall I could scarcely glimpse his ears as I lowered my head and focused on the stones under my bare feet. It was that or watch Laurent, and I couldn't bring myself to watch him be drawn down the hill.

There were no villagers present tonight, no angry Vassian subjects throwing apple cores and stones. I puzzled over their absence as the walk wore on. Surely Damir wouldn't have ordered them away now. But as we proceeded into Windersay proper and through the still-empty streets, I realized where they had gone.

They were waiting in the square, anxious to witness an execution.

I had prayed in the tower that this wasn't the end, and even as I followed Laurent down the road toward the sea, I still hoped. This was the last piece of Damir's puzzle, though—Laurent wouldn't be executed in the capital. No, that kind of infamy alone would bestow too much honor upon him. He would die in this no-name seaport, and few would remember the story once the generation that had witnessed it had passed away. One last humiliation of the king who'd refused to surrender his kingdom.

Thomas jerked me to a stop as I tried to blink back tears, tried to ignore the roar of the crowd. I failed, but my sobbing didn't seem to matter to Damir as his soldiers forced Laurent up the scaffolding ladder. I would have stumbled my way up, but my husband ascended as gracefully as though he was standing from the throne at Lochfeld, then straightened under the gallows. I stared at his composure, and in return his gaze focused on mine for the first time tonight. For a moment I thought his lip curled upward, but before I could question my own crazed imagination, his expression turned blank once more.

Why are you crying, Crownkeeper?

My stomach fluttered. I didn't hear the words, not exactly, but I felt them, somewhere deep, somewhere no one in Vassian could touch. My gaze wavered between the executioner and his assistants, between the rope hanging over the gallows and the whip hanging from his hand, between Laurent's calm visage and the villagers screaming for his blood.

All this, and I hadn't sensed a single threat to the Meirdrean throne.

It made little sense. If Father Gerritt was correct, I should have felt *something*, especially this close to the end of his line and my kingdom. Even if he was mistaken, I should have felt the map calling me, begging me to return to Lochfeld and avail myself of its magic.

But I didn't.

I felt nothing but rage.

Rage tinged with hope.

The executioner raised the whip. A crack echoed through the square, followed by cheers, applause, and shouts of *harder*. Laurent grunted, and I flinched, confusion overcoming my fury and grief. His feet were stable on the platform now, but that would soon change. Even Laurent, strong as he was, couldn't hold out like this for long. There was no rescue coming, no one to save him.

No one except—

A shimmer fell across the scaffolding, almost blinding me. The yearning I'd felt in Iraela took shape once more, tugging my feet forward with unimaginable power. I ground my toes against the stones, earning a quiet and unnatural laugh upon the breeze before the pull resumed. Only this time, instead of calling me toward Lochfeld, it summoned me toward the steps.

No one except me.

CHAPTER 42

A roar filled my ears as I reached the top step, like the thunder that swept over Elternow during the summer storms. But the night was clear, and the stars that watched from high above precluded any rain. Overcome by the sensation of not controlling my body, I didn't turn in the direction of the sound, though the executioner's head swiveled toward the bay. I was close enough to see his throat move as he swallowed, then he backed away from Laurent and waved at Damir. But his attention didn't fall on me. No, it was somewhere much farther away. Farther even than Damir and the soldiers surrounding him.

The gleeful shouts of the crowd died away, fading to an anxious buzz as I stopped and faced Laurent. Several of the villagers at the back of the group spun around and took off running up the street in the tower's direction, shouting for the rest to follow. I couldn't understand their words through the sound coming from the ocean and the dizziness inside my own brain. Seemingly oblivious to my presence, the executioner dropped the whip and met Damir's eyes. The king nodded, though his glance continually shifted up the cliffs, and the executioner jumped to the cobblestones below, only to dash off into the dark streets.

Laurent blinked at me as he wavered on his feet, silently pleading with me, but some unfamiliar power kept me frozen, just paces away from him. The roar of not-thunder grew louder, joined by hoofbeats, as a flood of horses galloped through the streets, heading for the cliffs. Some drew carts, some carriages, and some only carried frightened villagers, clinging for their lives. I had the vague, indistinct impression that I should follow—or at least grab Laurent and follow—but my feet held as fast to the wood beneath them as though they'd been nailed.

Damir circled the gallows on his horse, his eyes wide with horror—though somehow, there was no shock in his expression.

Like he'd known I'd lied, just as he'd accused me of. It was then that I realized *I'd* done something, that whatever the sound was, whatever had caused so much fear throughout the streets of Windersay—

I'd done it.

Damir galloped away as the shimmering light fell away from the scaffolding, the rest of the soldiers behind and around him. The smoke of a hundred torches disappearing along with them filled the square, but I couldn't even turn to watch him flee up the hill. A silence overtook the square as they vanished into the streets, heavy and powerful, broken only by faraway shouts and the distant whinnies of frightened, overloaded horses.

"Riette."

I swayed on top of the scaffolding as Laurent's whisper freed me from my immobilization. The noose still hung heavy around his neck, and I darted toward him, lifting him up the best I could. My fingers pried at the rope securing his hands, but outside of stabbing myself with a thousand splinters, I made little progress in freeing him. A knife, it was a knife I needed, but whatever had frightened everyone off, it hadn't seen fit to leave me with a weapon.

"I can't free you," I sobbed at him. "Not without a knife."

He leaned heavily on me, though not enough to put any pressure on the noose. I knew I had to leave him, to run into one of the nearest inns or houses and find something I could use, but I couldn't leave him.

"You don't need to." He pointed toward the wharf—at least, as well as one could point with their shoulder. "Look."

Water.

It flowed through the empty streets, rushed past the scaffolding, under our feet. I had heard of such things—huge, violent waves that had devastated our coastal cities in Meirdre long ago, but this wave hadn't destroyed anything. It simply surged forward, clear and placid, leaving standing buildings in its wake.

A terrified horse that hadn't been seized for the villagers' retreat stood frozen just outside of the plaza, not floundering to its death, but watching the water flow harmlessly about it.

I squinted over the tops of the village, toward the bay. The ships in the harbor must have been destroyed, smashed against the wharf, but masts and sails were visible in the moonlight, floating back and forth as on a windless summer day.

"What is this?" I whispered.

Before he could answer, the water receded, as pure as when it had come. No debris marred the retreating swell, no buildings had collapsed, so unlike the old stories I'd heard—and the earthquake I'd survived in Haszen. The horse shook off its feet and sauntered across the plaza, disappearing on the side, the cobblestones under the scaffolding dried in a heartbeat, the silence returned, though peaceful this time.

And a group of men drifted out of the shadows, dry as the hay on a warm autumn afternoon in Elternow. The peace flashed away, but we hadn't come this far to be trapped in Windersay now. I stepped in front of Laurent, but he only kissed my cheek and called out toward them.

"Cadaval," he said, his voice stronger than I'd heard it in a long time. "Would you be kind enough to cut these ropes, please? It seems my wife can summon enchanted water but not a sword."

Laurent was silent as I placed another rag full of peppermint on his torn back, but I could tell I was causing him even more pain. His jaw worked back and forth as I dumped another handful of leaves into the bucket next to me, so I worked quicker, tossing the occasional order over my shoulder to the soldiers in worn leather breeches and the clean shirts of Vassian peasants who lingered in the room of the inn a few blocks away from the main square.

Willow bark, whiskey, boiling water—nothing I requested was denied, though I recoiled each time the door opened, expecting more of Damir's soldiers instead of Laurent's. Eventually, having satisfied themselves their king would live another day, the soldiers departed, minus Cadaval, who watched me minister to Laurent with the eyes of a wary, beaten dog.

"You can trust me," I finally snapped. "I didn't save him to murder him."

"Of course, Your Grace." He glanced backward at the bucket of water on the fire. "But someone should remain in case you need anything else."

"I don't know who you are, but I can tell you're hardly a servant." I dumped the last bloody rag in the bucket and stared at Laurent's back. He hadn't attended to me like this the night of our wedding, and though I would have never left him here to suffer alone, I wished he hadn't done so to me. "I don't believe waiting on us is what you're here for."

Laurent sighed. "Captain Cadaval has been at my side since we left Lochfeld. I doubt even an order from me would shake his protection now. Not from you—but you can't forget we haven't made our way back to Meirdre yet."

"By your side the entire time, was he? It seems like you shook his protection yourself long enough to get yourself captured." My voice broke, and it wasn't from homesickness.

"Riette." His rebuke was quiet, but I knew I'd gone too far. "There are things—"

"I know." I settled back on my heels and basked in the fire's warmth. I was truly too stiff to sit like this, but I couldn't force myself farther away from him. "You had to get yourself and a small raiding party past the Vassian border. As a captive you could do so with much less bloodshed than an all-out attack."

Laurent rolled to his side, grimaced, and fixed me with a wary expression. Behind me, embers crackled as Cadaval stoked the fire.

"When we neared the Illrus River," he replied, "the scouts returned with unwelcome news—the Vassian Army was assembling at their outpost near Edrista, just like we'd feared. It was only days until they crossed the border, if that, and once that happened, they'd have flattened Meirdre as they proceeded north. So, I decided. If it was my death Damir wanted, he would get it—or at least, I'd let him think he would. We already knew Vassian had their own scouts heading toward Brannitz, so it was a straightforward matter to separate from the rest of the army and find them. Cadaval thought I was an idiot, I might add."

"I did, sire." Cadaval coughed, and a flash of pity rushed through me. Reporting directly to Laurent like he did must be as exasperating as being married to him. "And might have said as much to the stars when you retired to bed that night."

Laurent's eyes crinkled. "And now, Captain?"

"I suppose you were right, sire." A small smile broke through.

"But they—Thomas—suspected nothing when they found you?" I asked as Laurent's laugh faded. "You riding off on your own?"

Laurent forced a smile. "Perhaps a little. But they didn't question their good fortune. Of course, at that point I realized I needed you as well, so I convinced them they'd have to bring me to Lochfeld first. I said I knew Damir wanted you as well, but that you'd never go with them, however unwillingly, if you thought I was dead. Naturally they argued with me when I told them—they were certain I was lying, so I told them your secret. After that, they couldn't risk not believing me."

"But you could have told them anything else but that!"

"Hardly. You'd never have been able to hide your confusion if Thomas Wennink would have accused you of being anything but a crownkeeper. Telling the truth saved both our lives."

I swiveled my head toward Cadaval, but he must have known my secret, for he didn't look remotely shocked at the word. Though I suppose if he hadn't, my feat in the plaza would have erased all doubt. I turned back to Laurent, and tears filled my eyes. The image of him kneeling on the floor of the throne room, a sword at his throat . . . it would never leave my imagination, grand plan or not.

"I am sorry I frightened you." Laurent reached out a finger and brushed a tear from my cheek. "But I knew he would never hurt you without Damir's permission, and I knew—"

"You knew Damir couldn't hurt you as long as I wished otherwise." There. It was said. The accusation I'd been wanting to make since I'd realized why Laurent wasn't afraid. "As long as I fulfilled my duties."

He nodded.

"Why didn't you ever tell me what else I'm capable of?" I asked. "That water—the way it simply ran through the streets without harming anything—I've never seen anything like it. It's frightening to think I did that."

He stared at me, then rolled to his stomach once more.

"I didn't know until not that long ago. The map—yes, my father told me about that when I was a child, just after I first received the lecture regarding my duty to marry and produce heirs. But the other magic, the more secret magic, I didn't know about that until Father Gerritt told me just before I left Lochfeld. And even then, I wasn't certain how it could manifest—just that it would."

"I felt it." I lay my cheek on my hand, acutely conscious of our bystander. "On the ship. I tried to throw myself overboard, but before I could, we hit a wave. Out of nowhere, the sea turned from glass to something I can't even describe. It was terrifying. To know that *something* wanted me alive that badly . . ."

"You did promise you'd protect Lochfeld. And Meirdre. And me." Warmth filled his reminder. "The map—or more precisely, its magic—wasn't going to let you get away that easily."

"I suppose not." I took in a deep breath. "I need to refill the water."

Cadaval jumped to his feet. "Please, Your Grace, allow me."

"As I said, you're not a servant—and I'd be more comfortable if he had you here watching over him. I'll be fine." I brushed my fingers over Laurent's. "It's not as though I've never hauled water before."

Laurent raised his brows at my argument, and Cadaval nodded, so I grabbed the bucket and headed downstairs, swinging it from my hand. There was a pump out the back in the alleyway—I'd seen it when we'd come in—and the fresh air was calling me like it hadn't in a long while. It would be safe enough. While some of the villagers had trickled back into town, drawn by the stories of the wave that had destroyed nothing, most of the rest were still hiding in the cliffs, too fearful of a recurrence to chance coming home quite yet.

A few of the Meirdrean soldiers I recognized from upstairs glanced my way and nodded respectfully, but even my presence wasn't enough to tear them away from their well-deserved meat and ale. I slipped out the door, leaned against the wall, and took a deep breath of night air tinged with smoke from the surrounding chimneys. The stars were bright, and even if I was viewing them from a small village somewhere in Vassian, they looked almost the same as I'd seen every night in Elternow. And when I closed my eyes . . . I could almost believe I was still there. Except the scent of the peppermint and whiskey I'd used on Laurent's wounds wafted up from my hands, and my lips still stung with the taste of his. No, this was definitely not Elternow—it was something much better.

With a sigh of longing, I opened my eyes and trudged toward the pump. A shadowy figure turned the corner as I moved off the wall, and I stopped, the hair at the back of my neck prickling. Maybe we didn't need more water. Maybe Captain Cadaval or one of his men could get it. I shouldn't have felt afraid—it was evening, and the air was cool, so the figure's cloak wasn't out of place—but even so, I turned on my heel and headed for the back door of the inn where dozens of Meirdrean were waiting.

Just a few steps to safety . . .

A hand clamped over my mouth; the other shoved something hard and sharp against my side. The breeze turned cold as I tried to reconcile the sensation with the elation I'd felt just a few hours before, but I could feel nothing but heat. I gasped, and the pistol pushed harder.

"Hello, Riette," Thomas said.

CHAPTER FORTY-ONE

THOMAS PUSHED ME AGAINST THE WALL WITH HIS KNEE, HIS PALM still over my mouth and the pistol pressed against my stays. I gagged at the taste of the sweat on his palm, then swallowed enough of my fear to stop fighting him. It wasn't as though I could overpower him, and I didn't want that gun any closer to me than it already was.

"You're smarter than I thought. And more powerful." His fingers eased up on their pressure, just enough that I could breathe again. "Now, we're going to discuss our next steps. Don't move and don't scream."

"They'll come looking for me," I tried to mumble through his hand. "Soon."

"Unlikely." He flipped me around, my back against the wall, and leaned toward my ear. "If you were stupid enough to scream, you'd have done it already, not that there are many people left to hear you, thanks to that grandiose display of yours back at the plaza. Besides, those Meirdrean soldiers in there are too concerned with their ale to realize you left and didn't return."

"Who—"

"Oh, please." Thomas cackled. "They stick out. I don't know

what your sovereign has planned, but if he thinks he's going to escape back across the border with less than twenty men, he's wrong."

The heat that insisted on filling my gut turned to ice. I didn't know what Laurent had planned, but Thomas was right. Any strategy he could have come up with on his way to Vassian would likely be futile.

Or would it? He'd intentionally let himself be captured by Vassian troops, after all. He couldn't be planning to take an entire kingdom with the men who'd made their way across the river, singly and in pairs, so he must have had a plan. If only he'd suggested it to me before I'd come downstairs.

I shook my head. "I don't know his plan either."

A slim figure, shrouded in shadows, caught my eye. I held my breath as it slipped around the corner and seemed to stop to watch me. It was entirely possible a bullet would end up in my side if he was startled by a resident out for a late evening walk.

"That doesn't surprise me." Thomas's lip curled—it was obvious he was unaware of our audience in the shadows. "Did you really think he'd mention it to *you*? A peasant girl from Elternow, who he refused to make his queen?"

I licked my lips as the slight wormed its way into my soul. The fact was, Laurent had said nothing to me. I hadn't questioned it before, but why should I? He had soldiers with him. I was only here to keep him alive, and I would have done that regardless of his intentions.

"His Majesty's military strategy is of little consequence to me, anyway," I whispered.

He laughed as he jerked me from the wall. "You can't lie to me, Riette. Never could. What girl wouldn't want more than he's given you? Especially now. You must already be wondering how much he truly appreciates your power. Or maybe he only appreciates you for your power—you can't believe he respects you, as much as he's kept you in the dark like he has."

With a shake of my head, I tried to twist from Thomas's grip, but he gave a jab of the pistol as he pulled me down the alley. A few Vassian women stepped outside to dump the remains of cooking water outside, but no one said a word—and I wasn't going to beg one of them for help. No, I would have to wait until I had a chance at overwhelming Thomas, before he could bring me somewhere from which I would never escape. The inn faded into the distance, but footsteps behind us grew louder.

"Riette?"

Thomas and I both froze. Well, he froze, then shoved the gun against me so hard I gasped, then spun me around to face our follower. I squinted at her—for the voice was undeniably feminine—but the moon had set, and she was hidden in the shadows.

"You have the wrong person," Thomas growled. "Now leave us, before you regret it."

"I think it's you that has the wrong person, Thomas Wennink."

My breath caught.

Oh, heavens.

Elsanne?

There was no way Laurent's mother could be standing here in a dark alley in Windersay, in the Kingdom of Vassian, but she'd been at Lochfeld long enough that I knew her voice, and now, the familiar posture of a woman who'd long ceased to fear anyone like Thomas. Did she have a sword under that cape? Probably. Knowing Elsanne, it might even be a musket.

Thomas jerked me closer to him. I swung my free hand at him, momentarily forgetting the pistol. He must have done the same, for when he reached out to catch my wrist, the gun clattered to the cobblestones. I kicked it away as he grabbed me, catching my shoe in my skirts and tripping backward, away from him.

Elsanne's shadow grew larger in the dim alley, and before I could find my feet, she'd yanked me back into a doorway behind us. Finally, I scrambled up, searching for the pistol somewhere out on the darkened stones, but there was no use. Thomas gave us one last look and took off north, giving me only a brief glance over his shoulder as he sprinted.

She turned to me and put a cool hand to my cheek. "Are you injured?"

For a moment I could only stare, trying to figure out if I was imagining her. Was this another of Laurent's games? Not likely, I decided. No matter what it gained him, Laurent would never involve his mother in something like this.

"No—he didn't hurt me."

"Surprising, given how poorly you fight." Her eyes glistened in the shadows as she focused on me. "And where might my son be?"

I gawked at her. "An inn."

"Well? Are you going to take me there or just stand here?"

"I—yes, of course, Your Majesty."

I skulked back into the alley and led her toward the inn where I hoped Laurent was still waiting safely, the hair still standing on the back of my neck. Though desperate to know how and why Elsanne was here alone—and how she'd found me—I didn't dare question her after she'd asked for Laurent in that tone. I didn't even dare to fill the bucket I'd left near the pump when Thomas had grabbed me. Cadaval could do so, since he'd been so motivated before. Maybe he could take Elsanne with him, for I wasn't sure I wanted to see how Laurent was going to react to her appearance—or the fact Thomas had grabbed me.

Four soldiers meandered about the hallway outside Laurent's door when I climbed the stairs, and I didn't look any of them in the eye as I slid inside and approached the bed. Laurent's eyes were closed, a blanket pulled up over his bare chest, and I placed a hand on his, ignoring Cadaval's critical expression. He could try telling Elsanne she couldn't enter if he felt like it.

"Sire? There's—there's someone here to see you."

He brushed his fingers over mine, smiled, then cracked one eye.

"She made it, did she?"

"Indeed I did," Elsanne broke in before I could formulate any kind of stunned reply. "Only to find Riette here being dragged off by that Wennink creature. All these soldiers milling about, and you couldn't assign one to protect your wife? What were you thinking, Laurent?"

Laurent sat bolt upright, a man on his throne instead of a dirty bed in a foreign inn.

"She what?" he asked, his eyes landing on mine.

"When I went to get the water." I collapsed in the nearest chair and placed a palm where Thomas's pistol had been. "He was right there. Like he was waiting for me. He—they've returned to the village. They must be watching the inn. Why they haven't yet barged in here, I can't begin to imagine."

Laurent snapped his fingers, and two of the soldiers who'd followed Elsanne and me inside vanished out the door. "And then?"

"She tried to hit him when I showed up." Elsanne's voice dripped something. Not scorn, but certainly not approval. "And he ran."

"To Damir, most likely," Laurent replied. "And if he recognized you, he'll know exactly why you're here, and we won't have that much time. We must move quickly."

"Much time for what?" I asked foolishly.

My chest closed in, but I wasn't sure it was from the utter fatigue or Thomas's suggestions regarding my marriage. Maybe Thomas was right. Laurent had told his mother his plans but not me? Did he not trust me? Not love me? Not think me capable of acting as a crownkeeper? Or worse, his wife?

"Marius—" Laurent began. Cadaval shot him a sharp look, so he paused, glanced at Elsanne, and then back to me. "He's been leading his army toward Vassian since . . . well, for several weeks now, I would imagine. Ever since my mother used my departure from Lochfeld as an opportunity to run home to Iraela like I expressly ordered her not to."

Elsanne's mouth dropped open. "I—"

"Are predictable, Mother, yes." He winced as he shifted. I stood and moved toward him, but he waved me off. "And your arrival in Iraela was enough to tip off Marius that things had been set in motion, enough to let him send a rider to his men waiting in the wastes of the Coalwood Basin. Tobias Erstad is with them, in case you were wondering," he said to me. "Vahl's men chased him out of Meirdre, and he stumbled across Marius's army, terrified he'd fated you to death. I'll let you apologize."

A shudder of relief ran through me. I'd long believed Erstad dead.

"As for Marius," Laurent went on, "I may owe him the next seven generations of my children, but at least Meirdre will be safe—and I'll have cemented an alliance with Iraela as well. Properly this time. Splitting a conquered kingdom between each other tends to do that."

I straightened in my chair and stared at him. "You mean to say—"

"That we intend on taking Vassian?" Laurent gave me a brilliant smile. "Yes. We unlocked the door. Marius and the Iraelan Army will knock it down."

CHAPTER FORTY-TWO

THE ROOM GREW SILENT. ELSANNE STARED AT LAURENT, HER LIP twisted in a disappointed expression—but even she knew to be silent when her son had made such a declaration. Me, I had no such restraint, not anymore. If Laurent wanted to reprimand me, at least now he knew exactly who he was reprimanding—a crownkeeper who'd just proven she could control the tides.

"You don't mean that," I breathed out.

Cadaval cleared his throat.

Laurent's brows rose. "What part of this plan was confusing for you, my dear?"

"None of it, sire. I only . . ." I stopped, finally aware of my foolishness. "But where is King Marius? If he'd been here, I wouldn't have had to—do what I did."

Laurent shrugged, casually, like I hadn't just saved him from further whipping and death. "He's heading this way, I would imagine. Round south the Bolcour Mountains or taking care of that stronghold at Edrista first, I have no idea, but they'll be here, and soon."

"You said *unlock the door*," I began hesitantly. "What exactly did you mean?"

His smile fell. "The plan was for Damir to let his guard down a bit at the border once he had me. Makes Marius's job of passing through the Basin easier—our own soldiers following behind as well. But it seems he was too impatient for my death—that's changed the timeline a bit, as you've probably figured out. We've bought ourselves tonight, after what you did in the plaza, but after that, we're going to have to come up with something different."

"And Thomas. He found me and he'll know you're close by." My heart began to pound again. "It won't be long until they find you."

"Likely." Laurent glanced up, as if he'd just remembered Cadaval and his mother were still in the room. "I need to speak with Riette alone, please."

Cadaval simply nodded as he disappeared out the door, but Elsanne straightened.

"You used me." Her tone was low with fury. "Once more. I should—"

Laurent sighed, cutting her off. "I am righting a wrong, Mother. One I was partially responsible in creating."

"You were thoughtless," she snapped back at him. "And now you've wrapped two kingdoms up in your careless plot."

"You'd prefer to kneel to Damir?" It sounded like a threat that should have been shouted, but Laurent's voice was terrifyingly even. "Because you would, eventually. Yes, even with Marius's army. You know Vassian won't stop at Meirdre, especially with us having the most tenuous connections to another kingdom. I did what I had to do, and Marius agreed. If this all ends poorly, it ends poorly, but history will not accuse me of not doing everything I could to protect my land and people after so foolishly doing the opposite before."

I swallowed at his mention of the bargain with Iraela. Elsanne gave a small huff, no doubt annoyed at the reminder of being sold as a hostage as well.

"Do you trust me?" he asked. "Do you trust Marius? You travelled all the way here on his order after all—alone, no less—apparently knowing very little of why he commanded it of you."

"I try." Her shoulders sagged, making her look less like a queen in costly traveling clothes and more like a woman accepting the inevitable. "But this plan of yours is difficult to trust."

"Your loyalty will not be in vain." He struggled to his feet and gave her a quick kiss on each cheek. "I promise you that, Mother."

"Then I will not question you again." She cupped her hand on his jaw, and I suddenly saw him as the beloved child he must have been at one time. "But this had better be the last time I fall into one of your plans. Next time I will not be so understanding, sire."

Regardless of her words, I doubted Laurent had seen the last of her, but she disappeared into the hall with a respectful nod. I threw a cautious glance at the door, then guided him back to bed.

"I would never have said it in front of my mother, or even Cadaval, but things happened too quickly," he said, collapsing. "Fool I might have been, but I didn't realize Damir was so eager for my death." He angled toward me, and I leaned against his chest, avoiding several whip marks. "I doubt Marius is as near to Windersay as he should be at this point. And now that Wennink knows where I am—there are precious few places we can hide until the Army of Iraela arrives."

"And Vassian soldiers are protecting the Meirdrean border, no doubt." I reached for another rag, but he waved me off.

"There is no going home now." He sighed once more. "Not yet."

"So, we need to delay." I matched his sigh with a deep exhale of my own. "For how long?"

Laurent ran a hand through his hair. "A week, possibly."

Heavens. A week. He was wrong. He had to be. I doubted we had another day in this inn.

"You must have an idea," I replied. "You wouldn't have said anything to me if you didn't."

He reached for a glass of water by the bedside and drained it in one gulp. "A few bad ones," he admitted. "Cadaval suspects the direness of our circumstances. He wants me to make a run for it, but I won't leave my men—or you. And I fear our other options are similarly poor. Make no mistake, this is not the end, but things have become rather complicated."

I stared at the floor for a long while. A tower flashed into my mind, a stone window and the feel of the ocean breeze on my skin, a too-recent memory I'd rather have forgotten. But could it be the answer? I didn't want to broach the subject, but Laurent almost seemed to be asking for my thoughts. And mine was certainly better than Cadaval's ideas of running, well-intentioned though it was.

"Damir still wants me," I said quietly. "I'm sure of it. When the water came, he was watching me as I stood, and he wasn't surprised by what was happening in the least. I don't believe he expected the water, but he expected something. He wants my power for himself, and badly. My appearance would startle enough to distract him from his plans for you."

"No." If it was possible after his whipping, Laurent's face paled even more. "I know what I said before, but now—I forbid it."

"Do you have a better solution?" My mouth was dry with fear, but I pressed on. "He was desperate to see if a crownkeeper's power will work outside of Meirdre. Now he knows—the only question remaining in his mind is if he can make it work for him."

"It could work." He stood and paced to the far wall before dropping on the bed again. Blood seeped through the bandages, but I knew better than to tell him to rest. I watched him instead, trying to decipher his expression, but his face was stone. "But I will not permit it."

"But sire—"

"I will not risk your life like that."

I ran a finger down his jaw. "Isn't my life already at risk?"

"It is." Laurent turned my face toward his and leaned against me, cheek to cheek. He was silent for a long time. "And because of that, I'm inclined to let you do this, however ill-advised it may seem. But I must ask you one thing . . . is it Thomas Wennink you want? Is that what this is about?"

For a moment I thought he had slapped me, such was the heat that passed over my cheeks before taking over my entire body.

"Sire, I would never—"

"Perhaps not. But I wouldn't be a man if I didn't question it." There wasn't anger in the statement, not even an accusation. Fear? Yes, some of that. Fear and desperation. And I understood. I hadn't ever truly loved Thomas, but I couldn't blame Laurent for wondering. Especially not now. "Especially since you left with him once before," he added.

Tears filled my eyes at his decidedly unregal fear. I had been stupid, naïve, untrusting. Had hurt a man who'd only wanted a loving marriage. Was it any wonder he was worried about my intentions now?

"I love you." The words were so easy to say now. "No one else. Ever."

"Prove it." His voice grew husky. "And once we return to Meirdre, you will wear the crown that started this all."

"I don't care about the crown." I shifted toward him, suddenly frantic for his touch. "Just you."

His command wasn't a challenge, I knew. More of a desperation to love me like he hadn't been able to bring himself to do the night of our wedding. He pulled me onto his lap with only the slightest flinch. The fire crackled as he drew my dress over my head, and he didn't speak as my lips lingered on his, promising something unsaid, something too insistent to be uttered with words. I shrank back then, wordless and afraid of his wounds, but he gripped me so fiercely that I almost forgot to breathe as I gave in to desire—though I wasn't sure which one of us needed and wanted it more. I'd meant to reassure him, but he'd ended up comforting me.

Still, I knew, while I watched his chest rise and fall in exhausted slumber afterward, that when he woke, all those reassurances would mean nothing.

CHAPTER FORTY-THREE

THE BACKSTREETS OF WINDERSAY WERE SILENT WHEN I SLIPPED along a row of houses several hours later. Even the wharf was quiet, though a sailor who'd been brave enough to return was singing somewhere in the distance, a melody of homesickness and loss. I had stopped shivering once I turned and the buildings blocked the wind, but I still shook as I hurried along, turning backward every so often to check for pursuers. Nothing could block the fear.

Nothing could block my feeling of failure, either. I'd been wandering around the village for almost a half hour now, and surely someone would have seen me by now. Surely someone would have recognized me as the woman who'd summoned water to rescue the king of Meirdre, and they wouldn't hesitate to turn me back over to Damir. I certainly didn't want to show up at the front gate of his clifftop fortress. Confused and angry was the plan, not immediate surrender.

Even so, I turned west, toward the colossal tower that loomed over the thatched roofs and sails. The soldiers would be more numerous the closer I got to the fortress, and perhaps Damir wouldn't question it. A scorned woman, wandering in circles, trying to decide if she was going to commit treason tonight . . . yes. And Thomas, finally useful, could confirm that *yes, Riette has a tendency to abandon her duties, run off and follow her childish emotions. Even when they lead to treachery.*

The idea of seeing him again made my stomach churn, so I focused on the cobblestones I'd walked just hours before, so certain I would witness Laurent's death. He'd made it out of that, hadn't he? Without me knowing the extent of my crownkeeper abilities, no less. Not that I was certain I knew the full extent now—what else was the magic hiding from me? I didn't feel it now, but perhaps that meant nothing. I'd felt nothing but despair watching Laurent ride down the hill in that wagon, after all—until I hadn't.

I mused over that as two Vassian soldiers passed me by. They looked me up and down, but their interest appeared personal instead of professional. That alone was enough to set my hair on edge once more. I quickened my step, trying to decide how I would explain to Damir that I'd passed up several of his soldiers before deciding to surrender. But no matter how suspicious that was, I couldn't turn around and speak to them now without them asking questions themselves.

Lights and voices inside an inn ahead caught my eyes. Early morning it might be, but at least some residents of Windersay were still up—likely ones who were celebrating their survival and drowning in ale their sorrows over Laurent's escape, I hoped. Just . . . just not too much ale. I crept closer to peek inside, staying in the shadows of the alley. The magic, I hoped, would tell me if this was the place to make my appearance. It was difficult to tell through the fogged-over window, but it appeared most of the patrons were sailors and workers from the docks—though a few soldiers were visible in the corner, their uniforms obvious through the condensation dripping down the glass.

"What's this?"

I started at the voice. It was a tavern worker who'd caught me staring.

"You look familiar." He peered at me through the shadows, and I held my breath. "That Meirdrean girl! The one who—"

My legs acted without permission, and I darted toward the left, away from his grip. Suddenly, with my goal within reach, I was too terrified to follow through. I would have to run back to the inn, would have to find Laurent, confess my failure. He would forgive me, I was certain, but . . .

Would I forgive myself?

I froze at the internal question, my chest heaving. The man was beside me in two steps, and when his fingers curled around my upper arm, I didn't fight back. I didn't protest as he led me inside the tavern, my appearance stopping all conversation immediately. I had, apparently, found a group of Windersay residents who recognized me at once.

An officer in the corner rose, interest written all over his face. "Where'd you find her, Leontiou?"

"Skulking around out back." He pushed me forward, into the center of the tavern. "Listening in who knows what. Probably trying to decide what dark magic to use on us next."

"I wasn't listening to anything," I replied, rubbing my wrists in a vain attempt to calm myself. "I couldn't have heard through the glass even if I wanted to."

"Then why are you here?" he asked.

I shook off the tavern owner's hand on my arm. "I have information for King Damir."

The room fell silent, except for the distant calls of birds, disturbed from their nightly slumber by the rising sun near the horizon.

"What kind of information?" The officer circled around me, as though he'd discover the information just by staring at me. Looking through me. "Surely you can't expect me to disturb His Majesty on nothing more than your word."

"That"—I lifted my chin, if only to convince myself of my non-existent bravery—"is only for King Damir's ears. If you know who I am, you will not risk arguing with me."

A roar of laughter. It filled my mind, along with a certain sense of purpose I'd been missing since Thomas had pushed me onto that ship way back in Vistel. And suddenly, somewhere deep inside me, I realized Laurent and I had made the right decision by allowing this foolish endeavor. The map? Some other magic? My own soul, letting me know I was finally doing something right? Maybe it didn't matter.

"Then by all means," the officer said, gesturing me toward the front door, "let's get you to King Damir."

In the early morning darkness, the tower I thought I'd never see again was cold, even with the window closed. I paced from it to the door and back, sometimes counting my steps, sometimes simply walking, my mind elsewhere. Was it fear? There was some of that threatening to bubble up, but also a certain giddiness— Damir no doubt knew I'd turned myself in, which meant Laurent was safe for now. And the longer he waited to see me, the longer it took for him to debate my intentions and power, the closer King Marius and his army would be to Windersay.

A flicker of gilded sunlight appeared through the window as the sun rose, and I yawned despite myself. Sleep was tempting, but I knew I'd dream of Laurent if I could find a comfortable position on the stone floor, so I continued my pacing. No one came, not Damir, nor Thomas, nor any of the soldiers, and by the time the sun set once more, my stomach was growling.

But that was one much-needed day down. One day to allow Laurent to heal. To allow King Marius's approach. Or had Damir ignored my message totally? Had he headed back into Windersay, searching each inn and private home for Laurent?

My eyes burned as I leaned against the wall and let my imagination take control. It was difficult to dream with the smell of salt on the breeze, but if I concentrated, I could feel Laurent's hands on my skin. The earthy scent of horses in the Lochfeld stables. The breeze through the apple orchards outside Elternow. Would I live to experience them? Would Meirdre exist in another month? All of it was too much to think about, so I stood on the stone bench and tried to yank the window shut. It would make the tower room claustrophobic, but if I could only ignore the perfume of the sea, perhaps I could ignore the entire situation—especially since the door creaked open just as I hopped down.

"Are you planning on jumping?" Damir asked, closing the door behind him.

"I hate the smell of the ocean," I replied. "It smells . . . rotten."

"I doubt that, after what I witnessed last night." He gave me a sullen smile. "You told my soldiers you had something to tell me?"

I took a breath. It would be the most difficult lie I'd ever told, and yet the most important. But the shadows of the tower embraced me as I swallowed, calming me somehow. Like they know my motive and were holding me in their own approval.

"I was wrong," I said, keeping my voice soft. Disappointed. Not distraught, for I doubted Damir would listen to a distraught woman, no matter what information or powers she held. "Wrong to do it, wrong to run afterward. Because even after what I did, he—he didn't want me after all."

His eyes widened a fraction. "And you're angry."

Tears wet my cheeks, so easy. "I sacrificed so much for him, and he threw it all away, all because he was afraid of my gifts."

Damir sank to the bench opposite me, half shrouded in darkness, half shimmering in the moonlight. Dusky circles under his eyes shadowed his expression, but the lines in his face had faded somewhat, like my appearance had been the answer to his prayers. A moonbeam hit the clasps on his cloak as he shifted, and a pair of dragons stared back at me, disappearing into the shadows as he leaned against the wall.

"I would not be," he replied. "The power you showed last night is not to be discarded out of fear. Any sovereign worth anything would see that."

"I thought you might understand." I looked out the window, like I was second-guessing my decision. Rushing would seem suspicious. In truth, I was searching for wherever Laurent might be, praying he might send me some of his strength somehow. Was that silly? It felt like it, but something told me Laurent wouldn't mind sharing. Not now. "And that means you deserve the power. Vassian deserves it."

"Then you confess that you lied to me before. That you do have powers. And you were well aware of them when we last spoke."

"I wouldn't think I'd need to confess after what happened down in the village." I gave him a choked laugh, one I didn't need to feign. "But no. Until last night, I wasn't aware that what I did there was possible. It surprised me as much as it must have surprised you."

"Hmm."

He studied me so long that the glint of moonlight drifted across the floor. Time was both my friend and enemy—the longer I sat here, the closer I was to losing my nerve, but the more chance Laurent and King Marius had of seeing things through. The very idea made me shake, the responsibility too heavy to bear.

"Then we shall see what else you are capable of," he said, slapping his palms on the bench. "But not here."

"Not here?" I stammered.

He smiled and pointed toward the door.

"Not here."

CHAPTER FORTY-FOUR

THE CARRIAGE DAMIR SHOWED ME TO WAS AS UNLIKE THE CART IN which Laurent had ridden as possible. Though I hated to admit it, it could have been called more luxurious than the one in which I'd ridden to Iraela so long ago. If only I didn't have to share with Damir and Thomas, it could have been . . . almost enjoyable.

But Thomas's sneer had grown old long before we'd settled into our journey on the road from Windersay to Damir's principal palace outside Heosta. I couldn't help but wonder if he knew my true motivation for being here, but he hadn't said anything to Damir yet, so I had to assume I was safe—for a while, at least. I leaned my head against the side as Damir made small talk with me about the spring planting season, and I tried to ignore his voice as the sun came up and filled the carriage with an unwelcome warmth.

He had claimed, when we'd departed the tower, that the trip to the palace would take less than two days. By the way the driver was whipping the horses, I believed it. Still, I couldn't help wishing he'd urge them on faster, if only because I couldn't stand the idea of spending the night in a strange inn in Vassian, Thomas in a nearby room. But we came to a stop as the sun dipped low in the distance, outside a squat building built around what looked like a courtyard. Strange trees surrounded it—plain, brown trunks with a set of fanlike leaves on top. I'd never seen such a thing except in books, and despite Thomas's presence, I couldn't help staring at the exotic sight.

Damir jumped out of the carriage into the sand below, all silk and fine leather and unnecessary bluster toward the innkeeper, and I pressed myself into the velvet seat, hoping he would forget about me. But he motioned me out, Thomas at my side, and I trudged upstairs to a small, spartan room. The cracked window overlooked the road, enough that I could see anyone coming to my rescue.

But that was silly, for there was no rescue coming. I'd volunteered for this, hadn't I? And I was succeeding—I'd tempted Damir away from Windersay. It was a waiting game now.

"We leave early in the morning for Heosta," Thomas said before shutting the door. "Don't do anything stupid."

I ignored him and deadbolted the door. Despite the dust from the road that needed to wash off, I curled up on the ancient bed, still in my stays and gown, and stifled a yawn as it creaked. I wanted Laurent's arms around me, and I wanted to go home, so I closed my eyes and let sleep take me. If I couldn't see either right now, at least I could see both in my dreams.

I woke to the sliding of the deadbolt on the inside of my door. I must have dreamed the intrusion before it woke me, for my heart was already pounding. I told myself it was simply Thomas come to wake me up to resume my journey—not that I approved of that familiarity of him entering my room at all, but it would have been a *reason*—but moonlight still cascaded across the floor when I opened my eyes and tried to focus in the darkness.

It wasn't Thomas who'd entered, though. Damir stood there

in the moonlight, but I could tell in an instant that his intentions were . . . well, not noble, but also not what I'd initially feared. The curiosity was simply too plain on his face.

"What do you want?" I clutched the blanket to my chest as he stood there, staring.

"I couldn't wait until we reach Heosta to see what else your powers allow." He took a step toward me. "I have to know now. Please."

The desperation in his *please* threw me. Laurent had sounded that desperate once, back when I had thought little of him. Could Damir possibly have some compelling reason for wanting access to my powers?

I shook off the question. Pity was the last thing I needed to feel for him now. Even if the dragons of old themselves were raiding Vassian, his fate was not my business. Damir would deserve his scorched farmland, and even as a farmer's daughter, I would be happy enough to watch.

"It's the middle of the night," I replied, drawing up my most regal tone, "and I would have assumed to be treated with more propriety than this. You couldn't have waited until the morning, at least?"

He shook his head and took another step forward. I sighed and swung my feet to the floor. Maybe it didn't matter. There was no magic floating through the inn that I could sense, so he was likely only wasting his time and my sleep. I padded along next to him as he led me to the courtyard, brighter than I would have expected in the moonlight. The fountain in the center bubbled as we entered, and I sank to the edge, letting the cool water flow over my fingers. Now that the time had come, it scarcely calmed the heat I felt in my soul.

"What exactly are you expecting from me?" I asked.

"I saw you call for the water, even if you didn't know what you were doing." He circled the fountain, his gaze never leaving mine. "Perhaps something with the fountain. What do you think? Is it calling to you?"

I jerked my fingers out of the water and wiped them on my skirts. Finally, it had to come to this. I had known when I'd left Laurent in Windersay that I was taking a risk—that he might not catch up to me once Damir's soldiers had vacated the town, leaving Laurent safe. Nausea rolled through my gut. Damir was seconds from calling my bluff, and once he did—

"I don't feel anything," I said. "Maybe if you were in danger, I might. We should continue on the road to Heosta and see if anything changes." Fear prickled a warning in my gut, but I couldn't help issuing him an order. "If there are bandits, or a flood, or even a sandstorm, then perhaps that would put you in enough danger to—"

"I may be desperate for your power, but I am not a fool," he interrupted. His leathery face smooth in the moonlight as he peered at me, then shouted over his shoulder, words I didn't understand until three soldiers appeared in the shadows behind him. "I think you've been playing me, and now I want the truth."

Fear.

I might not feel the magic that had sometimes inundated Lochfeld, but I felt raw fear now. It was the only thing I could sense, actually, and as the soldiers came closer, I made my decision. I'd saved Laurent this time, hadn't I? If I died, he would be forced to remarry, and perhaps it wouldn't matter if his next wife was a crownkeeper or not. Perhaps I'd only been fated to meet him to save his life in Windersay.

"I told Thomas the magic is limited to Lochfeld," I whispered to my feet, "and I thought I had spoken the truth. But I was wrong. It's the Kingdom of Meirdre it protects. Meirdre and her sovereign. I cannot serve you, even if I wished." I lifted my head and met his stare. "And I do not wish."

If he felt rage, I couldn't see it in his expression.

"I see," he replied, his voice level. "So, you have betrayed me."

I knew I should stop talking before I made things worse. But then, could there possibly be a worse situation than the one I was currently in? I wasn't escaping, that much was certain, and that meant—that meant Damir needed to know exactly how I felt about him.

I steadied my feet. "My loyalty was never to you, sir."

For a long while, he said nothing.

"No? I suppose I should have expected nothing less from a Meirdrean peasant girl." His lips twisted in a sort of cruel smile. "You have made your decision. You shall die as your husband should have."

Before I could imagine how that would be, the soldiers grabbed me and flung me to my knees in front of the fountain. I screamed and kicked and tried to stand, but they spread my arms to my sides and held me, throat-first, against the stone. My fingertips clawed against the stone, but their weight and the position in which they held me was too powerful to fight. Images of the night the executioner had chained me to the whipping block in the dungeon of Lochfeld flooded my mind, but this time—this time I wouldn't survive.

Damir pushed my hair to the side and stroked the back of my neck with his palm as he knelt beside me.

"Laurent is in pursuit, no doubt," he whispered into my ear, drawing a chill down my spine. "And I will be kind enough to let him find your body here. Give him something to bring back to Meirdre and mourn—do not think I cannot show some mercy to him. Maybe, if he searches long enough, he might even find your head as well."

I choked down a cry as the surrounding darkness grew. It didn't make sense. The moon hadn't set yesterday until well into the morning, which meant it shouldn't be gone now, so soon before sunrise. Was this what sheer terror did to a soul?

A breeze brushed over my skin as he stood and unsheathed his sword. I pressed my mouth against the stone to hide my sobs and closed my eyes as the shadows turned to a glittering gold brilliance. Finally, there was the sunrise that I'd prayed would bring hope. Moonlight or not, I wouldn't die in darkness at least, and that was something. Executed on a clear night was a traitor's death at home. Dying in the light, that I could handle. Laurent would be relieved when he learned how it had happened. He would understand what it meant to me—and to him.

"What is it they say in Meirdre?" Damir asked. "Godspeed into eternity? Well, it'll have to do."

It wasn't what they said in the least, but I could scarcely remember what they did say, for the sun's heat on my back had turned to fire as he spoke. I flinched into the stone, more at the hope welling up than at the sword I knew he'd raised above his head. I opened my eyes, and my breath caught at the familiar shimmering glow that bathed the courtyard in light.

The sword whistled through the air.

I tensed as my teeth slid against each other, my muscles so painful that death would be a blessing. But it was shattered metal, cool and smooth and tiny, that fell against the back of my neck like rain. What didn't wind up tangled in my hair cascaded to the sand beside me. Glitter, like some of my visions had been. I turned my head to the side just as the hilt bounced harmlessly off my hip and landed on the ground. The glow faded as it did, leaving me with an aching head—but one which was still attached to my body.

Laurent had done this.

Tears welled up as I remembered those last hours in that room in Windersay. He'd promised to make me the queen of Meirdre, and his vow had saved me—for whatever magic flooded our kingdom now saw me as worthy of its protection as Laurent was. Had he known the power he was giving me when we said goodbye?

Damir backed toward the archway that led to the front of the inn, his right hand curled as though he still held the sword that lay in a million pieces next to the fountain. Eyes wide and wild, he muttered a prayer—or maybe a curse. I gasped for air, and then, finding my hands free, pulled myself to my feet with the help of the stone wall. I could barely move to defend myself, but the soldiers had already disappeared, too afraid, apparently, of the power I'd finally demonstrated.

The sun's rays crested the roof of the inn while Damir and I stared at each other, and as I shook off the headache, shouts and the whinnies of horses replaced the sound of my labored breathing. Outside the courtyard, figures hollered at both each other and nothingness. Laurent and his men? Or simply bandits who would kill all of us if they had the chance? Though I'd suggested it to Damir, I wasn't nearly educated enough about Vassian to know if there was a common threat on this road as it was in parts of Meirdre.

The shouts turned to musket shots. Bellowing for a new sword, Damir took off running. I backed to the other side of the fountain and slid to the ground, praying it hid me from whomever had arrived. If I was lucky, they would take what they wanted and simply head off down the road.

My eyes threatened to close out of sheer fatigue, but my heart refused to cooperate as I slumped over. A dreadful quiet overtook the courtyard, then the slamming of doors and windows overtook it. No voices joined the sound, so I pressed myself against the ground and dragged a finger through what remained of Damir's sword. The rising sun illuminated some of the courtyard but left the rest shrouded in deep shadows, enough that I hoped whoever had arrived would give up and go away before finding me—for I was now certain that it wasn't Laurent.

I lay motionless as the voice shouted for me, though I didn't know why. Whoever they were, they knew who I was and that I was here. Had they tortured someone for the information? There was no way to know. The one thing I did know was this: if it was one of Laurent's men, there was no threat. If it was one of

Damir's men—or Thomas—well, how many times could I rely on that magic? Possibly an infinite amount, though I had no desire to test that prediction.

"Where the hell is that girl?" the voice continued when I didn't reply. "They said she was here in the inn—how hard could she possibly be to find? If I found out Damir's men lied—"

My heart skipped a beat. I tried to pull myself upright, but the headache hadn't faded in the least, and my strength seemed to have disappeared along with that dreadful sword. Not caring any longer how disheveled I appeared when they found me, I collapsed back into the sand and sobbed in relief.

It wasn't Damir coming back for me.

Or Thomas.

It was King Marius of Iraela.

CHAPTER FORTY-FIVE

"Laurent is perhaps a half-day behind us," Marius told me as I leaned against the archway in the garden behind the inn. The rising sun cut through the early chill, so I didn't argue about his chosen place for this discussion. He hadn't removed his palm from the pommel of his sword since they'd found me behind the fountain, and I knew the anxiety of battle would take more than an hour to dissipate—especially since more was likely to come. "But his wounds are likely slowing him, so we will stay until he reaches us."

"And I appreciate that protection, my lord. But Damir—"

"Fled south toward Heosta. My men caught him before he reached the river. He should have not tried to make a stand there —the animals will take care of his body."

"And Thomas Wennink?" My knees shook as I spoke. I couldn't celebrate Damir's death, but I hadn't known relief could make one so weak.

"I don't know the name." He shrugged off my question. "Likely escaped with the rest of them who separated from Damir. None of them will get far."

I wasn't so certain about that, but I gave him a respectful nod and wandered back inside, intent on that bath I'd scorned last night. If nothing else, Laurent would appreciate the scent of clean skin instead of horse. The inn's owner and servants had gone missing as soon as the army of Iraela had appeared, so I lugged a few buckets of hot water into the washing room off the main kitchen and stripped my grimy clothing off. The only soap I could locate was cheap kitchen lye, but I ran it through my hair. It was better than nothing.

When I dressed in a new gown—pilfered from the carriage Damir had left—and reentered the kitchen, the soldiers who'd been filling their stomachs earlier were gone. I could see them outside in the courtyard, laughing and cleaning their swords and muskets. I couldn't help a smile at the ordinariness of it all, despite the shards of metal that still lay in the dust.

I began to hum as I dug through the cupboards for some spare bread, anything to stave off my growing hunger. Even though they'd run off, I was sure the owner and his staff would be back, and I didn't want to take much from them, even if they were Vassian. Elternow was too recent in my memories, and I knew how sacred food could be in a remote place like this. Finding a pomegranate, I polished it with my skirt and headed to the court-yard to watch the soldiers spar with each other.

The rear stairwell creaked as I approached, and the hair on my arms stood up. It was likely nothing, just another soldier coming downstairs, but my chest grew tight as I backed into the kitchen, the only place I could think to hide. Marius's men made noise. They didn't slip silently around an inn they now controlled.

Footsteps resonated down the stairs and just outside the kitchen, and I gasped for air as they came closer.

As the fire behind me, untended for hours, gave a dying gasp.

As a gleeful shout echoed outside, an Iraelan battle cry of victory.

As Thomas slipped in the kitchen with a broad grin and a sword in his hand.

The apple fell to the floor.

"You'd best run, Thomas," I said, swallowing hard. "They will not treat you kindly if they find you in here. And they will."

"Unlikely." He glanced down at the sword, then back at me. "The fools are celebrating their success, too stupid to realize they've been too hasty in their festivities."

"And what? You think killing me will solve anything?" *If you're even able to.* "You think it will prevent Marius and his army from taking the castle at Heosta and making sure no one replaces Damir?"

"Maybe not." Thomas shrugged. "But solutions aren't my goal at this point—revenge is."

I backed against the stone wall, ash coating the bottom of my skirts. Thomas hadn't cared about Damir and Vassian after all. They were a means to an end.

"Your argument is with me," I said. "Not Laurent. Leave him out of it."

"It's with both of you." He took a step toward me. "You've taken everything from me."

"You didn't even want me," I whispered. I'd have shouted it, but I didn't trust him to not run me through with that sword if I let the soldiers outside hear me. "And he did!"

"And you didn't mind turning your back on Elternow, did you?"

Right before I died was a strange time to bring up my supposed sins, but I couldn't let him criticize that decision. I wouldn't let him speak of my marriage like that. And though I could be silent around Laurent when protocol demanded it of me, Thomas had earned no such respect.

"You turned your back on Elternow," I ground out. "I protected Mama and Papa, especially after you destroyed their home. I gave them a life. A future. I sacrificed everything to protect Meirdre!"

"It's hardly a sacrifice if you parade around Lochfeld in pretty gowns on the arm of a tyrant, is it?" He glanced at my current attire as he stepped even closer. "Though I suppose even a queen has to give up the pretty gowns and beg for charity eventually."

"I would back off if I were you, Thomas." I slid against the wall toward the fireplace, wondering if I could climb up the chimney. "Unless you want to see for yourself exactly what happened here earlier this morning. You do not want to cross Lochfeld's magic."

By the look on his face, I realized he *had* been there, somewhere in the background.

"Then maybe I won't try to kill you. Or maybe I'll wait until your power fades one day." His lip curled up. "Right now, I was more thinking I'd sample Laurent's goods before I destroy his life —I've always wondered what he saw in you. The fire pit isn't ideal, but it will do."

"Leave me alone," I whispered. "Go away and leave me alone."

He grinned. "I don't think I will."

"You will do what she says, Wennink."

Laurent's order echoed through the kitchen. Thomas spun around, but not before I caught the look of horror in his eyes. His sword fell a fraction, then his fingers went rigid on the grip. I didn't know which one of us was more surprised, but surprised or not, he clearly intended to fight.

"After all," Laurent continued, a smile playing about his lips, "she is the Queen of Meirdre. As such, you are subject to her commands."

Thomas scoffed. My eyes floated to Laurent's gaze, but he wasn't looking at me. His attention was solely on Thomas, and when Thomas lifted his sword, he took a graceful step backward, the picture of a swordsman who'd been accomplished since he was old enough to lift a weapon.

But I'd seen the whip marks on his back, knew how badly it must hurt to stretch his skin to heft a sword like he was. Thomas followed him out the door, and though Laurent didn't stumble, his smile faded as he steadied himself on the wood floor of the main room.

"You've been played for a fool." Thomas snarled the accusation, then darted toward him, tossing a chair out of the way before slamming his sword against Laurent's. I flinched at the sound, praying it would draw the attention of the soldiers outside. They had to know Laurent was in here, didn't they?

Laurent lunged to the side. Thomas dove toward him once more, but Laurent's feet were too light for him to be caught off-balance. They'd both had plenty of practice in the past few months it seemed, and I flinched each time metal hit metal—and even more when several figures in Iraelan red burst through the back door. Thomas gave them the briefest glance, then thrust at Laurent once more, with a furious scream that time.

I held my breath. Part of me wanted to plunge right into the middle of it, but Laurent was holding his own, and the soldiers, after a moment's hesitation, moved in on both. Thomas turned his head at the sound, then twisted back toward Laurent a second too late—one well-placed slice on his upper arm and he stumbled backward. It wasn't a fatal injury, but the chair in his way took him down as surely as a stab to the lungs.

Laurent wiped the sweat on his forehead and approached Thomas, his blade landing on his chest. "Fool," he said calmly, waving away Marius's soldiers. "Whatever will they say about you once you're gone? Think of how they'll mock you—that you died after falling over a chair."

Tears filled my eyes. Relief or fear or some misplaced sadness or long-ago loyalty, I couldn't tell. All I knew was that I didn't want to see Thomas die. After everything . . . I still couldn't watch his life leave him.

Laurent must have sensed my emotion, for he looked toward

me with a certain resignation. "Are you going to plead for his life again?" he asked. "Beg me to spare him?"

"I will not, sire." I shook my head, and the tears fell harder at the unexpected mercy—if that was in fact what it was. "Not this time."

Laurent's stance grew unyielding, his shoulders square and firm. The tip of his sword slid from Thomas's heart to his stomach, and there it stopped. I put my hand over my mouth and looked away. A painful, slow death it would be, and I was so tired of death.

"She may have decided that you are no longer worthy of mercy," Laurent said, "and I would never blame her for that decision. Your crimes against her are a thousandfold more than the ones you have committed against me." He forced a swallow, after giving me the briefest of looks. "But I will not become what Damir was. I will not cause more violence hoping to end it."

I gaped at him. All this, and Laurent was still willing to show him mercy?

"Fool?" Thomas asked. He twitched, lying there on his back. "You dare call *me* a fool?" His hand twitched toward his side, bringing out a dagger I hadn't seen before. "You have no idea—"

Laurent's blade pierced his stomach before the scream left my mouth.

CHAPTER FORTY-SIX

THE CARRIAGE JOLTED ONCE MORE AS WE HIT ANOTHER ROCK.
Wedged between Laurent and the door, I scarcely shifted on the
velvet seat, but my joints were aching more with each hour that
passed.

Laurent reached for my hand. "We'll stop soon."

"It's still three days back to Lochfeld, though."

I let his fingers drift over mine, though I wasn't as blasé about
the remainder of the trip as he seemed to be. I'd thought riding a
horse was painful, and perhaps it was, but it wasn't nearly as bad
as riding in a carriage like this. I'd only been on a trip this long
once before, on the way to Iraela, and those roads had been
smoother.

"Yes, three days." His mouth met my ear. "And you can't leave
me this time."

"Laurent!" I didn't quite swat him away, but as one of the
soldiers escorting us came into the view out the window, he
backed off himself. "I would never, anyway. That carriage ride
with that man—it was one of the worst experiences of my life. I
much prefer my husband beside me."

He did kiss me that time, and I sank against him, all soreness forgotten. Much as he might believe otherwise, I hadn't lied in the least—and the comfort he now provided, though a surprise, was more than welcome. His fingers stroked my cheek, and I closed my eyes, willing away the roughness of the road.

"Well, I prefer you here as well." His gaze grew deeper. "I meant what I said, you know—in the inn. When we return to Lochfeld, the crown will be yours."

A single tear welled up, and I brushed it away. Today was not the day for such feelings.

"I know," I replied. "The magic of the map knew, too. But I would stay beside you without it, though."

"Oh, Riette." He laughed, and the spell of the moment was broken. "You really haven't learned."

My own laugh burst out in return. Perhaps I hadn't—or perhaps I had. It was difficult to catch my breath, so long had it been since I'd laughed like this. A strange scent drifted through the carriage as I inhaled, and I sat upright, his wit forgotten.

"Laurent, that smells like—"

He interrupted me with a whistle, and the horses came to a stop atop a rolling hill. To the south was undulating farmland, soft and green, with all the trappings of spring in southern Meirdre. In the distance lay a small town I didn't know the name of—it didn't seem important enough to be placed on the map.

I pressed myself against the window as Laurent hopped down from the opposite side of the carriage. Exiting by myself would be improper, and I was learning . . . but patience was another matter. Soon enough though, he opened the door himself and helped me down.

"There's something you need to see," he said cautiously, guiding me off the dirt road and into the grass.

My slippers sank into the supple dirt, and I clung to his arm, pretending soldiers weren't surrounding us. Protection they might be, but after Vassian, I had little desire to pay them much attention. Laurent led us around the front of the carriage, and then I saw it—

Haystacks.

Haystacks in flames.

My heart threatened to leap into my throat, and I gripped his arm. Because down the hill, tossing flaming torches onto an entire field's worth of hay—an entire season's work for that farmer—were soldiers in blue Meirdrean uniforms. A single figure in brown stood to the side, likely the farmer, and my cheeks grew hot in the sun as he began to pace.

Thomas had been right. He'd told me the soldiers had burned the hay.

Soldiers burned them. Soon as they were stacked. Starve the people and their livestock and they can't rebel.

My throat grew tight. I looked up at Laurent. After all this, he'd stopped to let me witness . . . what? It didn't make any sense that he'd let me watch atrocities as they happened, did it? Not after what we'd been through. I squeezed his arm though I backed away, a question and promise at the same time.

"They're helping to destroy the stem rot," he answered quietly. "Did you really think otherwise?"

"I—" I couldn't admit that I had, not now. Nevertheless, by the way his face fell, I could tell he knew my suspicions. "I am sorry, sire."

"Apology accepted." He didn't make a move toward me. "It had to be done, my dear. The rebels spread the fungus too far and wide, and it must be stopped."

"But at what cost?" Too agitated to rein myself in, I took a step away. "You know they can't afford to replace it!"

"We certainly can't let it spread between farms." He sighed. "That's a hay merchant down there. If he had sold it, it might have reached throughout the entire region. He's been compensated for the hay, as well as for the work he did last season that was all for naught."

"But—you compensated him? You order the soldiers here?"

"Guilty." Laurent lifted a shoulder. "An entire squad—led by Captain Erstad—is crossing the kingdom, carrying coin and burning what needs to be burned. It was the least I could do. And lest you think you had no part in those . . . it was all due to you."

I blew out a breath and stepped close to him once more. "I'm sorry I doubted you."

"I don't blame you. I could never blame you for that. Wish that things had been otherwise from the start, yes, that I do."

I looked up at him, and his eyes were dark, even though the sun was still hanging above the horizon. He had hurt me, and I had hurt him, but somehow, we'd survived it all. And the future? It drew me toward it like the map in Lochfeld did, and the idea of it had ceased to be frightening.

"I think I'd like to watch a bit longer, if you don't mind," I said. "It's beautiful, in an odd way."

Laurent pulled me close, and I leaned my head on his shoulder.

"For as long as you want," he replied.

And so we stood there on top of that hill, arm in arm, as the sun set and embers danced into the sky.

EPILOGUE

LAURENT

THE SMILE ON RIETTE'S FACE FLICKERED UNEVENLY AS LAURENT knelt before her in the throne room at Lochfeld. Whether she was thinking of the apple blossoms in the orchard outside or the hundred pairs of eyes on her, he didn't know, and he didn't care. She had agreed to this ceremony, and that meant more than he had words for. He would have avoided it of course, had she wished it, but agreeing meant so much.

He smiled at her, perched uncomfortably on her throne, and her eyes grew solemn with duty and love as he knelt before her. She stretched out her hand without his prompting, and he kissed the back of it, wishing he could kiss so much more of her. He contained himself though and reached for the crown on the small table next to him. Riette's lips parted as he stood and placed the crown on her head, and his heart skipped a beat. Had it hurt her again?

But she gave him the slightest nod, the agreed upon sign that the magic was cooperating, at least for tonight. Like a wave, it was, retreating and advancing—at least, that was how she'd tried to describe it. He doubted he could ever fully understand the gift she'd been blessed with, and maybe that was for the best. The guilt would fill him forever . . . already did, to some extent. He didn't deserve her, not the crownkeeper, not the wife.

Giving her one last bow, he helped her to her feet and watched her waver on unsteady feet before catching herself and smiling at him. Laurent could tell she was pretending the applauding crowd didn't exist, and that was just fine with him, too. He would never complain that she was focused on him and no one else.

"We walked like this once before," she whispered as he took her hand, and they strode toward the doors at the back of the throne room. "Do you remember?"

Laurent raised her hand to his mouth and kissed it again, a violation of protocol that he couldn't bring himself to care about. What would his courtiers do? Talk? They'd been doing that for years, and now that rumors of the *occurrence* in Windersay had almost certainly reached Meirdre, he doubted Riette's part in it was much of a secret any longer.

"I remember how nervous you were to dance with me," he replied. "And how much I wanted an excuse to put my hands on you."

"I was." Her cheeks flushed, and he looked away for an instant to gather emotions more proper for a public event. "And I suspected as much of you."

"And now?"

She lowered her voice even further. "I wish all these people would go away so we could dance all night without having to stop for politeness's sake."

His smile split his face, even though it wasn't dancing that first was on his mind. As a consolation prize, yes, it was that. "Duty first, my darling." His mouth met her ear. "But I suspect we can still fit some dancing in. Who am I to deny you what you want on a night like this? But first—"

Her nose wrinkled. "But first what?"

"Captain Erstad!" he called. Riette's eyes widened as the

captain approached, and Laurent both loved and hated what he was about to do. "I believe my wife has something she'd like to say to you."

Riette glanced backward, as though escape was possible, then forced a smile. "Captain. It's so very nice to see you again. Are you enjoying the evening?"

"I am, Your Majesty." Erstad forced his own smile. "Especially at Lochfeld."

Laurent squeezed her hand. He'd already reprimanded Erstad for losing her, but part of that accountability fell to her as well.

"About that—" Her smile became more natural. "I am sorry about the position I put you in. I was reckless and foolish and not becoming of one chosen to lead Lochfeld in the king's place. I should have trusted you."

"Never mind that." He cocked his head to the side. "It was a learning experience—enemy armies, I can handle, but queens are something altogether different, I have learned. And for my part, I am sorry I failed you. If will not happen again, Your Majesty."

"Then we are even?" Riette asked. "For now?" she added with a glint in her eyes.

"We are indeed." Erstad gave her a short bow before disappearing once more—for more wine, Laurent was certain.

"Your Majesties!" The crowd gathering in the ballroom parted as Juliana scurried toward them. His sister curtsied before taking Riette's hands in hers and kissing each of her cheeks. "I'm so happy for you."

Riette brushed her palms over her skirt, a heavy gold velvet embroidered with red silk. "King Marius," she replied, "returned some of your mother's dowry. A fraction of it went to the dress. The rest—"

"Yes, yes." Juliana tossed her hair. "To the treasury, to allow my dear brother to suspend taxes for five years. I wonder who could have possibly convinced him to do that?"

"At least you used your time in Iraela wisely," Laurent cut in, "though I suspect I'll be hearing about how you convinced Marius to return the dowry money for much longer than those five years."

It was a polite lie. He didn't only suspect—he knew, because he knew Juliana. But if that was what it had taken to solidify the union with Marius and gain some of his own coin back, he would consider it an even exchange and then some.

"Perhaps." Juliana grinned at him, then curtsied again and vanished into the crowd.

Laurent brushed his fingers against Riette's, an apology and promise. The musicians departed, but he scarcely noticed. And once the courtiers drifted out of the ballroom, Juliana and her husband disappeared to whatever room upstairs they'd appropriated this time, and the map became visible under his feet, he wound a hand around Riette's waist and drew her against him.

"You can see the map now," he said, tugging her backward into a casual waltz. "Not so many feet."

"I could see it before." She leaned her head on his shoulder and closed her eyes, as though the power of the place was overwhelming. "It made sure of that."

"Does it ever leave you alone?" His fingers alighted on her hair.

"Well—" Riette missed a step, and he gripped her hand while she caught her balance. "Yes. Most of the time, at least. But it seems to know I'm here now, and it's leaving me alone for the most part—though it's letting me know that there's so much more I need to learn."

"Father Gerritt will help you with that." The priest had cornered him earlier that morning and all but ordered him to send Riette to his library every day next week to pore over whatever texts he could find. "Though something tells me you know more than you think."

"I'm learning. But I'm afraid I'm not very good at interpreting the magic yet—and using it is something completely different.

Maybe I'll never figure it out. The water—I scarcely knew what I was doing in Windersay. Even worse, the sword." Her voice grew quiet. "I'm afraid of letting the map work through me like that again."

"Hmm." He let his lips drift down her jawline as he hummed a folk song, a traditional Elternow melody. "Somehow I think you will learn."

"Laurent!" Riette pulled away, her eyes wide with delight. "Where did you learn that?"

"Your parents," he admitted. They'd appeared at Lochfeld last week when summoned, then fled back to Elternow immediately after. Their new farm needed managing, they'd claimed, and Laurent had let them go, realizing that accepting their daughter as their new queen wouldn't be an immediate happening. "Though I wasn't able to convince them to attend tonight, I convinced your mother to teach me the melody."

"I wouldn't imagine even you could convince them to celebrate a coronation. The very idea would intimidate anyone from Elternow—including me." Her face fell for a fraction of a second, but then she recovered. "I will pay them a visit as soon as the farm work allows, and until then, I will satisfy myself with you."

"Shameless." He drew her against him once more. "And yet I shall do the same."

Riette closed her eyes and laid her head against his chest. He hummed the rest of the melody as he led her around the ballroom, over the map that would protect Meirdre for the rest of his reign.

All thanks to her.

ACKNOWLEDGMENTS

I'm so very grateful to everyone who helped Crownkeeper become a book: Meghan, Hope, Cathy, Ed, and Taf. You all made my experiment in fantasy a success.

ABOUT THE AUTHOR

Anne Wheeler grew up with her nose in a book but earned two degrees in aviation before it occurred to her she was allowed to write her own. When not working, moving, or writing her next novel, she can be found planning her next escape to the desert—camera gear included. She currently lives in Georgia with her husband, son, and herd of cats.

For more information:
www.anne-wheeler.com

www.ingramcontent.com/pod-product-compliance
Lightning Source LLC
Chambersburg PA
CBHW030358200726
48286CB00015B/1538